THE GOOD NEWS GAZETTE

JESSIE WELLS

One More Chapter
a division of HarperCollins*Publishers* Ltd
1 London Bridge Street
London SE1 9GF
www.harpercollins.co.uk

HarperCollins*Publishers*
Macken House, 39/40 Mayor Upper Street,
Dublin 1, D01 C9W8

This paperback edition 2023
1
First published in Great Britain in ebook format
by HarperCollins*Publishers* 2023

A catalogue record of this book is available from the British Library

ISBN: 978-0-00-847584-0

Printed and bound in the UK using 100% Renewable Electricity
by CPI Group (UK) Ltd

Jessie Wells lives with her husband and two children in Merseyside. She has always written in some form, and previously work ̣ as a freelancer for various national women's mag ̣ ̣ ̣ ̣ ̣ ̣ ̣ and newspapers before moving into finance. She loves nothing more than getting lost in her imaginary worlds, which are largely filled with romance, communities bursting with character and a large dose of positivity.

For my family

'Alone, we can do so little; together, we can do so much.'

Helen Keller

Chapter One

'You've been robbed again, haven't you?' Ollie smirks, using the camera app on his phone to check his reflection as he fiddles with his blonde quiff.

'What?' I sling my Primark bag down onto my desk, catapulting it against yesterday's cup of coffee, a cardboard take-out container which meets the challenge with all the resistance of a plastic skittle.

'Robbed,' repeats Ollie, who is dutifully adhering to his ethos never to do any actual work during the first hour of the working day. 'It's Friday. That's always your excuse for being late on Fridays. Mondays tend to be road traffic accidents, Tuesdays are the days you leave your straighteners on, Wednesdays are always the fault of the Head not opening the school on time, Thursdays your car tends to break down and Fridays – 'he dips his head slightly to examine his razor-sharp cheekbones – 'Fridays are the days the burglars call.'

I tune out, distracted by the coffee currently flooding my workspace with complete abandon, drowning piles of council meeting agendas, old newspapers and sticky notes that keep falling off my monitor in thick, brown liquid.

Thrown by the fact that I haven't immediately hurled an insult back at him, Ollie shifts his blue-eyed gaze from the phone to me, enjoying every second of watching me try and fail to mop up half a cup of coffee with three multi-coloured Post-It notes.

'Look out,' he mutters, as something behind me catches his eye. 'Stevie boy approaching from the rear. You have approximately three seconds to come up with a new excuse for being late that he might actually believe. Three … two … one…'

I chuck the soaking Post-It notes in the bin, cover the pool of coffee with the newspapers and turn to face my greasy-haired, scruffy twenty-something news editor as I wait for the onslaught to begin.

'Good morning, Zoe,' he says loudly, enjoying the attention his booming voice commands as some of the more junior reporters slump even deeper into their seats in a bid to avoid whatever's about to come my way. 'Let me guess, you were caught in a terrifying hostage situation and despite your most ardent pleas, the kidnappers simply wouldn't accept that you had to be at work by 9am.'

I smile sweetly, a move that's meant to charm but that I suspect looks more like I'm planning ways to assassinate him. I pause for a moment and wonder whether I could get away with it, then rule it out on the basis that I keep myself to myself, which seems to be a prerequisite for a murderer.

'Good morning Stephen.' My tone is authoritative; an attempt to suggest I'm in control of the situation despite all evidence pointing to the contrary being true.

'I'm so sorry I didn't make it in earlier.' I try to adjust my smile into something a little less serial killer and more office angel. 'But I did call the newsdesk to say I was running a bit late. We were burgled last night and I've been dealing with the police.'

Over my right shoulder I hear Ollie attempt to stifle a snigger. Stephen flicks his dark, beady eyes in his direction then eyes me suspiciously.

'You were burgled last week, weren't you?' he says, a frown creeping across the shiny forehead and resting in two vertical lines between his eyebrows.

'I was,' I nod gravely. 'There's been a lot of burglaries recently.'

'And the week before?'

I carry on nodding, which is starting to feel like a safer course of action than speaking.

He nods in tandem with me. 'Hmmm. I suppose there *have* been a lot of break-ins lately. But in the nicer areas like Presthill. Nowhere near where *you* live.' He says this with such relish I want to pick up the soggy mass of sticky notes and newspapers and dump it on his head.

'You are also clearly unaware that we ran a story yesterday about how the police have nailed a group for the burglaries, which you'd know if you *read* the paper now and again.'

I bite my lip.

'So, I trust you won't be experiencing any more burglaries from now on?'

Ollie snorts. I shake my head.

'Good. Now we've got that out of the way maybe you can make a start on some work.' He spins on his heel and slithers off towards the newsdesk. 'Oh, and Zoe?' he shouts over his shoulder. 'Maybe you could call when you're going to be on time in the future. That seems to be the exception rather than the rule these days.'

In the time it has taken to clean up my desk, Ollie's done a round of the female trainees, set up a date on Tinder and completed a round trip to the canteen. He hands me a fresh cup of coffee, blue eyes twinkling in amusement.

'So your house *has* been burgled eh?' he chuckles. 'And on a *Friday* too. What are the chances of that happening? Do you have a crime reference number? Have you called the insurance company? Anything of particular value been taken? Oh, please say they've nicked that flowery top that looked as though it had been pinched from the Chelsea Flower Show.'

'Shut up, Ollie', I snap. 'It was Charlie's homework. We were on our way to school when I remembered—'

'Don't even attempt to blame your tardiness on your son,' Ollie cuts in. 'Anyway...' He checks who's around, then leans towards me, dropping his chest down to his desk like a spy evading the secret service. 'Have you heard the news?'

I shake my head.

'Stephen's about to be promoted to head of digital, which means that the news editor job will soon be up for grabs. Why don't you apply for it?'

A rush of air fills my lungs as I inhale sharply. 'Is it official?'

'Too right. And this opportunity has got your name written all over it. Seriously, Zoe, it's been what, nearly nine years since you trundled back from the nationals with your tail, not to mention a massive baby bump, between your legs? Surely you don't want to write about drug raids and Westholme's desperate need for wheelie bins forever?'

'But I'm rubbish. You heard Stephen. I don't even *read* the paper.'

He bites a huge chunk off his burnt sausage then leans back in his chair, making grotesque facial movements as he grinds it up into small pieces.

'No-one reads the paper,' he says between chews. 'It's crap.'

'I don't know...' I start. 'I mean...' I trail off, not exactly sure what I mean.

'Come on Zoe,' Ollie cuts in. 'You might as well go for it. After all, you're no spring chicken. You're nearly forty—'

'I'm thirty-three,' I interrupt, indignance creeping through my tone.'Exactly. You're not getting any younger. You need to crack on, do a bit of ladder climbing if you don't want to get left behind while the likes of my good self steam on ahead of you and dominate you from above.'

He looks at me now as though appraising a prize cow. 'You're a good-looking girl, nice hair, good teeth, great legs. Make a bit more of an effort and dress a bit more,' he glances at my paisley midi-dress, 'well, a bit less like *that*, and you'd have the bosses fawning all over you. Even *I'd* take you out if you weren't old enough to be my mother.'

'I'm eight years older than you!' I exclaim.

'If you say so,' he says, winking before turning back to his computer to update his social media status.I glare at him, envious of his ability to be twenty-five with no responsibilities, then, at a loss as to how to respond to that statement with words, I tut and focus my attention on checking my emails instead. The subject headings do nothing to lift my spirits. From *Rat infestation in Moorland Road* to *Why the council are screwing us all* – which, on closer inspection, is far less erotic than it sounds – none of them imply a story full of cheer.

'Wait a minute, what's this?' I click on one promising heading: *Letter from my grandad arrives fifty years after it was sent*.

I scan through the contents. 'Listen, Ol,' I say. 'A woman's grandad sent a letter from America half a century ago, and it finally arrived this week. Isn't that incredible?'

Ollie pulls a face. 'Sounds like a nice story, but you know Stevie-boy won't go for it.'

'Why not?' I ask, though I already know the answer.

'Because all he wants is vandalism, drug deals in the park, low OFSTED ratings. He thinks the good stuff is just fluff.'

'But people need the good stuff. They need to be reminded that great things are happening as well as bad. Light and shade, isn't that what they taught us at journalism college?'

Ollie shrugs. 'Don't shoot the messenger. You know as well as I do it won't get past him.'

Looking over my shoulder to check Stephen's whereabouts, I spot him through the floor-to-ceiling windows of the editor's office, his head tilted to one side as Ray, editor of *The Northern News* and our not-very-esteemed boss, speaks.

'What's going on in there?' I say.

Ollie glances past me and frowns. 'I don't know, but I don't like the look of it.'

We watch as Stephen nods, stands up and leaves the office, closing the door behind him. He pauses, rubs his forehead then looks directly at Ollie and me. It's not a look that screams instant promotion.

Within seconds, he's behind me again.

'Ollie, the ed wants a word.'

Phew. At least it's Ollie who's about to get a rollicking rather than me.

I raise my eyebrows, wondering what antics Ollie's been up to that might have landed him in trouble with our pint-swilling editor Ray. Maybe it's to do with Becky from Advertising and that store cupboard business last week. Then again, Ray would probably steer clear of any involvement in the romantic entanglements of his employees. From what I hear, he has enough of his own to deal with.

Ollie follows him into the office and, satisfied the three of them will be tied up for a little while, I pick up my purse and head to the canteen for a very naughty but very needed breakfast. The weight of my heaving backside as I walk is a reminder that I should really opt for fruit, but sod it. I don't care.

In fact, given that not only is it Friday, it's also payday, I might even have a hash brown and some fried bread too.

———————

I've just swallowed the last bite of my full English when Ollie returns to his seat, his face ashen.

'What's going on?' I ask.

Ollie looks at Stephen, who has resumed his place at my shoulder.

'Zoe,' he says, his hushed voice a marked contrast to his earlier ear-wincing tones. 'The editor will see you now.'

My heart does somersaults all the way down to my stomach. *Everything will be fine,* I tell myself. *Everything will be fine.* Except what if it's not?

———————

'Zoe.' Ray issues a tight smile as he gestures for me to sit on the green fabric couch facing his. 'How are we today?'

Ray always addresses his employees as 'we', his attempt to convey the message that everyone is in 'it' together. Whatever 'it' is.

I clear my throat, smiling nervously at him and wondering if he seriously only has that one blue tie with the red slashes all the way down it. And whether it's ever seen the inside of a dry cleaner.

'Um, good thanks, Ray. How are you?'

'I'm fine, fine,' he says cheerily, examining a spot on the floor for a moment before looking up at me, broken spider veins popping out across his bulbous red nose.

'Actually, Zoe, I'm not fine. I'm devastated.'

I try to feign concern. 'Oh no, Ray, what's wrong?'

'Zoe, it's awful. Possibly one of the worst moments of my career if truth be told.'

Good grief, what on earth's happened? I stay silent and adopt my most sympathetic look. Perhaps one of his numerous affairs has been revealed. Maybe he's been fiddling his expenses. Whatever it is, it must be bad if he wants to confide in me about it.

Ray shuffles forward in his seat and looks directly at me.

'You know we've been struggling with a decline in advertising for a long time now.'

I nod and feel a pang of sympathy. Poor Ray. The big bosses must finally have given him his marching orders.

'And you'll remember we had to let Alf go last year.'

'Yes,' I say slowly, remembering the kind-hearted arts correspondent who was unceremoniously dumped from the paper in a cost-cutting exercise.

'Unfortunately, Zoe, the powers-that-be have been at work again.' He raises his eyes to the ceiling in reference to the Finance team that reside on the floor above.

'They've crunched the numbers and they've told me I'm going to have to lose two people. One, sadly, is Ollie. The other,' he pauses for dramatic effect, 'is you.'

My brain freezes, unable to grasp the enormity of what Ray is telling me. His voice rolls into one long, meaningless noise as the room begins to spin. I hear a few random words. Restructure, garden leave, lump sums...

Ray is still talking. 'I impressed upon them how valuable you are to us. I even explained you were a single mum.' He shakes his head. 'None of it did any good.'

He's wearing a patronising expression that makes me want to punch him. 'There's a lot of hungry new entrants willing to work for next to nothing. And they've got more social media followers than you.' He coughs. 'Not that that makes a difference of course. We couldn't actually *replace* you. That wouldn't be allowed.' He shakes his head as if to emphasise his total commitment to employment law.

I gulp. 'I'm pretty sure *this* isn't allowed, Ray. Aren't we supposed to have some sort of consultation exercise or something?'

Ray looks uncomfortable. 'We did have a consultation exercise, Zoe. Last year, when Alf was made redundant. We mentioned we might have to make more redundancies then.'

'Yes, but—'

'Anyway.' He leans back and crosses his short, stumpy legs. 'Let's not worry about the semantics. We are where we are, after all.'

A wave of horror passes over me. 'Ray, is this about the staff Christmas party?' I can't even look at him as I say it.

'Gosh, no,' he roars, throwing his head back in laughter. 'I think most of us would sleep with the managing director, given half the chance.'

'But I didn't *sleep* with him. I didn't even speak to him. I just—'

'Told his wife you would,' he says, the tone of his voice far too upbeat. 'And who can blame you, as I say, even I—'

'I thought she worked in Payroll,' I say, the familiar heat rising in my cheeks. 'I didn't realise it was his wife. And I had had a few when I said it.'

'Anyway.' Ray waves a hand as if to dismiss the entire incident. 'I can assure you it's nothing to do with that. Honestly.' He shakes his head and chuckles, then checks himself. 'Now, Tracey from HR will be down to speak to you shortly, but in the meantime … is there anything else you'd like to ask me?'

'Not at the moment,' I say quietly, a jumble of thoughts whirling around my head.

He slaps his thighs as if to indicate that the meeting's over and I stand up to leave.

'So…'

He's smiling, relieved I haven't cried and clearly congratulating himself on his sensitive handling of the situation.

'Leaving do for you and Ollie? The Pig and Whistle?'

'I'll think about it,' I say, my voice trembling ever so slightly. I make my way out of the door, a lot less confident in the strength of my own legs than I was five minutes ago.

'Okay!' Ray shouts cheerfully behind me. 'But don't leave it too long to decide. We'll have to give them plenty of notice if we want a decent buffet, or we'll all end up eating crisp butties like we did at Alf's do...'

I leave him, still going on about the inferior quality of the last redundancy spread and head straight to the ladies' loos, where I lock myself inside the cleanest cubicle I can find, drop my head in my hands, and let the tears fall.

As if what I've done to my son isn't bad enough already, I can't believe I've failed him once again. Except this time it's worse. Because this time there is no back-up plan.

Chapter Two

Approximately one Filet-O-Fish Meal (plus a few extra chips nicked from Charlie's Happy Meal) a Fry's Chocolate Cream, a grab-size bag of Monster Munch and a bottle of Diet Coke (to offset the other calories) are consumed within an hour of me reaching the sanctuary of my home. And now that my two oldest friends and support network, Emma and Beth, are here, I've thrown a few glasses of Pinot Grigio and a box of deliciously gooey brownies into the mix too.

When I'd eventually left the haven of the foul toilets to return to my desk, I'd immediately texted the girls with the words 'Code Red' – our emergency distress call. It's rare that we need to issue such a text, but when one of us sends that message, the other two know to drop everything and provide whatever's needed.

They'd responded immediately, of course, and have kept me in constant supply of tissues and hugs since they turned up on my doorstep earlier this evening.

Because while I haven't technically been fired – Ray called it redundancy with gardening leave – it stings just as much as if I'd been sacked on the spot. It seems to have hit me harder than Ollie. He was shocked by the news but also confident that redundancy was part of the earth's grander plan to unleash him from the confines of paid employment and allow him to pursue his best life. He isn't entirely sure yet what this new best life will entail, but he knows it's on its way.

But then Ollie lives in a studio flat above the parade that costs him eighty quid a week in rent. I have a house that's prone to flooding, a clapped-out Toyota, Charlie – whose eighth birthday celebrations alone are still being paid off – and approximately fifty-nine school charity days a year to shell out for. Not to mention a hedonistic cat, Lola, who treats the house like a hotel, returning only to eat and sleep before disappearing again, leaving behind a deposit in her litter tray to confirm her continued residence – if we're lucky.

At least I've still got a couple of months' wages and a redundancy payment to come. That will see us through a bit longer. But after that…

I kick off my slippers and take another gulp of wine; a move that triggers a fresh round of tears.

'Beth, she's off again.' Emma throws her arms around me and squeezes me tight. The distinctive scent of false tan mixed with perfume that should never have got through Quality Control wafts up my nostrils.

'I can't believe this. I have seriously not seen you cry this much since Neil Daveson drew on your fake UGG boots at school,' she says. 'After everything you've been through, I can't believe it's losing your job that's finally caused so many tears.'

'I really loved those boots,' I say, my words muffled by her thick blonde hair extensions.

Emma gives me an extra squeeze then releases her grip, rescuing the wine glass from my hand before its contents slosh over onto either my couch or her gym top.

'Don't worry, chick,' she says. 'It'll be fine, really.'

I press my fingers into my eyeballs in a bid to stop the tears that have been falling intermittently since I left Ray's office just hours before.

'Sorry,' I mumble through my palms. 'I'll be alright in a minute.'

Beth moves from the armchair and initiates a new group hug and together, both her and Emma form a protective human shield around me that is even more comforting than a roaring fire on an icy cold day.

'We understand,' she says, her soft voice and arms soothing me as she presses her enviably straight caramel brown bob against my own long dark waves. 'To lose your job in the current climate, well … it's terrifying. But you're a hard worker. You're resourceful—'

'You're also broke,' Emma interrupts. 'You could do with a career that brings in a bit more cash and, anyway, I always thought you made a mistake going back to *The Northern News* all those years ago. Now this questionable redundancy business has made me even more certain. This might be just the push you need to make a change.'

I instinctively know that gentle, calming Beth is issuing her with a stern look over the top of my head.

'You don't need to worry about money right now,' she says, her voice like soothing balm to my raw nerves. 'You'll have your redundancy payment and, if the worst comes to the worst, you can pitch up round the corner at your mum and dad's. You'll be fine.'

'But the redundancy is next to nothing,' I sniff, dabbing at my nose with a crumpled piece of kitchen roll. 'Plus, I can't start a new job until I'm at the end of my notice period anyway.

'And that's not even the worst of it.' I'm aware I'm hovering on the boundaries of the self-pity zone, but I ignore the flashing beacon and enter it anyway. 'It's Charlie I worry about. I've already deprived him of a proper dad. What if he ends up losing his home too?'

This time I actually see, rather than feel, the look that passes between Emma and Beth. 'Not to put too fine a point on it, but you did not deprive Charlie of a proper dad,' Emma says, her sympathetic expression hardening to reveal a glimpse of her inner core of steel. 'It's Ryan who's deprived himself of a proper relationship with Charlie.'

'He does ring him now and again.' I don't know why I do that, why I leap to Ryan's defence. Maybe I think that if I keep telling myself he cares about our son then Charlie will carry on believing it too.

Emma manages to hold in whatever retort is fighting to be set free. Instead, she says, 'Anyway, this isn't about Ryan – although it may be a good time to remind him of the definition of child maintenance – it's about you. You say Ollie sees this whole redundancy thing as an opportunity to do something else. What about you? What would you like to do?'

'Honestly? I don't know what else I *could* do. Journalism's all I've ever known.'

'Why don't you start up a magazine?' Beth says. 'One of those free ones that carry a thousand tiny adverts about garden landscaping and plumbers.'

I think about the dozens of beautiful magazines neatly filed in the bookshelves around my house. I love the upbeat nature of the women's glossies. The beautiful clothes, the inspiring stories, the 'go-get-'em' life-affirming articles. They're nothing like the advertising booklets that are sometimes posted through my letterbox that get immediately dumped in the recycling bin – the type of magazine Beth's talking about.

I shake my head and pull my feet up onto the couch, wrapping my arms around the battered fabric of one of the lumpy cushions. 'I don't think that would work for me.'

Emma reaches forward and grabs the plate of brownies. 'Here, have another. Just don't post it on the Slim City Facebook page this time. Ballbreaker Barb will definitely kick us out of the group if we do it again.'

I smile despite myself, remembering the dressing down our Slim City leader gave us the last time we posted pictures of ourselves eating a takeaway from The Lobster Pot, Liverpool's legendary Ranelagh Street chippy, after a particularly good drink and dance session.

Emma taps her head as if to indicate a lightbulb moment. 'Speaking of Facebook, why don't you become one of those social media influencers? They make a packet, don't they?'

'Pouting while hiding my mum tum? Imparting lifestyle advice at a time when my own world is falling apart?' I wrinkle my nose. 'I don't think that's quite me either.'

We all fall silent as we attempt to conjure up a new career out of thin air.

'The truth is, I don't *want* to do anything else,' I say, my eyes welling up again. 'I love being a journalist. I love hearing people's stories, finding out about their lives, highlighting their problems and shining a light on issues that would otherwise go unnoticed. It's what I do. It's what I've always done.'

Emma reaches for the wine bottle and tops up my glass. 'Correct me if I'm wrong, but the last time we met, weren't you telling me how fed up you were of reporting on bad news all the time? Didn't you say you missed writing about positive stuff? Maybe the time *is* right for you to move on, write something a bit more cheery, you know … get your mojo back.'

I take another gulp of my wine, then another, then finish it off.

'Hold that thought. I'll just nip to the loo,' I say, head spinning slightly as I propel myself off the couch, through the hallway and up the creaky stairs.

When I reach the landing I give my pelvic floor muscles a little squeeze, a silent request that they'll hold out a bit longer, and turn right into Charlie's room rather than going straight into the bathroom.

As my eyes adjust to the darkness, I look around my son's mini-empire. With posters of football players plastered to the walls, the former baby blue nursery where I once spent many a sleepless night is now a shrine to the beautiful game.

Over the years, Charlie's bedroom has played host to Postman Pat, Fireman Sam, Spiderman, and now footballing superheroes. It's the place that best reflects his journey of self-discovery, his passions, his world. It's also my favourite room in the house. And not just because it's filled with pictures of half-naked, toned, tanned men.

I tiptoe over to his bed where he lies, splayed out, arms thrown above his head in complete abandonment and I drink in his little face. The full, pink lips, the smattering of freckles across the bridge of his nose, the long dark eyelashes that mirror my own. 'It'll be okay,' I say, keeping my voice to a whisper as I stroke his forehead. 'I'll find a way.'

By the time I've been to the toilet, gathered my thoughts and wiped the black mascara off my cheeks, my usual fighting spirit has returned.

I walk into the lounge with purpose – at the exact moment that Emma and Beth drop their phones on their laps in unison, guilt etched on both of their faces.

'What are you doing?' I ask, instantly suspicious.

'Nothing,' replies Beth, pulling at a loose thread on the hem of her jumper.

'Looking at websites,' says Emma.

I flop on the couch between them, noticing the wine glass that's been refilled in my absence.

'What websites?' I'm intrigued by the secrecy.

'Over to you, Em,' Beth murmurs.

Emma straightens up. 'Oh, alright then,' she tuts. 'I was telling Beth about a woman in America who'd started up a good news website and we were just Googling it to see if it would be something you might be interested in doing.'

'What – launch a good news website? Here? In Westholme?'

'Well, yes.'

I scoop a handful of Monster Munch from one of the chipped cereal bowls I've set out on the table, the best attempt at hostessing I can muster tonight.

'That sounds like a great idea, Em, but I'm not sure it would take off here.'

'Why not? We've already established you've had enough of bad news.' She looks across at Beth. 'And we have a confession to make.'

'Emma!' Beth snaps, her voice sharp.

'Oh what the hell, we've come this far. Look, chick, neither Beth nor I read *The Northern News* anymore. Not even *your* articles. In fact, we haven't done in ages.'

I sniff. 'Alright, Em, talk about kicking me when I'm down.'

'Well I'm sorry, but we don't,' Emma says. 'It just became too…' she pauses, searching for the word, 'depressing.'

'Really?' I feel embarrassed, though given I've just been given my marching orders by the same newspaper, I'm not sure why.

'Really. Look at us. We get up, we go out to work, we come home, we run round after the kids.' She pauses to correct herself. 'Sorry, Beth, that was thoughtless.' Beth waves away her concerns and she continues.

'We go to the shops. We cook the tea. We iron our husband's

17

shirts, well, Beth and I do anyway. You have so far escaped that particular delight. All that's depressing enough. When we have a precious five minutes to ourselves, we don't want to spend it reading a newspaper that basically tells us all our hard work is for nothing because the area we live in is a hotbed of crime, delinquent kids and low educational standards and we're all pretty much doomed anyway.'

'Wow.' I stare at her. 'I had no idea you felt that way.'

'Well, now you know,' Emma says, her voice full of defiance. 'And I'm not the only one who thinks so.'

'She's right,' Beth admits, barely able to meet my eyes. 'Honestly, Zoe, you're better off out of there.'

'Oh.' I process their words. 'What *do* you want to read about, then?'

Emma purses her lips. 'I want to read news that makes me feel *good* about the area where I've chosen to raise my kids. I want to feel that living in Westholme isn't going to kill their career prospects or their soul. There are some amazing people in Westholme. I want to read about *them*.'

I let her words sink in. 'Mum was telling me last week about an eighty-nine-year-old woman at their church who runs the local food bank,' I say. 'How amazing is that, to be nearly ninety and in charge of making sure a community doesn't go hungry?'

'That's what I'm talking about,' agrees Emma. 'And there are so many people like her. There's a lady down our road who set up one of those schemes to provide homeless people with outfits for interviews.'

'One of my neighbours is running five marathons for charity,' adds Beth. 'He did approach *The Northern News*, but they weren't interested apparently.'

'And I don't know if you ever look at the Westholme Community Facebook page…'

Emma and I groan in unison.

'The Westholme Whingers' page more like!' Emma laughs.

'I know, I know.' Beth smiles, revealing the gap between her front teeth that she hates but I find so endearing, 'but a few people on there were having a real pop about *The Northern News* last week, including local businesses.'

I think back to my conversation with Ray. No wonder advertising revenue is down.

'Everything you're saying makes complete sense,' I say, a rush of ideas filling my head. 'This town is crying out for an injection of feel-good news.'

'It's not just about morale.' Emma twists her hair into a top knot. 'It's important for businesses too. If people don't feel good about Westholme, they're going to spend more time out of it in posher areas like Presthill or Lawton – something we know is already happening. That drives even more revenue away from the very few pubs we have left standing, not to mention places like the Westholme Parade.'

I stand up and start pacing the room, the laminate flooring cool against the soles of my feet.

Emma's still talking, lost in her own thoughts. '…And that will drive house prices down even further, fuelling the belief that Westholme's going downhill. It's a vicious cycle.'

'Exactly,' Beth says, throwing her arms up to emphasise her point.

Emma looks at me, like a bird surveying its prey. 'There are some great website templates out there that you can use for free…'

'But we'd need a newspaper as well as a website.' I'm still pacing, my feet unable to keep up with my mind.

'Not a problem,' says Emma, exuding exactly the kind of calm and authoritative manner you'd expect from the head of marketing for a large chain of hotels. 'A print newspaper would only enhance your advertising offering. And you're great with people, Zoe. A few months in, once you're freed from the confines of employment, you'll be able to convince businesses to advertise with you, I'm sure of it.'

My usual response to any kind of compliment would be to dismiss it out of hand, something I've only even realised I do because Emma and Beth have both pointed it out often enough. But tonight, adrenaline, combined with copious amounts of alcohol, is pumping through my veins and I let her words hang in the air, unchallenged.

I look at my two friends in turn. 'Do you really think I could do this?'

'Yes!' they yell in unison.

'But we'd need a name. Something that tells people that this is no ordinary newspaper. That it is a paper full of positivity, love, good news. What sort of name could convey all that?'

'The Positivity Paper?' suggests Beth.

Emma and I pull a face.

'The Happy Times?' Emma proposes.

This time we all groan.

I head to the kitchen to fetch more wine from the fridge and it's there, among the cracked floor tiles and the damp that keeps appearing around the back door, that the perfect name comes to me. I head back into the lounge, brandishing the wine bottle.

'I think I've got it,' I say, excited but also reluctant to say it out loud in case it doesn't sound quite the same. My friends stay silent, waiting expectantly.

I take a deep breath.

'*The Good News Gazette.*'

'*The Good News Gazette,*' repeats Beth slowly. 'That's brilliant.'

'Love it,' says Emma.

'*The Good News Gazette,*' I say again, enjoying the way the words roll off my tongue. 'That's it. That's the one. Now let's just hope there's enough good news in Westholme to actually fill a newspaper.'

I top up the wine glasses and we clink them together, three best friends, strong enough alone, but together an unstoppable force.

Chapter Three

Before I even open my eyes, I know I have The Fear.

I lie still, willing the low-level nausea hovering over my body to disappear and send back the usual deliciously relaxing half-asleep, half-awake haze through which I like to greet the weekends. But instead, the dark cloud that tends to appear the morning after the odd run-in with a bottle of wine envelopes me, filling my mind with anxiety and squeezing my chest so hard I can feel the reverberations of my own heartbeat.

I shift onto my side to ease the throbbing against my head, yet it continues.

'Mum.' A voice infiltrates the fog. 'Muuuuuuuum.'

As little fingers catch a section of my hair, it dawns on me that rather than being the physical manifestation of hangover hell, the throbbing is actually borne out of a far more human form; my son.

I peel open my left eye and reach out to ruffle Charlie's thick mop of dark brown hair, but he jerks away before I can touch it.

'Morning, love,' I mumble.

'It's eight-o-one. You've slept in. Can we go downstairs and put the TV on?'

Rolling onto my back, I open my other eye.

'Have you brushed your teeth?' The question comes from a force of habit rather than any particular concern for hygiene at that moment.

'Yes.' He moves quickly towards the door.

'Let me smell your breath.'

Charlie stops in his tracks and walks backwards into the centre of the room.

'Come closer,' I say, reaching out to him.

He turns and moves gingerly towards me.

'Urgh, Mum, you stink.'

I gesture for him to open his mouth so I can smell inside, then breathe deeply. 'So do you. Don't tell fibs. Go and brush your teeth and get dressed, then we'll go downstairs.'

Grateful for the two-minute respite, I watch Charlie as he pads along the landing towards the bathroom, whilst I try to gather my thoughts.

My job. Or, more correctly, the fact that I no longer have one. Yesterday's events form a collage in my mind, like a particularly unattractive Instagram grid.

Tears in the toilets, frenzied texts to the girls, their instant promises to call round as soon as they could. Managing to hold it together until Charlie drifted off into a deep sleep, then letting the tears fall again, slowly and heavily, a river of tears unleashed by the news that Zoë Taylor, whose career was once so full of promise, is now surplus to requirements.

One two three four, one two three four... I try to practise a breathing technique I found on YouTube to deal with the anxiety that rears its ugly head from time to time. But The Fear is too strong to fight today.

I remember wine ... lots of wine. Excited chatter about a good news newspaper. Waving goodbye to the girls. Cooking and eating an entire goat's cheese pizza. Opening up my laptop.

At the end of the bed my computer is balancing precariously on the heap of clothes I dumped there last night. My anxiety levels move up a gear. Facebook stalking? Almost certainly. Emailing? Messaging? Social media posting? Or something much worse? The Fear turns into full-blown horror as the full scale of my nocturnal activity dawns on me.

I've started a good news website.

I throw back the duvet and scramble to retrieve the laptop. As soon as I open up the screen, I see it. The result of last night's alcohol spree which looks remarkably like the homepage of something called *The Good News Gazette*.

One two three four, one two three four. I try to keep my racing mind in check. It's okay. It's only one of those free template sites Emma told me about. No-one will have seen it. I can easily delete it.

A sliver of light breaks through the gap in the faded curtains, casting a spotlight on the various small make-up stains that have appeared on the beige carpet over the years, and highlighting the phone lying on the bedside table next to me.

I reach for it, swiping off Airplane mode.

Within seconds, a flurry of beeps and flashes alert me to the numerous messages that have accumulated overnight. I frown, scrolling through them. Texts, WhatsApps (including eighteen messages from my Slim City group alone), Facebook notifications… They're all about the website.

'Well done, you.'

'About time someone did something good for Westholme.'

'Good luck finding good news in this dump.'

'Can't wait to read it.'

I turn to the laptop again and click onto the website dashboard, my eyes flicking backwards and forwards over the jumble of numbers on the screen. I'm no data analyst, but it appears that one hundred and eight people have already looked at the site in the few hours since I launched it and there are seventy-four comments waiting to be approved.

'Come on, Mum, I'm starving!' Charlie yells from downstairs.

'On my way,' I lie, still staring at the screen.

The ringtone of my mobile interrupts my thoughts and Emma's name flashes on the handset. She knows I'm normally long up by now, and, as the mum of nine and eleven-year-old boys, so is she. I answer instantly.

'Bad head?' How Emma's voice retains its sparkly, upbeat tone even after a night of booze is way beyond me.

'Urgh, it's more the nausea that's bothering me.'

'Aw, still struggling with those hangovers, chick?' Emma says. 'Anyway, push that aside for a minute and let's talk about the website. You didn't waste any time, did you? We only came up with the idea last night and by the time I woke up this morning I had an invite to 'like' *The Good News Gazette's* Facebook page. Well done!'

I don't know what to say, so make the mistake of saying nothing.

'Zoe? What's up? Wait a minute, don't tell me you've gone cold on the idea?'

'Well...'

'Zoe, no. Seriously. Remember what we chatted about last night? That the bad vibes around Westholme are being made so much worse by the constant flow of negative news stories about the place? How a newspaper that only focuses on good news would help give Westholme – and possibly you – its mojo back? What's changed?'

I pick at a loose thread on my quilt cover as I picture my daily school run. Mums – and some dads – making their way to work from school. Another mum trying to hurry along a young uniformed child while also navigating a pram with a toddler who is balancing on the buggy board. All parents like me, all desperate to feel they are giving their children the best life chances they possibly can.

That was the passion I'd felt last night when I'd agreed that Westholme and the people in it needed a better press. That there was more to the town than drugs raids, dog muck and gangs. I feel my resolve soften. As does Emma.

'If it's the money you're worried about, why not try your hand at a bit of PR while you're waiting for this to take off? I'm sure you've mentioned a few other journalists who've done that and I might be able to give you a bit of work out of our marketing budget too.'

'Thanks for the offer,' I say. 'But I can't officially work 'til I'm no longer employed – and that's going to take a couple of months.'

'Right,' Emma says carefully. 'What do you think you'll do after that then? It's going to be tricky finding another job where they're as flexible with you hours-wise as *The Northern News* was, isn't it?'

The Fear raises its head again. 'I know.' I'm trying but failing to hide the tremble in my voice.

'Whereas if this worked, you'd be able to choose your own hours. You'd be your own boss. *Ethan, stop that!* Sorry.'

'I suppose that's true,' I admit.

'I can even give you a nice little lead to start you off,' she continues, aware that the promise of a story is a carrot I've never been able to resist.

'What is it?'

'The boys go to the Westholme Football Academy and the bloke who runs it has just won a national grassroots volunteer football coach award for all the time he puts into running free football teams for local kids.'

'Emma, I'm really not sure about this.'

'If you don't do it, I'll set up a Tinder account for you, and I'll use that photo of you with your legs in the air in Ibiza.'

'That was fifteen years ago!' I shriek.

'Hmmmm, I'm just typing Tinder into Google now... *Ethan, you're strangling your brother! Get off him. NOW.*'

I sigh, trying to drown out both the screams from the other end of the phone and the incessant banging coming from downstairs as Charlie repeatedly kicks his football against the front door in an attempt to torture me out of bed.

'Okay,' I say. 'Text me his details. I'll give him a call.'

'Will do.' Emma sounds unashamedly triumphant. 'Oh and, Zoe?'

'What?'

'Not that you'd be interested in this small fact, but he's fit.'

I roll my eyes. 'Emma?' I say as I end the call, 'you're right. I'm not interested. Not at all.'

I sink back into my pillow, pull the covers over my head and groan. A good news website. I'll soon have the wrath of Westholme upon me. And like it or not, there's no going back now.

Westholme Community Facebook page:

Eileen Birch: Anyone seen this – a new website about Westholme that only reports good news?

Pete Owen: Going to be the shortest-lived website in history then!

Chapter Four

Westholme is an unquestionably unremarkable town whose only saving grace is that it has the good fortune to be located in the north-west of England, so not a million miles away from Liverpool, Manchester, the Lake District, or indeed Scotland or Wales. Other than its proximity to prettier, livelier and infinitely more interesting places, it has very little going for it.

In the sixties it was apparently an estate agent's dream; a salubrious location favoured by the well-heeled, thanks to its shiny new shopping centre – The Westholme Parade – and well-connected rail links.

Fast forward six decades and the well-heeled have long since gone. The auspicious shopping parade is now agreed by all who live here to be an assault to the senses and the train station has become the town's most popular bring your own bottle venue for teenagers looking for more excitement than TikTok can provide.

I look across at the Westholme Parade as Charlie and I walk around to my parents' house and wonder for the fifth time today whether launching a good news publication in Westholme, when its town centre looks like this, would be like offering free mixers in a dry bar – great in theory, but pretty pointless in practice.

Everything about the parade – three blocks of shopping units wrapped around a pedestrianised square – screams 'past its best'. With the exception of the young magnolia tree that stands proud in the middle of the flagged space the concrete concourse that lies before us is the sort of image that those with a downer on 'The North' would point to as confirmation that it truly is grim up here.

Granted, there are some colourful planters dotted around the place with plaques attributing their beauty to the efforts of an anonymous, but clearly enthusiastic, group called the Westholme Gardeners, but despite their labours the overwhelming ugliness of the parade still shines through.

Soulless flats and offices sit above both occupied and empty retail units. Cardboard boxes can be seen resting against some first-floor windows while net curtains hover over plastic flower arrangements in others. Below them, disparate shops conceal their varied fortunes.

The bookies, which seems immune to recessions, periods of austerity and the continued death of their hard-living customers, boasts a constant flow of characters wandering in and out of its premises.

Two doors along, travel agents browse the net to book themselves on to cheaper versions of the very holidays they're trying to sell. Meanwhile, locals head to the mini-supermarket at the centre of the main row of shops, which offers every item of discount biscuit and confectionary under the sun yet rarely has anything anyone actually needs in stock.

There are a few charity shops which come and go depending on the number of volunteers they have at any given moment. Standing between two of them is my all-time favourite place, The Lower Story, which was once filled to bursting point with new and second-hand books but these days appears to be becoming more and more depleted by the week.

If that retail offering wasn't enough to inspire a coach trip to Westholme, there's also Pink Performers, a dance shop run by an eccentric former dancer, Wilson's the Butcher's, Bob's greengrocer's and a cafe run, ironically, by the town's least hospitable woman.

They're the shops that are open, of course. The other fifty per cent of units are closed, with their graffitied shutters down. Visible evidence, if any were needed, of the slow and painful death of the high street.

Even on a Saturday footfall is low, with many shoppers opting to drive three miles to the nearest retail park where they can use their credit cards to buy throwaway clothes before heading into Costa for coffee and cake. Others head up to Presthill, where fancy boutiques sell designer clothes and posh handbags. Not that I'm complaining. It means there's less competition for me when snapping up the best buys at the parade's charity shops.

None of the retailers make use of the square which, with its overflowing bins and graffitied benches, has long been written off as nothing but an eyesore.

My eyes fall on the *Big Issue North* seller who's become something of a permanent fixture at the parade, where she stays close to the magnolia tree as though it might offer her some protection from the elements. She's young, perhaps in her early twenties, but other than polite small talk about the weather, I've never seen anyone engage in meaningful conversation with her. Maybe it would open their eyes to a world they would rather not see. Or maybe they have enough of their own woes to deal with without taking on someone else's. A pang of guilt squeezes my insides as it strikes me that I've never had a proper conversation with her either. I make a mental note to do it when I have more time.

'Come *on*, Mum,' says Charlie impatiently, pulling at my hand. 'I want to watch the match on Grandad's dodgy box.'

'Shhh, don't call it that,' I whisper, noticing the cool April wind wafting the scent of bacon butties from the cafe in our direction. 'It's not dodgy.'

'That's what Grandad calls it.'

'No, he says the digi box.'

Charlie looks up at me, his expression indignant. 'He doesn't, he definitely calls it the dodgy box.'

'Well he shouldn't.' I quicken my pace. 'Let's go.'

'Sue!' Dad hollers from the lounge. 'Are you streaming chick flicks again? The box is buffering in here.'

'Stop distracting us,' Mum yells back, looking up from the pine kitchen table on which the iPad is balancing precariously on top of a pile of junk, held up by a chipped coffee mug on one side and a tin of spaghetti hoops on the other. 'We're watching *Poldark*.' It's her best attempt, I know, of taking my mind off the job situation and, so far at least, it's working.

Dad's voice rises by a few decibels. 'What the— Well, turn it off, woman, you're overloading the internet and messing up the match.'

I rub my forehead with the palm of my hand. This is not helping my hangover.

My parents' small semi is always like this. Loud, chaotic, a little bit volatile, but always full of love, especially for their only child and grandson.

A collective roar can be heard in the room next to us, then Dad dances into the kitchen, Charlie hot on his heels, both of them punching the air like *X-Factor* contestants who've just been told they've made it through to boot camp.

'Half-time and we're two up,' Dad says, pulling his red t-shirt up over his gut and scratching his beer belly. 'It's in the can.' He takes one last swig of beer and crushes the can in his hand, holding it up to emphasise the joke. 'In the can! Get it?'

We all ignore him.

Hurt by the lack of attention, Dad puts his arm around my shoulders and squeezes me, pressing his cheek against mine. Then he lets go and looks me up and down. 'Have you put on weight?'

'No I haven't.' I push him away, feeling a heat rise in my cheeks. He's right, I have. 'Well only a bit. Anyway, I'm back at Slim City.' I poke his tummy. 'Maybe you should join me.'

Dad clutches his gut with both hands, blubber spilling out through his fingers. 'Nothing wrong with this. Sign of a real man, eh Sue?'

Mum, who has the priceless ability to be able to eat what she wants and remain a petite size eight, rolls her eyes.

'Slim City,' he continues. 'What a waste of money that is. Paying a fiver to moan about how you can't stop eating, then coming here and polishing off two packets of Hob Nobs.'

'Leave Mum alone,' Charlie says, immediately at my side, his arms around my neck, 'She's not fat, she's cuddly. Like a cushion.'

My own mum picks up the closest thing to hand, which just happens to be a copy of *The Northern News*, rolls it up and swats Dad. 'Yes, leave your daughter alone. She's beautiful.' She looks at me. 'You're beautiful,' she repeats, her dark brown bob swishing around her ears as she lays her weapon down on the table. 'Take no notice of him.'

I watch her for a moment and notice her hazel eyes, surrounded by crow's feet but still as striking as they must have been when my dad first had her in his sights, opening even wider as the realisation of what she's just been brandishing sinks in.

'Piece of rubbish,' she says quickly, picking up the newspaper again and swiftly depositing it in the recycling bin. 'Should have burnt it after speaking to you last night. Nothing but bad news anyway.'

'Your mum's right,' says Dad. 'You're better off without them. I always knew you were too good for that rag; it's a depressing read these days.'

I take one last look at a half-naked Poldark and issue him a silent promise to return later before closing down the screen.

'It's interesting you should say that,' I say, then take a deep breath. 'I've decided to launch a newspaper and a website that only focuses on good news.'

Dad snorts and scratches the three remaining hairs on his head, as red and shiny as his cheeks. 'In Westholme? Good luck with that one.' He pauses for a moment, then grins. 'Why don't you bring back page three? Now *that* would be good news. The lads at the factory would love that.'

'Dad!' I say. 'There will *be* a page three. But you can forget about there being any topless models on it.'

Charlie releases his grip on me and wanders off to the treat cupboard. His face looks a little more rounded today and I remind myself to make a renewed effort to cut back on his snacks.

'That sounds like a great idea, love,' says Mum, her voice muffled as she roots through the contents of the freezer, looking, I know, for something she can whip into a meal for her grandson, despite the fact I've told her he's already had lunch. 'But won't it cost a lot of money to start up a newspaper? I know things are a bit tight at the best of times - although you know you can always borrow some cash off us if you need to.'

'Thanks, Mum, but I'm fine,' I say, far more confidently than I feel. 'There's a printer I know who'll probably do me a deal on the first issue in return for a few adverts dotted throughout the paper and then hopefully within the next two or three months I'll be able to secure some other advertisers as well.'

'So, let me get this right,' Dad says slowly, 'you want local businesses to pay for an advert in a newspaper that doesn't exist yet and that only tells *good news*? In Westholme?'

I feel like a balloon that's starting to deflate. I take a sip of my coffee and wish I hadn't mentioned anything.

'Um yes, Dad, that's pretty much it.'

I brace myself for the criticism that is no doubt heading my way. But instead, Dad looks thoughtful for a minute then says, 'Why don't you try that salsa place? The bloke there might take out a little ad.'

'What salsa place?' I watch as Charlie helps himself to a Wagon Wheel and I stretch out my hand so he can pass me one.

'Colin from down the road told me that he and Lynne have been having salsa lessons in the back room of Bob the greengrocer's at the parade. I think it's Bob's son that's doing the lessons. He's a proper ballroom dancer, apparently. His partner's been injured or something, so he's taking a break. You should write about him.'

I smile as I picture Colin and Lynne, both in their sixties and pretty straight-laced, gyrating among the veg. 'Why don't you go along, Dad?' I say, nodding at his tummy in an attempt to give as good as I get. 'Might help you lose a few of those rings.'

'On your bike,' he snorts. 'You wouldn't get me doing any of that carry on.' He taps his head. 'My activity is all up here.'

'Typical of your father,' Mum shouts over the noise of fishfingers clattering onto a baking tray. 'Suggest anything that involves him getting off his backside and he makes out he's busy being Einstein.'

'Go on then, Sue, why don't you go?' Dad winks at me. 'Maybe you'll come back looking like one of those Strictly dancers. That'd suit me down to the ground.'

I chuckle as my mood lifts momentarily. Strangers are always horrified at the way my parents speak to each other, but I recognise it for what it is – a secret, ongoing joke between the two of them that only they understand.

Not that you'd think it to listen to them.

'Right then,' Mum rants. 'Maybe I *will* go and I'll take that Italian guy with me.'

I look up. 'What Italian guy?'

'You know Cath from Cath's Caff at the parade? Her sister moved to Italy years ago and married an Italian guy.' She shoots Dad a look. 'Pity I didn't see him first. Anyway, her son's taking a gap year as part of his business studies course and he's going to spend it here working in the cafe.'

'Ooh, an Italian man in Westholme,' I say. 'The locals will be queuing up to have him serve them pie and chips.'

'He's only about twenty I think, so too young for you,' mum says, patting my arm in consolation, 'but he'll be nice to look at all the same. Cath said he's convinced her to fork out for one of those fancy coffee machines too. So maybe soon you'll be able to get hold of that posh coffee you like so much without having to drive to the retail park to get it.'

I'm about to respond when we're interrupted by the unmistakable sound of Tom Jones announcing his sex bomb status from somewhere beneath the chaos on the table. I dig through the pile, retrieve a mobile phone from under a Balti House menu and pass it to Dad.

'Hello? Hello?' he bellows into the handset, despite the screen clearly displaying that it's 'Dave the roofer' calling.

'Alright, Dave, how are you? Sorry about that. I've got our Zoe here and we were chatting.' He pauses for a minute, listening, then laughs. 'Yeah, Zoe, that's the one … oh yeah, it's been years since she came back from London. Got up the duff, didn't she, silly cow.' He spots Charlie's shocked expression, covers the handset and mouths to him, 'only kidding' then turns back to his call. 'Anyway, about this roof…'

As he wanders out of the kitchen, scratching his backside with his free hand, I rest my head on the cluttered table top and wish I could climb back into bed.

Zoe, the girl who blew the chance most people around here would give their back teeth for.

I close my eyes and remind myself that I made the right choice, even if it does mean a lifetime of jibes, crappy jobs and struggling to keep my head above water.

Back teeth I could have managed. But my son?

He had been non-negotiable.

Westholme Community Facebook page:

Bernard Phillips: To the scumbags who kicked down my front wall after the match today. I hope you rot in Hell.

Chapter Five

M y first day of gardening leave has been a strange one. In theory, it wasn't even supposed to start for another month, but, in practice, Ollie and I both had so much holiday to take we'd been able to finish work immediately.

It started as usual. Get woken up by Charlie tapping my head, try and buy myself five more minutes before he forces me to get up, finally admit defeat and get up, shower, dress, drink three coffees while waiting for Charlie to get ready, take Charlie to school, but then … nothing.

I spent the first few hours watching morning TV and drinking more coffee, but by the time *Loose Women* had finished I felt the urge to do something proactive with my day. Plus, all that caffeine was starting to make me hyper so I really needed to get moving.

My initial task had been to get Ollie onboard with my new venture. It had taken a little persuading to convince him to design a newspaper with no guaranteed income, but I'd reminded him that a) he had nothing else to do, and b) it was part of the earth's grander plan for him. Eventually, in the absence of any other options, he'd agreed to join me.

Then, after trying and failing to Marie Kondo my wardrobe (I think the method only works when you can identify more than two items of clothing that bring you joy), I dumped its contents into one big 'to be hung' pile and made it to the school gates with only seconds to spare.

Now, having deposited Charlie safely with Mum and Dad, I'm on my way to my first *Gazette* assignment to interview the footballer Emma told me about.

I turn onto the long main road that runs through the town. The route alone tells a tale of mixed fortunes and histories with shops, old cottages and new-build homes making unlikely bedfellows.

The first part of the journey takes me past the parade, the town hall and the old cinema, a beautiful Art Deco building that was boarded up and left to rot over twenty years ago and looks as though it's been untouched by human hands ever since. This being a negative story, *The Northern News* has fully embraced its downfall over the years, filling the paper with page after page of headlines about its fate being a metaphor for that of the town, and even though I think that might be overegging the pudding a little, I do agree that it's an absolute travesty such a gem should be left to decay.

I continue on, whizzing over the bridge that arches across the small river snaking around the town, passing cul-de-sacs filled with an assortment of houses and the odd old farmhouse that acts as a nod to Westholme's heritage.

The further away from Mum and Dad's I drive, the less attractive my surroundings become, with detached houses and cherry blossoms gradually giving way to metal railings and takeaways. I motor past the small cul-de-sac where I live, a close of just ten identikit 1960s houses marked by a street sign that said 'Tucker Close' before one of the local gangs made the unilateral decision to give it a DIY name change. Then, fifty metres or so later, I reach the huge tree on the corner of the side street that acts as a gateway into an area where perfectly manicured gardens sit alongside boarded-up houses, where houseproud women clean their windows as lads let their lurchers defecate on the pavement and where hard-working families go out to work while the less well-intentioned sit on garden walls drinking cans of Special Brew. I drive under a pair of trainers strung over a telephone wire. This, my friends, is the Orchard Estate.

After weaving through the maze of streets, I eventually pull up at the town's playing fields where kids in football kits are banging their dirty boots on the floor in a cacophony of sound. I look through the windscreen at the scene before me and curse Emma under my breath.

A couple of dozen young boys and a group of middle-aged men are all focused on one thing and one thing only – their balls. For the younger boys it's all about kicking them, for the older guys it's about how they kick them. The whole ground is pulsating with testosterone and it's all I can do not to restart the engine and get Tilly – my ageing Toyota – and I the hell out of there.

Instead, I take a deep breath, step out of the car and head towards a small opening on to the playing field. Mud squelches from the wet grass onto my black biker boots as I edge around the perimeter of the ground, hiking up the skirt of my midi dress and keeping well away from the dozen or so balls flying around various pitches marked out on the grass.

In the distance a rugged bloke in navy tracksuit bottoms and a hooded-jacket yells instructions as he watches the players from the sideline.

'Come on, Kieran, tackle him…'

'Jacob, remember to pass…'

'Well done, Sean, great goal.'

A little boy with dirty-blonde hair that I take to be Sean breaks into a grin as he runs back to his starting position on the pitch and I slow down as it strikes me that I haven't got a clue who Sam is.

I look around, trying to pick him out from the numerous male figures in my line of vision. My eye is drawn again to the tall guy in the tracksuit with the light-brown hair and I find myself hoping it's him. He looks over and stares for a few seconds, then smiles and waves.

'Guys, carry on playing, I'll be back in a minute,' I hear him shout, and he breaks into an effortless jog as he makes his way towards me.

I try not to gawp as his long legs cover the pitch and for the last few steps in particular I make a point of watching the training session with intense focus, as if I have a clue as to what any of them are doing other than trying to boot the ball.

Then he's standing right in front of me and I can no longer pretend I haven't noticed his presence.

'You must be Zoe,' he says, extending his hand, a statement rather than a question.

It's only then that I allow myself to look at him and I'm almost certain my pupils must be dilating like some sort of cartoon character in appreciation of his attributes. He has green eyes, gently spiked hair and the cutest dimples which go some way to soften his high cheekbones.

I shake myself. If I were the type of woman who noticed all that stuff, I might admit that Emma's description of Sam was accurate. But noticing these things in living, breathing men as opposed to footballers on posters tends to lead – in my experience anyway – to trouble, so I'm determined not to. Instead, I focus on working out where I recognise his face from.

'Hi.' I smile, hoping he doesn't pick up on the strange quiver that's hijacked my voice.

'Let's grab a coffee. Tommy,' he shouts at an older guy doing drills at the side of the pitch, 'look after the kids for a few minutes, will you?'

Cupping my elbow in his hand, Sam steers me towards a battered white van where a handful of bored-looking parents are sipping hot drinks in polystyrene cups.

'Hey, Tracey,' he greets the young woman serving up the beverages. With her smooth forehead and straw-like white-blonde hair, she reminds me of a Barbie doll. 'I'll have my usual and Zoe here will have…?' He looks at me, awaiting a response.

'A strong coffee please,' I say. 'One sugar.' I inhale the heavenly scent of salt, vinegar and chip fat.

'Do you want anything else?' Sam gestures to the menu. 'Burger? Fries?'

'Oh no, thank you.' I feign a look of disinterest. 'I'll have a salad when I get home.'

Sam turns his attention to Tracey, winking at me as he says with an easy charm, 'And how is life at the best coffee bar in Westholme?'

Tracey's over-inflated lips seem to grow even bigger as she pushes them into a pout while attempting to make eyes at him through unnervingly thick black eyelashes that bear no relation to the colour of her hair.

'Great now,' she purrs, shooting me a sideways glance that seems to suggest life would be even better if I buggered off.

Tracey makes the drinks then plonks the cups down on the counter, their contents sloshing over the sides and onto her weaponised glossy black nails. 'Yours is on the house,' she smiles at Sam, before turning to me. 'Yours is a quid.'

I fish around my bag for my purse as Sam hands over the money, hushing my protestations, before leading me to a bench overlooking the field.

Once out of Tracey's hearing range, he takes a sip of his drink and wrinkles his nose. 'Bless her, her coffee-making skills never get any better.'

I take a tentative sip of mine. It's disgusting. I lean down and put it on the floor.

'So,' I begin, taking my notepad out of my cross-body bag and focusing on being completely professional. 'Congratulations on winning the coaching award. You were nominated for the amount of time you put into running free kids football teams I believe?'

'That's right,' Sam says, rubbing a hand across his clean-shaven chin. 'I've been running the football academy for a few years now – that's where people pay for their kids to receive individual or specific coaching – but the football teams are completely free and open to everyone.'

'Even girls?' I smile.

He nods. 'Definitely. Football really can change lives and I want to make sure that as many kids as possible have the opportunity to play the game. In fact, one of the best players in this team is Erin. Can you see her? White top and ponytail?' Sam gestures to the group, still playing energetically on the field. My eyes pick out the little girl zooming up and down the pitch, tackling the boys with ease and I wonder how I missed her when I arrived.

'Wow,' I say, my eyes still on the human dynamo before me. 'She's amazing.'

'They all are.' Sam nods slowly. 'The very fact that they're even here is a feat in itself.'

I watch the players, struggling to understand why their presence would be considered an achievement. 'What do you mean?'

Sam lowers his voice.

'Most of the kids I coach at the academy are from stable families. They go to school, come here, head home for a decent tea and are basically well cared for. Some of these,' he gestures to the players in front of him, 'on the other hand, have pretty tough lives. A lack of cash, unstable homes ... this football team gives them a sense of normality, a place to belong.'

His voice is ignited with passion now, and I scribble frantically, noting down his words in shorthand as he continues.

'For every game they win, these kids come a step closer to believing in themselves, to believing they can achieve, that they are worth something and most importantly in believing there's more to life than what they see at home.'

'You know about the Orchard Estate gang, right?'

I nod without looking up, still trying to commit every one of his words to paper.

'Some of these boys have already been caught up in that gang culture.'

My jaw drops. 'But they're only, what,' now I look up, 'seven? Eight?'

'I know.' Sam shrugs. 'It's the way it is. They're getting into trouble with the police, in school ... and they're being egged on by the older boys. These football teams are my attempt to stop all that. To give them something positive to focus on. Which is why we're going to participate in the regional league next season.'

'It sounds brilliant,' I say, 'and perfect for *The Good News Gazette*. I'd love to add in a bit about you and your background too. Have you always coached, for example?'

My question seems to cause a shift in the atmosphere. I can't put my finger on what exactly changes, but it's there.

'In recent years,' he says, looking back towards the players. 'I spent eight years working in Spain, coached a youth team in America...' He smiles. 'It's been a busy time.'

'Ooh, that sounds interesting,' I reply, aware that the very mention of life outside of Westholme has caused me to react like an overexcited puppy. 'Tell me more.'

He ignores my question and I'm not sure if he's being evasive or kind.

'But then my mum got sick and needed me here,' he continues, 'so I moved back and started up the football academy with a special focus on kids like these.' He nods at the team.

We sit in silence as I digest his words. I want to know more about his work abroad but it seems callous to press him in light of this new piece of information.

Instead, I say, 'I'm sorry to hear about your mum. Is she okay now?'

'She died unfortunately, a year ago. Complications arising from dementia.'

I kick myself. 'That's awful. I'm sorry.'

Sam shrugs, the smile that has been ever-present on his lips since I arrived momentarily absent. 'One of those things. Anyway, by that time I'd already started up the football academy and I could see it was having an effect, so I decided to stay and see what happened.'

He turns to face me. 'That's my sorry story. What about you? What brought you to Westholme?'

'I grew up here,' I say, still scribbling to capture the last of his words.

'Oh really, which school?'

'Moorlands Primary, then Westholme Comp.'

The smile returns then, reaching his eyes so I know it's real. 'I was in Westholme Comp too. What year did you leave?'

'After my A-levels – 2005.' I feel my cheeks colour as I realise that's where I recognise him from. It hadn't clicked when Emma had mentioned him, but I can recall his face, his gait, the way his golden-brown hair, now short and spikey, used to flop in his face as he passed the ball around the field to his friends, oblivious to the small group of younger girls watching him from afar. It must have been nearly twenty years ago, yet I still feel just as shy and awkward in his presence. He, on the other hand, is as ignorant of that fact as he ever was.

'Ah, that's why I don't remember you,' he says, nodding as though he's working it all out. 'I left in 2002, four years before you. Did you stay in Westholme after that?'

I rest my pen and notepad on my lap and pick my coffee cup up from the floor. The drink itself may be foul, but at least the cup is warm.

'No,' I reply, trying to regurgitate my past while ignoring the emotions that go with doing so. 'I went to uni in Lancaster, got my first job on *The Northern News*, then one of my editors landed a position in London for one of the national newspapers, so I followed her and worked there for a while.'

Sam lets out a low whistle. 'That sounds pretty impressive. Was it all film premieres, fancy meals and celebrities?'

I shift on the bench. It's very strange, this feeling of being interviewed and not one I particularly welcome. 'There was some of that involved, yeah' I say. 'Other not so nice stuff too, mind. But then I fell pregnant with my little boy, Charlie, and staying down there on my own wasn't an option. I needed support and my parents were still here, so I moved back. Believe it or not, life as a tabloid reporter doesn't really go hand in hand with motherhood.'

I pause, surprised at how much I've just revealed and I look at him, wondering whether he realises the enormity of that fact.

He's watching me, his full lips forming a crescent moon which, in turn, is setting off those dimples again. I shiver.

'Are you cold?' he asks, looking around. 'I'm sure we have a few spare jackets if you want me to get one?'

I shake my head. 'I'm fine thanks,' I lie, taking a sip of coffee and inadvertently knocking my knee into his thigh. For a split second I see his eyes glance down at the point of contact and I move away quickly, the schoolgirl in me embarrassed at the touch.

'So,' Sam says, his voice casual and his eyes back on me. 'Is Charlie's dad not around?'

'No, he's…' I shake my head. 'No.'

Thankfully, Sam doesn't pursue it and an easy silence settles between us as we watch the players, huffing and puffing, in their pursuit of the ball.

Sam chuckles. 'I know there are a few red faces out there. It's early days. But look at them. They're having fun. And some of them are actually pretty good too.'

As if on cue, Sean kicks the ball down the centre of the field where it lands firmly in the back of the net. 'Amazing, Sean!' Sam shouts. Sean practically inflates with pride.

'Charlie would love to be in a team like this,' I think out loud, wondering at the same time how my timid, gentle son would fare in a team of tough kids. I worry enough about him at school, and that's under teacher supervision. 'He's obsessed with football. He just hasn't got anyone to play it with. I do what I can, but…'

Sam laughs. 'There's only so long you want to kick a ball around in the garden for?'

'It's not that so much. More the fact that football's like a language that boys need to be able to speak in order to be accepted by other lads, isn't it? I want Charlie to be able to speak that language.'

Sam tilts his head to one side as he considers my words. 'Have you thought about getting him football coaching?'

I look down at my biker boots, scuffed through age and wear rather than by any fashion forward element on my part and pull my fake leather jacket across my chest. 'It's on my "to-do" list. It's just, well, it can all add up…' I trail off.

Sam nods. 'I get that,' he says thoughtfully, then adds. 'Why don't you send him here, to this team? I could keep an eye on him, make sure he's okay. He'd certainly toughen up while he was playing with the kids here, but in a safe environment.'

I bite my lip.

'I'm not sure he'd last five minutes here.'

Sam laughs. 'Children are tougher than you think – and the players don't *all* have ASBOs.' He winks. 'Why not let him try it at least?'

I watch as another goal flies into the net and a triumphant Erin performs a victory salute to her cheering teammates. I take a deep breath.

'Go on then,' I say. 'What harm could it do?'

Regular contact with my schoolgirl crush, signing my timid son up to a team full of wolves and doing a U-turn on one of my red lines – never to accept help from a man. Of course there's no harm in it. No harm at all.

Westholme Community Facebook page:

Paul Gregory: Wasn't there meant to be a good news website starting in Westholme? I haven't heard anything since that woman announced she was going to do it a few days ago.

Lisa Sheldon: That's cos there's no fecking good news in Westholme!

Chapter Six

I t's been four days since I set up the website and so far the good news contributions from the local community have amounted to a handful of press releases, an offer of sex from an ageing rocker called Roger and some social media comments so vile I wonder how the trolls who wrote them find the positivity required to get out of bed in the morning. Or maybe they don't.

Not that it matters, because despite the trolls and the slow response to my call for happy news stories, I'm feeling surprisingly upbeat as I switch on my computer this morning.

While suggestions may not exactly have been flooding in, at least readers seem to like the articles I've posted so far. Sam's story, which was illustrated by a headshot I took of him the other day, has done particularly well on social media, generating hundreds of likes and shares along with numerous expressions of appreciation for his physical attributes, so at least I can count that as a win. Hopefully it will be the first of many.

Scrolling through my inbox, my pulse quickens as I see a few new messages and realise that people have actually been in touch with leads. The first is from a member of the public urging me to write about the elusive Westholme Gardeners, who appear to be big – but as yet unidentified – names on the town's underground horticultural scene. I've made numerous enquiries over the past few days to try and find out who exactly creates the pots of brightly coloured floral displays that prettify grotspots around the town, but with no success. Even today's email contains no mention of who they are or how I should go about rooting them out and, short of setting up surveillance on one of the planters, I'm at a loss as to how to track them down.

I click on to the next message, a fascinating note from a woman called Margaret who runs a meals on wheels service for mums with newborns, alongside a less-fascinating one from a guy who mansplains, using bold capital letters throughout, just why *The Good News Gazette* is destined to fail.

But it's the final email and accompanying video that really makes my day. It's from an elderly lady who calls herself Starr but who I actually recognise to be Edna who runs the shop selling dance stuff at the parade. Her curly, vivid-red hair stands out like a cloud over her head, her oversized glasses have sparkly silver rims and she's dressed in an outfit Beyoncé would probably find too revealing, twerking the hell out of 'Crazy in Love'.

As my body shakes, surprised by an unexpected bout of giggles, I feel a sudden burst of hope that maybe good things *are* happening in Westholme. If these emails are anything to go by, there are at least one or two people working together, helping each other and twerking as though their life depends on it. And let's face it, whose life wouldn't be improved by a twerk or two? So far, it's turning out to be an extremely successful day. Now all that's needed is for my good fortune to extend to this morning's weigh-in.

The Slim City class is busier than I've ever seen it and consultant Barbara is in fine form, her voice echoing around the town hall's function room as she issues last-minute instructions to those waiting for weigh-in.

'Remember, ladies, a trip to the loo could be all you need to get that extra pound off, so if you haven't paid one last visit, go now,' she barks, her short light-blonde bob firmly intact around her razor-sharp jaw.

'Have you been?' I whisper to Emma, shuffling forward along the heavily marked carpet as several attendees drop out of the queue and head towards the toilets.

'Nah, can't be bothered with all that,' Emma says. 'Anyway, it's my working from home day,' she winks, 'so I've got to keep an eye on my phone and there's no reception in the loo – oh excuse me a minute. Email from the new boss.' She dips her head and her blonde mane throws a veil over her features as she starts tapping away at her handset.

Beth, Emma and I joined Slim City a few months ago in order to shift some of the excess weight we'd gained over Christmas – and in my case for quite some time before the festivities began.

Beth's job as a financial adviser usually gives her the perfect opportunity to arrange client 'meetings' at exactly the same time as Slim City occurs, but today she has a real client meeting that she hasn't been able to escape, so it's just Emma and I.

I cast my eyes to the front of the room, where Barbara's waving a bony finger at the slimmers who queue silently, their eyes fixed on the scales as though they're facing the stocks.

'Maureen, that cardigan will put at least an extra two pounds on you. Get it off,' she orders.

'Sandra, look at the size of that belt buckle. Off.'

Edging closer to the scales, I feel a growing sense of panic at the thought of seeing the digital numbers flash up. It was easy staying slim in London when I barely had time to eat, but since having Charlie and moving back home, I've gained two dress sizes – at times verging on three – despite an eternal but somewhat fruitless determination to drop them again.

The conversation of two slimmers somewhere in the queue behind me catches my attention.

'Beaten to a pulp apparently, just so that they could take his phone,' the first woman says. 'Poor little lad, just ten years old.'

'And they know for sure it was the kids from our estate?'

'Oh, you know what it's like, Pat. Even if it isn't, they'll blame it on us anyway. I'm sick of it. Alright, yeah, we've got our problems with the gang. But we're not all like that. Look at the people in our street; we all go out to work, we've all got great kids. Our Michael's looking for a job right now and I'm worried sick that the minute he says he's from the estate, employers will just write him off – all cos of that group of lads.'

Their words echoing in my ears, I slip my boots off and hand my weigh-in book to weight monitor Wendy, whose face never reveals even a flicker of judgement, regardless of the figures – both physical and digital – that appear before her.

'Two pounds on,' she says, pursing her lips upwards to make a sympathetic upside-down smile. 'Don't worry, you'll have that off in a jiffy.'

I grin as I repeat my weekly refrain. 'I thought it would be worse than that to be honest. I'll get back to normal this week.'

'Of course, love,' Wendy replies, both of us aware that any kind of a weight loss would be an anomaly, rather than the norm.

———

The weigh-ins have been completed, the figures counted, and Barbara is not happy. She's standing in front of the class, a formidable figure in wide black trousers and a stylish cropped purple jacket.

'Ladies,' she says, her voice stern. 'We haven't managed to lose a single pound between us today. Worse than that, we've actually collectively *gained* weight. For the fourth week on the run.' She sighs.

'Look, it's great that you all get on and it's lovely that you're using the Slim City Facebook page to arrange your socials, but it's supposed to be about losing weight, not planning meals out. And I don't want to name names, but when one of you posts a picture of yourself consuming a very large chocolate brownie while flashing the 'V' sign, things have gone way too far.'

Emma prods me in the side, giggling as I look at my knees.

'My team leader has seen these incriminating photographs, and let's just say she's not happy. Not at all. Ladies, you're paying a fiver a week to be part of the Slim City community. Don't you want to try at least?'

Around the room indignant faces murmur denials to their neighbours.

'Now, you know I never single anyone out but, Zoe—'

I feel my buttocks shift forward as I sink deeper into the plastic seat and wonder, not for the first time, why I continue to pay for this weekly public shaming ritual.

'Zoe, you've put on another two pounds.'

'Sorry, Barb.' I'm hopeful that a humble apology will be the quickest way to get this over and done with.

'You've been averaging half a pound a week weight gain since you joined us,' she peers over her glasses at the screen in front of her then pushes them back up her nose as she resumes her attack, 'just over three months ago. Zoe, that's roughly half a stone on in three months. Don't you *want* to lose weight?'

I sink even further into my seat, trying to ignore Emma's body jolting into mine as she shakes with laughter.

'Yes, Barb.'

'Are you happy being you, Zoe? Do you look in the mirror and like what you see? Do you really feel you're achieving your full potential?'

Good grief, I think my cheeks are actually on fire. Plus, I don't remember psychology being included in the membership package. Maybe Barb's been on one of those Slim City leader training courses again. She always returns eager to share her new 'skills'.

'Erm, maybe not, Barb.'

Barbara pauses for a minute and looks at me. I think even she realises she's gone too far this time. Her expression softens.

She sighs. 'Okay, so what are you going to do this week to turn things around?'

I consider my answer, wondering whether I should tell her about the article I read on Weight Watchers last weekend, before settling instead on the standard Slim City motto.

'Eat less, Barb.'

'Right.' She smooths her hair down with her left hand and a large sapphire on her ring finger, nestling into a smooth silver band below it, catches the light. 'Might I suggest you eat a *lot* less.'

And with that she moves on to the next offender as I issue a silent vow that over the next seven days I'll turn it all around. I'll stick to the diet and lose half a stone. I won't eat any chocolate or drink any wine. In fact, I'll be so good that maybe I'll even scoop next week's City Slimmer award too.

———

After what seems like an eternity, Barbara finally dismisses the class. I'm still clear on my course of action for the week, but as the other members head over the road to Gregg's for the traditional post-class treat, I decide I'll join them for my very, *very* last supper.

'Phew, I bet you're glad that's over,' says Emma, checking her phone again as we head to the back of the queue. 'She gave you a bit of a roasting there, didn't she?'

'Tell me about it.' I roll my eyes. 'Although I suppose I did deserve it. I've been an absolute pig lately. Even Beth admitted I could do with reining it in a bit when she saw how quickly I devoured a plate of biscuits at hers yesterday.'

Emma's smile fades. 'How did she seem after the appointment?'

'A bit upset. I think even just going to the IVF clinic really brought it home to her that conception is unlikely to happen naturally. She seems to be trying to process it all at the moment.'

'Poor Beth,' Emma says. 'I *so* hope it works for her. She and Tony would make the best parents.'

I nod. 'Life can be so unfair sometimes.'

We fall silent as we move along in the queue.

'On another note,' I drop my voice to a whisper. 'I don't suppose you've heard anything about a boy being beaten up for his phone, have you?'

'No. Round here was it?'

'I think so.'

Emma shakes her head. 'This place is getting worse. I'm just hearing one bad story after another at the moment.' She winks. 'Thank goodness we've got *The Good News Gazette*. Speaking of which, how did it go with Sam?'

'Great. He's a nice guy and he's doing some brilliant stuff in the community. His story was a hit on the site too. Don't you remember him from school?'

'He went to Westholme Comp? I didn't realise that.'

'Yeah, we used to watch him playing football at lunchtime.'

'Did we now?' replies Emma, watching me closely.

'What?' My cheeks tingle.

'Nothing, chick.' Emma grins. 'Nothing at all.'

'Aside from that,' I say, keen to change the topic of conversation, 'I do actually have some other good news for you. Have you heard about Cath's Caff?'

'The Italian nephew? The checkout operator in the mini-market told me the other day. Who would have thought good old Cath would be hiding a hunky Italian up her sleeve? No idea why he'd want to leave Milan for here, but there you go. I think he's arriving tomorrow so we'll probably see him around soon.'

Emma turns back to the glass panel that protects the pies, biscuits and cakes from the herd of starving slimmers. 'What are you having? My treat.'

'A vegan sausage roll and a strawberry tart please.'

Emma raises her eyebrows.

'Why are you looking at me like that?' I ask.

'Just the one vegan roll this week?'

'I'm cutting down.'

Emma snorts as she waves goodbye to a group of girls leaving the shop, laden with boxes of cakes.

'You're the only one of us that is then,' she says. And with that, she takes her pasty from the woman behind the till, pulls it out of the paper bag and tucks right in.

Westholme Community Facebook page:

Simon Crossley: Called in at the parade to put a bet on last night. Never seen the place in such a state. Graffiti all over the place and litter everywhere. Disgrace.

Rob Horton: Horrible, isn't it. The wife and I won't even go there anymore. We go to Lawton instead. There's a better class of graffiti up there.

Chapter Seven

I tread carefully through the greengrocer's and round to the
back room of the shop, feeling cabbage leaves crunch under
my feet as I move. With the scent of fruit and veg lingering in the
damp, dark room, it really couldn't be any less like Havana.

But the strains of salsa music and chatter that filter through the
air confirm I'm at the right place and as I push the fly net at the
back of the store aside, my eyes adjust to a scene that, while not an
exact replica of the staff party in Dirty Dancing, does share some
similarities.

Empty crates have been moved to one side to create room for a
makeshift dance floor and over a dozen people of all ages chat
while a redhead who I'm pretty sure is Starr (The Artist Formerly
Known as Edna), the octogenarian dancer from the home video,
bumps and grinds to the beat.

A man in a white shirt and black trousers that match his very
shiny black hair is doing a shuffle step by the back door, next to a
box of wonky parsnips. He looks completely at home in the
chaotic mix of vegetable remnants and South American music

that's doing a surprisingly good job of bringing a taste of Cuba to Westholme.

Even I, who can only usually be tempted anywhere near a dance floor after the consumption of copious amounts of white wine and a couple of shots of vodka, can feel my legs twitching involuntarily to the beat.

'Laaauura,' bellows the white shirt man as he spots me, embracing me in a tight squeeze as he kisses both cheeks. 'You came!'

I smile self-consciously as all eyes turn to me. Even Starr stops dancing for a second then, reassured that there is no immediate competition, returns to her own little world of happiness, moving seamlessly from her X-rated grind into a variation on the rainbow floss.

'Of course,' I say, accepting the plastic cup of brown liquid that someone thrusts into my hand. 'There's no way I was going to miss out on Westholme's version of *Strictly Come Dancing*.'

'As I said on the phone, I'm Lawrence,' says the white shirt man, who is suspiciously tanned considering the lack of sun so far this year, 'and this,' he gestures towards the room, 'is the Westholme Salsa Social Club. Not exactly the Buena Vista Social Club, I grant you, but we do serve rum by the gallon and some dodgy Cuban cigars.'

He flashes me a grin, luminous-white teeth shining like a beacon in the dim light, places his hands on my shoulders and spins me round to face the crowd.

'Let me introduce you to everyone. Everyone, this is Zoe. She's going to write a story about us for her new publication, *The Good News Gazette*.' A few people raise their hands in a subtle wave. Others grin. They seem like a friendly bunch.

'There's Colin and Lynne, who I think you know…' I nod and smile. 'Lisa and Pete,' a pair of thirty-somethings raise their plastic cups and beam, 'Kate, Margaret, Paula … and tons more,' he trails off. 'We've only been going for a few weeks so we're still all getting to know each other. Oh, and there's Starr of course. She knows all the moves.' We tilt our heads to one side, watching as she starts to twerk again. 'Although admittedly she's better at some than others.' He claps his hands together three times. 'Right, everyone, let's begin!'

Within the first five minutes it becomes apparent that the world of Cuban dance has not been holding out for my arrival. Neither my left or my right foot seem to know what they're doing and the thought of throwing in arm action too is just a step too far.

The other dancers, however, are a revelation. They may be beginners, but they can still do the arm and leg moves at the same time, with some even adding a hip wiggle or two.

While I'm not quite at their level – or in fact anywhere near it – I have to admit that the whole thing is quite fun. The absolute focus required to learn the steps leaves no capacity to worry about Charlie, *The Good News Gazette*, my mortgage and how on earth I'm going to juggle it all, and it's a welcome relief.

When Lawrence instructs us to grab our partners, I find myself paired with Paula, a lady I recognise from Slim City. With her pasty skin, hair scraped back into a knot, baggy jumper and leggings, she's not exactly a poster girl for South American dance. But she's brilliant, flying through the steps and breaking down Lawrence's complicated dance moves into something even I understand.

After spending some time learning the routine, Lawrence turns the music up and we try and pair the routine with the music. It's not pretty, and my (mis)interpretation of the steps causes Paula to wince more than once, but she's endlessly patient and assures me that there's no lasting damage to her toes, even if the same can't be said for her shoes.

All too soon, Lawrence claps his hands again.

'Okay, everyone,' he shouts, 'that's a wrap.'

I look up, surprised and more than a little disappointed that the lesson has flown by so quickly. I'm out of breath and borderline disgustingly sweaty, but the adrenaline boost has kicked in and I can feel myself grinning at no-one in particular.

Everyone is so much more relaxed now compared to an hour or so ago and I exchange awkward but friendly comments with the others about my two left feet, my inability to master the steps and the other sort of self-deprecating put-downs that strangers – and especially women – often inflict upon themselves in an attempt to bond.

It's as we're chatting that I catch sight of something on the far side of the wall. The last rays of sunlight are bursting through a large hole in the frosted glass of the window which is covered up in part by a piece of cardboard and some Scotch tape.

'What happened there?' I ask Lawrence who, after checking I'm walking home, hands me a cup of rum 'for the road'.

'I'll give you one guess,' he says. I look at him blankly, not quite sure what my one guess should be.

'We're not one hundred per cent certain,' he continues when I don't answer, 'but we're pretty sure the Orchard Estate gang had a hand in this. Fortunately, we don't leave any cash on the premises overnight and they didn't bother with the fruit and veg, but, as you can see, they've made a right mess of the window.'

A hush falls on the group as the dancers let their own conversations trail off and start listening to ours. Paula, who, as it turns out lives on the estate, looks at the floor.

'We called the police,' he continues, 'there were fingerprints, faces caught on CCTV, everything.'

'And did they come out?' Colin asks.

'Nope. They weren't interested at all. Complete waste of time contacting them.'

'Zoe, maybe you should write about it,' Lynne says. 'Surely the police would have to give you a comment about why they haven't responded.'

I hesitate for a second. 'It's tempting … the only problem is that *The Good News Gazette* is really meant to be about just that. Good news. I'm trying to shine a light on all the great things that go on in Westholme, rather than focusing on the bad stuff all the time.'

We all fall silent for a moment, then Colin says, 'Where are your offices, Zoe?'

I smile. 'I'm currently working from the very impressive setting of my kitchen table. Which, although not particularly inspiring, has the bonus of being cheap.'

Lawrence frowns. 'There's a room upstairs that my dad has as part of his lease on this place. He sublet it up until a few months ago, but there's no-one in there now. You can use that as a temporary office if it helps at all? It needs a bit of a tidy but I'm sure he wouldn't want any money for it – it's only lying empty.'

My smile answers before I do. 'Are you sure? That's incredibly generous of you.'

'Of course.' Lawrence winks. 'Just write a few nice stories about our tasty food and our sizzling salsa classes. That'll be payment enough.'

'Talking about stories,' Starr chips in, 'don't forget you have the video of me dancing, which I know you'll want to use of course, and you must write an article on the Westholme Gardeners too.'

Several members of the group nod and grunt in agreement.

'So I've been told – on numerous occasions actually,' I reply, 'but I'm struggling to find out exactly who I should speak to about them.'

All eyes turn to a rotund lady with short curly light-brown hair, wearing a plain blue tunic and a pair of black slacks. 'You can speak to me,' she says.

'This is Margaret,' declares Starr, extending her hands with a flourish. 'She's Westholme's chief organiser. She gets things done.' I nod in Margaret's direction and start to say that I'd love to have a chat, when Starr interrupts.

'Anyway,' she says, satisfied that the necessary introductions have been made. 'Would anyone like to film me dancing before we go home? I'm okay with you sharing it on social media, as long as you tag me.'

Paula leaves soon after, citing the need to get to the supermarket where she does night shifts and after more rum and, for some, a few puffs on a Cuban cigar, our little group heads out of the greengrocer's and off to their respective homes.

An office, I think, looking up at the windows above the shop as I leave. Despite the warm evening, I feel a shiver ripple through my body as a long-lost emotion makes a fleeting appearance. It feels good. After a few moments, it dawns on me what it is. Hope.

Ollie stares around the office open-mouthed. Lawrence hadn't lied when he'd said it needed a bit of a tidy. Cobwebs hang from the corners of the ceiling, boxes of paperwork are strewn across the floor and I suspect we're going to need a spade to shovel the thick layer of grime off the window ledge.

'I'm thinking we shouldn't make this our first *Good News Gazette* Instagram post,' he says, with no hint of irony.

'I'll admit, it's not exactly what I'd expected.' I'm using the sort of faux cheery voice I adopt when I'm trying to cajole Charlie into doing anything that takes him away from his Nintendo. 'But nothing that's worthwhile ever came easy. Or something like that.'

I bat away the apprehension that's wrapping its tentacles around my stomach and put every ounce of energy I have into summoning up some enthusiasm.

'I'll run downstairs to the mini-market and pick up a few cleaning products,' I say brightly. I pick up my handbag and jab Ollie in the ribs. 'Come on, it'll be fine. Just needs a little TLC, that's all.'

Ollie fixes his eyes on a patch of black mould on the ceiling. 'It needs more than a little TLC.' His gaze moves to his white t-shirt and skinny jeans. 'And believe it or not, this isn't my cleaning gear. Can't we just pay someone else to do it?'

'Made of money, are we?' I tut. 'No, we can't pay someone else to do it. It won't take long. Why don't I grab the stuff and make a start and you can go home and get changed?'

Ollie looks at me as though I've just suggested he pops to the Outer Hebrides for a takeaway.

'Zoe, I have a to-do list as long as your arm,' he says, with the air of someone who doesn't spend their mornings doing their hair and their afternoons uploading photographs of themselves to Facebook. 'Cleaning the office from The Land That Time Forgot is not on it. I'll come back tomorrow when you've had the chance to give it a little tidy up.'

With that, he is gone.

'Right then,' I say out loud, feeling my energy wane. 'First stop, coffee and cake.' And I head down the stairs and straight out to Cath's Caff to drown myself in carbs.

I pick the most inconspicuous table in the cafe at which to devour the biggest, unhealthiest piece of Victoria sponge I can find behind the streaky window of the glass counter.

It is a beast. A mountain of synthetic cream, refined sugar, jam and goodness knows what else and I'm about to take a bite when I notice Cath pointing in my direction.

I pause, fork hovering redundantly in the air as I watch a tall slim lady with head-turningly smooth, Marilyn Monroe-style silver waves thank Cath before navigating the obstacle course of rickety wooden tables in her way to reach my spot.

'Many apologies for the intrusion, but I wondered if I could introduce myself?' she says, reaching out her hand, the lines around her mouth deepening as she smiles. 'Zoe, I presume?'

I look at my fork, so full of promise and lower it reluctantly as I nod, intrigued by what this woman with all the presence of a 1950s' movie star could be doing in Westholme – and what on earth she'd want to speak to me about.

'I'm Gloria. Gloria Bridges. Our good friend Cath over there has been telling me about your fabulous new venture and I wondered whether I could speak to you for a moment?'

I smile and shake her extended hand.

'Absolutely,' I say, gesturing for Gloria to sit down.

Nearby diners wince as the chair legs drag over the terracotta floor tiles and Gloria flashes them all a dazzling smile, creamy teeth framed by fuchsia-pink lips as she shrugs apologetically. I watch, fascinated, as one by one the locals smile back.

Gloria sits down. 'Congratulations on your new website,' she says, in plummy Joanna Lumley tones that suggests she's not from around here. 'I must say, your publication is exactly what this community needs.'

'Thank you.' I smile. I'd be lying if I said I wasn't enjoying the praise that *The Good News Gazette* is generating right now.

'I thought you might be interested to speak to the group of ladies I mentor,' she continues. 'I've sat on the boards of various companies across the country over the years and now I've returned home I'm using my skills to support women who need a bit of a helping hand. Most of the ladies have faced numerous challenges in their lives and many are without a regular income. I'm working with them to help bring about a change in their situation.'

I push my plate out of the way and retrieve my ever-ready notepad and pen from my bag.

'Now *that* sounds interesting,' I say.

'Really, my dear, they're the most fabulous bunch who are working on all sorts of business ideas. In fact, one of them is about to start up a bakery right here in the parade.'

My ears prick up. *A new bakery at the parade.* I'm picturing freshly-baked bread, pastries, cakes – I look at the slab in front of me – that don't need to be defrosted before consumption.

'The woman I'm talking about creates the most delicious goods,' Gloria continues. 'Really, they wouldn't be out of place in one of the patisseries in Paris. But, my dear,' she leans forward and lowers her voice, 'we have a little problem. My friends in elevated positions have informed me that moves are afoot to have the parade knocked down and the land leased out to a supermarket.'

She reaches into her bag and pulls out a leaflet advertising a public meeting.

'Over the next couple of days, these notices will go up in local shops and *The Northern News*. You'll probably have one sent to you, too.' I glance over it as she speaks.

'If the plans go ahead then all this,' she looks around the cafe, 'will be gone. As will any chance of the bakery, the vintage clothes shop and all the other business ideas those wonderful women have up their sleeves, ever seeing the light of day. To put it bluntly, Westholme will become little more than a supermarket.'

I shake my head, my brain working hard to catch up. 'But the owner would have to obtain planning permission. Westholme Council would never allow it.'

Gloria shrugs. 'You'd be surprised. As long as the developer agrees to rebuild the shops and update the public square, there's a good chance it could go ahead. And with your new venture shining a spotlight on our town, you are perfectly placed to lead the charge against it.'

I pick up a sachet of sugar and start flicking it against my fingers. 'I really don't think you need to worry. The parade's been here forever. It's the heart of Westholme. I'm pretty sure it's safe. Anyway, wouldn't a supermarket put our local traders out of business?'

Gloria nods emphatically. '*Exactly*, my dear. How would a greengrocer's, a bookshop and a butcher's fare when they're competing with a supermarket? And I really don't think Edna, or Starr as I believe she likes to be known these days, would start up her dance shop somewhere else at her grand old age, do you? That's why I need you to convince the council that there's more value in keeping the parade as it is than in knocking it down.'

'But if anyone was to be in with a chance of changing their minds, surely it would be you,' I say. 'You clearly have contacts in all the right places. Why don't you do it?'

'Gosh, no,' replies Gloria, aghast. 'My campaigning days are long behind me. I have a feeling that yours, however, may just be beginning.'

I hesitate long enough for Gloria to go in for the kill.

'The current owner is a firm called Lewis & Co., a large company that's currently exploiting the death of the high street by attempting to buy up great swathes of town centres, knock them down and lease the land to other businesses for ventures that produce a higher rate of return, such as retail parks and supermarkets. As long as they rebuild the shopping units that are currently in operation, they can call it "regeneration" and we're all supposed to applaud.

'People simply aren't shopping in traditional high street shops anymore,' she continues. 'Shops are lying empty, leaving commercial landlords with little or no rental income. Have you noticed how many units are boarded up in the parade right now?

The forecast is that it's only going to get worse, which is why many property investors are having second thoughts about retail premises. For many, selling up is the only option.'

I listen carefully, aware from stories that I've previously written for *The Northern News* that everything Gloria is saying is true.

She pauses. 'You say that the council wouldn't allow it. Unfortunately, we are living in difficult times. Councils are aware that the death of the high street is more than just a headline. Supermarkets are promising to be the new hub of the community. Planning committees are listening to what they have to say.'

I lean back in my chair. 'This company that owns the parade. Who's behind it?'

'Ironically, it's a man from Westholme,' Gloria says. 'He doesn't live here now, of course, he lives somewhere in Presthill. But his plans clearly show he holds no sentiment for the area.'

'He's from Westholme? Who is he?'

Gloria's forehead creases into a frown as she pulls his name from her memory. 'Daniel Lewis. Do you know him?'

I shake my head.

'I'm sorry, Gloria, but this just isn't for me. *The Good News Gazette* is about bringing good news to the people of Westholme. I can't see anything good about the potential demolition of the parade. I appreciate the vote of confidence, but I'm really not the right person for this job.'

Disappointment flashes across her face and she says nothing for a moment or two, then rallies. 'I quite understand, my dear. No need at all to apologise.' She stands up, handing me her business card. 'By the way, you should come along to our next mentor group and meet the women I was telling you about. It's quite a hotbed of stories.'

'I'd like that,' I say. 'I really am sorry I can't help you with the parade. But I promise I will be in touch about doing a story on your group.'

Gloria treats me to one more brilliant smile, issues a warm, 'Good day, Zoe,' and heads towards the door. Suddenly she turns back to me.

'It *will* happen, you know, my dear. These shops, businesses, livelihoods … we'll lose them all unless *someone* steps up to the plate. I won't give up hope that that person will be you.'

With that, she sweeps out of the cafe, leaving diners staring in her wake – and my plan to bring good news to the people of Westholme seemingly shot to pieces.

Westholme Community Facebook page:

Elise Harvey: Don't forget, ladies, the Italian Stallion starts at Cath's Caff tomorrow.

Eyelash Lucy: Been false tanning all night. Just got my gel nails to do and I'm ready to go. He won't know what's hit him.

Chapter Eight

I'm awake long before the alarm clock goes off, thanks to the nocturnal activity taking place in both my house and my brain.

First it was Charlie sleepwalking again, something he started doing about six months ago that the doctors insist is completely normal, then for the rest of the night I was kept awake by the dilemma that Gloria has posed. Well, that's not entirely true – I did doze off long enough to have a completely inappropriate dream about Sam, but I woke up at a key moment then, frustratingly, sleep completely refused to return.

I squeeze my eyes shut to rid myself of some surprisingly raunchy images and focus on the problem at hand – the parade.

Run-down, tired and hideously ugly, the parade is definitely past its best. But while its white elephant status might be one of the hottest topics on the Westholme Community Facebook page, I'm pretty sure no-one actually wants to see it razed to the ground.

I shift onto my side, flipping the pillow over and laying my cheek onto its cool surface.

Gloria's right – we can't just let the parade disappear before our eyes. But I need to put every effort into making *The Good News Gazette* work if there's to be any chance of it generating a living wage for Ollie and I in the long term and, the last time I checked, there are still only twenty-four hours in a day. Not quite enough to breathe life into both the parade *and* the paper.

Leaning over to my bedside table, I reach for my notepad and pen. It's filled with to-dos that I haven't crossed off yet, so I turn over to a fresh page and start a new list. Under the heading *Pros and Cons of Trying to Save the parade*, I draw a line down the middle and write *Pros* on the left-hand side.

1. *Could save businesses and jobs. Including, very importantly, The Lower Story;*
2. *Would help to establish The Good News Gazette as a positive force in the area;*
3. *If successful, there may be the potential to return the parade to its former glory one day. No such potential if it becomes a supermarket;*
4. *If successful, I could still go to salsa class;*
5. *If I continue going to salsa class, I may lose some weight.*

I rest my chin in my palm and sigh. I can't think of any more 'pros'. Moving to the other side of the page, I scrawl, *Cons.* This is easy.

1. *No time to do it;*
2. *No time to do it;*
3. *No time to do it;*
4. *New supermarket might have a coffee shop franchise in it – could miss out if it doesn't go ahead.*

I turn the problem over and over in my mind, trying to identity people with time on their hands who would be willing to fight the supermarket development, but no-one other than Gloria springs to mind and she's already ruled herself out.

I'm still musing over the problem when a series of creaks coming from Charlie's past-its-best bed in the room next door signal that he's awake.

Within minutes I hear the pad of his footsteps going into the bathroom followed by the flushing of the toilet, along with the distinct lack of sound – I notice – of the tap being turned on and him washing his little hands.

Then he's there, at the side of my bed, his eyelids still droopy with sleep, hair sticking out at all angles and the Barcelona FC pyjamas that he won't give up despite them being way too small for him, just about covering his tummy. My heart melts and I open my arms wide.

'Cuddle?'

He nods and clambers into bed, his little body still carrying the warmth of his own duvet.

I wrap my arms around his chest as I snuggle into his back and we lie like that for a few minutes until he's fully awake.

These moments, when Charlie's rapid passage towards adulthood slows temporarily, are so precious and I inhale them hungrily, holding on tightly to the seconds that are all too fleeting.

Then, with the words, 'Mum, who do you think is a better midfielder, Kevin De Bruyne or N'Golo Kanté?', the spell is broken and I'm brought crashing down to the football pitch with a bump.

Reluctantly, I open my eyes, inadvertently allowing the day to begin.

I yawn. 'I don't know, who do you think?'

Charlie hesitates. 'Probably Kevin De Bruyne.'

'Really?' I'm keen as ever to give Charlie the false impression that I understand what he's talking about.

'Because he can score goals as well as set them up, he's a classy dribbler and he's got nice skills.'

'Okay,' I say slowly, 'now it's my turn to ask you something.'

Charlie wriggles around to face me.

'What do you think of the parade?'

Confusion passes across his little features and he wrinkles up his nose.

'What do you mean?'

'What do you think of it?' I say, stroking his hair back from his face. 'Do you like it or not like it? What do you think?'

He wipes the back of his hand across his eyes and sits up. 'Why are you asking me this question?'

'I don't know, I just wondered whether you thought it was good or bad?'

'Erm, good,' he says, swinging his legs out from under the covers and shuffling off the bed.

'And would you be sad if it wasn't there anymore?'

'Why wouldn't it be there anymore?'

'I don't know, I just wondered.'

He stands on one foot and looks at the floor. 'Well then, Cath's Caff wouldn't be there anymore would it?'

I think for a moment. 'No.'

He moves to the other foot and swings his arms about. 'And she wouldn't be able to sell blue slush from the machine anymore, would she?'

'Well, no.'

He starts kicking my yet-to-be-used yoga ball at an imaginary spot on the wall. 'Would you still have your office?'

Even *my* heart sinks at that one. 'No. Stop that, by the way. You'll burst it.'

Charlie gives the ball one final, defiant welly, then looks at me.

'And how would we buy those strawberries that Bob sells?'

'I guess we'd have to buy them from somewhere else.'

71

He pauses, processing my answers.

'It's got to stay there then, hasn't it? Can we go downstairs now, it's seven-seventeen.'

He runs out of the room and makes his way down the stairs, just as he does every morning, with the sort of enthusiasm that suggests he's half-expecting to find Santa's sack waiting for him.

I throw on my dressing gown and follow him, wondering with every step whether I'm overcomplicating the issue of the parade – and whether the answer to the problem is actually staring me in the face.

Westholme's rumour mill had gone into overdrive in the days preceding the arrival of Cath's Italian nephew, so it's little wonder that on the day he's scheduled to make his first appearance it's all anyone can talk about.

Before the doors have even opened, a gaggle of women have collected around the cafe, pushing their daughters to the forefront as though they're in a retelling of a Jane Austen novel.

From jeans usually reserved for best to patterned gym leggings and crop tops, Westholme's best outfits are on display as the town's eligible and not-so-eligible alike wait for the Italian stallion to be unleashed upon them. And Emma and I are among them.

As usual, Emma's glued to her phone.

'Work?' I ask.

She rolls her eyes. 'It's my boss, Simon. He's *so* demanding, always wanting me to visit hotels with him that he hasn't seen before. As if he can't go on his own. I haven't even met him yet and already he's got me scheduled in to do four overnight stays with him in the next month alone.'

'That sounds awkward,' I say. 'Is Dave okay with that?'

'He's being great about it.' She smiles. 'Obviously some of

these hotels are hours away so I've been doing overnighters for years, but I'd never usually do so many in such a short space of time. I think Dave feels sorry for me more than anything else.'

I groan. 'Your boss sounds like a nightmare. An old bloke wanting to recreate the wheel I guess?'

She looks thoughtful. 'He actually seems quite young. Do you know, I never thought to Google him.'

'Why don't you check out his LinkedIn profile?' I suggest. 'Let's do it now while we're waiting.'

Emma taps his name into her phone and we wait while the handset does its best to root out a connection hidden somewhere within the surrounding concrete walls.

'Bingo.' Emma scrolls through the results, her eyes widening.

'What?' I ask, intrigued by her facial expressions.

'Oh my days,' she replies. 'Look!'

Emma thrusts her phone in front of my face to reveal the photograph of a man who wouldn't look out of place in a Next catalogue.

With his blonde hair, brown eyes and sexy grin, it's the kind of photo you'd be proud to have on your dating profile, let alone your LinkedIn one.

'Oh no,' I say. 'You're in trouble.'

She tuts, tossing her blonde hair behind her back, her normal composure resumed. '*He's* in trouble, you mean, chick. I'm immune.'

'If those words were coming from anyone else's lips, I wouldn't believe them,' I say grinning. 'But from yours? I'm inclined to agree. Good luck, Simon,' I pull the screen closer to me to make out his surname, 'Jennings. I've got a feeling you're going to need it.'

The hype has been incredible. Expectations are great. And after what seems like an interminable wait, the doors to Cath's Caff finally open and the women flood through, searching for the Italian Prince Charming housed inside.

But something's wrong.

There's no olive-skinned, dark-eyed hunk waiting for Westholme's finest behind the counter. Instead, a skinny, fair-skinned, red-haired young man beaming from ear-to-ear is throwing his arms open and welcoming them all inside. In a distinctly Italian accent.

'No way,' a teenage girl in a vest and hot pants says, failing to hide her disappointment.

The others look, at best, mildly irritated. Emma and I watch from afar as they mill closer to the counter, their narrowed eyes absorbing every aspect of him. Suddenly, they're turning round to whisper to each other, overplucked eyebrows shooting into hairlines as they register two unexpected details on his face.

He's wearing black eyeliner and a slick of gloss across his lips.

A silence descends on the women standing before him.

Eventually, a larger lady in a candy-pink hoodie and jeans that probably stopped fitting her two sizes ago, decides the situation needs to be addressed.

'Alright, Cath, where's your Italian nephew then?' While all evidence points to the fact that he's standing right in front of her, her tone implies that Trading Standards might be contacted if that indeed turns out to be the case.

'Here he is,' Cath beams proudly, throwing her arm around the young man's shoulders. 'This,' she pauses for dramatic effect, 'is Antonio.'

Though he's obviously painfully aware that he falls somewhat short of the mark when it comes to stereotypical expectations, Antonio still smiles broadly.

'*Ciao, belle*,' he says, disarming the group with his very typical

Italian greeting. 'It is so lovely to meet all of my Aunt Cath's wonderful friends.'

The women exchange glances. They wouldn't exactly call their relationship with Cath a friendship, but you can tell what they're thinking: he's foreign and friendly, if a bit strange-looking, so they'll humour him all the same.

'I am happy to be of service. Tell me, what can I get for you, ladies?'

One by one, the customers step forward, ordering from the menu and engaging in mild banter with Antonio. He might not be the rugged sex god they were expecting and his make-up application may put theirs to shame, but he's male and he's Italian. For some of them at least, it's enough..

Westholme Community Facebook page:

Chris Scott: Dog walkers – do us a favour and pick your dog's turd up when you take them for walkies. My wife got some on the pram today and it's a bugger to get off.

Lisa Sheldon: Council should provide more dog dirt bins then.

Chris Scott: Yeah, I get that, but in the meantime it would be good if people could just do their duty and pick up after their dogs.

Lisa Sheldon: Still don't see why the Council can't sort it.

Jimmy Hunter: Probably too busy putting their feet up and working out their coffee expenses.

Lisa Sheldon: Speaking of coffee. That new Italian fella in Cath's Caff – the one who's just come in and taken a job someone from round here could have had? He wears make-up. Just sayin.

Chapter Nine

I t's one of those blisteringly hot April days that always takes everyone by surprise despite them happening every year, yet there's barely a whiff of suntan lotion among the young footballers warming up on the pitch.

Charlie jerks his head away as I attempt to rub a white spot of excess lotion into his temple. 'Stop it, Mum,' he hisses, while simultaneously doing a quick recce of the playing fields to make sure no-one has witnessed such a mortifying act.

Spotting us, Sam grins and gestures for Charlie to join the others. 'Hey, Charlie, great to see you. I'm Sam. We're just getting warmed up before we start training.'

He turns to the group of boys – and Erin – making a comical effort to jog on the spot. 'Okay, guys, Charlie's joining us for training tonight, so I want you to make him welcome.'

My heart plummets as a couple of them practically snarl at my son.

Sensing my concern, Sam quickly dispenses with the niceties. 'Right,' he shouts, 'give me a lap around the field. You've got three minutes. Go.'

Nerves are hitting my stomach from all angles, dancing away like butterflies in a cage. Charlie was so excited about training this morning that I thought at one point he might actually combust, but then he was quiet in the car on the way and when I looked in the mirror to check on him, he was chewing at the skin around his fingernails. I have no idea how he's going to fare with this bunch of kids and I wonder again why I ever agreed to it.

Sam takes a few casual steps towards me. 'He's fitting right in,' he lies, nodding in Charlie's direction.

'Do you think?' It's easier to go along with the lie than speaking out loud the fact we both know to be true – that these kids could literally eat Charlie for breakfast.

In the old Liverpool kit, a hand-me-down from Emma's sons and football boots that are ever so slightly too big for him (also courtesy of Emma's sons), he couldn't look less at home in his surroundings. But I'm relieved to see that he's doing a decent job of keeping up with the others as they jog half-heartedly around the perimeter of the field.

'Definitely,' Sam says, and I look up at him, fighting the feeling of awkwardness that transports me back to high school and gives me the sense that I'm dealing with a teenage pin-up rather than my son's football coach. His eyes look even greener than they did last time we met and it strikes me that I could happily spend all day looking into them.

Shaking myself, I turn my attention back to the pitch. The boys are swearing, pushing and laughing as they try to trip each other up, their behaviour a direct contrast to that of Charlie, his little face set in concentration as he ignores their antics and keeps putting one foot in front of the other.

He has never looked more vulnerable.

'Oi!' Sam yells over to them. 'Are we here to play football or muck about? Because if you're here to waste my time, you might as well go home now.'

'Sorry, coach,' a couple of boys shout back. The others simply stop messing around and carry on running.

'They always start like this,' Sam says. 'They'll settle down soon.'

'Yeah, I'm sure they will,' I reply, my eyes fixed firmly on Charlie.

'Hey,' Sam puts his hand on my arm. 'He's going to have a great time.'

I try and smile as I meet his eyes, aware that all the other parents have scarpered and I'm the only one left on the field.

'I know… It will be good for him. I think I'm going to wait in the car, in case he needs me.'

'Zoe, stop. He won't need you. At least go and get a coffee. I'm sure Tracey would be delighted to see you again.'

I give him a look. He grins. 'Or maybe get in your car, drive away and enjoy a bit of time to yourself. I bet that doesn't happen too often. We'll be finished in an hour.'

I hesitate. 'It's just—'

'Go,' he says firmly, pushing me gently towards the edge of the field. Reluctantly, I give a little wave to Charlie – who pretends not to see me – head back to my car, stop off at the petrol station for a chocolate bar and a can of cola, then pull up around the corner and whip out my phone.

I'm becoming seriously addicted to checking the number of hits *The Good News Gazette* website is getting, but it's the only way I can really get a feel for whether this whole thing is working or not.

Encouragingly, there's been a lot of traffic in the past twenty-four hours, and a flurry of social media messages from people suggesting further story ideas. Which reminds me – I promised I'd call Margaret about the Westholme Gardeners. I find the telephone number I'd taken down from her the other night, tap the digits into my phone and wait.

It turns out that Margaret is seventy-nine, a former midwife and the powerhouse behind a number of Westholme's charitable organisations. Not only did she start up the Westholme Gardeners, she's also the very same Margaret who sent me the email about the meals on wheels operation for new mums and was given an award last year for her services in providing rooms for refugees. I can't even imagine how much caffeine a person would have to consume to cram that much productivity into each day, but Margaret puts her achievements down to one far less stimulating factor – loneliness.

'I lost my husband Stan five years ago,' she explains 'and the sad fact is I've been lonely ever since. My children live in different parts of the country and although they phone every week and come back and see me regularly, it's not the same as having company in the house.'

I murmur in agreement, thinking of the noise and vibrancy that Charlie brings to our own house, and how lost I'd be without it.

'It was when Stan died that I started doing what you're doing now,' she continues.

'Oh,' I say, surprised. 'I didn't realise you'd started a newspaper too.'

She laughs. 'No, my dear, I've never started a newspaper. I wouldn't even know where to begin with that. No, I mean reaching out to the community, trying to make things better for people. Just like you're doing.'

I'm momentarily speechless. I've never thought about it like that – for me, it's more about creating a job that doesn't kill my soul, but I suppose in a way she's right.

'It all started with the memorial tree, you see,' she explains. 'You know the magnolia tree in the parade's square? I planted it in memory of Stan, who used to have a barber's there. After that, it struck me that the parade would look a bit better with a few pots of flowers around. Some of my friends said they'd like to help and that led to the development of the Westholme Gardeners, then I decided to offer up one of my spare rooms to refugees – one of whom has just left me actually,' she says.

'You're welcome to write something about the Gardeners if you'd like,' she continues, 'but I wonder if you'd mind doing something on the Meals for Mums service first? We need more volunteers so a bit of publicity could work a treat.'

I glance at the time on the phone. I need to get back to Charlie. 'Tell you what,' I say, 'why don't I come with you on one of the days you're delivering the meals and you can tell me all about it then? That way, I can chat to some of the mums involved too.'

Margaret promises to email me with some potential dates and I sign off and head back to the playing field, smiling as I drive. There *is* plenty of good news in Westholme. And, piece by piece, I'm finding it.

By the time I pull up alongside the playing field, my emotions are ricocheting between the fear that I might find Charlie lying on the edge of the pitch with blood pouring from his head and the hope that I'll step out of the car just in time to witness him being high-fived by his teammates in recognition of his brilliance.

My eyes scan the field as I search for his dark hair and red top and a massive sigh of relief escapes me as I spot him. While the scene that meets me isn't exactly triumphant, it isn't the stuff of nightmares either.

Charlie is simply playing, running his muddy legs off and even enjoying a touch of the ball now and again. I wave at him and he gives me a little grin of reassurance.

Before long, Sam blows the whistle to call time on the game and beckons the group over for a post-practice analysis. It's then that I notice a small group of teenage lads hanging around the entrance to the field.

They're all dressed head to toe in black, despite the sun, with hoods pulled over the heads of some. On others, black caps complete the look. None are smiling.

Seemingly unconcerned by the presence of the group, Sam escorts the team to the edge of the pitch where half a dozen parents wait, chatting to each other and enjoying the sun.

'I'll see you Saturday. Okay, guys? Remember what we've talked about today and don't forget, practise, practise, practise.'

As the kids run to their parents, a boy with shaggy blonde hair who I vaguely remember seeing at the last session shouts, 'Charlie. Are you coming to the next practice?'

Charlie looks at him warily. 'Um, I think so.'

Catching the boy's eye, I flash him an appreciative smile. Then I realise the woman he's running towards is Paula from the salsa class. She shouts 'hi' and I wave back.

'How did it go?' I ask Charlie, beaming as he reaches my side. I pull him to me for a quick squeeze, before his shrug reminds me of the social ramifications of being seen hugging your mum in public when you're eight and I quickly release him.

'Good,' he replies.

'Good good or just good?'

'Good good.' He picks up his bottle, takes a swig, then looks over his shoulder. 'Can we go now? There's something important I need to ask you.'

We've just reached the car when Sam catches up with us.

'You had some great shots there today Charlie,' he says, his smile revealing a set of naturally but perfectly aligned teeth I haven't noticed before.

Charlie glances at the ground before looking up at him. 'Thank you,' he says politely.

'Did you enjoy it?'

'Yes, thank you. It was good.' Charlie's beautiful manners seem to jar with the testosterone-filled setting.

'Do you fancy coming again?'

'Um, I think so, yes please. Bye.' Charlie opens the car door and jumps into the car seat, a clear sign that he's ready to go.

He slams the door shut and I smile at Sam. 'Sorry about that, he's a bit shy.'

'He's eight,' Sam replies.

We stand there awkwardly, neither of us seemingly willing to bring the stilted conversation to an end. Eventually I speak. 'So how did it *really* go?'

A tiny frown creases his forehead, as though he had expected me to say something else, then he smiles.

'Honestly, he was great. There was a little altercation early on, but he held his own and I think that will have stood him in good stead.'

My heart misses a beat. 'A little altercation? What do you mean?' I glance at Charlie, playing with an old McDonald's Happy Meal toy that he's fished out from behind the booster seat.

Sam's smile falters. 'Right after you left, one of the boys headed over to him and started telling him to go home. At first Charlie ignored him, but then the boy started pushing him a little bit.'

I freeze.

'Now don't panic,' Sam says. 'The boy started pushing him, I was about to yell at them to stop, when I heard Charlie shout, "no, *you* go home," and he shoved him back hard.

'I think the other lad would have given him another shove at this point, but I split things up. Later on, I put them in the same team. Within minutes they were passing to each other as though they'd played together all of their lives.'

I frown. 'Which boy was it?'

'Sean. The little blonde lad. In the Mo Salah kit. Did you see him?'

I look at him blankly.

He tries to give me another hint. 'Messy hair?'

I think. Paula's son, the lad who's just waved at Charlie, has blonde, messy hair. It must have been him. 'I know who you mean now,' I reply, nodding.

An urgent tap on the car window commands our attention and I see Charlie's Happy Meal toy making repeated contact with the window before he catches my eye and looks away as if oblivious to his actions.

'You really think he'll be okay?'

'Honestly,' says Sam. 'He'll be fine. He obviously just needs to practise more. And he can do that here.'

I look him right in the eye, a gesture that feels intimate and brave, but I brazen it out anyway because I want him to understand just how grateful I feel. 'Thank you.'

Sam's cheeks colour. He kicks at a stone on the ground then looks at me and smiles. 'See you at the next practice on Saturday?'

I smile back. 'See you then.'

Charlie's quiet again on the way home. In fact, the only noise I can hear as I head through town is a kind of grinding noise underneath Tilly. I sigh. This happens periodically. A part falls off her, I take her to the garage and the mechanic charges me an extortionate amount to stick it back on again.

'So,' I say, working on the basis that if I ignore the sound it might go away. 'What did you want to ask me?'

'Well,' Charlie starts, then stops and says instead, 'it's nothing.'

I look at his reflection in the rear-view mirror.

'Charlie, if there's anything at all you're worried about, then it's something.'

'Is my dad dead?'

I slam on the brakes, almost causing the car behind to career into the back of Tilly.

'Of course not, why on earth would you ask that?' I say, flashing my hazard lights by way of an apology.

'It's just that there was this one boy,' Charlie says.

'Go on…' I'm using the softly softly approach, even though inside I'm screaming, *Where the hell did that come from?*

'It was the boy with the Jordan Henderson kit on – did you see him?'

'Umm, I'm not sure.' I wish people would stop referring to player's kits as though I could pick them out of a line-up.

'He asked where my dad was, and I said he didn't live with us because he had to live in London, and he said that my dad probably didn't live with us because he was dead.'

I wonder, not for the first time, why these in-depth conversations, the type that tend to require a comfortable knee and a big hug, always seem to crop up at the most inopportune times.

'Oh, Charlie, I promise you, your dad is not dead.' Although, I think, the infrequency of his child maintenance payments means he might as well be.

I look into the rear-view mirror again to check that this conversation isn't too much for him. 'He sent you a birthday card on your birthday, didn't he? How could he do that if he was dead?'

'I suppose.' Charlie sounds mildly reassured.

'He just works really hard in London, so he can't come and see you as much as he'd like. He'd be up here every weekend if he could.'

'But it's been ages since I last saw him.' Charlie's lips form the sort of pout only an eight-year-old can truly master.

He's right. Ryan has never actually managed to make his way up from London to Westholme to see his son. In fact, the last time they spent any time together was when I took Charlie to see him a year ago. Ryan had managed the grand total of fifty-five minutes with us at a posh restaurant (his choice) before announcing that he had a meeting to get to and disappearing without a backwards glance.

Most of the time Charlie and I bumble along quite happily, the absence of the dad he's never really known an insignificant fact. But now and again the subject crops up. And despite my best efforts to reassure him that the situation is entirely normal, every mention of his dad only feeds my insecurities about the fact that I happened to create my little boy with a man who was clearly never going to be father material.

'I have an idea,,' I say, aware that I'm grasping at straws but so desperate I do it anyway, 'why don't I message him and see if we can try and arrange to see him again soon?'

In the rear-view mirror I see a smile spreading across Charlie's face. 'Really?'

'Absolutely,' I reply, with more conviction than I feel. 'But listen, little man, it might take him a while to answer because you know his work keeps him really busy and sometimes he can't answer our messages for ages.'

'I know that,' Charlie's voice is indignant. 'But I'm pretty sure he'll want to come and see me. Maybe we can go to the safari park.'

'Let's do that. And if he can't come, let's just go by ourselves.'

'Okay.' Charlie seems to accept this compromise. 'But I think he'll come.'

Westholme Community Facebook page:

Lee Langdon: CCTV footage here of the little scrotes who robbed the disability scooter out of my mum's car last night. Faces clearly visible. Please share.

Chapter Ten

From the minute I step into the meeting room of the library, any preconceived notion I might have had that Gloria's mentees would be quiet, downtrodden victims of circumstance is blown out of the window.

They're sassy, rowdy, dynamic and together they have more potential than the entire England football squad – or at least that's what Charlie would say if he met them.

Granted, my newbie status means I'm eyed with suspicion at first, but as Gloria introduces me to each one of them, they start to thaw as they open up about their lives and business ideas.

I'm delighted to see Paula who – as it turns out – is as talented in the kitchen as she is on the dance floor. Gloria explains that Paula's the master baker she was telling me about, the one who's planning to open a bakery in the parade and as if I needed any more encouragement to overindulge, she's brought a tray of brownies for us all to sample.

Paula smooths the way for me, too, whispering assurances to the others that, so far at least, I seem to be alright and before long

I'm sitting with crumbs on my chin, transfixed by their stories of triumph over adversity.

There's the stunning Eva, a tall, slim twenty-something with flawless brown skin who was plucked off the street at the age of fifteen and signed to a modelling agency, only to give it all up a year later when she became pregnant. Her skinny jeans showcase her long, lean limbs and she repeatedly tucks her tight black curls behind her ears as she explains that she's working on a business plan for a vintage clothes store she hopes to open in Westholme.

Paula's hair is, again, scraped into a knot but she's swapped the leggings for jeans and is sporting a red shirt that's bold, beautiful and screams positivity. Her motivation, she explains, is to improve her fortunes so that she can move herself and Sean, the little boy that Charlie met at football, off the Orchard Estate.

'I've lived on the estate all my life,' she says. 'It's my home and I love the people that live there. But the gang frightens me. Now I want Sean out of there.'

Her friend Anita is also there, a slim, no-nonsense brunette in smart trousers and a white shirt who escaped domestic violence and is now working on a fantastic idea to create a home decluttering service for people who are either too busy or simply unable to do it themselves.

'If there's one thing I can do well, it's keeping my home in order,' she says, adding quietly, 'probably because of the punishments I used to face if I didn't.'

Paula reaches over and squeezes her hand and Anita throws her shoulders back and continues. 'Anyway, you can come into my house at any time and you'll find everything neat and tidy.'

I tell her I can think of a few women off the top of my head – myself included – who would jump at the chance of having someone overhaul their homes. 'That's the problem with most people these days. They've just got way too much stuff,' she says, matter-of-factly. 'It's far easier to keep on top of your house when you haven't got anything. I don't know why people find it so hard to let go.'

The next thirty minutes are spent photographing, taking notes and indulging in real, tear-inducing belly laughs as I hang out with these awe-inspiring forces of nature who may not have things easy but are forging ahead with their plans anyway.

Through a mixture of group discussion and one-to-one chats, Gloria presses them on their progress, pointing out flaws in some ideas, genius in others, and continually asks them to refocus on why they're doing what they're doing. Why it's so important.

'The women who don't already have jobs are desperate to work,' Gloria explains during the coffee break when we find ourselves alone for a few minutes. 'Many of them have been stuck in the poverty trap for far too long now and together we're finding ways for them to get out of it.'

We're interrupted by peals of laughter as the ladies huddle around someone's smartphone. They fall silent then gasp in unison as they stare at something on the screen.

'Is that what I think it is?' Paula looks horrified.

'Talk about hung like a donkey,' Anita says.

'Send him round to my house – I'll show him what he can do with his tools,' cackles an older lady and the women shriek with laughter.

'Keep it clean, ladies,' warns Gloria, rolling her eyes. 'Unless you've come up with an idea for a business that uses donkeys to carry out home repairs. In which case, I'm all ears.'

The calorie-laden dishes that Mum's force-feeding us for tea would, if Barbara could see them, undoubtedly result in the immediate and permanent termination of my already precarious Slim City membership.

Chips, deep-fat-fried to within an inch of their lives are set out alongside slices of pizza oozing enough cheese to block up every major artery and burgers sandwiched between plump, golden brioche rolls. In the unlikely event that we feel the need for yet more saturated fat, potato skins stuffed with even more cheese have been thrown into the mix too. It's a heart attack on a plate. Yet it couldn't look more beautiful.

'Yeeess, get in there, Nan.' Unsurprisingly, Charlie's delighted to find that my efforts at reaching anywhere near five-a-day have been scuppered once again.

'Mum,' I say in horror, 'this looks amazing. And very, very naughty.'

'I know,' Mum grins, wiping a spot of Red Leicester off her blue jeggings, 'but it's Charlie's favourite and,' she pulls Charlie towards her and squeezes him tight, only letting go when he pushes her away,'it's okay to spoil your only grandson now and again, isn't it?'

I roll my eyes. 'Now and again would be fine … but it tends to be more "again and again".'

'It's not Charlie we need to worry about though, is it?' Dad looks over the top of the *Daily Star*. 'Still enjoying those cream cakes a bit too much, eh, love?'

I pretend I haven't heard. For some reason his comments, which I can normally take in my stride, sting today.

'Anyway, look at this,' he leans over to where the iPad is propped up on the counter and gestures at the page it's still open on. 'You've put a few more stories on there, I see. Doesn't it look great? Almost like a proper website.'

'It *is* a proper website, Dad.' I steal a chip.

'I know. That's what I'm saying. I thought it might look like one of those local things. You know, a bit like that one your mum does for the Neighbourhood Watch – no offence, Sue. But it looks good. Could do with a few more stories on it, like, but I'm sure that'll come. When is the proper newspaper going to come out?'

I ignore the unintentional jibe.

'July, hopefully. I might even do a launch at the—'

'Ow!' An oven tray containing an assortment of pre-packed Chinese buffet food crashes out of Mum's hands and onto the worktop. 'Burney hot,' she says to Charlie by way of explanation. Sometimes I swear my mum thinks Charlie's still three years old. Maybe I'm not the only one who wishes he could stay little for ever.

Mum sticks her hand under the cold tap and looks at me over her shoulder. 'Sorry, love, what were you saying? A launch where?'

'I was thinking maybe the parade,' I say, uncertainty creeping into my voice.

'Yeah,' says Dad. 'It'll be like when Cath's Caff opened – she had a launch then, do you remember, Sue? It was sound until Maureen Lawson discovered her husband kissing Elaine Fowler behind the back of the kitchen.'

'Dad,' I say sharply, clapping my hands over Charlie's ears.

'The opening of Cath's Caff…' he continues, his eyes glazing over as he meanders into memory lane territory. 'It was a lovely do that. Must have been thirty-odd years ago now. We were made-up about having a new cafe open, weren't we, Sue? Shame it wasn't a pub, but there you go. Cath still slipped us whiskey under the counter every now and then. That all stopped after the council gave her that warning, mind…'

I pull a chair up to the table, eager to hear more.

'Do you remember the parade when it first opened then, Mum?'

'I'm not *that* old,' Mum laughs, naturally white teeth shining through rose-coloured lips. 'No, we weren't here when it first opened – that must have been back in the sixties. It was the seventies when we moved in, but it was still like new.' She sets the Chinese food down on the table, pushing the pizza out of the way with her elbow to make space.

'It was lovely back then,' she continues. 'All clean and sparkling, with white pillars in between each shop. It really was very grand-looking, even with the grey concrete.'

Dad's paper rustles as, drawn in by the conversation, he folds it up and lets it rest on his lap. 'Brilliant it was,' he says. 'There was a Woolies there then. I remember buying records there and every week when I got my pay packet, I'd treat your mum to some Pick 'N' Mix.'

'He hasn't changed.' Mum winks at me, gently slapping Charlie's hand away as he tries to sneak a piece of pizza. 'Always was the last of the big spenders.'

'Everything happened at the parade back then,' Dad says, openly taking the slice of pizza that Charlie's just failed to steal. 'We'd head there for New Year's Eve parties, for summer fetes … we even had a do for the Queen's Silver Jubilee. It was a proper' – he screws up his face as he reaches for the word – community. But then Westholme was much smaller in the Seventies. I suppose it's outgrown the parade now.'

I feel my heart sink. 'Do you really think Westholme's outgrown the parade? Doesn't it just need a bit of TLC to bring it back to life?'

'It needs a lot more than the flowery triangles Cath puts up now and again to resurrect it from the dead,' Dad says.

'He means bunting,' Mum explains.

'That's right. And then there's those flowerpot people. They do their best with their planters and hanging baskets, but what do I always say, Sue? You can't polish a turd.'

I think about my next words, careful not to betray Gloria's

confidence. 'Do you think it's had its day then, Dad? Is it time for the parade to be knocked down and something else built in its place?'

Dad considers this. 'I think we've all had enough of the parade the way it is. I mean there's beggars sitting outside the shops now, poor sods. Smackheads, some of them. You can spot them a mile off. Look like the living dead, they do. And that Eastern European girl. She's there every flaming day.'

'But should it be knocked down?' I persist, trying to focus on the parade rather than his bigotry.

'I don't think that's the answer. What would we end up with then? Another gym? A retirement village? A supermarket? The way it is now is the lesser of all the evils. We're stuck with it and that's just the way it is.'

'Take no notice of him, love,' says Mum, passing the cutlery to Charlie to set out on the table. 'It's not that bad. There's a few good charity shops there – I must show you the lovely Marks & Spencer's cardie I picked up the other week – plus Cath's managed to stay open all these years and Bob's still going strong. Things'll turn around soon. And maybe one day someone'll stick some nice white render on it and get rid of that grey concrete façade. Make it look good again.'

'That's right, Sue,' Dad sneers. 'We've got bins overflowing with rubbish in the square, fatties shaking their backsides at Bob's shop and an endless supply of second-hand tat for you to clutter the house with. Nothing that can't be saved by a bit of white render.' He picks up his paper and buries himself behind the its pages again. 'Render, indeed.'

But as I watch Mum laser a death stare into Dad's back, the realisation hits me that if Lewis & Co. has its way, the likelihood of emptied bins, cake shops or even *The Good News Gazette* emerging from the parade anytime soon is unlikely, to say the least.

In fact, unless someone does something pretty quickly, the best thing on offer in Westholme could well be a bag for life and discounted tubs of Cadbury's Roses.

I'm still thinking about Dad's words when Emma texts later that evening.

Have you seen The Northern News? *The parade is going to be knocked down and turned into a supermarket.*

I text back immediately.

You're kidding.

The screen lights up.

Not definite yet, but it'll probably happen. Front page news. Saw it in the mini-market earlier.

I grab my phone and search for the story on *The Northern News* website.

The headline, *Supermarket To Replace Westholme Parade*, confirms my worst fears and the details as Gloria described them are set out in full detail. There's going to be a public meeting and consultation, but with new retail units, flats and revamped public space promised as part of the development, it's not hard to imagine that the plans will be approved.

I head back to the couch and call Emma.

She answers immediately. 'What do you think?'

'I can't believe it. All those shops, the people who make their living out of that place. What are they expected to do?'

'I know,' she says. 'I mean, okay, yes, the parade is a dump, but they can't just knock it down and replace it with a supermarket.' She pauses. 'What are you going to do about it?'

Lola approaches her dish, sniffs at the food on offer and looks at me in disgust.

'What do you mean, what am I going to do about it?'

'It says there's a public meeting at Westholme Town Hall next week, so I assume you'll be going to that. And I just thought now you've got the paper ... you might want to start a campaign.'

'But it's supposed to be about good news,' I say, wondering if *anyone* is ever going to get the premise of *The Good News Gazette*.

Emma pauses for a second. 'Well it would be good news if you saved the parade, wouldn't it?'

Around my chest, the invisible band tightens again. 'But what if it doesn't work? What if we lose?'

Emma considers the possibility.

'But what if you win?'

Neither of us speak for a few seconds.

'I'm going to do it,' I say quietly, feeling the start of a long-lost sensation stirring inside me.

'You're going to do what?' There's a hint of anticipation in her voice.

Deep in the pit of my stomach, something fierce starts to unfurl, spreading a fire through my veins that, now lit, feels overwhelming and unstoppable.

'I'm going to fight this all the way. It's not right. Developers can't just destroy an entire community to line their own pockets. It's terrible. Think of all the businesses that'll have to relocate, the people happily living in the flats above, the magnolia tree... We've got to fight this, Emma, we've just got to.'

Down the line, I can almost hear Emma smiling.

'Too right we have,' she says. 'Go get 'em, chick. It's time to make some waves.'

Westholme Community Facebook page:

Kim Hughes: Parade gonna be knocked down. Final nail in the coffin for Westholme then.

Peter Mason: Final nail got hammered in when they closed the cinema down. This part's the cremation.

Chapter Eleven

The public meeting is well underway and despite his smart suit and slicked-back hair, the feathers of the man standing before us are looking distinctly ruffled.

The Lewis & Co. spokesman – who introduced himself what feels like a million years ago as Phil – is only two slides into his PowerPoint presentation and emotions are already running high.

People are heckling. Phil is trying his best to deal with their comments in turn. And watching the scene unfold is a tall, dark-haired man who's leaning against a wall at the side of the room, arms folded across his solid chest.

'Look, mate, you're missing the point,' shouts a bloke in tracksuit bottoms and a vest top, an eye-catching dragon tattoo snaking all the way up his arm. 'There are businesses that have been in the parade for years. If you stick a supermarket there, you're gonna kill them stone dead.'

A murmur goes up around the room as the hundred or so people scattered across the carefully set out rows of chairs nod and voice their agreement.

'But, sir, as I'll explain on' – Phil consults his laptop – 'slide five, we won't just be building a supermarket, we'll also be recreating the shop units.'

A middle-aged man stands up. 'You're not being straight with us. You won't be recreating all the shopping units, will you? Your plans show you'll only be building eleven of them – not the twenty-two that currently stand.'

Phil looks alarmed, as though despite this being a public meeting, he's surprised at being challenged.

'Legal requirements are that we only have to rebuild those units that are fully occupied,' he says. 'We are under no obligation whatsoever to replace those that have been vacant for years.'

A woman I recognise to be a mum at Charlie's school shouts out. 'But thanks to your extortionate rental rates, that's fifty per cent of them. You'll reduce the units by half.'

'And what about the square?' An elderly gent with a walking stick huffs and puffs as his neighbours help him to his feet. 'I suppose you'll turn that into a car park, will you?'

Phil takes a deep breath and smiles. I suspect he's delighted that he finally has the opportunity to talk about the proposed improvements rather than focusing on everything we're about to lose. He clicks through the PowerPoint to slide seven and addresses the room.

'As you can see from these graphics, public space will be recreated elsewhere in the form of a beautiful area where shoppers can sit and enjoy their surroundings, soaking up the ambiance of the new, regenerated Westholme town centre.'

He quickly clicks on to the next slide, ignoring the hecklers. 'Our plans set out the details of how we'll install a beautiful set of benches and a few planters which will improve the look and feel of the square immensely.'

'What about the tree?' A lone voice rings out from somewhere at the back of the room and Phil peers out into the crowd to find its owner.

Margaret, Westholme's organiser extraordinaire, stands up, her hairstyle held in place with extra-firm hairspray, the beige hue blending perfectly with her camel-coloured top and brown trousers. 'What about the magnolia tree?'

Phil's expression is blank. He clearly hasn't got a clue what she's talking about.

'My husband used to have a barber's at the parade,' she says, holding her own despite the beginnings of a croak in her voice. 'I planted that tree, *with Lewis & Co's express permission* in the centre of the square after he died. It's been there five years now and it's coming on a treat. Will that be destroyed too?'

'Absolutely not, madam,' Phil says hastily. 'We'll move the tree and take good care of it.'

'But how are you going to move it?' Margaret asks. 'What if it gets damaged in the process?'

Phil's mouth opens and closes like a goldfish. He's out of his depth now and he knows it. The man leaning against the wall moves quickly to rescue the situation. I feel a weird jolt of interest in this new figure. He's pretty rugged-looking, must be well over six foot, and wears glasses that only serve to emphasise his huge dark eyes. Add to the mix a well-cut navy suit and white shirt and he couldn't look more out of place among Westholme's residents if he'd turned up wearing a crown.

'I'm sorry, I didn't catch your name,' he says, his eyes fixed firmly on Margaret.

'Margaret Kemp. Lived in Westholme all my life. My husband, Stan, ran the barber's.'

He nods by way of a greeting. 'Mrs Kemp, thank you for your question. I'm Daniel Lewis, managing director of Lewis & Co.' My eyes widen. Gloria's description of Daniel Lewis had left me with the impression that he was an absolute ogre. This guy? Well, he's … not what I was expecting.

'While not included on our PowerPoint,' he continues, 'we're absolutely aware of the magnolia tree and have every intention of carefully removing it and replanting it in the new square.'

'But it won't be anywhere near Stan's old barber shop,' says Margaret, clearly long past being silenced by a good-looking man in a suit.

Daniel adopts a conciliatory expression and pushes his dark-framed glasses further up the bridge of his nose.

'Unfortunately, no. As knocking down the units is necessary in order to press ahead with our plans, it will be impossible to keep the tree near the shop. I'm very sorry about that, but repositioning it is the best we're able to do.'

He pauses. 'What we would like to offer you, however, is an improved area around the tree, with perhaps some seating nearby for when you visit it.'

Margaret presses her lips together to form a thin, straight line. 'Not really the same though, is it, dear?'

Daniel has the good grace to look embarrassed. 'I accept your point,' he says. 'And I'm deeply sorry that that is a part of the plans that I'm unable to change.'

Margaret raises her eyebrows as if to indicate her utter disappointment in his answer and sits down.

Daniel turns to his sidekick. 'Thanks, Phil, please continue.'

'I think it's safe to say that tree's about to meet the same fate as Stan,' Ollie whispers in my ear.

I give his thigh a disapproving tap. 'Ollie!' I hiss, looking around to make sure no-one's heard.

'Come on,' he whispers. 'Can you really imagine they're going to pay any attention to a tree when there's millions of pounds at stake?'

'I know, but it's about her husband. Show a bit of respect.'

He thinks for a minute, then leans back in his chair. 'It *was* about her husband,' he says thoughtfully. 'I've just remembered something about the council having to take stuff like this into account. Now, played carefully, this tree could be the very thing that stops the plans from going ahead.'

One of the benefits of being your own – as yet unpaid – boss is that you can take a lunch break without anyone commenting on your late return, so although I'm aware I've already spent way too long browsing the new releases in The Lower Story, Westholme's one and only bookshop, I allow myself another five minutes of self-indulgence anyway.

My head is still spinning a little from last night's meeting and I'm wondering whether I've been a bit hasty in accepting Gloria's challenge to fight the development of the parade. I need some soothing balm today. And, as always, I'm finding it here.

The Lower Story truly is my happy place. I love the smell, the unobtrusive classical music owner, Neil, plays quietly in the background and the hundreds and hundreds of shiny new books that sit alongside many more battered old ones. It's thrilling to know that each and every one of them are carefully preserving the secrets that will ultimately only be revealed to those prepared to set aside their busy lives for a while, take the author's hand and step inside the pages that lie behind the covers.

I'm moving along the bookshelves, making a mental wish list, when I spot an A4-sized notice I've never seen before advertising a new 'Classics for Beginners' book club that's starting up in the shop.

I take my phone out of my pocket, snap a shot of it then make my way around to the counter to ask Neil what it's all about.

He's serving a customer – which in Westholme these days is a rare occurrence in itself – and I give him a wink and a smile as he adopts his very best 'bookstore manager' persona, which for Neil means raising his voice by half a decibel as he advises a young woman on footballer biographies her husband might like for his birthday.

There are dark circles under his eyes and I could swear his frown lines have deepened. I'm not sure what colour his hair was in his younger years – possibly brown, if his eyebrows are anything to go by – but now it's a thick wave of grey, as is his sparse beard. His checked shirt looks old and his jeans even older. And while I'm unable to verify this, I'm pretty sure that if I asked him to show me the soles of his shoes, I'd find a few holes here and there. Call it a sweeping generalisation, but this does seem to be a common theme among single men of a certain age who find the idea of shoe shopping more terrifying than a root canal.

We've chatted in the past about the fact that times are tough, but looking at him today I wonder just how close to the edge his situation really has become.

Having chosen a suitable book for his customer and rung it through the till, Neil mumbles a grateful 'goodbye and thank you for choosing to shop with The Lower Story' and I smile and head over to him.

'Hey, Neil, how's business?' I ask, then immediately kick myself for being so insensitive.

He smiles. 'Oh, you know, could be busier. Although it may not be something I'll need to worry about if this place gets knocked down.' He looks around the shop, the little kingdom that he's spent the best part of fifteen years building up. I shudder at the thought of it not being here.

'Did you go to the meeting last night then?'

He shakes his head. 'Not really my sort of thing,' he says, and I have to admit he's right.

I purse my lips, wishing I could magic up a solution, then plaster on an enthusiastic smile. 'I saw your poster, about the Classics for Beginners. What a great way of attracting new customers.' I'm doubtful that Neil is *quite* the right person to talk at length in front of a crowd, but impressed that he's prepared to give it a go.

He gives a little cough then starts fiddling unnecessarily with the counter display.

'It's being run by a friend, actually. I'll just be here to observe. You never know, I might even sell a book or two.'

I'm intrigued. I never pictured Neil as a man with friends, other than the many characters he appears to know intimately through his dedication to his books. It's not that you wouldn't choose this kind, unassuming man to be in your gang, more a sense that he only participates in real life when he absolutely has to. I have a feeling that as soon as he turns the shop sign to 'closed', he steps through the wardrobe doors and back into Narnia, or a more fitting destination for a fifty-something singleton, and doesn't emerge until his alarm clock goes off again the next morning.

'Who's the friend then, Neil?' I tease, a clumsy attempt at getting him to smile. I regret it almost immediately.

'No-one,' he says, his ears and cheeks turning crimson as he starts manically stacking pens into a Perspex container. 'I mean, just someone I know.'

Whoever it is, he's clearly mortified at the prospect of discussing it. I feel cruel and immediately abandon my line of questioning. 'Anyway, I was going to ask whether you'd like me to promote the book club in *The Good News Gazette*? I'm sure lots of people would be interested in this.'

He coughs again, but does at least reduce the speed at which he's stacking the pens. 'That would be very kind of you, Zoe,' he says quietly. 'I would appreciate that.'

'That's decided, then,' I say firmly. 'When's the event again?'

'Two weeks on Thursday,' his says, rubbing his head. He grins now, revealing endearing crinkles around his eyes and for a moment I can see him as a young man; shy, studious and, in his own way, attractive.

'I'll make sure it's on the website by tomorrow morning then. Ooh and I'll share it on social media as well.' I think for a minute. 'Are you on Twitter? Instagram? Facebook?'

He looks at me as though I've started speaking a foreign language.

'Never mind. I'll make sure people hear about this, Neil. It's going to be great!'

———————

Westholme Community Facebook page:

Tori Hindle: Well up for this Classics for Beginners group at The Lower Story. Been dying to read *Twilight* for years!

Chapter Twelve

One by one, the newly formed Friends of Westholme Parade flock into *The Good News Gazette* office where I greet them all as Ollie, in a surprisingly cooperative mood, serves up coffee, tea and biscuits.

After Ollie made it crystal clear that he wouldn't set foot back in the office until it had received the sort of deep-clean treatment usually reserved for major crime scenes, I'd scrubbed it to within an inch of its life.

By the time I'd installed two new chairs and desks, positioned some pictures on the walls and added a few new cushions to a couch I'd found underneath the clutter, even he'd had to admit it had cleaned up beautifully.

Tonight, looking around at the room, I'm pretty pleased with the result. And with people other than Ollie and I in it, it could almost pass for a *real* office.

The group file into the rows of plastic chairs I've arranged in front of a flipchart, chatting amongst themselves, and . I congratulate myself for serving refreshments. It's amazing how compliant they all are once they have a cuppa and a chocolate digestive in their hands.

The turnout isn't too bad, considering it's a Monday night and the attendees are missing a gripping *Coronation Street* storyline to be here. There's Cath and Antonio from the cafe, Lawrence the salsa teacher, Paula, Colin and Lynne, also from salsa, Margaret, Starr and Mum and Dad. Gloria's here, of course, while Charlie's sitting in the corner, delighted at the opportunity to enjoy extra time on his Nintendo. Emma and Beth have texted to say they're running late but hoping to get here at some point and, unsurprisingly, Neil has avoided the whole thing like the plague.

I make my way to the front of the room and clear my throat.

'Ahem. Right, everyone, thanks for coming tonight.' I cringe at the sound of my own voice. 'As you know, the demolition of the parade and the subsequent creation of a supermarket is a move that will affect each and every one of us, not to mention the community as a whole, which is why it is so important that we stop this development from happening. The aim of this group is to achieve just that.'

'I assume that most of us have never been involved in a campaign of this kind before. But I'm also aware that we have some secret weapons in our arsenal, not least of all Colin, who, as a former surveyor, does have some experience in this field.'

Everyone turns towards Colin, a short man with two symmetrical patches of dark hair on either side of his head. Unaccustomed to being the centre of attention, he blushes and nods to acknowledge the reference.

'As anyone who was at the public meeting the other night will know, the developer is now working up his plans to submit to the council.'

I pause as the attendees give a collective tut, accompanied by eye rolls and head shakes to reaffirm their disgust at the plans.

'We'll then have an opportunity to make our voices – and our objections – heard, which is why these meetings are so important. I really do think that by creating an opposition strategy that reflects our passion for the parade, we can prove to the council why the proposed plans should absolutely not go ahead.'

Murmurs of agreement go up around the room and Mum even claps for a moment, then, realising she's the only one doing so, lets her hands drop to her side.

'So, first thing's first,' I continue. 'Let's start with a mind mapping session around the best ways to stop this development from going ahead. Who wants to kick off?'

'It's gotta be a petition, hasn't it,' says Cath immediately. 'Send it to the planning committee and our local MP.'

I nod, pleased that someone's taking the initiative. 'That's a great idea, Cath.' I write the point down on the flipchart, feeling incredibly organised and efficient. 'Are you happy to be in charge of the petition then?'

Cath pulls a face. 'Well, I can't commit to that – I was just making a suggestion.'

I take a deep breath. 'Okay, never mind, we can talk about responsibilities later. The important thing is to mind map potential actions so please, just shout out any random ideas you might have and I'll jot them all down.'

Lawrence puts his hand up.

'How about writing letters, testimonies, about the importance of the parade and how it would affect us and our livelihoods if it were to be knocked down?'

I turn to the flipchart. 'Brilliant, Lawrence.'

'Maybe we could get local residents to join in,' Ollie suggests.

Lynne, a slim woman with honey-coloured, shoulder-length layered hair and clearly the driving force in her and Colin's marriage says, 'Let's write to our MP. I'll find out who he is.'

The room falls silent. Then Margaret says, 'He's always in *The Northern News*. What's his name... Marcus something.'

'Marcus Stanford,' Dad jumps in quickly, looking around the room and smiling as though he's just won the million-pound question on *Who Wants to be a Millionaire*.

'Marcus Stanford is a dear friend of mine,' Starr interjects. 'A *dear* friend. In fact, he actually lives next door. So I'll speak to him.'

'Great, thanks, Starr,' I reply. 'Any other ideas?'

'Why not hold a community fun day at the parade to remind people how much we need it, too,' says Starr, clearly on a roll now. 'I could sing.'

Everyone looks at her. We're all aware of her dancing skills, but the fact that she considers herself to be vocally proficient too comes as something of an unwelcome surprise.

'Do you know what, Starr, that's not a bad idea,' I lie, reluctant to curb anyone's enthusiasm at this stage. 'In fact, I think the fun day in particular would be brilliant. When I was reading up on the Westholme Parade recently, I noticed that it was built sixty years ago this year. Why don't we hold a procession through the town, just like the ones we used to have when I was a kid, and then a community fun day at the square? I'm sure Lewis & Co. would give us permission to do that. They're looking for support for this scheme of theirs – what better way than to let everyone have a party in the square?'

Everyone voices their approval.

'That would be nice,' Mum replies. 'Give us all something fun to look forward to. The carnivals used to be great. It'd be lovely to bring them back.'

'I used to be involved in the Westholme Carnival,' Margaret recalls. 'It was run by the Rotary Club back in the day so I'm sure I could rope in some of the members to help out. Hopefully they'll offer to run it. I'll raise it at the next meeting and report back. It might be a good idea for me to contact Daniel Lewis over permission for the carnival to go ahead at the square too. I'm sure he won't refuse an old woman this request. You, on the other hand,' she nods in my direction, 'he might see as more of a threat.'

I feel my insides unfurl at the thought of the Rotary Club running the carnival rather than me and marvel again at this powerhouse of a woman with the organisational skills of a CEO.

'Margaret, that would be amazing, thank you.'

'Leave it with me, my dear,' she says kindly and I thank my lucky stars that I've found her.

'And just so you know, Margaret,' I add, 'I'm well aware of the significance of the magnolia tree and I'll make sure that that's highlighted in any dealings we have, both the developers and the council. It's a really important part of the need to save the parade and it won't be forgotten.'

She lowers her eyes, bites her lip and simply nods.

Gloria raises her hand.

'Yes, Gloria?' I say, smiling.

'There's the small matter of a budget. Carnivals tend to cost quite a lot of money to stage and I wondered what your thoughts were on how it might be funded?'

I'm stumped. 'Maybe crowdfunding?' I suggest hopefully.

'Crowdfunding could work,' Lynne replies. 'I was involved in crowdfunding when the arts organisation I work for staged an event in Liverpool a few years ago. We managed to drum up quite a bit of support.'

'I'm sure I could convince the council to pitch in with a small grant too,' adds Gloria.

'Great.' I feel a little more confident now people are starting to lift some of the responsibility for all of this from my shoulders. 'If both of you wouldn't mind researching those things, I'll look into the cost and we'll see what's possible.'

I jot it all down on the flipboard then turn my attention to the rest of the group. 'Now back to the supermarket development. I did think about lobbying the planning committee members.

Nothing too in your face and certainly nothing aggressive – just a way of impressing upon them the importance of the parade's existence.'

The group stares back at me in silence. 'How would we do that?' Cath frowns.

'Maybe an impromptu delivery of cakes to their next meeting?' I wink, hoping that Cath will pick up on my not-so-subtle hint.

To my surprise, Cath doesn't immediately object. Instead, she pulls a face that I take to mean she's prepared to give it some thought.

Then Colin, who speaks so quietly that the room has to fall near-silent in order to hear him, pushes up the sleeves of his fleece jacket and says. 'You could always try and create a bat house in the parade.'

Everyone looks at him. A few people – most noticeably my dad – smirk.

'I think *you're* the one that's bats, Colin,' he says, laughing more openly now.

Colin smiles gracefully. If he's embarrassed, he's not showing it. Lynne places a protective hand on his knee.

'As a matter of fact,' he continues, 'the presence of bats in a property can, in some cases, prevent the building from being knocked down. Even the mention of bats will result in a survey having to be undertaken to establish whether they're present. So – and this is completely off the record – if you could entice bats to roost in one of the buildings, or at the very least mention the possibility that they might be present, then it would throw some spanners in the works of the owners trying to get the site shovel ready and buy us more time.'

'Seriously?' I say, sensing possibilities.

He nods. 'It's an offence to disturb bat roosts, so demolishing one would be a big no-no.'

'That's brilliant, Colin.' My heart lifts at the glimmer of hope he's just cast my way. 'Okay, so who wants to look into bats?'

'I don't mind doing that,' Colin replies.

A few more ideas are bandied around before I call the meeting to a close and I promise to send out meeting notes and action points, well aware that the name attached to most of those will be mine.

'I guess I could provide some cakes for the committee members,' says Cath as they prepare to leave. 'Maybe throw in a few coffees too.'

'Thank you, Cath, that's really generous of you,' I smile, grateful for the offer.

Instant coffee and synthetic cakes. How could we possibly fail?

As far as I'm concerned, the first Friends of the Westholme Parade meeting was an overwhelming success. And as I am a strict believer that every achievement, no matter how small, should be celebrated, I've dragged Charlie into the mini-market on the premise of buying him a gingerbread man for being quiet during the meeting, when we both know it's really so I can pick up a bottle of wine.

I'm trying to work out whether pinot or prosecco would be more fitting for the occasion when I hear a man's voice addressing Charlie. Whipping around, my shoulders relax at the very welcome sight of Sam, looking casually fine in grey tracksuit bottoms and a black t-shirt.

'Hi, Zoe.' He smiles. 'How are you?'

'Good.' I nod, trying to look not at all perturbed by the muscles in the top of his arms that are all but doing a song and dance routine as his basket, laden with fruit, veg and various sources of protein, challenges the capabilities of every one of them.

I subtly move my own basket – and its not-so-impressive contents – behind my legs.

'Doing a bit of shopping?' he asks, his voice warm and familiar.

'Yeah. We had the first Friends of Westholme Parade meeting in the office tonight and I needed to pick up' – I wrack my brains to come up with something that isn't booze or biscuits – 'cat food before we go home or I'll have Westholme's feistiest feline to answer to.'

My eyes dart further up the aisle to check on Charlie, who's trying to work out the purpose of a cat toy hanging off the sort of plastic contraption that holds pork scratchings in pubs.

When I look back, Sam hasn't moved his eyes from my face. 'I've been meaning to text you actually,' he says, those muscles still flexing unconsciously.

'Have you?'

'I was wondering,' he glances at Charlie then starts again, his voice quieter this time. 'I was wondering whether you might like to go—?'

His final words are lost in the sound of footprints and Charlie calling my name as, bored of the cat toy, he chooses that exact moment to return, leaving me unsure of what the question was, so I am clueless as to what the answer should be.

I shift awkwardly, unable to ask Sam to repeat himself in case maybe, just maybe, he was about to ask me out, while he stands in front of me waiting for a response.

'Mum, I need the toilet,' Charlie whispers, pulling out what has become his trump card, so to speak, of late.

'Okay, we're going now,' I hiss. Turning back to Sam, I say, 'Kids, eh?' then quickly follow it up with, 'I'd better go.' He nods, taking a few steps backwards, a hint of disappointment in his eyes.

'No problem,' he replies. 'Just let me know if you change your mind.'

And I stare after him as he makes his way to the tills, wondering what it is exactly that I'm being given the chance to change my mind about.

———

Westholme Community Facebook page:

Paul Gregory: It's all kicking off now – that girl at *The Good News Gazette* has launched a pressure group to stop the parade being knocked down. I'll post the link to the article.

Jimmy Hunter: Pressure group? What a joke. Only brown paper bags with massive wads of cash in them is going to save that place now.

Chapter Thirteen

I have never been so active on social media and I have to admit, I'm quite enjoying it. Seeing the number of 'likes' each of the posts has generated is more than a little addictive and it's a great way of finding out which stories are are resonating with the readers.

So far, of course, it's been Sam and his dimples that have garnered the most positive feedback, but the Classics for Beginners post has been liked and shared dozens of times too.

Not for the first time in recent weeks, I've been pleasantly surprised by Westholme's residents. Who would have thought there was a group of people just wanting to be guided through Dickens, Gaskell and E.M Forster? All they needed was someone prepared to make it all a little more accessible.

I start wondering whether Sam enjoys the classics, then catch myself and focus on shutting down my laptop instead. I'm off to meet up with Margaret and hear all about her meals scheme today and hopefully interview some of the new mums too. My tummy growls. That's if I don't eat the dishes myself first.

I'd imagined Margaret's Meals for Mums service as a quiet, cosy, genteel affair, with ladies of a certain age in twinset and pearls doling out meat and two veg to new mums so harassed they'd have eaten dog food if someone had heated it up for them. The reality, it turns out, couldn't be more different.

They might be looking for more volunteers, but the force that is Margaret has already enticed a whole host of people to join her in distributing meals made up of leftovers donated by restaurants across the region.

Each night, this dedicated group collect food that would otherwise be dumped, then turn it into tasty dishes for low-income mums who are feeling overwhelmed by the additional pressures placed on them by a newborn.

In certain cases, Margaret explains, the deliveries are the only meal the families will eat that day. 'What happens on the other days?' I ask. She frowns. 'We try not to think too hard about the other days.'

As I jot down some details about the group, it transpires that Margaret's own experience as a community health visitor was the inspiration behind it all.

'For many mums of newborns – and in particular those whose babies aren't sleepers – eating well can be the last thing on their minds in the early days,' she says. 'It was always something that concerned me when I worked as a health visitor, the thought that mums were doing everything they could to make sure their families were well cared for, but they weren't taking care of themselves.'

'Then one day, a friend who owns a restaurant told me about the amount of food they had to dispose of at the end of the day and asked whether I knew of any charities that would be glad to take it. Making meals for mums seemed like the perfect answer and so I started up this service.'

The white van that they've borrowed from the local scout group is jam-packed with meals, so rather than clamber in alongside the boxes, I follow in my car, snaking behind them through the town as we start on our route.

The first stop is a one-bedroom flat a few minutes away from the parade into which a mum, a newborn, a toddler and a pre-schooler are crammed. Within seconds of stepping inside I feel claustrophobic – as, it appears, does mum Ali who looks as though she'd do anything to hand over the kids and escape for a few hours.

'I'm sorry I can't offer you a cuppa,' she says when I explain who I am. 'I've just run out of milk.'

She brushes toast crumbs off her dressing gown with one hand,while the other hand holds the legs of the baby cradled in the nook of her arm. 'Sorry about the state of me as well. I look a mess, don't I? I haven't been able to get a shower in ... a while.'

Margaret sets the box of meals down on the kitchen counter and checks her watch. 'Fortunately, we have plenty of time today, don't we, Zoe?' she says briskly.

I sense where she's going with this and nod vigorously.

'So why don't you use the opportunity to have a shower while we keep an eye on the children? Zoe's a mum, she knows what to do.'

The woman looks as though she doesn't know whether to protest or kiss us. In the end she simply nods and scuttles off to the bathroom. And I spend the next thirty minutes on the floor, being used simultaneously as a climbing frame, gaming partner and then a mediator when the toddler presses the wrong button on the pre-schooler's Nintendo Switch. All with a newborn in my arms.

Clearly having concluded that she's contributed more than

enough to the country's childcare services over the years, Margaret stays firmly in the kitchen sorting out the food. By the time Ali emerges looking almost human again, I've managed to coax the children to turn off the TV and sit down while I use all my powers of imagination to regale them with a story about a dinosaur and a one-legged lion.

When we leave, the children are tucking into a home-cooked lasagne, Ali is feeding a very contented baby and I am hit with an overwhelming sense of satisfaction at how we've turned her day around. The fact that I also managed to grab a few quotes from her about the importance of Margaret's Meals for Mums only adds to my general feeling that, today at least, I'm winning at life. Ollie would be proud.

Our next visit is to a two-up, two-down on the Orchard Estate. One of the few remaining inhabited houses on a row that's been boarded up for years, the small front garden is thick with overgrown grass and weeds, and paint is peeling off the windows. There's a brick-shaped hole in the downstairs window with duct tape plastered over it and I start to wonder whether Margaret and I should be venturing inside alone, but then, reminded that I escaped from far worse locations during my time as a reporter, I take a deep breath and stand behind her as she knocks on the door.

We hear the inhabitants of the house long before we see them. There's the sound of an older boy shouting, combined with rap music playing loudly in the small front bedroom. Somewhere in the midst of the chaos I can hear the cry of a newborn and a mum yelling at them all to keep the noise down so she can put the baby to sleep. It's a plea that is clearly falling on deaf ears.

After endless rounds of knocking, the door is wrenched open

by a teenage boy. 'Alright,' he says, acknowledging Margaret's presence with a nod. 'I'll get me ma.' And he disappears back inside, a quick flash of the wording on the back of his t-shirt confirming my suspicions of what he'd really like to say to us, and indeed the rest of the world.

The front door leads straight into the lounge and from where I'm standing I can see two boys, probably a year or two older than Charlie, watching a YouTube video. At the back of the lounge a door frame with no door leads through to the kitchen where a woman with a baby in her arms acknowledges the presence of the lad who's just left us with a disinterested glance. Even from our position at the front of the house she looks exhausted.

The boy murmurs something and, seeing Margaret, the mum makes her way towards us. Most of her hair is blonde, but there's a good inch or so at the roots which is mousey brown and slicked with grease. A patch of dried sick is splattered on the left shoulder of her grey sweatshirt and her black leggings have been worn so much without washing that they look more like tracksuit bottoms. A line of smudged black eyeliner that I suspect has been there for a few days sits under one hollowed eye and dots of mascara have made their way onto the space just under her eyebrow. It's clearly been one of those weeks.

'Alright, Margaret,' she greets us, her voice thick with weariness, possibly at the effort it appears to be taking her to summon up a smile.

'Hello, love,' says Margaret. She pats her on the arm that's holding the crying baby. 'We've brought you some supplies.' She nods in my direction. 'This is Zoe. She's from *The Good News Gazette* and is accompanying me today to find out a bit more about what we do. Zoe, meet Fiona.'

I grin then, hoping that that one gesture will convey so many things; the sense of understanding that one mum can offer another, the sympathy I feel at the chaos she's having to endure

119

and the fact that she really, really needs to get that front window fixed.

Even as Fiona blinks back at me I can tell she's not really seeing me, or indeed picking up on any of my hidden messages. In fact, she seems to be so preoccupied that I truly think a green man with two heads could be making his way inside her house right now and it wouldn't register.

We follow her into the kitchen with our food, the scent of hot fare far preferable to the smell it's replacing, and Margaret sets the dishes down on the table.

'How've you been, dear?' she asks, forcing her naturally gentle voice up a few decibels in order to be heard over the rapper who is promising to carry out all sorts of unsavoury and illegal actions in the background and the baby whose cries are getting louder by the minute.

That one simple question pushes Fiona over the edge and her eyes become glossy with tears as her face crumples.

'Not so good today, Margaret,' she replies, stroking the baby's forehead in a bid to settle it. I peer at its face. It's wearing a pink Babygro with blue mitts and knitted cardigan so it's hard to work out what sex it is, but it's cute all the same.

Margaret guides Fiona towards a chair and sits her down in it, then fills up the kettle as I hover awkwardly, marvelling at the ease at which these mums simply let her take over and do exactly what needs to be done.

'Why don't I make us a cup of something and we'll have a little chat,' Margaret says, a subtle movement of her head indicating that I should sit down. I transfer a pile of socks from a chair to the table where it joins a pile of crumpled washing, which could either be clean or dirty and take a seat.

A cacophony of noise erupts from the lounge as a row breaks out between one of the boys in there and the gruff teenager we met before.

Their voices are like a red rag to the woman, who has tried so hard for so long to settle the child in her arms. 'Will you just. Shut. Up,' she yells, her voice piercing a delicate spot somewhere between my ear drums. The baby starts crying again. And I find myself wondering exactly which part of this whole scenario comes under the heading of 'good news'.

Westholme Community Facebook page:

Rosemary Jenkins: I volunteer for a group called Meals for Mums, which delivers food to mums in need, in and around Westholme. We're currently looking for more people to help, so if you'd like to get involved, please message me.

Alan Boyd: I volunteer for a group called Dishes for Dads, which delivers pizza and beer to stressed dads within a one-mile radius of Westholme. We're currently looking for donations of pizza (preferably pepperoni), beer (preferably Bud) and women (any kind). DM me for details.

Rob Horton: Now *this* is a group I want to join.

Chapter Fourteen

M argaret has the air of someone who's seen thousands of domestics, and as a former health visitor, she probably has.

'I'll go and have a word,' she says, quietly slipping out of the kitchen to talk to the boys.

I suddenly feel very much in the way and I look around the room, trying to pretend I'm not there in order to give the woman the head space she so desperately needs.

'Do you have kids?'

I turn to her. 'Just one,' I nod. 'Charlie. He's eight.'

'Good age,' she says, resting her elbow on the tale and putting her forehead on her palm. 'Not like mine.'

'How old are yours?' I ask, raising my voice to the point of shouting in order to be heard over the baby's wails. I really feel for Fiona's neighbours.

She frowns as if trying to recall the names and ages of her children.

'Johnny is fifteen, Kendal's eleven but acts as though she's twenty-one, Reuben's ten and then there's Sammy,' she says, her expression softening as she looks down at the baby.

Sammy. Well at least now I know it's a boy.

'How old is he?'

The woman looks at me, incredulous.

'Sammy's a girl, short for Samantha, after my mum. Look at her – can't you tell?'

A prickly heat dances around my cheeks and I look again.

'Of course…' I say. 'That's what I meant, she.'

Mercifully, Margaret re-enters the room at this point, saving us both from any further potential foot-in-mouth moments.

'All sorted,' she says, patting Fiona's arm. 'Now, let's make that tea.'

———

A cup of tea (coffee in my case) and a sleeping baby later and Fiona is finally ready to talk … and cry.

'The boys are at that age where they want to kill each other,' she sobs, 'all Kendal's interested in is uploading dance videos to TikTok and I'm terrified she's going to be groomed by a paedophile. As for their dad…' She casts a glance at Margaret. 'You know what he's like. Only comes back when he's run out of money and his bender's come to an end.'

I shudder, reminding myself how glad I am that I don't have to put up with any of that. When I close the door at night, it's just Charlie and me. I don't need to worry that someone's going to come staggering through the door – except maybe the cat.

'I don't know from one week to the next how I'm going to pay for everything,' Fiona continues, 'and I've got Johnny's birthday coming up next month. He's good like, knows not to bother asking for much but I feel like such a rubbish mum. And now I've got her,' she nods her head at the baby, 'and I'm getting no sleep, I'm just snapping at them all the time too.'

Tears spill out of her red-ringed eyes and I reach out and squeeze her hand. She looks at my notepad that I've, perhaps over-optimistically, placed on the table. 'Don't write about any of this, like.' She sniffs.

'Of course not.' I shake my head.

Margaret pulls out a chair and sits down opposite her. 'It sounds as though you have an awful lot on your plate. I noticed the front window too. What happened there then?'

Fiona rolls her eyes. 'Johnny had a run-in with someone. Probably best not to ask.'

Margaret presses her lips together then says, 'Have you been onto the housing association about it?'

'No.' Fiona shakes her head. 'I don't want them to kick us out.'

'Leave it with me,' Margaret says. 'I'll have a word with them. Now, you also mentioned money being an issue. Have you spoken to the Money Man at all?'

My ears prick up.

'Sheila down the road mentioned something about him but I didn't take much notice,' the woman says. 'What did you call him – the Money Man?'

'Barry, The Money Man,' Margaret repeats. 'He'll look at your finances and work out whether you're entitled to any more benefits or grants. He'll also go through your incomings and outgoings and help you to draw up a budget so that you can manage everything each month.'

The woman looks at her dubiously. 'What about debts – credit cards, overdrafts … stuff like that?'

'He can help you with those too,' says Margaret. 'Tell you what, why don't I have a word with Barry? He can give you a call and make an appointment to come round and see you.'

'Barry, Money Man,' I jot down on my notepad, so I don't

forget to ask Margaret about him later. That sounds like exactly the kind of story I want for *The Good News Gazette*. And maybe he can help me with my finances too.

Next to me, the woman's tears – and those of the baby – have finally stopped. She sniffs again and even manages a small smile. 'That would be great,' she says. 'Although maybe I could go to him.' She looks around her. 'The less people that see the house in this state, the better.'

———

I'm thoroughly inspired by Margaret's Meals for Mums service, but there's one small problem – so far, no-one's wanted to pose for a photo.

'Don't worry, dear,' says Margaret confidently. 'I'm sure our next mum will jump at the chance.'

Our final stop is still on the estate, at a little close a few roads away from Fiona's. 'Our last mum of the day is Stacey,' Margaret informs me. 'I think you'll like her.'

From the moment Stacey flings open the door to her two-up, two-down, dressed in a pink jumpsuit while simultaneously dancing to Stevie Wonder with a laughing baby on her hip, we're completely engulfed in her whirlwind of happiness. Tall, blonde and beautiful, she looks like the sort of mum I've always dreamed of being, and I know instantly that compared to our last house call, this one's going to be a blast.

'Sorry.' She giggles as she ushers us inside. 'I thought it was the baby's dad – he's due to call in soon. I promise I usually open the door in a much more refined fashion.'

Her house is sparse but she's upcycled practically everything she can to create a warm and cosy home for her and her four-month-old, Ted.

Glass food jars have been painted to create a cluster of vases that, when holding a simple bunch of flowers, look like something off Instagram. Twigs stuck into pretty former perfume bottles holding various oils make diffusers which fill the small house with a sweet, floral scent and an old square bookcase has been painted and dressed up with logs and fairy lights to create a false fireplace. The whole place looks fabulous.

'How on earth do you keep your home like this with a baby in tow?' I say, taking it all in. 'My house has never, ever looked like this and I suspect it never will.'

'Stacey, meet Zoe,' says Margaret. 'She's accompanying me today to write a story for *The Good News Gazette*.'

'Nice to meet you.' Stacey smiles, a slick gloss highlighting her plump lips. 'And as for this place? It's amazing what you can do when you have to.'

I make a mental note of which of her inspired touches I can pinch for my own tired decor. Ted gurgles, grinning in delight at the arrival of new visitors.

'Don't be fooled though,' says Stacey. 'I may have a tidy house but I can't cook to save my life.' She grins. 'I'm working through one domestic goddess goal at a time.' I take to her immediately.

I like her even more when she readily agrees to pose for a photograph, on the condition that we hold the baby first so she can stick some more make-up on. She emerges twenty minutes later looking as though she's had a MAC makeover.

'Ready,' she declares, grabbing Ted and falling easily into a series of poses.

On the surface, it appears there's never been anyone who's needed Margaret's services less, but when we open the fridge to put away some of the ingredients, I realise why her intervention is so important; apart from some milk and a couple of past-their-best carrots, it is literally bare.

'We're going to the shops tomorrow,' she explains, 'but I don't like to buy in more than I need – it's too easy to waste food and money that way.'

She's clearly got very little, but this woman is just so *on* it. I think of the amount of food I throw away each week and feel a wave of shame.

With the fridge stocked with meals, photos stored on my phone and the pages of my notepad filled, Margaret and I head down the little hallway, picking up our coats on the way out.

Stacey gives us both a squeeze and kisses our cheeks in turn. 'Thank you so much,' she says. 'If it weren't for you, I don't know what I'd do. I've tried to keep hold of some of my hairdressing clients but it's tricky with Ted right now and it's not like I can rely on Ted's dad for anything.'

And as I open the door, commiserating with her on the failings of men, I come face-to-face with the one man I'd hoped was the exception.

Standing on the doorstep, right in front of me, is Sam.

Westholme Community Facebook page:

Heidi Ho: Does this black and white cat belong to anyone (see pic)? She's been hanging out in ours with our tomcat for the last couple of days but there's a tag around her neck that says Lola so I'm sure someone'll be looking for her by now.

Jason Kline: That cat was in our house last week. Pinched my steak right off the kitchen worktop. Seemed quite cute though so we gave her some food and she spent the night in front of the fire.

Mark Mitchell: I had to chase her from our garden a few days ago. She kept terrorising my Rottweiler.

Zoe Taylor: Sorry, all, this is my cat. If she turns up on your doorstep doing a good impression of a stray, please don't be fooled – she's a con artist. Heidi, can you DM me your address and I'll come and get her. Jason, DM me your address and I'll replace the steak.

Chapter Fifteen

'I need to ask you a question and it's a serious one.'

Ollie is standing before me, a grave expression on his face. 'Go on then, hit me with it,' I say, taking a sip of coffee as I prepare for what's to come.

'Are you about to have a nervous breakdown?'

I splutter the contents of my mug onto the keyboard and grab a tissue, trying to simultaneously save myself from choking and my laptop from drowning.

'No!' I shriek through coughs. 'Why would you ask me that?'

Ollie smacks me on the back just that bit too hard. 'No reason, except that you seem to be miles away at the moment. You've taken on quite a bit recently – maybe too much if we're being entirely honest. Oh – and you put the kitchen roll in the fridge.'

'Ollie,' I say in my most dignified manner. 'I can assure you that I am not having a nervous breakdown. Although I might if you ever ask me anything like that again.'

'Alright, alright,' he says, holding his hands up in mock surrender. 'But if you ever need to talk.'

I shake my head, but I know he's right. Since seeing Sam on Stacey's doorstep the other day, I probably have been acting strangely. In fact, I've thought of little else. How could he not have told me he had a son? A son who's just *four months old*. More importantly, *why* would he hide something like that from me? I'd thought he was one of the good guys, but according to Stacey that couldn't be further from the truth. And to think I might have gone on a date with him if Charlie hadn't intervened.

Turning back to my computer, I resolve to get over it. He's a man. It's what they do. Any failure to ignore that small but important fact was mine and mine alone.

I'm uploading a story about the fact that the carnival is returning to Westholme when an email headed 'Invitation to meet' pops into my inbox.

Dear Zoe,

It has been brought to my attention that you are behind the recently formed Friends of Westholme Parade group.

I think it would be in both of our interests if we were to meet to discuss the group's plans and to explore whether there might be a way that we could work together to benefit both Westholme and its residents.

Please can you let me know your availability and we can schedule a date in the diary.

Best wishes
Daniel Lewis

'Wow,' I say, under my breath.

'You okay?' Ollie looks up.

'I'm okay,' I start chewing the skin around my thumbnail as I read over his words again. 'But look at this!'

Ollie wheels his chair around the desk to read the email. He lets out a long, slow whistle.

'He's got some front, I'll give him that.'

'I know. I can't believe he'd think I'd want to meet with him. As if that would change anything.' I shake my head as my eyes hover on his words again.

'Well, you never know,' says Ollie as he scoots back to his desk.

'What do you mean?'

'You can be very persuasive when you want to be. After all, you managed to get me here, working for next to nothing, when I could be at home with my feet up in front of the TV.'

'Hey!' I exclaim, my voice filled with indignance.

Ollie laughs. 'Seriously, maybe it would be worth meeting up with him. Tell him the parade is like a caterpillar. An ugly old bugger but once you peel its wrapper off there's a beautiful butterfly waiting to be set free.'

'I don't think even I would buy that one.'

'Why not put forward the economic arguments around keeping the parade open then?'

'That's the problem,' I reply, the feeling of defeat creeping in again. 'I'm not sure there is an economic benefit.'

Ollie throws his hands in the air, exasperated. 'Then appeal to his better nature. Impress upon him what this means to the community. Look at it this way – what have you got to lose?'

I turn back to my computer screen and read the email once again.

Inhaling deeply, I say, 'Okay, let's do this,' and begin to type.

Dear Mr Lewis

Thank you for your email. I would be happy to meet you and discuss the next steps for the Westholme Parade.

I pause, choosing my next words carefully and then start tapping on the keyboard again.

My availability is limited this week, but I do have space in my diary tomorrow morning at 10am, if that time would suit you. We could meet at Cath's Caff?

I look forward to hearing your thoughts.

Kind regards,
Zoe

'What do you think?' I ask, after reading it out to Ollie.
'Perfect. Short, polite, to the point. Press Send.'
I jab the Send button on my keyboard. 'Done.'
Within minutes, a reply flashes up on my screen.

Dear Zoe,

Tomorrow at 10am would suit me perfectly. In the absence of other coffee establishments around these parts, Cath's Caff will be entirely adequate.

Best,
Daniel

'All arranged. I'm meeting him tomorrow at Cath's Caff.'

'Interesting,' Ollie says, nodding slowly. 'Well, I'll await the results of that particular rendezvous with bated breath. For now, I'm popping out for lunch. Do you want anything?'

'No, I'm fine thanks – brought my own today.'

I think of the squashed sandwiches inside my bag, the best option I can afford right now, and bury my longing for a freshly baked French stick filled with my favourite toppings.

Saying no to shop-bought sandwiches might be an unavoidable consequence of being a single mum with no income but, good grief, it's a painful one.

As soon as Ollie is out of the door, I reach for the letter that's been haunting me all morning. I didn't have time to read it before dropping Charlie off at school, but I know what it is – a VISA bill reminder. I also know that my minimum payment is overdue.

I unfold it slowly, groaning as I see the balance. I've almost maxed out my credit card, there's very little left in my bank account, and most of the cash I'd had in the house was sent into school this morning to pay for Charlie's forthcoming zoo trip.

I don't know how this happens, but somehow it always does. At the start of every month I diligently work out a budget for the month and pledge to stick to it. But within days, I've usually been hit with unexpected costs. A friend's birthday here, a car repair there. Always unexpected, always unaffordable.

Right. There's nothing else for it. I need to do the one thing that, in normal circumstances, I would use every tactic in the book to avoid. I need to contact Charlie's dad, Ryan.

It's not as though he refuses to give me any child maintenance – he'll usually cough up eventually if I put enough pressure on him. But I hate asking him for money and he knows it. So, the unpaid payments tend to go unacknowledged by both of us until the odd occasion when, like now, the situation reaches breaking point.

My fingers move quickly across the touchpad of my phone as I check when Ryan last made a payment into my bank account. Eight months ago. He's definitely due a text.

Cursing myself for having to do it, I tap a message into my phone.

> *Ryan, it's been a while since your last payment and I've lost my job. Can you let me know when the next one's coming so I can organise my finances please?*

I then remember the promise I made to Charlie and, against my better judgement, add:

> *PS – Charlie's asking if he can see you again soon. Let me know.*

As I stare at the calculations in front of me, the long fingers of anxiety reach up from my stomach to squeeze my pounding heart like a sponge. This is bad. Really bad. I bury my head in my hands, wondering what to do. Then I remember the Money Man. What was it that Margaret said to Fiona about him? *He'll go through your incomings and outgoings and help you to draw up a budget so that you can manage everything each month.* Turning back to my phone, I scroll through my contacts, find his number and make the call.

The Good News Gazette

Westholme Community Facebook page:

Claire Phillips: Has anyone seen *The Good News Gazette* site? It says they're bringing back the Westholme Carnival this year to celebrate sixty years of the parade.

Johnny Miller: Sixty years of rubbish shops housed in a concrete heap that's going to be knocked down soon anyway? Can't wait.

Chapter Sixteen

The following day, I drop Charlie off at school and head straight for the cafe so I can fit in a little work time before my meeting with Daniel.

As I drive through town, a nineties pop song comes on and I crank it up, singing at the top of my lungs as the sun warms the side of my face through the window. I'm feeling great today. The site's heavily populated with content now, with Sam's article still garnering the most hits and, so far at least, I've managed to avoid using Starr's twerking video – a move which I suspect will protect both her and me from a world of embarrassment.

Ollie and I have agreed on a publication date for the print version at the end of July and although there's a lot to do, I'm excited about the idea of creating a newspaper again.

But perhaps the best news is the fact that, in the two days since we launched the online petition against the supermarket plans, more than a thousand people have signed it. Maybe, just maybe, there's a chance we can fight off Lewis & Co. after all.

Thirty minutes later, I'm sitting in Cath's Caff, still riding high on the idea of defeating Daniel and his posse when raised voices at the counter interrupt my daydream.

'I do not know how to use it,' Antonio is remonstrating in broken English, pointing despairingly at a huge shiny coffee machine that has been dumped on the counter. 'I only said you should get one.'

'But you're Italian!' Cath yells back indignantly.

'So what!' he shouts. 'You are English but you don't drink tea. At home I buy coffee, I don't make it.'

'What am I supposed to do with that thing now?' Cath points accusingly at the contraption.

Her nephew throws his hands up in the air. 'Read the recipe,' he huffs, thrusting a book of instructions in her hands before muttering something about a cigarette break and storming off into the kitchen. I take a sip of the instant coffee that, along with tea, comprises the hot drinks offering at Cath's Caff. I grimace at the bitter taste and wonder again how the deluge of coffee bars that have engulfed the rest of the UK have so far managed to avoid Westholme.

A movement at the front door marks Daniel's arrival and as he approaches the counter warily, I suspect he might be thinking the same thing.

'Do you have a menu I can look at?' he asks Cath.

'You're looking at it. I'm the walking talking menu. What do you want?' Cath snarls in response.

I turn my attention back to the site, wondering how best to indicate that I'm the person he's supposed to be meeting, when a polite cough causes me to look up.

'Zoe?'

With a five o'clock shadow grazing his jaw and another impeccable suit jacket gracing his shoulders, he looks far more Italian than the only real Italian in here.

Scraping back the chair, I stand up and shake his hand. 'Hello,

Mr Lewis,' I say, trying hard to present a cool exterior despite feeling uncomfortably and unexpectedly flushed. His skin has a golden tone to it and his brown eyes are so dark they're almost black.

'Daniel, please.'

I sit down and he pulls out the opposite chair, wincing at the torturous sound of wooden legs scraping against tiles, just as Cath bangs down a mug of coffee on the table, contents sloshing over the side. He watches her storm back to the counter then turns to me. 'Customer service is not high on the agenda, I see,' he says.

'You get what you pay for.'

Daniel looks around. 'Hmmm, it's certainly one of the *cheaper* establishments.' He nods at my drink, then gestures to his own. 'The owner clearly saves the cups and saucers for her regulars,' he quips, taking a sip. 'Nice coffee though.'

I smile, sure he must be being sarcastic but also thrown by the straight line of his mouth and I begin to wonder if he actually does like the coffee.

'You have to earn Cath's trust before she'll let you anywhere near these,' I joke in an attempt to start the meeting off on a friendly footing.

'In fact, I know a great way that you could do just that…' I let my words trail off as I wonder whether I've dispensed the niceties far too quickly.

'It's a business decision,' he says firmly. 'And let's face it, Westholme could do with a big supermarket.'

'We already have a big supermarket on the road out of town. And then there's the mini-market of course.'

He raises an eyebrow, but I carry on undeterred.

'How would we benefit from a new one?'

'For a start, the supermarket chain I'm partnering with wants to invest a lot of money in this. It wouldn't just be a supermarket. It would be a *hypermarket*.' He says this last bit with such aplomb, you'd swear he'd just announced he was about to bring Harvey Nichols to Westholme.

I frown. 'There's a cafe, a butcher's and a greengrocer's in the parade, as well as numerous other independents in and around town. Not only would you be putting the parade's shops out of business, you'd also be killing other local retailers too.'

'I appreciate,' says Daniel, 'that progress is not always welcomed—'

'Or even required,' I cut in.

'But it is necessary,' he resumes. 'Look at the state of the parade. It's a mess. I presume you live around here? What do you think it's doing for your house price and for those throughout Westholme? Don't you realise it's dragging them all down?'

'And what would a steel and glass supermarket construction do? Put them up?' I argue back, feeling a heat spread across my face as a passion I didn't realise I even possessed lays itself bare. I know he has a point, but it's not one I'm willing to concede.

He shrugs. 'It may well do.'

I urge myself not to rise to his bait.

'Getting back to why we're here,' I say. 'Was there a reason you wanted to meet me?'

For a moment he colours slightly, a look of embarrassment fleeting across his face, before the mask returns.

'This group you've started—'

'The Friends of Westholme Parade,' I clarify.

'Yes, that one. It strikes me that, unfortunately for its members, who I'm sure are very keen to preserve the status quo, the supermarket development is ninety-nine per cent likely to go ahead. Which means that in a few months, your little bunch of well-meaning residents are going to look back and kick themselves at all the time they wasted. The new supermarket—'

'I thought it was a *hypermarket*,' I cut in. I know I'm being immature, but he's pushing all my buttons.

'The *hypermarket*,' he says slowly, as though he's talking to a child, 'will mean new jobs, new offerings, and even new commercial units for local businesses. No-one has to lose out on anything. It will be just like it is now, only better.'

I snort. 'How on earth will it be in any way like it is now? The parade won't be here for a start. Are you seriously telling me that the butcher's and greengrocer's are going to be able to operate from retail units next to a supermarket?'

'I understand you feel strongly about this,' he says, 'but you must understand that whether it's in Westholme or anywhere else, progress is inevitable. The fact that it comes at a price is also inevitable. By trying to oppose it, you're wasting your own time and everyone else's. This development is going to go ahead whether you like it or not.'

'Really,' I say, pushing my chair back and causing the most ear-piercing screech on the tiles in the process. I zip my laptop into its case and thread my arms through the sleeves of my jacket, shoving my fingers repeatedly into them until they're freed from one of the folds. 'We'll see about that. You may have written off Westholme, but I certainly haven't.'

Daniel looks at me, smug, condescending. 'You're making this too personal.'

'Mr Lewis,' I say, my voice shaking with rage. 'For the past fifty-odd years, the parade has been more than just a shopping centre. It's been a meeting place for friends, in fact it's been a place to *make* friends; it's been somewhere that new mums can enjoy a conversation with someone who actually responds in words rather than gurgles, where people can start their own businesses, take their first steps into employment, escape the loneliness of being alone.' I continue, so enraged that I'm oblivious to the hush that has fallen around the cafe in direct contrast to the increasing volume of my voice.

'People have found a passion for gardening here, they've

found love here, they've challenged prejudices here, they've even...' I say, looking at Antonio, who has abandoned his own strop in order to listen in on this one, '...moved countries to be here. So, don't you dare tell me I'm making it too personal. If anything, I'm not making it personal enough. Now I think we've said all there is to say, don't you agree?'

This time he doesn't answer. He just sits there, staring into his instant coffee.

'I thought so. Goodbye, Mr Lewis.'

As I turn my back on him and direct my trembling legs through the maze of tables and chairs, a slow clap starts up. I turn around and see Cath, hands making repeated contact with each other, behind the counter. Antonio follows. Then, one by one, the entire cafe joins them, nodding at my words. I pause at the door and watch as all eyes turn to Daniel.

Aware that he's in a minority of one, he stands up, straightens his tie and picks up his briefcase.

I'm about to leave when I see him stop by the counter. 'I don't suppose I can get another of these to go, can I?' he says, raising his mug.

Cath steps forward, arms folded. 'Tell you what, how about I *don't* get you another of those and you just go?'

Daniel looks around the room, at the expressions of disgust etched on the faces of those watching the scene unfold, all defiant in the face of the man who is about to destroy their community.

'You know, I'm trying to make things better. *This* better,' he says, throwing an arm up so violently I fear for the carefully handstitched seams of his jacket.

'I think you must leave,' Antonio says quietly. And me? Well, I make a dash for it and head back to the office. Daniel Lewis may have money, but I have the people of Westholme on my side. And I'm going to stop him from knocking down the parade if it's the last thing I do.

Westholme Community Facebook page:

Alan Boyd: Massive showdown at Cath's Caff today. Think the owner of the parade might have a fight on his hands with that *Good News Gazette* girl.

Jonathan Partridge: Yeah it's Zoe Taylor who's behind it, isn't it? Made the mistake of standing her mate up once. Zoe let me have it with both barrels. Let's just say I never stood anyone up again. That parade bloke doesn't stand a chance.

Chapter Seventeen

B arry Swift, a.k.a the Money Man, is not your typical superhero.

He has a very round tummy, wears a thin grey polyester suit, blue shirt and red tie, and when he moves in his chair I can see Father Christmas socks peeping out from underneath his trouser legs, despite the fact that it's May.

But he also has a smile that makes his whole face light up, is a whizz with figures, and could be about to save my life.

We're sitting at my kitchen table, the surface almost covered in old-school paper bills and documents that I've chucked in storage boxes over the years. I wasn't sure whether I'd ever need them again but always worked on the basis that it was best to save them anyway. Now I'm so glad I did.

Barry taps a few numbers into his calculator, scratches the fuzz that covers his head, dark on top and grey at the sides, then says, 'I'd need to look into it further, but I'm pretty sure we could reduce your outgoings by a few thousand quid if we shopped around for better deals.' He winks. 'Maybe even more if you reign in your coffee habit.'

JESSIE WELLS

One by one he dissects each of my direct debits, searching for better deals and generally trying to find ways to help me cut costs. By the end of our session, he's saved me the best part of £3,000 a year.

Finally having a plan in place to manage my money is like opening the door to a sunnier, shinier world. I can literally feel my spirits leap. It's as though they're

setting off fireworks and hosting their own little celebration party inside my body or wherever it is they reside.'This is incredible,' I say as I thank him. 'I can't believe I've been over-paying by so much for so long.'

'You're not the only one,' he says, rubbing his forehead with his chubby hand. 'It was only a few years ago that I was doing the same.'

He's agreed to let me do a story on him for *The Good News Gazette*, as well as giving me some good news of my own, so I make us another cuppa, pick up my trusty notepad and sit, transfixed, as piece by piece, Barry reveals the story of his life.

'Eight years ago, I drove a Range Rover, wore expensive suits and had a house in Presthill that I could only have dreamed of back when I was growing up here in Westholme,' he says.

'I was married to my childhood sweetheart with two fantastic sons and a job in medical sales that I loved. But then, out of the blue, I was made redundant. My income stopped, but the spending didn't. Meals out, holidays, nice clothes … none of that changed – until the money ran out.'

He pauses now and I try and picture him in his former life, wearing fancy suits and socks that didn't have Santa faces on them. It's a challenge.

I hear him take a deep breath as he prepares to relive what came next, then he continues.

'Within a year, I'd lost everything. The house, the car … my family.' He looks down, his face expressionless as he recalls the most painful part.

'We had a bit of equity left over when we sold the house, so we rented a small place on the Orchard Estate. My wife started doing a bit of cleaning work but I struggled to get anything at all. The stress was immense as the money started to disappear. We didn't know what was going to happen. Then one day she went out to work and never came back.'

His voice cracks a little as he tells me this and I stop taking notes and wait while he sips his drink, steadying his emotions.

'I was left alone with my boys and suddenly, it really was a case of sink or swim. We had no food and no money to buy it. So, I got creative. Every weekend, the three of us traipsed around Presthill and Lawton, offering to wash windows, houses … anything we could to earn a bit of cash. During the week I contacted every business for miles around, begging for work.'

'We just about managed to cover the rental payments and the kids never went without food, but…' He points at his belly and smiles ruefully. 'One of the casualties of the whole experience unfortunately,' he says. 'Now I *can* afford to eat, I tend to do too much of it.'

I'm scribbling as fast as I can, trying to capture every word that falls from his lips.

'Anyway…' He leans back in his chair, visibly more relaxed now the worst part of the story is over. 'Slowly but surely, I started bringing the money in again. Then I got an office job on the outskirts of town and I'd learnt enough by that stage to know I needed to stick to a budget if we were to get by.'

'As I started looking into it all – where to find the cheapest groceries, how to get the best deal on services – I was shocked to realise how much money we'd wasted before. And once I was back on my feet, I realised there were plenty of other people in my position who would probably benefit from knowing some of the money-saving tricks that I'd learnt.'

'So far,' he grins, 'I've helped two-hundred-and-eighteen people – nineteen including yourself – to sort out their money. My target is to get that figure up to a thousand.'

'Wow,' I say. 'I can't even imagine how much cash that would equate to over the years.'

'Half a million at the last count,' he says, his chin raised now, shoulders back. 'Half a million quid just by doing a bit of shopping around.'

'I see.' I smile. 'So *that's* why they call you the Money Man?'

He nods. 'Well, that and the fact that all the money I've saved means I'm now sitting on a shedload of cash of my own. The difference is, this time I'm not blowing it.'

I pack the bags of groceries into my trolley, quietly yet triumphantly high-fiving myself because, empowered by the Money Man, I've successfully managed to avoid the chocolate and sweets aisle, the cakes section and the wine department in the parade's mini-market. I've even convinced Charlie to pick up a piece of free fruit on offer.

One last stop at the kiosk for a newspaper and a National Lottery ticket (for investment purposes) and we'll be home free.

I join the queue, averting my gaze from the selection of chocolate on display. As well as conserving cash, I simply *have* to lose 1lb at Slim City this week so I'm determined to cut out the treats. As Charlie takes a few steps away from me to look at the football magazines, I feel a wave of temptation threaten my good intentions. Trying but failing to keep my eyes focused on the cover of the *Men's Health* magazine, I make the mistake of allowing them to stray back to the chocolate display.

All of my favourites are there, just centimetres away from my grasp. *Mars bars, Cadbury Dairy Milk … they even have Fry's Chocolate Creams, for goodness sake. How on earth am I supposed to resist those?* But I won't give in. I'm a strong, healthy woman. And I'm absolutely determined not to fail.

I'm trying to stuff the Fry's Chocolate Cream I've just bought into my jacket pocket so I don't have to explain to Charlie why I'm allowed one but he's not, when I feel a tug on my sleeve.

'Look, Mum. What's happening over there?'

I turn to see what's captured Charlie's attention. Beyond the sliding-glass doors, Margaret and some of the other gardeners are watering the planters on the other side of the square. But that's not what's caught Charlie's eye. A few feet away from where we stand, the *Big Issue North* seller who I'd planned and failed to speak to is cowering on the ground, arms wrapped tight around her knees and head buried into them as a dozen or so teenagers in black tracksuits with their hoods up, hurl empty bottles, cans of booze and insults at her.

My heart starts racing as I wonder what to do – whether to alert the supermarket staff to the horror unfolding outside or step in before the gang do some serious damage and help her myself.

I cast a glance at the security guard watching the scene with disinterest.

'Right.' I pass Charlie my handbag and check that the chocolate is still firmly in my pocket. 'Don't move,' I say, before marching briskly through the doors towards the boys.

'Hey,' I shout, 'what do you think you're doing?'

The boy at the front, who I guess to be around sixteen or

seventeen, turns to face me. A scar runs down the side of his face and his top lip curls up as he glares at me. 'Mind your own business,' he snarls.

He raises his arm and prepares to throw another bottle, but I grab it and stand in front of him, suddenly aware of my own physical vulnerability as he towers over me.

'Stop it!' I yell, a hail of debris continuing to fly past me towards the girl.

A look of pure hatred flashes in the boy's eyes. He wrenches his arm away, knocking me to the floor as he shakes his arm free and continues his torrent of abuse.

I lie on the floor, stunned. Then, vaguely aware of the shoppers finally trying to intervene, I notice Charlie out of the corner of my eye, terror etched on his face as he drops my handbag and runs towards me.

'Mummy.'

'Charlie, stay there,' I yell, anxious to stop my little boy venturing into what is quickly becoming a ring of fire. It's too late; he's determined to reach me. *'Stay there.'*

Suddenly Charlie disappears from view as someone scoops him up out of the way.

Panic pumps through my veins as I scramble to my feet, my eyes desperately following his little frame. Then I realise who has hold of him. It's Daniel Lewis.

Swiftly depositing Charlie back inside the supermarket, he returns to face up to the ringleader and they stand nose to nose as Daniel speaks quietly to him.

'The lad's got a knife. Call the police,' a voice shouts, and I reach for my phone before remembering it's in my handbag.

Sensing trouble, the other gang members pause their assault on the girl and surround the pair of men.

A hush descends on the group as Daniel starts to speak again, his words inaudible to the onlookers. Then, something

148

strange starts to happen. The boys withdraw, moving slowly backwards until the ringleader himself issues a final, defiant spit on the ground and the gang skulk away from the parade.

I race over to Charlie, enveloping him a bear hug and clutching him tightly. For once, he doesn't protest.

Releasing him, I bend down so I can see his face. 'Are you okay?'

Charlie brushes the back of his hand over the tears that are trickling down his face and wipes his nose on his sleeve.

'I thought that boy was going to hurt you.'

'You're kidding, aren't you?' I force a smile. 'I could have taken them all out.' I retrieve my handbag and look over at the *Big Issue North* seller. She's shaking her head as she talks to Daniel, who is now crouching in front of her.

I watch the scene with grudging fascination as he helps her up, takes off his coat and wraps it around her. He then pulls some notes out of his trouser pocket and presses them firmly into her hand.

'What's going on? Are you okay?' Curious to find out what has caused the kerfuffle just yards away from her cafe, Cath has entered into the fray, closely followed by Margaret and a couple of the other Westholme gardeners.

'I'm fine,' I say. 'But I'm not too sure about her.'

'Let's go and find out,' says Cath, her jaw set in grim determination.

We walk over to them, Cath, Margaret, Charlie and I, an unlikely but well-meaning support crew.

Daniel starts speaking into his mobile while the girl presses her fingers against her eyes, in a pointless attempt to stem the tears that won't stop coming.

Cath puts her arm around her, revealing a compassionate side she usually keeps well hidden from view. 'Come on, don't cry.

They're nothing but animals.' She looks at Daniel. 'Is he calling the police?'

The girl nods.

'What's your name, love?' Margaret asks, her voice gentle.

'Adina.'

'Why don't you come into the cafe, Adina, and we'll get you sorted out? Antonio can make us all a nice cup of coffee too.'

Adina lets Margaret and Cath lead her into the cafe. I'm trailing behind them, trying to appease Charlie with the promise of a blue slush, when I hear a low, rough voice.

'Did they hurt you?'

I turn around and come face-to-face with Daniel, still impeccably dressed, despite the loss of his coat and his run-in with the Westholme mafia.

'I'm fine, thanks.' I'm trying to ooze standoffishness following yesterday's meeting, but gratitude overtakes me. I gesture towards Charlie. 'Thank you for moving my son out of the way. He should have stayed in the shop ... he was just worried about me.'

Stepping forward, Daniel takes hold of my left arm and turns it to reveal a bloodied patch spreading through the elbow of my white cotton top.

'He was right to be – you're bleeding. Do you regularly do battle with Westholme's gangs?'

I smile self-consciously, surprisingly aware of the touch of his hand around my arm and the intensity of his dark eyes. He holds my gaze for a little longer than is comfortable, before I gently pull my arm away. 'No this is definitely a one-off.'

'Don't do that again, okay?' he says. 'Those boys ... you don't know what you're dealing with.'

Don't know what I'm dealing with? I try to ignore the wave of indignance that rises fleetingly and instead say, 'I have a good idea.'

Daniel frowns. 'Then you'll know exactly what I mean. I've called the police, but I wouldn't expect them to rush to the scene of the crime. They didn't sound particularly concerned.'

He starts to walk away and then turns back.

'Oh, and you'll be glad to know your son wasn't the only thing I rescued.'

I raise an eyebrow, still smarting from his comment.

He reaches into his pocket and pulls out the Fry's Chocolate Cream I had hidden so carefully.

'I think this is yours?'

An unpleasant heat spreads across my face as he returns the offending item.

'Oh, thanks,' I say. 'It's for Charlie.'

'Yeees,' his little voice hisses triumphantly from my side.

Daniel nods, keeping any hint of a smile in check. 'Thought it might be.'

As he turns away he throws one last retort over his shoulder. 'By the way, they're my favourite too.'

I'm huddled around a table with Margaret, Adina and Ollie, who, despite only appearing after any threat of physical violence had been averted, seem to be aware of every detail of the event. Charlie, sitting next to me, is staring at my phone and slurping blue chemicals out of a straw.

'I can't believe it,' says Ollie, feigning surprise, after he's been brought up to speed by Margaret. 'I knew those lads were trouble, but I didn't realise they'd go that far.'

'They did it before,' Adina says in quiet, stilted English, 'but the bottles were plastic then. This time...' She looks down. 'I was very scared.'

'Do you mind me asking where you're from?' I ask.

'Bucharest, Romania,' she says, looking as though she's half-expecting me to tell her to go home.

'And how long have you been here?' I'm probing, but I'm doing it carefully. I know I need to tread gently.

'For just one year.'

'And is selling *Big Issue North* your main source of income?'

She frowns to indicate that she doesn't understand and I rephrase the question. 'Is selling *Big Issue North* your only job?'

She nods.

I look closely at her, taking in her thick, long dark hair that, now free of her beanie hat, cascades across her shoulders and her deep-brown eyes. She is universally beautiful – a fact that is clearly not lost on Ollie, who is gazing at our new friend as though she is the most fascinating creature he has ever had the good fortune to come across.

Underneath her clothes – a pair of skinny jeans now sporting lager stains that stand out like brown raindrops against her long legs and a plain black jumper that narrows around the waist – it's clear that she's hiding an impressive figure too. In any other situation, I'd be envious of this woman. But as she sits alone, totally dependent on the kindness of strangers, my heart breaks for her.

'What did you do in Bucharest?' Ollie asks and I'm taken aback by the soft tone of his voice. No sarcasm, no irony, just real concern.

'I work at coffee bar,' she says.

I look around the cafe, at the counter where Cath is fixing our drinks, at the Formica tables and the red floor tiles that lie underfoot. 'I bet it was nothing like this one.'

Adina smiles. 'It was very different.'

'So where are you staying now?' Ollie asks.

'Anywhere I can… Shelters if I can get in … or I sleep on the streets.'

'Oh, my dear girl,' Margaret interrupts. 'That's awful. A young girl like you, you mustn't be more than what, twenty-one, twenty-two?'

'Twenty-three,' Adina replies quietly.

Margaret shakes her head. 'So dangerous,' she says, almost to herself.

A moment passes before she speaks again.

'Well, there's no question about it. You'll have to sleep at my house.'

We all hold our breath, hoping Adina will opt for this solution rather than any of the less appealing alternatives.

'I could not,' she says.

'You absolutely could.' Margaret is resolute. 'I have a big house and no-one to share it with. You don't have a home. It makes perfect sense.'

After some to-ing and fro-ing, Adina reluctantly agrees to stay at Margaret's for the next few nights on the condition that she pays her way.

And while Charlie's repeated kicking of the chair leg indicates he's ready to go home, Ollie is clearly keen to keep the conversation going.

'What are coffee shops like in Bucharest?' he says.

Adina's eyes open wide as she's reminded of what she's left behind and she uses her hands to make up for the words she doesn't know how to say. 'Busy, lots of talk, laughing, good coffee … happy places.'

I look at the man beside us, shovelling an all-day breakfast into his mouth while feasting on his tabloid and can't help but wonder what she makes of the closest thing Westholme has to a coffee bar.

'Lots of different coffees,' Adina continues wistfully. 'Cappuccinos, lattes, espressos. And, of course, teas and food too.'

'Sounds amazing,' I say. 'It might be a bit more like that here if someone could work the coffee machine.'

'Which type is it?' Adina asks.

'Absolutely no idea. I just know that it's big, silver and behind the counter next to Antonio.'

Adina cranes her neck to identify the machine. 'Ah yes, I know it,' she says confidently, her whole demeanour changing as she finds herself on familiar territory. 'It's similar to the one they had in the place I used to work in back home. Maybe I show them how to use it?'

I grin. 'I'm sure Cath would love that. Let's ask her.'

I don't think I've ever seen Cath let anyone tell her what to do before, but under Adina's tutelage she's as docile as a lamb.

She and Antonio listen intently as Adina explains as fully as her limited English will allow her, how to work the silver contraption. Eventually, there's a clinking of glasses as the three of them raise their picture-perfect cappuccinos together in a congratulatory 'cheers'.

'Hey, Zoe,' Cath yells across the cafe. 'Say hello to my new – what did you call it again love?'

'Barista,' Adina says. She's smiling, her eyes shining, almost unrecognisable from the terrified girl we brought in here an hour ago.

'That's it, my new barista. Adina's going to start tomorrow, isn't that right, Adina?'

Adina looks at Margaret and I, and shrugs, already aware that Cath's not the type of woman who takes 'no' for an answer. 'I guess yes.'

'Finally,' says Cath, 'I can serve up posh coffee like the best of 'em. Cath's Caff is going to move up a gear,' she addresses the diners stifling giggles,'and you're all going to love it.'

I cheer along with them, trying to silence the voice in my head reminding me of one, small fact. If I fail to save the parade, there's more to lose than the possibility of posh coffees. On top of everything else, I could now be responsible for the fate of a homeless Romanian girl too.

Westholme Community Facebook page:

Lisa Seddon: Anyone see what's just happened at the parade? That *Big Issue North* seller nearly got her head kicked in.

Bernard Phillips: By who?

Lisa Seddon: A group of lads in black tracksuits. Don't know who they were.

Bernard Phillips: Orchard Estate lads. Got to be.

Lisa Seddon: Not being funny, but what's she doing here anyway?

Julie Morehouse: And we're off…!

Chapter Eighteen

'Right, Colin, what do we know about bats?' I'm standing at the front of the office, no more comfortable with my role as leader of the opposition, as I've come to refer to it, than I was at the last meeting, but still giving it my best shot all the same.

Colin stands up and adjusts his glasses. He's sporting a pair of dad jeans and yet another fleece. 'I've been on the website of the Bat Conservation Trust, and it appears that the planning authorities must consider whether a proposed development could affect any bats before a decision can be made.'

'This means a bat survey may need to be carried out to make sure there are no bats on the site. If the survey indicates that bats are likely to be affected by the development, then various other measures need to be taken, all of which would delay the process. But from what I understand from my other contacts, even if the bats don't roost, if we write to the team detailing our concerns that bats could be present then the relevant survey will have to be carried out over a period of a few weeks.'

'Which would give us more time to build our case,' I say, my mind racing.

Colin gives a little cough and nods. 'It would appear so.'

'Are you happy to put together the letter, Colin? It seems like you're the perfect person for the job.' I realise I sound a bit over-enthusiastic and make a mental note to rein it in.

He writes something on his notepad. 'I can do that,' he says.

'We also need to try and attract bats to the building, don't we? If we can get them to roost there it will cause even more problems for the developer.' An idea is forming in my head, but it turns out Colin is one step ahead of me.

'I've had a go at knocking a bat box together so they've got something to roost in. I can get it from the car if you'd like to see it?'

'Brilliant, Colin,' I say. 'We'd love to.' As he moves at a snail's pace towards the door, I turn to Starr who is resplendent in a gold bomber jacket, massive star earrings and a red beret.

'Starr, did you manage to talk to Marcus Stanford at all?'

Starr's thin lips part to show off her beautiful set of false white teeth, the kind I hope will eventually replace my own slightly crooked natural ones. Not that I'd ever tell my dentist that.

'Well, as you may know,' she starts, more than ready for her turn in the spotlight, 'Marcus is a dear, dear friend of mine – I don't know if I told you that he lives next door to me?'

I smile generously. 'You may have mentioned it.'

'I had a chat with Marcus about the matter when we were at a dinner party together last week. It was a lovely event. Four courses. Lots of wine. We all had a little dance afterwards.' She dips her head and smiles up at us all coyly, like a debutante at a ball. 'I think everyone was quite impressed that I could move the way I can despite the fact that I'm in my eighties.'

We wait for her to get to the punchline.

'So where was I…'

'Marcus Stanford,' Margaret offers.

'Oh yes. Thank you, lovely. Dear Marcus. Yes, I was quite

disappointed when I spoke to him, as it turns out he is on the side of Mr Lewis.'

I stay silent as the members voice their disapproval, trying to rearrange my facial features to hide all traces of dismay.

'That's unbelievable,' I eventually reply. 'Are you saying he actively *wants* the parade to be knocked down?'

'Well,' Starr says, looking sheepish, 'I'd had two glasses of wine – maybe three – so I don't remember every word, but I do recall something about jobs.' She taps her head. 'That's right, he said Westholme needs jobs more than it needs empty shops.'

I sigh. 'Right, well, let's cross Marcus off our list and move on to the next point, which is…' I peer down at my agenda, 'the carnival. Margaret, did Daniel Lewis approve the use of the parade and square?'

Margaret strokes the fingernails of one hand with the fingertips of the other, as if trying to smooth out the ridged lines set deep within them.

'He did,' she replies, smiling. 'And, as promised, I raised it at the Rotary Club meeting. While no-one actually wants to run it, a few people said they'd be happy to help out independently of the group.'

'Oh,' I say in a small voice, relieved they're offering to help but disappointed they're not taking the whole thing off my hands.

'I spoke to my contact at the council too,' Gloria adds, 'and they said they would expect the cost of staging a carnival to amount to around £10,000.'

'£10,000?' I repeat, my face falling as the others gasp. 'Where on earth are we going to get £10,000 from?'

Gloria continues, her voice silky smooth and reassuring. 'Not a problem, my dear. The council have agreed to provide £5,000 towards it, if we can crowdfund the rest.'

'I've looked into the crowdfunding set-up,' says Lynne, 'and

I'm sure we could raise the money that way. I'm happy to take that on.'

'Brilliant, thank you.' I'm buoyed again by enthusiasm and the unfamiliar sense of things going my way. 'In that case, assuming no-one else wants to do it, I'll take on the role of carnival co-ordinator.'

I look around the room, hoping for a last-minute reprieve, but no-one objects.

A little line appears between my mum's eyebrows. 'Don't you think you have enough on at the moment, love?' she says in that voice she uses when she's trying to sound casual but she's really worried sick.

I now know how Charlie feels when I try and hug him in front of his friends.

'Don't worry, Mum,' I say, keeping my voice firm in an attempt to retain the impression that I'm in charge. 'I'm good at multi-tasking and it sounds as though I'm going to have plenty of helpers.'

The line between her eyes is still there. 'Yes, but still,' insists.

'I'm more than happy to provide as much support as you need.' Trust Margaret to come to my rescue. 'You must be so busy, whereas I have time on my hands.'

'Thank you, Margaret, you are a godsend. Right, that's settled then,' I say as Colin returns, conveniently bringing the whole carnival business to a close.

We watch expectantly as he resumes his seat and delves into his Marks & Spencer carrier bag.

'This,' he says, pulling out a small wooden construction, 'is what I've managed to come up with so far. It's not perfect, but it might work.'

A series of appreciative oohs and aahs circulate around the room.

'Colin, this is fantastic,' I exclaim. 'You must have put an awful lot of time into making it.'

Colin colours slightly, and looks at his shoes. 'It didn't take too long.'

Lynne snorts.

'Brilliant work, thank you,' I say again. 'Now, where would this go?'

'It needs to be mounted on one of the outside south-facing walls of the building. Ideally near a hole under the eaves that the bats might accidentally make their way into.'

'But surely we're not allowed to start nailing bat boxes to the side of the walls,' says Ollie. 'We don't want any accusations of property damage levelled at us, do we?'

I put my hand out to silence him. 'Look, I'm pretty sure they'll be playing dirty, so I think it's fair enough that we do the same. Besides, no-one needs to know. We could install it late at night, in the dark. Now, who wants to do it?'

'I'll have a go,' Cath grunts, looking unnervingly enthusiastic about the idea of taking a hammer to the wall of the parade.

'Aunty Cath, you fell off the chair last week putting the new menu up,' says Antonio. 'I think your balance is maybe not what it was?'

'Rubbish,' she says indignantly, then adds, 'Well you're not doing it. I don't want you going off sick.'

Ollie is starring intently at a spot on the ceiling, a subtle signal that I should remove him entirely from the list of potential candidates.

I sigh. 'Why don't you leave it to me. Mum, if you're alright to babysit Charlie while I sneak out, I'm sure I'll be able to put it up in no time. After all, I've nailed enough pictures to the wall. How hard can it be?'

Mum pulls a face. 'Zoe, I really don't think this is a good idea.'

Colin agrees. 'The bat box does need to be at least fifteen feet high you know – in fact as close to the eaves as possible – so you'd need a very long ladder.'

'Guys, don't worry,' I say in my most soothing voice. 'It will be done in no time. Colin, it's no problem. I've got a good head for heights. Any other word on what we should put in the bat box? Food? Drink?'

'I've got some ale we could throw in,' cackles Cath. 'A sip of that and it won't be getting them in that'll be the problem – it'll be getting them out!'

I look to Colin for a more sensible answer. 'I don't think so,' he says. 'We just need to try and place them on the south, south-east or south-west side of the parade – somewhere that's exposed to the sun for part of the day.'

We all pause for a minute and try and work out which side of the parade that might be, then agree it would be the left-hand side at the end of the row.

I smile, excited at how the plan is coming together. 'They're going to come – I can just feel it. I'll put it up tomorrow night.'

I've been doing all I can to avoid Wham Bam Sam, as my inner voice has been referring to him, since discovering the existence of his love child, but tonight at football he finally caught up with me.

Every time he tried to make conversation, I found a reason to be distracted and at times he looked so confused by my sudden distancing tactics that I almost felt sorry for him.

Were it not for Charlie, who let the cat out of the bag about my bat box plans, I would have succeeded at keeping him at arm's length. But once Charlie had regaled him with what were meant to be the top-secret details of Mission Bat Box, Sam had insisted he accompany me, despite my assertions that I was perfectly capable of going it alone.

The fact that I needed his ladder to reach the required spot on the wall eventually sealed the deal and now, as we walk along the parade, I have to admit that the twilight eeriness of the place is making me glad he's here.

'Will you *please* let me do it,' says Sam, for what must be the twentieth time.

'Sam, it's just a case of banging a nail into the wall,' I say. 'I do it all the time at home.'

We reach the far end of the parade and carefully extend the ladder, whispering instructions to one another as we go.

After a final, failed attempt to convince me to let him take on the job, Sam resigns himself to being my wingman and places his hands on either side of the rungs.

Mercifully, he keeps his head bowed as I heave my huge backside up the thing, hammer in hand, with the bat box hanging around my neck like an oversized pendant.

The ladder shudders a little as I climb awkwardly, like a baby monkey learning compulsory skills.

'Are you okay?' Sam hisses, cranking his head back to check on me.

'Absolutely,' I say firmly, my words almost lost in the breeze that's starting to pick up speed.

Sam puts his head down between his arms. I suspect it's making him feel queasy just looking that far up while I, fortunately, am completely unfazed by the task in hand.

'Right, I'm here,' I say. 'I'm going to make a start.'

'Just be careful,' Sam whispers.

Resting my full weight against the ladder, I take the nail out of my left pocket and carefully position it against the façade. Moving my right hand slowly away from the rungs, I move the hammer into place, bash the nail into the wall and hook the bat box onto it.

Leaning back slightly, I admire my handiwork. It looks pretty good, even if I do say so myself. Time to start my descent.

I'm about a third of the way down when a sudden gust of wind nearly knocks me to the ground. My knuckles turn white as I clutch the sides of the ladder, waiting for the violent shaking of what are essentially only two pieces of metal and a few rungs to pass.

But while I hold firm, the bat box doesn't. The angry gale rips it off the wall, its sharp edge stabbing into the side of my head as it careers to the ground.

I cling to the rattling ladder, resting my spinning head against the rungs.

'Zoe?' Sam shouts, no concern for noise levels now.

I'm too stunned to answer.

'Zoe, are you okay?'

'I can't move,' I mumble, scared now that I'm going to pass out. Or be sick. Neither of which count as appropriate behaviour when you're two-thirds of the way up a ladder with a fit bloke standing below.

Sam, for his part, is still holding on to the base as though his life – let alone mine – depends on it. 'What do you mean you can't move?'

'I think I'm going to faint.'

He pauses, then says, 'Zoe, stop messing around, come down.'

I try to shake my head but feel a warm trickle down the side of it. A drop rolls down my temple, then my cheek, then my jaw, before splashing onto the concrete flags below, spreading outwards into a tell-tale vivid red splodge that can be seen even in the half-light.

Sam swears as he realises what's just landed next to him. A loud crunch of thunder only serves to up the stakes.

'We need to get you down,' he says, his voice more urgent now.

'I'm fine,' I murmur, a cold sweat spreading across my face and neck. 'Just stay there, I'll be fine in a minute.'

And then, the first few drops of rain hit me – along with the realisation that I might *actually* faint.

'Zoe, you need to do exactly as I say, okay?'

'Okay.'

'Can you feel your right leg?'

'Yes.'

'Then move it down onto the next rung.' He sounds authoritative. In charge. I, on the other hand, sound as weak – and wet – as I feel.

'Okay,' I whisper again.

I take a step down, the damp rung slippery underfoot.

'How about your left leg?'

'Yes.' I'm feeling really, really scared.

'Now move that one down onto the next step. Look at that, you're on your way, only a few more of these to go and you'll be done.'

Rung by rung, Sam talks me down the ladder as I slowly but steadily make my way to the ground.

After what seems like an eternity, I take the final step needed to reach the floor. The moment my feet touch the ground I am spun round and pulled so tightly into Sam's chest that I wonder whether suffocation might be the more pressing threat to my life.

'Are you okay? Let's see where you've been hurt.' He holds on to my shoulders as he gently pushes me away from him. The rain is now lashing at both of our faces and mixing with my blood to create a particularly attractive look. Sam's usually jovial expression looks different, serious, as the streetlight casts a half-hearted glow across his face. He cups my chin in his hand as he manoeuvres my head to get a better look at the gash. 'You're bleeding badly, Zoe,' he says, his frown transporting him even further away from the Sam I've come to know. Then he drops his hands. 'Do you have the keys to your office?'

I nod, clinging to him as I register the growing weakness in my legs.

He moves my arm around his shoulder and puts his own around my waist. 'Right. Let's go there and we'll get you cleaned up.'

The office is in darkness and, by now familiar with the layout, I feel my way to the freestanding lamp and switch it on, illuminating the corner of the room.

'I can't stand fluorescent lights,' I say, by way of explanation, shivering in my wet clothes.

'I'm the same,' Sam agrees. He walks to the sink and starts making a gauze out of a few sheets of kitchen roll. I stand still, watching, listening to the rain lashing against the window, until he beckons me over.I head across the room, suddenly very conscious that he's the one in control of this situation. It's an unfamiliar and not entirely welcome sensation. 'Come closer,' he says and I shuffle forward a few more steps.

His eyes flash over me and for a second, I can see him take in the contours of my body through my wet shirt. As he bends down and starts gently wiping my head, I'm very aware of just how close my face is to his. Of how easy it would be to reach up and pull his head gently towards mine; a move that would allow me to do so much more than just look at those very kissable lips.

He pauses for a minute and looks deeply into my eyes. It's like a jolt of electricity, bringing me back to life and I suddenly feel exposed, naked.

So instead of reaching for him, I reach for the kitchen roll.

'I can do it,' I say, my voice sharp. But Sam's not playing ball. As I move, he grabs my wrist and holds it for a second, his face still just inches away from mine.

'It's okay to let people help sometimes, you know,' he says quietly, leaning in towards me and stroking the wet hair out of my eyes. I fix my gaze on the hand holding my wrist, taking in the veins that run beneath the scattering of fair hairs, the tan that fades towards the underside of his fingers, the swollen joint of one of his knuckles.

Almost every part of me wants to give in to this overwhelming desire to lose myself in him and suddenly I'm not sure whether my light-headedness is a result of my injury or of Sam's presence.

And then self-control kicks in and I clutch at my only available barrier.

'Why didn't you tell me you had a son?'

'A son?' Confusion flits across Sam's features. 'You mean Ted?'

I nod.

'Ah yes, Ted's great, isn't he?' He hesitates, then says, 'Any dad would be proud to have a son like him.' A slow smile spreads across his face.

I feel the hairs rise on the back of my neck as he talks and suddenly I remember why I'm so angry with him. I can't believe the nerve of this man. Making out he's Father of the Year when I know the opposite to be true and choosing *exactly* this moment to do so. My eyes narrow as he continues.

'And his mum, she's absolutely gorgeous, isn't she? Such a stunner. Amazing legs.'

I glare at him and wrench my wrist away. And just as I'm about to tell him where to go, he bursts out laughing.

'What?' I ask, my voice hard.

'Ted's not my son, Zoe,' he replies, still smiling. 'He's my second cousin.'

I try and envisage the family tree. 'So that would make Stacey your…'

'Cousin,' he says, that smile looking far more appealing than it did a minute ago. 'She's my cousin, which you would know if

166

you'd stuck around long enough the other day for me to introduce you. I've never seen anyone disappear so quickly.'

I look down, trying to hide my relief – and my burning cheeks.

'She gets very little help from Ted's dad, so I do what I can to make life a bit easier for her. Interesting that you thought otherwise though,' he adds. 'It's almost as though you're jealous.' I glance up at his teasing smile and he spots my humiliation. If my cheeks were burning before, they're positively alight now.

He moves towards me again, leaving such little space between us that I can barely breathe. '*Are* you jealous?' His warm green eyes flicker over my face, my cheeks, my mouth and he cups the side of my face with his hand, tracing the outline of my lips with his thumb. I catch my breath and for a moment I think I might explode with pent-up frustration. Then, as I'm about to lean in, he drops his hand and takes a step back.

'Course you're not, are you?' he says, breaking the moment. His voice is husky and there's a gravel to it that I'm finding hard to ignore. 'From what I know of you so far, I'm pretty sure you don't do jealousy.'

Uncertain of how to answer and still reeling from unfulfilled desire, I take the makeshift gauze from him and dab the side of my face myself, careful to keep my eyes well away from his for fear they might betray me.

I look instead at the kitchen roll I've just used on my head. The amount of blood on it takes me by surprise and I'm suddenly reminded of the bat box, lying in pieces on the floor. 'The bat box!' I gasp, all thoughts of what might have been with Sam are momentarily suspended. 'After all the hard work Colin put into making it, he can't find out it's broken.'

Sam shoots me one last passion-filled look, then says. 'I know you pride yourself on being Miss Independent, but will you let me do this one thing for you; will you let me fix this bat box and get it on the wall?'

I smile, grateful that, for once, I can hand over a problem to someone else. And unsure as to whether I'm disappointed or relieved that we've moved on from what could have been a very steamy moment. 'Okay. And, Sam?'

He looks at me hopefully.

'Thank you.'

Nodding, he retreats through the door and I flop onto the couch feeling unsettled and confused by the exchange. As *if* Sam Milner, with his heartbreaker smile and footballer body, would be interested in a single mum with a weight problem.

The confusing thing is, he's doing a very good impression of someone who might be.

Westholme Community Facebook page:

Cath's Caff: We're pleased to announce that from next Monday Cath's Caff will be launching our new menu, complete with all your favourite speciality teas and coffees. We're also now delighted to offer the most delicious cakes by Paula. Please call in and you'll be guaranteed a warm welcome.

Rob Littlewood: A warm welcome? By Cath? That'll be the day!

Chapter Nineteen

I'm standing in front of a 1960s greengrocer's shop window. Fruit, veg and pies are arranged in a mouthwatering display on the other side of the glass, set out in trays that are tilted to face the hungry eyes of those looking in.

'It's not exactly as it was sixty years ago, but it's not far off,' says Mark, the care home manager whose idea it was to create Memory Lane, a mini-village at the back of the building, in order to support the dementia and Alzheimer's patients that live there.

Further along the 'street', there's a cafe where residents can enjoy a cuppa and a catch up, a post office and a hairdresser's, all of which, Mark explains, are fully functional two days a week. He leads me to the last unit and waves his hand with a flourish. 'And this,' he says proudly, 'is the pub.'

I peer in through the glass panes and allow my eyes to adjust to the darkness inside. The whole thing is like a replica of the Rovers Return. There's a bar complete with pumps and optics, a jukebox and brown circular tables with beer mats. A red swirly carpet covers the floor and old framed photographs of the local area adorn the walls. It's all I can do not to rush in there and start pulling myself a pint.

As I move away from the window, my eyes rest on a huge padlock on the door. 'Oh yes,' says Mark, looking sheepish. 'There was a small incident a few months ago when some of the residents, led by one in particular, decided it was payday and entered the pub unsupervised. It's all non-alcoholic stuff of course, but still...' He rattles the lock as if to demonstrate its efficiency. 'We've kept it locked ever since.' He coughs. 'Might be best not to mention that in your article though.'

The familiar feeling of excitement that I used to revel in when I knew I'd found a great story rises up inside me as I snap away at the 'street', filling my phone with gorgeous images of times gone by that'll look fantastic online. Once I've photographed everything in sight and made Mark promise we can come back later when the 'village' is open, I pop the phone back in my bag and swap it for my notepad.

'I can't believe no-one's ever written about this before,' I enthuse. 'It's brilliant.'

Mark's face lights up at the praise. 'There was some initial interest when we started doing the fundraisers for it,' he explains, 'but then it all died down and we didn't think to tell anyone when the construction work came to an end. It wasn't until we saw your call for good news on the Westholme Community Facebook page that we thought it might be something people would want to read about.'

'Brace yourself,' I say. 'I have a feeling that once it's been in *The Good News Gazette*, you'll be inundated with media requests. I'm sure the TV news channels would love this.'

Mark looks stunned. 'I genuinely didn't think anyone would care – except of course the residents and their families. We just thought it might help. We're not too bothered about making a name for ourselves.'

'But that's why it's so special, Mark. Because it's truly about making life better for the residents.'

We head into one of the lounges to continue our chat then, making way for the staff members who are starting to open up the shops, ready for that day's session.

Mark was clearly born to do this job. He beams with pride as he talks about the different and imaginative ways in which the care home staff have been able to reach the residents, giving many a quality of life that few would have thought possible. In fact, I'm so impressed that I almost ask whether I can put my own name down for a place now, on the basis that it never hurts to be ahead of the game.

Half a notepad later, we return to the village to see it all in action and as I follow a little old lady with a walking stick into the land of yesteryear, a lump forms in my throat.

On entering the village, residents are given bags of old-fashioned money – the type they're familiar with – to spend at the village, and they make their way around it, chatting to friends, stopping off for a pint and a cuppa and picking up the groceries they think they might need. One woman is pushing a baby doll in a pram, another dragging a battery-operated dog behind her. There's even a man sweeping the 'street' who I presume to be a caretaker until Mark informs me otherwise. Their eyes are sparkling, their expressions are animated, they look happy.

I photograph Mark and his team with a few of the residents whose families have agreed to it in various different parts of the village, then make my way back to the car park.

'This is a very special place, Mark,' I say as he waves me off. 'You should be so proud of yourself.'

It's his turn, then, to well up, and I wonder how many tears will have been shed by the time the first edition of the *Gazette* comes out. 'It's definitely been a labour of love,' he sniffs. 'But we got there in the end.'

Just then his walkie talkie goes off. 'Mark to the village, Mark to the village,' a voice crackles through the handset. 'Assistance required. Arthur's got behind the bar again.'

I decide to stop off for a coffee before I go back to the office. I might be breaking my 'no caffeine in the afternoon' rule, but after staying up until well past 1am searching the net for a dummies' guide to staging a town carnival, I need all the legal highs I can get.

Before I've even stepped through the doorway of Cath's Caff, I can tell something's different. Jazz filters through the doorway, providing background music to the loud chatter emanating from beyond. But it's not until I'm inside that I realise how much has really changed.

Running along one wall is a long table where a disparate mix of people sit chatting. A mum cradles a latte while two older ladies next to her coo at her baby, who is giggling in his buggy. Alongside them a middle-aged woman in a suit nods as a young lad in jeans and a scruffy jumper shows her something on his phone, while two men in their thirties chat on and off with all of them. I've never seen such a mixture of people on one table – and certainly not in Westholme.

Good grief. This is almost … trendy.

'Wow,' I say, soaking up this new, vibrant atmosphere.

'It's our Chatter and Natter table.' Cath grins. 'Adina said they have one at the place she used to work at in Bucharest, then Antonio did a bit of digging and found out there's actually a scheme called the Chatty Cafe here. It's for people who want to have a gab with others, you know, as opposed to just staring at their phones. Alright, isn't it?'

'Cath, this is brilliant,' I say, looking around in awe. 'What a fantastic idea.'

"Of course, if his lordship has his way then this will all be over before it's even begun, but you've got to give it a go, haven't you?'

'Too right,' I say forcefully. 'In fact, I'd like to write about this for the website – and the paper, too, if that's okay?'

Cath shrugs. 'No problem.'

'Do you think anyone would mind if I took a quick picture of it in action?'

Cath checks to see who's sitting at the table, clearly trying to identify willing participants. 'Give me a minute, I'll ask them.'

Everyone agrees, and I spend the next half an hour chatting and snapping, marvelling at the way in which people will open up to strangers and reveal intimate details of their lives, while I feel I've taken a leap of faith if I tell someone what I'm planning for tea.

Eventually I say goodbye to my new friends and am about to leave when Antonio calls my name. Today, I notice, he's wearing a deep-purple lipstick while rocking a Rolling Stones t-shirt, ripped jeans and biker boots and I find myself studying his look and wondering whether there are any elements of it that I could pull off.

'*Ciao*, Zoe,' Antonio's welcome is always warm and, despite having heard it on numerous occasions now, his accent remains little short of delicious. 'And how are we today?'

'I'm fine thank you, Antonio.' I nod at Adina, who's doing something complicated-looking with the coffee machine. 'How's the new recruit?'

'She's doing spectacularly,' he says, gesturing to a tray of coffees waiting to be taken to a table. 'Cath's been helping her improve her English. And look at these fabulous creations – have you ever seen anything like it in Cath's Caff?'

I smile as I take in the creamy foam dotted with chocolate

powder that tops the cappuccinos and the shots of espressos being served up alongside them. Long gone are the NHS-style thick-rimmed cups and chipped mugs; in their place are clear tall glasses and stylish cups and saucers.

'Your idea, I presume?'

'Adina's, actually,' Antonio says. 'We sat down and came up with a few suggestions we thought Aunty Cath might be interested in. I thought she would say no, but she loved them. Now we're starting to put them into action.'

I wonder whether I'm pushing him one step too far by asking whether they've considered offering any coconut milk or other dairy alternatives and after a long explanation as to what that means, it turns out my initial assumption is correct.

Antonio scrunches his nose up as he considers my question. 'No, we don't have those right now. Do you think we should?'

'There could be a market for them among vegetarians and vegans,' I say. 'It's what I drink at home. Veganism's quite the thing now, you know.'

Antonio rubs his chin. 'You think people would buy it if we offered it?'

'I think they might.'

Antonio leans forward and clasps my hands in his. 'Thank you, *bella*. I will look into it. So, what can I get for you today?'

I examine the new slate menu, trendy chalk writing spelling out what's on offer. Flat whites, cappuccinos, mochas, macchiatos … it's as though Cath has reproduced the entire Starbucks menu. I'm like a child in a sweet shop trying to choose which one to opt for.

Eventually I settle on one. 'I'll have a flat white please.'

'And will you have a cake with that?' Antonio gestures at the selection of varied cakes that sit behind the new glass counter window. 'We have a new lady, Paula, who makes them.' The mass-produced synthetic concoctions have gone. In their place are homemade cupcakes, brownies, a Victoria sponge, some sort of magnificent-looking chocolate cake and a salted caramel tart.

'Paula?' I repeat. 'I know her. Her cakes are amazing,' then, looking longingly at the creations on display, I add, 'enough to derail any diet.'

Antonio nods enthusiastically. 'After just one bite we were all sold. They are simply *deliziosa*! Now which one would you like?'

I quickly calculate the contents of my purse and factor in the night out I'm supposed to be having with the girls tonight. I can barely afford a coffee, let alone a cake. And anyway, I'm trying to be good.

'Do you know what, Antonio, I think I'm just going to stick with a drink today.'

'Nonsense. You must try one of these. The first one is free.'

Despite my protestations, Antonio is absolutely insistent that I must have a sweet treat and I pick out a chocolate cupcake with an After Eight chocolate strategically placed on the top of it.

It's Friday. No-one's ever good on a Friday. I'll start the diet again tomorrow.

———

'Hey, you.' I wave at Ollie, catching my breath. I swear those stairs are getting steeper.

He clicks away from his Instagram page and starts waving a sticky note around as though it's a winning Lottery ticket.

'Listen to this. A new Spanish place is opening down the road. They want to take out – wait for it – a full page advert in the paper.'

'You're kidding. But they don't even know how much it'll cost.'

'And guess what – they didn't even ask. Just wanted you to call them upon your return.'

'Oh my goodness, this is amazing, Ol!' I grab the sticky note from him and make a rough calculation of how many weeks I have left until my gardening leave officially ends and I can register myself as a new business. Only then will I be able to start sending out invoices to advertisers.

'It was probably my sexy phone voice that did it,' Ollie continues, smoothing back his hair. 'But I've got a date tonight and I'm feeling good about it, so I'll let you take the glory.'

I hang my coat up and sit down at my desk with my goodies, then take a bite out of the cupcake. The dark mint chocolate frosting oozes across my tongue, awakening my taste buds and giving way to the chocolate sponge below. It is, quite frankly, one of the best cakes I have ever had in my life.

Emboldened by the promise of an advert – not to mention the sugar rush – but also aware of the fact that if it weren't for Antonio's generosity there's no way I'd be working my way through this culinary delight, I decide the time has come to put some pressure on Ryan.

As soon as I've finished the cake, I wipe my hands on a napkin, take a gulp of coffee and pick up my mobile.

Did you see my texts about the maintenance? I tap into my phone.

Within a matter of moments, the familiar ping indicates a reply.

Yeah sorry. Just had a bonus actually, so I can drop some money in your account. I'll do it tonight.

I blink as I re-read his message, then tell myself not to get my hopes up. After all, we've been here before. But seeing as he seems so amenable today…

How about a trip up here to see Charlie? He keeps asking me if you'll be coming to watch his first football match.

This time it takes a few minutes before he replies.

When and where is it?

I type out the details and press 'send', sure that he'll come back with an excuse as to why he can't make it.

After half an hour he still hasn't replied, and my spirits are starting to wane considerably when my phone issues one final, triumphant beep.

That sounds good, just need to check I'm not double-booked. I'll let you know.

Westholme Community Facebook page:

Paul Cross: This situation with the parade is a disgrace. Gonna write to that Lewis bloke and voice my objections. Anyone know how to get in touch with him?

Lisa Seddon: No idea, but if you find out can you pass his details on? Wouldn't mind having his number in my little black book ♥

Chapter Twenty

'We're starting IVF next month.'

Emma, Beth and I are in The Piano Lounge in Presthill, a beautiful little bar with white panelled walls, pale parquet and urns of the most stunning pale-pink peonies in every corner. There's also, perhaps predictably, an ornate white piano taking centre stage with a highly skilled male pianist going largely ignored by the identikit young men and women taking selfies in front of it.

Its clientele is as pretentious as it sounds, but the bar itself is beautiful and our favourite haunt for a Saturday-night escape from Westholme.

Emma and I try to read Beth's expression, pausing to work out what the right response might be.

I speak first. 'Well, that's good … isn't it?'

She spins a beer mat around in her fingers, like a homemade fidget spinner.

'Is it?' she asks, apparently genuinely unsure of the answer.

'If it results in a baby it is,' says Emma, who, in her leather leggings and spikey boots is the only one of us who looks truly at home in her surroundings.

I glance down at my own outfit, a floral tea dress that shows what I had hoped was the right amount of cleavage and heels. I was pleased with the result before I left the house. Now, sitting next to Emma, I'm not so sure.

'I just never imagined it would come to that,' Beth says, looking more casual than Presthill tends to require in jeans, a t-shirt and a bomber jacket. 'I always thought that, given time, it would happen naturally.'

'But it's been what, two years since you started trying?' Emma retorts. 'How much time were you planning on giving it?'

Emma is loving, caring and utterly fabulous. But sometimes, even among her closest friends, her boss lady attitude can sting.

I squeeze Beth's hand. 'Look at it this way – a year from now, you could be a mum.'

She nods. 'That's the way I'm trying to think. Imagine it, me, with a baby!'

'You'll be fantastic,' I say. And she will. Beth's one of those people who was clearly born to be a mum. Out of the three of us, she's the one who had it figured into her life plan at school, the one for whom it took priority above career, a gap year to Australia or any of the other aspirations we had. The fact that she and Tony haven't been able to conceive is a cruel example of how good things don't always happen to good people.

Loud, tinkling laughter cuts into our conversation and I look over to the bar where a tall, slim woman with a hint of a tan and hair that falls over her shoulders in long, auburn curls touches the arm of her companion. She's jaw-dropping, but it's him who really catches my eye; an even taller figure with the darkest of brown hair clad in a thin-weave jumper that clings gently to the rounded muscles of his upper back and arms.

I'm about to shift my eyes back to the girls when the man turns, bringing his profile into full view.

I freeze.

It's Daniel Lewis. Minus his glasses.

I drop my head and peek up in time to see him put his hand on the small of the woman's back and guide her towards the door … which is positioned right next to where we're sitting.

'Keep talking,' I hiss to Emma and Beth as I duck down low, my chest pressed firmly against the table as I try to remain under his line of sight.

'Chick, what's wro—' Emma begins, before the unmistakably deep tones of Daniel's voice cut through the airwaves.

'Zoe Taylor,' he says stiffly, 'I thought that was you.'

I start stroking the table as if examining it for marks. 'Yes, it's definitely mahogany,' I say to absolutely no-one, ignoring the perplexed expressions on the girls' faces. Slowly, I shift my body back into an upright position.

'Oh, Daniel, hello,' I say airily, feigning surprise.

Next to him the model girl gives me a half-smile, clearly uncertain as to how or indeed why Daniel would know this strange creature engaging in bizarre moves in a Presthill bar.

His dark eyes have lost none of their intensity as they wash over me, taking in the 'glammed-up' version of the bane of his existence.

'Having a drink, I see,' he says, nodding at my half empty or half full – depending on which way you look at it – glass.

'I am,' I reply, my head nodding in a souped-up version of his own move.

'Right.' He's clearly unsure of where to go next with this conversation. 'Well, have a nice evening.'

I'm still nodding.

'Have a nice evening.' I beam at the model girl as if to convey that I am no threat – a gesture I suspect is entirely unnecessary –

and wait until they leave the bar before I collapse again on the table.

Emma looks from me to Beth.

'Erm, what the hell was that – or should I say who?'

I sit up, not even bothering to move my carefully crafted waves out of my face and groan.

'That, ladies, was Daniel Lewis.'

Their faces are blank.

'Daniel Lewis,' I repeat again. 'The owner of the parade. Which, I might add, you'd know if you'd turned up at any of the meetings.'

'Ooohh,' Beth says, ignoring my jibe. 'He's gorgeous.'

'I'd sleep with him,' adds Emma.

And as they start with a barrage of questions, I watch forlornly through the window as he ushers model girl into his BMW, casting one last and unexpected look back at the bar before he drives away.

———

'I don't believe it.'

'What?' Ollie looks up from the page design he's working on.

'He's sent me a press release about his company winning an award for giving back to the community.'

Ollie scoots his chair around to my side of the desk to read the email. On the screen is a photograph of Daniel and some of the members of his team shaking hands with the people that he's supposedly helped.

'I can't believe the nerve of that man,' I rage.

'Hmmm,' Ollie says, scooting back around to his side.

I fix him with a stare. 'What's that "hmmm" supposed to mean?'

He holds his hands up in a mock surrender pose. 'Nothing, oh great one. Nothing at all. It just seems like the sort of super-fluffy story that would be perfect for *The Good News Gazette*, that's all.' He swings his chair back to face his computer.

'Are you kidding me? Self-centred businessman cons awards body out of community accolade?'

Ollie keeps his eyes on his computer screen, clearly deducing that that's probably the safest place for them. 'I take it you're not going to use it then?'

'No way. In fact—' I pick up my phone and start tapping the number on the end of the email into the handset.

'Zoe…' says Ollie, looking at me now. 'What are you doing?'

'Shhh,' I hiss, putting up my index finger to indicate that silence is required. 'Oh, hello, I'd like to speak to Daniel Lewis please. Yes, I'll hold.'

His voice, when it comes, is deep and impatient.

'Ms Taylor. How are you today?'

I dispense with the niceties. 'Mr Lewis, you appear to have mistakenly sent me a press release. I say mistakenly because I can't think of one good reason why you'd send it to me on purpose.'

Eyes wide, Ollie scoots over to me at breakneck speed so he can listen in to the response.

'First of all,' says Daniel, 'please don't call me Mr Lewis. It makes me feel as though you're speaking to my dad. Secondly, your newspaper is called *The Good News Gazette*, right?'

'Well, yes, but—'

'And this is a good news story, is it not?'

'Well, yes.'

'And in fact, it is a good news story about your community, isn't it?'

I look at Ollie, hoping his expression will convey a degree of sympathy that I'm having to deal with such a complete tool. It doesn't.

'In which case, can I ask you why you wouldn't use it? I trust that your news operation is completely independent and wouldn't deliberately exclude news of a local company that has been found by an independent assessor to have carried out good work in the community purely because you disagree with a planned development which will create even more opportunities for the community?'

I bristle. 'No, of course not.'

'In which case, I take it this call is to thank me for asking my PR agency to include you on their contacts list. I'll make sure they continue to send you press releases such as these in the future. Now if that's all, I'm in the middle of a meeting. Good day.'

And with that, the line goes dead.

I stare at Ollie, unable to process the conversation that's just taken place.

He lets out a low whistle. 'You sure told him,' he says. 'Made it clear you're not a woman to be messed with. Right before he ended the call with one serious mic drop.'

Then he scoots back round to his side of the desk again before I can inflict serious injury.

———

I'm still stewing over Daniel Lewis an hour later when Ollie stands up and announces, for what must be the ninth time this week, 'I'm going to Cath's, do you want anything?'

'Do you know, he's not as clever as he thinks he is,' I reply.

He looks confused. 'What do you mean?'

'Daniel Lewis,' I say impatiently. 'This scheme he's worked on elsewhere – the one he's supposedly been given this award for—'

Ollie sinks back down into his seat. 'I think he probably *has* been given this award, Zoe – in the photograph, he does appear to be holding a plaque to prove it.'

'Never mind that. If he's dealt with other people then they'll know how dodgy he is. And they might be willing to provide testimonies to prove it.'

Ollie sighs. 'What's wrong with you today? You seem stressed again.'

'I'm not stressed,' I snap. 'Even though there's no sniff of a story good enough to make the front page of our launch issue, I'm trying to organise a carnival for the entire town when I can't organise my washing basket, I have no idea what I'm going to put in the sports pages, Charlie keeps asking me why his dad hasn't replied to my text yet and this idiot is wasting my time with self-promotional press releases.' I inhale deeply, exhausted with the effort of that speech alone.

Ollie walks around to the back of my chair and starts massaging my shoulders. 'Woah, easy tiger. I thought we'd agreed, after you tried to suggest that Jürgen Klopp was the manager of Everton, thereby confirming your complete ignorance of all sporting matters, that I'd take on the sports pages?'

I shrug his hands off me, exasperated. 'Yes, but all I ever see you doing is updating your social media. Have you even written any sports news yet?'

He recoils, hurt, and a wave of shame hits me. 'Ollie, I'm sorry,' I say in a quiet voice.

Ollie goes back to his seat and starts searching for files on his computer. 'I've written plenty of stories, actually,' he says sulkily. 'I'll send them over to you so you can see them.'

I stand up now and walk around to his side of the desk. 'Look, I'm sorry, I shouldn't have snapped. I'm feeling the pressure – on a number of levels. Ollie, I couldn't do this without you, I know that. It won't happen again.'

He looks up at me. 'Zoe, why are you so determined that this guy's dodgy? We haven't seen anything at this point to suggest that's the case.'

I try not to roll my eyes. 'Ollie, you're such a decent person, you always see the best in everyone. But haven't you seen those comments on the Westholme Community Facebook Page? There's a general consensus that he must be giving out backhanders left, right and centre to make this happen.'

I move back to my computer 'No, he's definitely dodgy, and I'm going to talk to these people he's worked with to prove it.'

With that, I start Googling the company that's mentioned in the press release, ready to find the evidence I know will result in Daniel Lewis's downfall.

Westholme Community Facebook page:

Stephanie Porter: That Romanian girl in Cath's Caff is lovely. Made a nice little space for me in the corner today when I was trying to breastfeed my screaming baby.

Beryl Twistle: Are you one of those new-age mums who thinks it's alright to get your bosoms out in public? It's really not done in Westholme, you know.

Stephanie Porter: Welcome to the twenty-first century, Beryl. Maybe I'll see you there one day!

Chapter Twenty-One

'So, you're here to talk about Daniel Lewis? Come this way.'

Jim Steiner types a code into the keypad and leads me through the staff entrance into the corridors of the college beyond, eventually reaching a door with the words 'staffroom' printed on it. The scent of coffee wafts up my nose as he passes me and I instantly know we're going to get along.

'Drink?' he offers, rubbing the bald patch that makes up a perfect circle at the crown of his otherwise grey-haired head.

'A coffee would be great, thanks,' I reply, perching on the arm of a couch. 'Milk, one sugar.'

He busies himself making it, boiling the water and spooning the coffee into the cup before serving it up with a Rich Tea biscuit that I don't even pretend to refuse. He pulls up his baggy jeans at the thigh before sitting down on the chair opposite.

'Thanks again for your time,' I say, 'I'm sure you must be very busy.'

'No problem,' he replies, his weather-beaten face crinkling up to reveal a gentle and fatherly smile. 'Anything to help Dan.'

I frown slightly before continuing. 'Anyway, as I said on the phone, I'm putting together a story for *The Good News Gazette* about the award that Mr Lewis, I mean Dan, won for his work on your building skills academy, and I'd really like to find out a bit more about it.'

He takes a gulp of his own drink before placing it on the coffee-stained table in front of us.

'I'll give you a bit of background,' he starts. 'I worked for Dan's dad many moons ago, so I've known Dan for years. When we won the grant to build the academy, I suggested Dan's company put in a tender.'

My ears prick up. 'Just out of interest, what line of work is his dad in?'

'He's in the property business, just like Dan. Haven't you heard of his company, Lewis Stone?'

I think quickly, Lewis Stone, Lewis Stone. And then it comes to me. 'Lewis Stone … is that the firm that's just built that massive retail complex over in Manchester?'

He nods. 'That's the one – and much more besides. Not short of a bob or two, let's put it that way. Anyway, the Chair had heard about Dan's venture and what he was trying to do with the business, so agreed that he should submit a tender. Don't get me wrong,' he adds quickly, 'he had to go through the procurement process like everyone else, but we wanted to work with an ethical company on this and we knew his credentials were good.'

I pause my notetaking. This is not going according to plan at all.

'What do you mean, his credentials?'

'We knew that Dan wanted to try and create local jobs for local people. We knew he'd already invested a lot in apprenticeships for the long-term unemployed and young disadvantaged kids. So, his ethos fit well with what we were trying to achieve here.'

My spirits plummet. It appears I've inadvertently gatecrashed a Daniel Lewis fan club.

I try a new line of questioning. 'So, what do you think of the work he's done for you? Was it in any way shoddy at all?'

Jim grins. 'No problem, love – in fact, why don't I show you?'

Trying to muster up the appearance of interest, I nod my agreement and follow him of the staffroom and down the shiny new corridor.

'As you probably know, the idea behind the creation of the building skills academy was to give young people, you know, those who might have messed up at school, the chance to train in an industry that was likely to offer long-term opportunities.

'Dan gave us an extremely competitive price. If I'm honest, there were days when I wondered whether he was even making a profit on it, and, good on the lad, he's given us loads of work placements and apprenticeships within his firm to a lot of our graduates.

'For Dan, it's all about job creation. He seems to have a good handle on the damaging effects of long-term unemployment and how easy it is to lose kids without prospects to crime and gangs. He puts a lot of time and effort into setting them on the right path.'

I'm surprised to find I'm listening intently, and, against my better judgement, I want to know more.

'And is his father of the same mind?' I ask.

'I think so. Dan's the first to admit he's grown up with a silver spoon, so to speak. Private school, big house, property abroad, the lot. Although it wasn't that way for his dad. He was a bit more normal – one of us. But he was switched on up here.' He taps his head. 'He could see there was money to be made in property, and make it he did. He worked hard for every penny. Maybe that's why he's always been so hard on Dan. I don't know if he thinks he's had it easy compared to him. Anyway ... sorry,

I've lost my train of thought. Let me show you what we're doing here.'

Jim leads the way into a classroom where teenagers, both male and female, are busy doing something with plaster and a trowel.

'We try and provide our students with basic skills in all areas of construction,' he explains. 'That includes plastering, plumbing, tiling, bricklaying … even kitchen fitting.'

Turning his back to the class, he speaks quietly, 'A good proportion of these kids come from deprived backgrounds. Their families are broke, their schoolgrades were poor and there's sometimes domestic problems too. We hammer it home to them that none of it is a barrier to carving out their own success.'

He turns and makes his way over to a quiet boy in a dirty white t-shirt, his forehead creased in concentration as he moves his trowel across a piece of plasterboard, spreading it on in a smooth, thin layer.

'Meet Luke, one of our trainees,' he says. 'He's one of Dan's apprentices. Do you know the Mounthouse development?' I shake my head.

'It's a big new office complex in Liverpool. Luke spends every Thursday working on it; the lads there are really showing him the ropes, aren't they, Luke?'

Luke nods enthusiastically. 'They've been great; the boss has even been showing me how to do my own books for when I get going – I was never any good at maths.'

I'm confused. 'You mean Mr Lewis?'

'Who? Oh, Dan, yes, him. Top fella.'

'I see,' I say, finding it more and more difficult to ignore the uncomfortable knot that's settled heavily in the pit of my stomach.

Jim's tour takes me to a number of different classrooms, each at least as impressive as the last, all filled with shiny pieces of equipment and happy-looking students.

He rounds off our tour with the impressive lecture theatre,

then turns to me and says, 'You can probably see now why Dan's firm won that community award. It's a big deal you know, a national thing.' He smiles. 'Yeah, he's a good lad really. Bark's worse than his bite. I'm glad you're flagging up the great work he's doing.'

I feel a flash of anger strike me.'You know, it's interesting, his firm is also involved with a proposed supermarket development that would involve wiping out our town's shopping parade. I can't help but wonder how the great work he's doing here ties in with his plans to demolish our own town centre?'

Jim looks at me, his kind smile fading.

'Well, I don't know anything about that,' he says. 'But knowing the way the high street's going and assuming your local shopping centre is heading the same way, I wonder whether Dan sees an opportunity to create more jobs. I don't know, you'd have to ask him about that.'

I give him a half smile, promise I'll contact him when the story's online, and sign out of the building.

As I get back in the car and start to drive away, I try and marry together the praise that's just been heaped on Daniel Lewis compared to my own experience of him. The two just don't sit right together.

There's something fishy about this, I decide. And while he may have conned those guys into thinking he's some kind of plastic working-class hero, there's no way *I'm* going to be taken in by him.

Westholme Community Facebook page:

Steve Crossley: What's the latest on the parade business? Anyone know?

Judy Short: Planning committee meeting in a couple of days. That's when they're going to make their decision. I think tomorrow's the last day to sign the petition against the supermarket – I'll post the link here.

Chapter Twenty-Two

There are just two days to go until the planning committee meeting, so tonight's the final Friends of Westholme Parade rendezvous. This time I've arranged the chairs into a circle formation, so although I still feel like someone pretending to be in charge, at least I no longer feel like a teacher.

'Hi everybody,' I say. 'Once again, thanks for your hard work this week. I understand you're all very busy and I want you to know it is very much appreciated.'

Everyone nods and smiles, encouraging me to go on. I consult my clipboard and try to look efficient, while also trying to ignore the nerves I'm feeling at Sam's presence. It's the first time I've seen him since the night of the bat box, and I can't help but feel nervous. Something's definitely shifted in our friendship, and I'm not sure how to deal with it – or even how I feel about it.

Sam, on the other hand, appears to have decided that the bat house debacle has made him a fully fledged – if late to the table – member of the group and while I'm experiencing the emotions of a teenage schoolgirl all over again, he seems completely unfazed by our encounter.

'So, first of all, I'd like to welcome Sam,' I say. 'Sam's been very supportive of our efforts so far and I'm sure he'll be an important part of our team going forward – depending, of course, on what happens at the planning meeting.'

A collective 'Hi, Sam' goes around the room.

'Now,' I continue. 'Updates from the last meeting. Lawrence, you very kindly agreed to take on the task of collecting signatures for the petition and sending them on to the council. How many did we manage in the end?'

Lawrence nods. 'I've been asking people to sign it when they've come into the shop and I've also been pushing the online petition. We've managed 506 written signatures and over 2,000 online ones, which isn't bad, all things considered.'

I smile at him, trying to hide my disappointment that we didn't get more, and bite my tongue so I don't ask him exactly what things should be considered. 'Thank you, Lawrence. Cath – any feedback on your cake delivery?'

'Nothing,' she says. 'I dropped them off just in time for the last planning committee meeting, but the way the security guy looked at them, I'd be surprised if they ever got past reception.'

'How did he look at them, Cath?' says Colin, genuinely intrigued.

She stares at him. 'Like someone who wanted to eat them.'

'Shall we move on?' I say cheerfully, checking my agenda. 'Bat boxes. Now, I was responsible for that and Sam, ahem, Sam…'

'He helped with the erection, didn't he, dear,' says Starr. My cheeks colour as various members of the group start to snigger, revealing a very smutty side to these upstanding citizens that I never suspected was there.

Fortunately, Sam is unperturbed. Sensing my pain, he steers the conversation back to somewhere near clean.

'Hi, guys, great to meet you all. Yes I did,' he gives Starr a wink, 'help with the *erection*, but there's no sign of any visitors just yet. Call me pessimistic, but I would suggest we put that idea on the backburner for now.'

I'm lost in his words, wondering at what point he became part of the 'we', when I realise everyone is looking at me expectantly.

'Okay,' I say, snapping back to attention. 'Now you're all aware that Lynne has been working incredibly hard to crowdfund the money that we need for the carnival and I'm delighted to reveal that she's done more than hit our £5,000 target. In fact, Lynne, would you like to tell everyone what the final amount came to?'

Lynne consults her notes. 'Thanks to everyone's generosity, and the many plugs on *The Good News Gazette* website, we managed to raise £5,763.'

A gasp goes up around the room before we all break into an impromptu round of applause.

'That's excellent, Lynne, thank you so much. And from what I understand, the council have confirmed they will match that, haven't they, Gloria? Gloria beams and nods.

'As you know,' I continue, 'I'm in charge of the carnival and Margaret –' I look at her gratefully, 'has also taken on a huge chunk of the organising. At the moment, all the plans are falling nicely into place. Margaret's spoken to the council, carried out a risk assessment and arranged insurance. She's also liaised with the Rotary Club who are assisting in the organisation of the stalls, I've hired a stage and some speakers...' I check my list and say, almost to myself, 'I just need to sort out a bouncy castle.'

'I can do that, love.' I look up in surprise at the fact that my dad, the one member of the group (apart from Charlie) who has looked as though he's been dragged kicking and screaming to each and every meeting, is actually making a contribution.

'A lad in work hires out bouncy castles on the side so he'll probably do me a good deal.' Inexplicably, he taps the side of his nose. 'Leave it with me.'

'Okay ... thanks, Dad,' I say, making a mental note to grill him on the specifics later. 'So, for now at least, it appears we've done everything we can do.'

I then make a short speech, thanking the group for their efforts and reminding them that no matter which way the decision goes, we should be proud of everything we've achieved.

Which, right now, amounts to precisely nothing.

———————

I don't need an alarm clock to wake me up on the morning of the planning committee meeting. All night, I've stared at the ceiling thinking about nothing else.

And now, with the golden glow of the rising sun announcing that the day has officially begun, I push my duvet aside and tiptoe to the bathroom. My attempts at silence are motivated by the promise of some alone-time with a cup of coffee and some breakfast TV before Charlie crashes onto the couch and demands the immediate return of CBBC.

After a quick toilet stop, I take a deep breath and step onto the scales. As expected, it's not good. I promise myself I'll try harder after the stress of today is out of the way and step off, just as Charlie is making his way into the bathroom. Eyes still barely open and hair sticking out all over the place, he sits down on the toilet and sighs.

The sight of my half-asleep/half-awake little boy makes me smile, and as I turn to leave him to it, I catch sight of my reflection in the mirror above the sink.

Usually when I look at myself in the mirror, I'm concentrating only on segments; my eyes as I'm putting on my mascara, my mouth as I'm brushing my teeth, my hair as I'm blow-drying it. There's rarely time to examine any area as a whole.

But today, I look at my face as the sum of all its parts. It's different now, from what it was ten years ago. It's no longer the face of the young woman who moved to London, her whole life before her. It's the face of a woman who's back where she started, her heart worn outside of her body in the form of a little boy, having experienced love and loss, but ultimately still standing. It might not be the most beautiful face on earth, but it's my face. The face of a warrior. The face of a survivor.

A little voice emerges from the toilet seat. 'Mum, can you help me? It's a messy one.'

I take a deep breath, arm myself with toilet roll and head into battle.

The face of a bum-wiper.

The past few months have seen meetings, emails, petitions and, in my case, concussion, in our bid to convince the planning committee to reject Daniel Lewis's proposal. And, today, the Friends of Westholme Parade are finally going to find out whether we've succeeded in our goal.

The whole gang is here; Starr, who has deemed it perfectly appropriate to wear a red-sequinned cocktail dress for the occasion; Sam, Ollie, Cath, Lawrence, Antonio, Adina, Mum and Dad, Gloria, Margaret, Colin and Lynne. Our little group is sitting in one of the wood-panelled meeting rooms in the town hall where we're currently thrashing out the details of the application and, in council speak, 'expressing our views'.

Johnny Wall, a *Northern News* reporter is here, making copious notes as he documents the proceedings and I'm hopeful that our shared past means he won't completely destroy me in the write-up.

The first to speak is Daniel, who is typically eloquent as he puts forward his argument, wheeling out all sorts of legal and planning jargon I can barely understand but I accept sounds impressive nonetheless.

As the nominated speaker of the Friends of Westholme Parade, it's then my turn to speak on behalf of the group.

After receiving a letter just yesterday from the council confirming, to no-one's surprise, that no presence of bats has been found at the parade, we've agreed to drop the subject from our argument, despite Dad's objections. He's become weirdly attached to the bat idea and has said repeatedly that he thinks it's our best hope, but now that the survey has come back negative there's really little point in pursuing it.

Instead, when I stand up to speak, I emphasise the detrimental effect the new supermarket will have on the current retailers, as well as the emotional significance of the magnolia tree.

It's a nerve-wracking, exhilarating experience and although I was consumed with nerves before the meeting, I'm on a high when my part is over.

The fate of the parade rests in the hands of the committee members, and, as the Chair starts to speak, there's a collective intake of breath. But her announcement is not what any of us are expecting.

'We have heard all the arguments,' she says, 'and with so much residential opposition, there is clearly a lot to consider. With that in mind, we will need to carry out another site visit and move the item to the agenda for next month's meeting, which is scheduled for,' she consults her notes, 'exactly four weeks today.'

It is probably the biggest anticlimax I've ever experienced – and it's had to compete with some serious competition to claim that title – and our spirits are somewhat dampened as we leave the room.

'Well, love,' says Dad, 'you've done everything you can. I'll be honest, it's not looking good for you – not when you've got the likes of him and his mates in their designer gear. But you know, you gave it a good go.'

'Let's not give up just yet,' says Sam. Despite his words, he seems to be keen to escape the confines of the town hall and he's walking a few steps ahead of us. 'Westholme Council may well vote against the plans.'

'I don't think so, lad.' Dad shakes his head. 'He'll be giving them backhanders, you see. They'll all be in it together, you mark my words.'

As we reach the car park Sam seems on edge. 'Sorry, Zoe, I'm going to have to go,' he says. 'Got a training session straight after school with some of the footie boys.'

'Oh, okay. Well, thanks for coming, Sam.'

'No problem,' he replies, climbing into his car. 'Speak soon.'

And with that he zooms out of the car park.

I watch him go, wondering what caused him to leave so quickly, before being distracted by the sight of Daniel Lewis making his way towards his car.

'It's not over yet, hey, Zoe?' says Mum, squeezing my shoulders.

'What?' Lost in thought, I barely hear a word she says. 'Er, no, it's not over yet. Just give me a minute, will you?'

Walking quickly, I catch up with Daniel as he reaches his BMW. He's still chatting with a few of his cronies and I hover behind him for a minute before cutting in.

'Mr Lewis?' He breaks off from his conversation and looks at me in surprise.

'Do you have a moment?'

He hesitates, then tells his colleagues he'll catch up with them later and turns back to me, one eyebrow raised.

'So,' I begin, 'did any of what I said back there make you stop and think?'

He purses his lips and crosses his arms, his stance screaming alpha male.

'This is business,' he says. 'We're knocking down something that's just not fit for purpose anymore in order to create something that's needed, even if not necessarily wanted, in this community.'

I take a deep breath. 'Look. I understand this is about the money for you. So, what if I showed you how there's potentially more value in keeping the parade intact rather than knocking it down and building a supermarket?'

He shakes his head. 'You're sentimental about this. I know those figures inside out. There's no way that keeping the parade is a better proposition.'

'I think I might be able to change your mind.'

A smile plays across his lips.

'Oh really? And how do you intend to do that?'

'Give me two weeks,' I say, my voice displaying a confidence I don't feel. 'Two weeks, and I'll show you why you should keep the parade and ditch your supermarket plans.'

He looks at me, as if he's trying to work out whether or not I'm being serious.

'Two weeks,' I repeat, a hint of desperation creeping into my voice.

He opens the passenger door, placing his briefcase down onto the leather seat. Then he turns back to me.

'Two weeks,' he says.

'Seriously?'

'Yes. But two weeks only, no more.'

'Okay.' I smile, despite myself. 'So, I'll drop you a line about the next steps and we'll go from there?'

He nods. 'You do that.'

And as I walk away, using every bit of restraint I have to stop myself from punching the air, I wonder whether I've finally bitten off way more than I can chew.

_____

Westholme Community Facebook page:

Rita Hollingworth: Does anyone know what happened at the planning committee over the parade today?

Eric Hanson: Decision delayed by a month.

Jimmy Hunter: Council's obviously dragging it out in the hope that we'll all eventually stop fighting against it.

Eric Hanson: A few years ago, I would have said Westholme Council were above that sort of funny business. These days? Anything goes.

Chapter Twenty-Three

I'm standing outside Cath's Caff, my tapping foot helping to ease the annoyance I'm feeling at having to wait for Daniel Lewis. It's 9:40, ten minutes after he and I had agreed to meet. He might be a smooth, sharp operator with stylish clothes, but he's a late one.

'Oi, Zoe.' I turn in the direction of the voice to find Cath, her weathered cheeks flushed pink and a sheen across her cheek and nose, standing in the doorway.

'If you're looking for that idiot, he's in here. I wasn't going to let him in, but he said he was meeting you. He's asked me to get you your usual, so Adina's made you a flat white with coconut milk,' she says, adding a wink in case I haven't clocked that my request has been passed on.

The place is already buzzing, with informal business meetings taking place, friends catching up over breakfast and the Chatter and Natter table is already full.

Daniel's at a table to the back of the room. He glances up from his phone and our eyes lock for a second. I look away quickly, take a deep breath and make my way over to him.

'Good morning, Zoe,' he says, standing up and extending his hand. He has another suit on today, this one a single-breasted grey affair, a white shirt open at the collar enhancing the golden skin that peeps out from underneath it.

'Good morning.'

We sit down and he clasps his own hands together, curling and uncurling his fingers awkwardly like a little boy who doesn't know what to do with them.

'I'm surprised she let me in,' he says, nodding towards Cath.

I bite my lip. 'I must admit, I didn't think she *would* let you in without me. That's why I suggested meeting outside.'

'I name-dropped you to barter for a coffee.' He raises a new cappuccino mug, set out neatly on a saucer with – unbelievably – a shortbread biscuit resting on the side, and almost smiles. 'There's been quite a few changes here, I see.'

I beam. Try as I might to remain cool and collected, I can't hide my delight at the new and improved version of the cafe.

'Have you noticed the Chatter and Natter table?' I gush. 'And the new menu?' I hold up the beautifully designed card detailing a range of mouth-watering – and distinctly twenty-first century – dishes. 'Don't the drinks look great?' I gesture to my own cup, containing a caramel-coloured coffee with a perfect latte art heart – courtesy of Adina – created from the foam, then add, 'thanks for mine by the way.'

I know I sound like an over-eager child begging to be liked, but I can't help it. I am so, so desperate for Daniel to be impressed.

But when I look back at him, he isn't taking in any of the changes I've talked about. Instead, he's still watching me.

He takes a sip of his drink, then starts to speak.

'I'll admit, the changes have certainly improved the place. But has it created any additional jobs?'

I gesture over to Adina, laughing behind the counter, her face glowing.

'Well, it's certainly created one for Adina.'

Daniel clears his throat. 'I noticed that. How is she doing?'

'Great. Thanks to the *community spirit*, she not only has a new job, but a place to live too. Margaret from the Westholme Gardeners – do you know her?'

He frowns. 'Is she the one who asked whether they could put those planters and baskets around the parade? The one with the—'

'That's the one. Margaret invited Adina to live with her, so she has a home now, too.'

'And did she hear any more from the police?'

'They interviewed her but I don't think it progressed any further than that.'

'Typical,' he says, setting his cup down on its saucer. 'Anyway, my secretary tells me you've scheduled in a few appointments over the next few days. Which of the parade's many delights are you planning on showing me today?'

'Actually, what I'm showing you today is nowhere near the parade,' I say, feeling a shot of victory at having surprised him. I stand up. 'Are you ready for your tour?'

Daniel gives me one of those smiles that doesn't quite reach a person's eyes. Like when you go to someone's house for tea as a child and they put carrots on your plate and you have to act as though you like them or they won't invite you again. 'Ready as I'll ever be.'

'Okay then,' I say. 'I'll ask Antonio to pour our drinks into take-out cups on the way out. 'We'll need to travel by car for this part. We could go in mine…' I trail off as I realise I forgot to do a sweep of it before I dropped Charlie off this morning, which means that the discarded crisp packets (Charlie's, not mine), undelivered bags of charity clothes and empty coffee cups that I'd vowed to clear out last night are currently still making their presence felt in a variety of unpleasant ways.

'I'll drive,' he says. 'I need to fill up on petrol anyway.'

I'm in love. I've never actually been inside a BMW – or any luxury car for that matter and it's just, well … perfect.

The black leather seats, the fancy screen that sits on the dashboard, the unbelievable spotlessness of it all collude to result in something so beautiful it should be an exhibit in a modern art museum.

As Daniel drives smoothly through the streets of Westholme and then away, up towards Presthill, I start to relax, my body melting into the seats like butter into warm bread. It's so comfortable, so warm. In fact it's too warm, much too warm.

My senses move to high alert as I tune in to the heat enveloping my buttocks, then feel an icy-cold wave roll along my entire body – except my bum, obviously – as I realise what it is.

The presence of this unusual heat can mean only one thing. Something has gone very, very wrong with my pelvic floor muscles. And there is absolutely nothing I can do about it.

Keeping one eye on Daniel, I shift a little as I try to establish the seriousness of the situation. Out of the corner of my eye I glance down at the seat. No sign of a wet patch yet, thank goodness. But I'm going to have to get out of the car in a minute. And then what?

Another damp sensation is now gathering under my armpits. I grip the side of my seat and am so, so close to losing it when Daniel's voice cuts into my near-meltdown.

'In case you were wondering, the seats are heated,' he confirms, barely able to hide the amusement in his voice.

I deliberately give him a haughty, sideways look and spot the corners of his mouth twitching as he tries to hide a smile. 'Of course they are.'

My gaze lingers as I take in his sharp profile, the scar that marks his cheek, the freckles on the side of his nose, the designer glasses that frame those dark eyes. He looks almost human. But within seconds the mouth twitch has disappeared and the furrowed brow is back as he concentrates on the road ahead.

'You told me to head towards Presthill. Where, specifically, would you like me to go?'

'The top of the hill,' I say. 'By the Makeout.'

The minute those words leave my mouth I want to shove them back in. Why, oh why hadn't I picked another spot? Everyone around here knows that the Makeout is where young lovers go in the evening to, well, make out.

Daniel raises his eyebrows but, thankfully, says nothing. Within a few minutes the car purrs, literally purrs, to a stop and I unfasten my seatbelt. 'Okay, this is us,' I say, climbing out of the car. Daniel follows, retrieving his suit jacket from the back seat and pushing his arms into the smooth fabric of the sleeves. He takes a cursory look around then says, 'Can I ask why, exactly, we're here?'

'We're here, Mr Lewis – Daniel – to see Westholme in all its glory. To forget about the levels of deprivation, the challenges, the problems and instead see it in the context of this beautiful setting.'

I lead him to the precipice of the hill and we both look down on the town below, farmers' fields taking up much of the landscape between us and Westholme and then way in the distance, wind turbines punctuating the River Mersey skyline. I never get tired of this view, no matter how many times I see it. Even Daniel isn't immune to the beauty of the panoramic. He's probably taken in this picture-perfect shot one thousand times or more on his drive to and from Presthill. So many times, in fact, that maybe he barely registers it at all anymore. But right now he's looking intently, as if seeing it anew. It's quiet at the peak, with the only noises being the rustling of the breeze and the lively chatter of the birds. Eventually I break the silence. 'It's so easy to get caught up in the nitty gritty of Westholme life which, admittedly, isn't always pretty. So, I thought I'd start here, well away from the town, to remind you of how beautiful the area actually is and how important it is that we don't just give up on it.'

I swear I see his lip curl, but I carry on, undeterred.

'Growing up, I remember Westholme as a fun place with so much community spirit. I'm convinced that all it needs is a little TLC and a lot of conviction to put it on the right track again.'

'And that's what you're trying to do with *The Good News Gazette*?'

I look at him sharply, expecting a sarcastic snarl, but his expression is surprisingly gentle.

'That's what I'm trying to do with *The Good News Gazette*,' I repeat.

Daniel looks at the town again, before signalling for me to sit down on the bench usually reserved for over-amorous couples late at night. Gingerly, I perch on the edge.

'You might be surprised to know that I actually did spend a fair amount of time in Westhill growing up,' he says, sitting down next to me. 'My family lived there before moving to Presthill.'

I look at him. 'How old were you when you left?'

'Ten or eleven, I think.' He hesitates. 'Westholme wasn't the happiest place for me. I was glad to get away, to be honest.'

Well. This is a revelation.

I shift and my eyes catch on the curves of his well-rounded shoulders, his slender stomach and the muscular thickness of his thighs. It's hard to marry the vulnerability of the young boy he's referring to with the undeniable manliness of the figure before me. I feel so sorry for him, I'm almost tempted to give him a quick squeeze.

But then he straightens his back and with that one small action, he closes the door on that particular line of conversation.

'Remarkable how things change, isn't it,' he says, his arrogant demeanour back in full force.

I roll my eyes, almost relieved to see him return to type. This Daniel is a lot easier to deal with. 'It obviously hasn't held you back.' I check the time on my phone. 'Right, we'd better go. I promised your secretary I'd have you back for your midday meeting and the last thing I want is for your car to turn into a pumpkin.'

He looks at me for a minute, trying to understand my reference, then gets it and smiles. A real smile, like he actually finds my joke funny.

'Okay,' he says, the smile still hanging around his eyes, 'let's go. But we're scheduled to meet the day after tomorrow anyway, aren't we?'

'Absolutely,' I reply, in my most business-like tone. 'Let's reconvene at the parade at 10 am then.'

I picture the group of feisty women he's about to encounter at our next meeting, then mutter under my breath, 'You won't know what's hit you.'

Westholme Community Facebook page:

Bernard Phillips: Just phoned the council to order more garden waste bags. Had to pay £2 for each one. Daylight robbery. Why can't we have wheelie bins like the rest of the UK?

Chris Scott: Don't you know? We're the town that the rest of the UK forgot!

Chapter Twenty-Four

There is something very strange going on with Ollie. I've turned a blind eye to the sudden introduction of some truly eyewatering aftershave and the recent injection of new clothes into his wardrobe, but when he offers to buy me coffee for the third time today, I can't ignore it anymore.

'What's going on?' I say, my fingers hovering above the keyboard like seagulls waiting to swoop on their prey as I stop writing up an article on a local marathon runner for a moment in favour of tormenting Ollie instead.

'What do you mean?' he asks, his cheeks colouring slightly. At least, I think they're colouring. It's hard to make out his actual cheek colour through the dark shade of sunbed-generated tan he insists on maintaining despite my stern warnings about the dangers of a) skin cancer and b) looking like a total prat.

'I mean,' I say slowly, 'what's. Going. On?' I pause between each of the words, as if an increased emphasis on each syllable might encourage Ollie to open up.

It fails to have the desired effect.

'Nothing,' he says airily, picking up his man bag. 'Nothing at all.'

'Then what's with the constant offers – lovely as they are – of coffee?' My eyes narrow instinctively. 'Has your redundancy come through?'

There's no mistaking the redness in his cheeks this time.

'Of course not,' he says, indignant, backing towards the door. 'You'd be the first to know if it had.'

As he tries to make his escape, a small book falls out of his jacket and onto the floor. He seizes it in record time, but not before I've spotted the title.

Ollie stares at me for a split second, his face the very picture of guilt.

Suddenly the penny drops. The numerous trips to the cafe, the lingering chats over the counter and now, most tellingly, the possession of a Romanian phrase book.

I gasp. 'It's Adina, isn't it?' I clamp a hand over my mouth then let it fall as the giggles kick in. 'You've got a crush on her!'

It's so interesting how grown men with the cockiness of a tomcat can be reduced to a quivering wreck by the unveiling of a secret crush. And in accordance with that truth, Ollie's usual relaxed, confident demeanour disappears before my eyes.

Whereas the Ollie I know and love usually has a quip for every situation, now he is literally speechless, his mouth opening and closing but no sound coming out.

'Awwww, Ollie … come here.' I push my chair back and envelop him in a big bear hug, a mother hen protecting one of her chicks.

'Don't say anything,' he mumbles into my shoulder. I hold my breath for as long as I can, fearful that, if inhaled, his potent aftershave might irrigate my nostrils, then lead him back to his chair and pat him on the arm as he sinks, defeated, onto the seat.

'I promise I won't,' I say, using the same soothing voice that placates Charlie when he's having a tantrum. 'Now, why don't I make us a nice cuppa and we'll come up with a plan to get her attention that won't result in you going bankrupt.'

Between yesterday's efforts to convince Daniel to save the parade and the hours spent this afternoon counselling Ollie over Adina, I've fallen behind on finishing off the first print issue of *The Good News Gazette*. And with a week to go before the publication date and still no story that's strong enough for a splash, I'm feeling the pressure.

My working hours are ramping up as we creep closer to the deadline, which means Margaret and her Rotary Club friends are taking on the lion's share of the carnival activity right now, but even with their help I'm still struggling to edit the first edition of the paper and create new content for the website too. So finally, worn down by tiredness and defeated by the knowledge that it's the only thing I have to hand that I can upload that day, I call Starr to tell her I'm going to add her twerking video to the website.

She's over the moon of course, so I ignore my deep concern that it's going to turn the site – and Starr – into a laughing stock and hope for the best.

It's at that point, the point at which time has become so precious that I've hung an old lady out to dry in order to save a bit more of it, that Emma sends a Code Red text.

And in that instant, every other urgent matter becomes little more than noise as I immediately message back, *come to mine for eight x*

By its very definition, I'd known the Code Red text meant something serious had happened. But it's not until I open the front door that the severity of the situation becomes clear.

Emma is standing on my doorstep looking as though she's been on a week-long bender. Black mascara streaks her cheeks and her eyes are red and puffy, but it's the presence of the comfy pants that makes me realise something is very, very wrong.

With Beth just metres behind, I put my arm around Emma and usher her through the hall and into the sanctity of my lounge. And it's only once she's there, curled into the very couch on which I shed so many of my own tears just weeks ago, that Emma finally falls apart.

'It's Dave,' she manages through hysterical sobs, 'he's cheated on me.'

I gasp. 'Dave? No way.' I pause for a moment. 'Who with?'

'A-a-a colleague,' she splutters, her breath catching as she spits the words out.

I look over at Beth who's perched on the edge of the other couch, her hands cupped over her mouth.

'I can't believe it,' she says, her voice muffled beneath her palms.

'Oh, Emma, I'm so, so sorry,' I say, unable to believe that kind, steady Dave could have committed the ultimate bad boy act.

'They had a work-do a fortnight ago.' She sniffs. 'He came home a bit late but said he'd struggled to get a taxi and I thought nothing of it at the time. But the reality was,' her whole body shudders as she takes in a jerky gulp of air, 'he was HAVING SEX with the little tramp. SEX,' she repeats loudly for good measure.

I throw a glance at the lounge door to make sure there's no little head peeping around it, torn between a desire to show support and a greater desire not to have to explain exactly what sex means to Charlie in the morning.

'Emma,' I say, 'are you sure?'

'He's admitted it. He's admitted it all.'

Confusion is etched into the contours of Beth's naturally smooth skin. 'But I don't understand,' she says, shaking her head. 'You seem so happy together. You get on, he does the dishes … he buys you *flowers* for goodness sake.'

Emma pulls a tissue out of her sleeve and blows her nose loudly. 'It wasn't enough. The constant juggle to stay on top of everything, the need to keep Simon happy at work and my kids and husband equally happy at home, the 11pm ironing sessions to keep everyone neat and tidy … none of it was enough.'

'Did he give any explanation?' I am at a loss at how to comprehend how the unstoppable force that is Emma could be anything *less* than enough for a man.

'He said he felt as though he'd lost me,' she says between sobs. 'As though we'd lost each other. But the worst of it is this – Dave then accused *me* of having an affair with Simon. Can you believe the cheek of it?'

I think back to the photo of Emma's jaw-dropping new boss, his insistence that they spend time away visiting each branch in the chain of hotels, the boredom I've suspected Emma's felt with her own life for some time now. Was Dave really that wide of the mark in suspecting that Emma might be having an affair? Hadn't she cut many of *our* conversations short to answer an urgent work call or email?

I extend my arm and squeeze it around her back.

'Em, you know what I'm about to ask you I'm asking you out of love.'

She looks at me. I hear Beth gasp.

'What chick? What are you asking me?'

'Does Dave have any grounds to suspect something might be going on between you and Simon?'

Briefly, Emma breaks eye contact on the premise of rearranging her position on the couch. It causes only a second's delay in her response, but it's a second too long. 'No.'

I pull my arm away and squeeze both her hands in mine instead. Looking her in the eyes, I simply say her name. 'Emma?'

That one word unleashes tears which fall like torrents now, seemingly from every orifice on her face. Water gushes from her eyes, gunk from her nose and dribble from her mouth. I think about the many times I've reprimanded Charlie for spilling his drink on that same couch and it crosses my mind that if Emma were to lay a finger on it right now, the deadly combination of mascara, foundation, tears and snot would probably do far more damage than a simple glass of water ever could.

I push the thought from my mind and concentrate on being a good friend.

'Honestly?' She squeezes her tissue into a ball, then starts tearing bits off it, letting them fall to the floor in one, big heap of white feathers.

'Something nearly happened. It was a month ago. Simon and I had a meal in one of the hotels and drunk more wine than we should. When we went up to our rooms he invited me in for a nightcap.'

'You didn't go, did you, Em?' Lovely, naïve Beth.

Emma nods. 'I did. The food, the wine, it had all been so perfect, so *romantic*. He was saying the nicest things and it felt good. I *wanted* him to kiss me. I *wanted* something to happen. And it very nearly did.'

Beth and I wait, holding our breath.

'But then his car alarm went off in the car park and while I was waiting for him to come back I fell asleep. I woke up at the end of the bed the next morning to find I'd had ten missed calls from Dave. He'd been worried when I hadn't called to say goodnight and I couldn't think up a good enough excuse to explain where I'd been so I told him the truth – well, an economic version of it.' She takes a breath. 'But that doesn't justify sleeping with someone else, does it?'

Beth and I shake our heads vigorously.

'Is he sorry?' Beth says carefully.

'He *says* he is,' scoffs Emma. 'But how am I meant to look at him every day, knowing that he's broken the most basic of our marital vows? How can I wave him off to work, knowing that he'll be seeing *her*, wondering if he's still sleeping with her, if he *wants* to sleep with her?'

We all fall silent, none of us having an answer to the question at hand.

'How did you find out?' I ask after a moment or two.

Emma sniffs. 'He confessed. We'd just settled down to watch TV last night when he came out with it. I honestly thought he was joking at first. I mean, I know things haven't been *perfect* since we had the kids, but who does have the perfect relationship?'

'No-one,' Beth and I reply together.

'Exactly,' says Emma, her black-ringed eyes looking sadder than I've ever seen them. I watch her, knowing she'll be sadder still when she realises how much make-up has made its way onto her top.

'So where is he now?' I ask.

'He's staying at his mum and dad's. The kids are staying with *my* mum tonight to give me a break. It's hard being Fun Mum when you're dying inside.'

Beth slips from the couch onto the floor and curls up at Emma's feet, her silky hair spilling across Emma's knees as she rests her head on them. 'What are you going to do, Em?' she asks gently.

'I don't know, chick. Before he told me, there were a few times when I woke up in the night to find him downstairs sitting at the kitchen table just staring into space, but ... I don't know. Infidelity isn't something we're meant to tolerate, is it. Isn't that what we always said? If a man ever cheated on us, that would be it?'

'But this is *Dave* we're talking about,' Beth says.

'He's always been such a good husband,' I agree.

'And he's a great dad,' Emma admits reluctantly. 'But he's also a cheater. And *that* is something I don't think I'll ever be able to forget.'

'But what about you and Simon?' I ask, tentatively. 'If it weren't for the car alarm business, wouldn't *you* technically be a cheater too?'

We talk well into the night, pondering the technicalities of infidelity, going over the past, trying to predict the future. The three of us have been through so much together. Yet, at thirty-three and with three kids between us, none of us are any the wiser when it comes to negotiating the highs and lows of this strange thing we call life.

———

I'm still thinking about Emma's situation when I wake up the next morning, wondering what I'd do if I was her. For the past eight years, there's only ever been Charlie and I. No-one else to worry about, no-one else to consider, no-one else to fear. When it comes to love, my heart has been well and truly closed for business.

It's a policy that, so far at least, has served me well. When I'm planning our busy lives, I don't have to consider anyone else but Charlie. I don't have to text anyone if we go out for the day and stay out longer than planned, I have all the wardrobe space I could ever need and thanks to the intensive training imposed on Charlie from an early age, the toilet seat is *never* left up.

But there's a flip side to that. There's an emptiness to knowing that if we *are* back late, the only one who cares is Lola – and that's only because it means she has to wait an extra hour or so for her tea. Sometimes I look in the other wardrobe in my bedroom, the one that contains just a few of my coats and some boxes of my old size tens, and wonder whether I'll ever open the doors to be hit by a musky, sexy, 'male' smell and find a selection of men's jeans, jumpers and jackets inside.

Hard as it is to believe, there are even times when I'll listen to women complaining about their husbands or partners leaving bath towels on the floor and wish, just for a second, that I could join in. That I could roll my eyes while picking up the soaking wet towel of the man I love and remind myself to chastise him for it later.

None of those things happen for me. And the ability to shut myself off from the possibility of love has been a godsend since I had Charlie and my life changed from fast-paced but ordered to a whirlwind of activity mainly powered by elements beyond my control. But there are times when I wonder how it would feel to love again. To be kissed, slowly and gently. To be held and cared for. To be loved.

I shake my head to rid it of those thoughts. They're dangerous and painful. They've also become all too frequent of late. I think of Emma again. Life is far simpler when you're alone. And that's the way I intend to stay.

Westholme Community Facebook page:

Beryl Goodwin: I'd just like to thank the two gentlemen who've been running the Classics for Beginners classes at The Lower Storey. Since starting the lessons I've read *Emma* and *Great Expectations* and am now halfway through *The Great Gatsby*. It's given me a whole new appreciation for the books I used to be forced to study in school. Thank you, Neil and John!

Tori Hindle: I went to the first session when they started on that *Emma* book which, by the way, is a total rip-off of the film *Clueless*. Decided not to go back when they said *Twilight* wasn't a classic. Think Robert Pattinson might disagree?!

Beryl Goodwin: Give me strength.

Chapter Twenty-Five

Gloria's mentoring group are on their very best behaviour for Daniel's visit, with not a wolf-whistle or a heckle between them. In fact, they are the very image of professionalism as they carefully outline their business plans and explain how the parade's empty retail units could be used to help get their start-ups off the ground while also generating a rental income – if only he'd reconsider the rental charges.

For his part, Daniel manages to shake-off some of that pole-up-his-backside haughtiness that always makes him seem so unapproachable, asking questions at the appropriate moments and displaying a far greater interest in the business propositions than I would have given him credit for. He even makes helpful suggestions as to how they can be improved, causing Gloria and I to exchange glances more than once throughout the morning.

By the time the session has come to an end, the room is buzzing with creativity and even Daniel seems excited by some of their ideas.

'You do know that all of these women will be looking for office and retail spaces in the very near future, don't you?' I say as we drive back towards the parade, again, thankfully, in Daniel's car. 'Which could mean that, if the rent was set at an affordable price, you could have all of these units occupied, all of them full, rather than the weird one open, one closed thing you have going on right now.'

'They're a resourceful lot,' he replies brusquely. 'I'm sure they'll find units elsewhere that will suit their needs.'

I bite my tongue to stop any one of the hundred cutting retorts that are on the tip of it from escaping and instead use the 'isn't it all exciting!' voice I wheel out for Charlie at times when the situation is anything but.

'Why don't we have some lunch?' I suggest. 'We can go to Cath's and I'll ask her to whip us up something special.'

Daniel purses his stiff upper lip. 'Hmmm, a request for Cath to give me something special,' he says, as if pondering my suggestion. 'What could possibly go wrong.'

I try not to smile. 'You're not saying you're actually *scared* of Cath, are you, Daniel?'

He pretends he hasn't heard.

'Don't be a wimp.' I chuckle. 'Anyway, there's something else I want to show you. Come on, I promise I'll protect you.'

Daniel looks around at the hive of activity taking place before him. At least a dozen freelancers and homeworkers type away at their laptops on what could loosely be termed 'hot-desks' in the bright, airy space above the cafe, accessed by the stairs at the back of the dining room.

In the corner, Antonio has set up two sofas and a coffee table to create an informal seating area and a woman in a suit is sitting there with a man in jeans and a pair of Converse.

A TV on the wall is showing a muted version of the BBC News

channel with subtitles. Jugs of water and glasses are set out on a table at the far side of the room. Cups of coffee and pots of tea are only an order away. It's a homeworker's dream.

Antonio heads up the stairs then, tray in hand.

'*Ciao,*' he says, nodding to us both before tapping me on the shoulder as he walks past.

'Exciting news about Starr, hey, *bella,*' he says, flashing me a grin.

I smile and nod back, then realise I haven't got a clue what he's talking about.

'Er … what do you mean?'

'Her dance video. The one you put on your site. It's been shared something like – 40,000 times,' he says. 'It's gone – how you say – viral. Check it out on social media.'

'What?' I reply, hardly able to believe what I'm hearing, then remember Daniel's standing next to me. 'I mean, I'll look at it, thanks, Antonio.'

I feel Daniel's eyes on me. He coughs. 'I saw that video actually,' he says.

'You read *The Good News Gazette*?'

He looks away quickly.

'Well, not *every* day, but sometimes I take a quick look at it. It's not too bad.'

'Thank you,' I smile. 'Faint praise indeed.'

Turning back to the room, I begin my pitch. 'Antonio suggested turning this storage space into a place that people could come and work,' I'm suppressing the high-five I'm desperate to give each and every one of the lovely homeworkers who have taken advantage of the idea on this particular day. 'As you can see, the idea has been very popular.'

He's trying to hide it, but I can tell Daniel's impressed.

'It's quite the twenty-first century workspace.'

'Works well, doesn't it?' I say, trying but failing to keep a note of triumph out of my voice. 'And there are all sorts of professions working alongside each other here. Gareth over there,' Gareth raises his hand, his eyes fixed firmly on his laptop,'is running a website design start-up while Kate, who you can see on the couch in the corner, is an accountant.'

Neil is sitting at a table with another man, but their heads are almost together, deep in conversation, so I decide not to disturb him.

Instead, I point out Sam sitting at a desk in the far side of the room.

'Sam runs Westholme's football academy. He's doing a great job, particularly with kids who've come from challenging backgrounds.'

I look up at Daniel to gauge his expression, expecting to find him bowled over by the many different workers choosing to hot-desk here, but something's wrong. He's not looking at the workers anymore. Instead, a shadow has set across his face and he's glaring at Sam.

At first, Sam is oblivious, typing away at his computer, but then he catches my eye, takes one look at Daniel next to me and freezes.

Daniel picks up his briefcase. 'I think I've seen enough, thank you, Zoe. Was there anything else you wanted to show me or should we call it a day?'

Abruptly, he turns and heads towards the stairs. I search Sam's face for answers but, finding nothing, move quickly to catch up with Daniel. Once outside, I put my hand on his arm.

'Hey.'

He continues walking, striding quickly towards the car park.

I watch him for a second, then start to run – okay, maybe it's more of an ungainly jog – after him again and tug at his sleeve, aware of how unprofessional and unsophisticated I am looking right now.

'HEY!'

Finally, he stops and spins round to face me.

'What's wrong?'

He looks embarrassed now, almost shaken in fact. But as he starts to speak, his expression is blank.

'Nothing. But I have an extremely busy schedule today, so if it's just people working on laptops that you want to show me then I think we're done. There's plenty of communal workspaces in far grander places not too far from here. There is no cause for one in Westholme.'

He blinks then, as if he's just played back his words in his head. He looks longingly towards the car park where, just yards away, sits the peaceful haven of his beautiful BMW. Then, exhaling deeply, he turns back to me.

'I'm sorry, that was out of order. Was there anything else you wanted to show me?'

I'm deflated, as if I've been winded by some invisible force – or maybe invisible words.

I shake my head. 'Let's leave it for today.'

He takes a step towards me. 'Zoe, I—'

'Let's leave it for today,' I say more forcefully this time. 'We're scheduled to meet again tomorrow anyway. We can pick it up then.'

And I walk past him towards my own car, start up the engine and ignore the sound of what I strongly suspect to be the exhaust pipe dragging along the ground as I drive away with as much decorum as both Tilly and I can muster.

Once again, Mum has created a banquet of comfort food that immediately throws a spanner in the works of the short-lived success I've been having in my ongoing battle with self-control.

But after the abrupt way today's meeting came to an end, it's exactly the sort of self-medication I'm looking for.

Cheese-topped lasagne and oily garlic bread are the perfect distraction to take my mind off the day's events. Well, those and the fact that, despite having managed to fill the newspaper with a wide range of positive stories I'm convinced add up to a fantastic read, I still haven't found an exclusive story that has enough punch for our first front page.

'Where are the recycling sacks, Dad?' I say, as I attempt to make myself useful by gathering up the empty food containers.

'Just outside the back door,' says Dad from behind his newspaper. 'They're a right nuisance. Always blowing away. Can't wait 'til we get the wheelie bins.'

I pause, boxes in hand. 'What wheelie bins?'

'Oops,' Dad says, scratching his head. 'Forget that, I'm not meant to mention anything.'

'Dad, what wheelie bins?' I press him, my news radar picking up signals.

Dad looks at Mum, who rolls her eyes. 'Oh, just something I heard on the factory floor,' he says. 'One of the blokes' sons is a binman, and he told me every house in Westholme and the surrounding areas is going to get a set of wheelie bins rather than these rubbish bags.'

I drop the containers on the counter. 'Dad, this is huge news. People have been demanding wheelie bins for years. Does anyone else know about this?'

'I don't think so,' says Dad. 'It's all hush-hush. Bobby told me not to mention it to anyone and I haven't – well, other than you of course.'

'Oh my goodness, Dad, this could be my splash. Now, think carefully. Did he say anything else? Anything else at all?'

Dad presses his temples with his fingers, silent for a minute. 'Yes, he did … it's just coming to me now… That's right, he said

... that you should definitely have a topless model on page three.'

'Urgh,' I say, shaking my head. 'Glad to see bin collection services are moving on in Westholme, even if misogynistic attitudes aren't. I'll phone the council first thing tomorrow for the full story.' Alarm flashes across Dad's face. 'And don't worry, Dad.' I smile, pinching a piece of garlic bread. 'I always protect my sources.'

I'm helping myself to another jam tart when Ryan texts.

After endless pressure from Charlie, I'd finally messaged Ryan again to ask him whether he could confirm his mooted attendance at Charlie's first football game. And, in a huge departure from form, he actually replies within twenty-four hours.

Unfortunately, it's Charlie, playing a football game on the handset, who sees his message come in, so my usual tactic of keeping any arrangements to myself in case they don't come off is shot to pieces.

'Mum,' he shrieks from the lounge, 'Muuuuum!' I jump to my feet, ready to save him from whatever is causing the hysteria, when he hurtles into the kitchen.

'He's coming!' he yells, throwing his arms around my waist, the phone still clasped tightly in his little hand. 'Dad's coming to watch me play football. I knew it! I knew he'd come!'

And the rest of my evening is spent veering between delight at the fact that Ryan has finally agreed to give him this, a dad who watches his football matches and the very real fear that he may not turn up at all.

The Good News Gazette

Westholme Community Facebook page:

Kev Lawson: Can anyone recommend a personal fitness instructor please?

Leah Moreton: Hollie Cross in the square at the parade every Monday lunchtime 12 noon.

Hollie Cross: Hilarious, Leah. Just hilarious.

Chapter Twenty-Six

A missing pair of trousers, a spilt orange juice and a forgotten lunchbox all conspire to make me just a teeny bit later than I said I'd be in meeting Daniel at the parade car park, so when I pull up he's already there, leaning against the bonnet of his BMW, head tilted towards the clear blue sky to greet the Friday morning sun.

At ease and off guard as he soaks up the warm rays, he doesn't notice my arrival and I watch him for a moment, taken aback by the sight of *this* Daniel rather than the one with the furrowed brow concentrating on his phone or his driving or whatever else it is that's requiring all of his powers of focus at any given moment of the day.

His five o'clock shadow has grown into a rough, dark stubble, the casual direction of his hair suggests he may have run out of gel and without his glasses I can see that those intense eyes are framed by eyelids trimmed with thick, dark eyelashes.

I'd told him to prepare to get dirty – the implication of which shocked us both for a minute, before launching into a long and babbling explanation of the fact we were going to spend some time with Margaret and the Westholme Gardeners – and he'd certainly delivered on his brief.

Gone are the James Bond suits and pristine shirts; today he's wearing a battered pair of jeans, a loose grey t-shirt that still manages to cling firmly to the curves of his shoulders and a pair of lumberjack boots. I catch my breath. He's like something out of a Diet Coke advert. Then, sensing my arrival, he shrugs off his moment of self-abandon, greets me with a nod and sticks the pole back up his backside.

I nod back and pocket my phone before getting out of the car. Thank goodness he's so dull. Throw any kind of personality into the mix and spending so much time with him might become a little more challenging.

Admittedly, my plan for us to muck in with the Westholme Gardeners isn't purely to do with proving the worth of the parade; it's also so I can find out more about Margaret's green-fingered team and put together a story on them for the *Gazette*.

While Daniel doesn't look overly thrilled at the prospect of hanging out with some of his fiercest critics, he doesn't object either and I'm intrigued to watch how he interacts with normal people as opposed to men in suits.

Not that anyone could call Margaret 'normal', and from the moment I introduce Daniel to her, it's clear that while we may be on his turf, Margaret's the one who's in charge.

They've had dealings before of course; a slight dip of the head when he shakes her grubby-gloved hand indicates that he remembers her publicly taking him to task over the memorial tree and he's since approved her request for the carnival, so he's more than aware of who she is.

Still, I'm pleasantly surprised when he dons the gloves she

gives him, follows her to her car and starts transporting huge bags of compost to the parade without so much as a hint of objection.

'That's right,' she shouts as he walks past for what must be the tenth time, biceps enlarged as he easily carries the plastic sacks of soil, 'put your back into it, plenty more where they came from!'

Daniel clamps his lips together, looks over at me tending to a hanging basket and shakes his head as I gently pull out some past-their-best blooms. But there's a twinkle of something in his eyes and I suspect he's secretly amused by this five-foot-nothing figure issuing him with orders like an over-eager Sergeant Major.

'About time he found out what real work is.' Margaret winks before continuing with her torment. 'Yes, keep going, young man,' she instructs. 'Once you've finished with my car there's hundreds of plants that need moving from Jack's. That's it, speed up a bit … don't want to be here all day now, do you?'

———

Margaret leans over the pot of sunshine-yellow daffodils and lilac hyacinths, reaching out to the disfigured petal of one of the flowers and tutting loudly.

'Slugs,' she tells me over her shoulder. 'It's a big problem with daffs.'

I brush a gloved hand across my forehead, pushing away strands of hair that have fallen out of my ponytail and into my eyes and look across at the injured flower. It's not the only one that's looking less than perfect. They've all been affected one way or another by the insatiable appetites of hungry slugs.

We've been working at the parade for a couple of hours now and I've noticed more than one business owner's jaw hit the floor when they've spotted Daniel getting his hands dirty, in ways they'd never imagined.

After he's proved his worth by transporting enough

compost and flowers to fill a small removal van, Margaret allows Daniel to join us at the planters where, although he's not exactly gushing with conversation, he's not shying away from it either. He seems particularly amused by Jack, a seventy-something in blue dungarees and yellow wellies whose raison d'etre appears to be to wind Margaret up to bursting point.

'Hey, Margaret, are you ready for me to put those slug pellets down yet?' he shouts over, giving me a wink.

'Absolutely not,' Margaret growls back. 'What a silly suggestion. Imagine if a child got hold of them. Not to mention what it would do to the slugs.'

'Ah give over,' Jack says. 'You're going soft in your old age. Nothing wrong with taking out a few slugs. Or a few kids for that matter.' He chuckles at his own joke as Margaret turns to him, somehow managing to make her eyes wide, her chin jut out and her forehead frown, all at the same time.

'Will you stop that,' she reprimands him sternly. 'That's not at all funny,' she glances over at Daniel and me, 'and not at all reflective of the ethos of the Westholme Gardeners.'

Jack grins, his perfect set of false teeth gleaming in the sunlight, the glint in his bright blue eyes suggesting an attractive combination of looks and personality that must have made him quite a catch back in the day.

'Oh, don't be going all la-di-da on us, Margaret Kemp,' he says. 'You forget, we go back a long way. In fact, I remember the days when your jokes were dirtier than mine.'

Margaret's already ruddy cheeks turn a brighter shade of puce and, stumped for an answer, she simply turns back to her planter. 'Ridiculous old man,' she mutters under her breath. 'I've a good mind to kick him out of the group.'

I steal a glance at Daniel, indulging in a rare chuckle, then look around at the other gardeners working within hearing range, all of whom appear as amused by the exchange as he is and I feel my shoulders relax.

Despite the fact that my own gardening skills are limited to borrowing the lawn mower off my dad once a month to fend off potential complaints from my neighbours, I'm having fun.

The sunny morning has turned into a beautiful day, the banter between the multi-generational crew is making me smile, and I have to admit that getting out of the office and into the fresh air feels really, really good. Even Daniel seems to be loosening up.

I turn back to the pot Margaret's given me to liven up.

'How often do you work on the planters here?' I ask, wondering not for the first time if I'd be such a committed volunteer so far into retirement, or whether I'd be more inclined to watch TV and drink gin all day.

'Every Wednesday,' she replies, wiping the back of her glove across her nose. Most of our planters and hanging baskets are here and it takes a fair amount of time to keep on top of them. Then on Mondays we pop along to weed and water the planters in the other parts of Westholme – the train station, outside the library and the like. Thursdays, as you know, tend to be reserved for Meals for Mums.'

I breathe deeply, inhaling the air that encompasses the scent of rubbish, bacon butties and manure from the farmers' fields on the outskirts of town. The sun is warming the back of my neck and the chatter of the group is ringing in my ears. It feels refreshing, this. To be outside, fingers buried in soil, laughing with strangers and, bizarrely, Daniel. It's what I always imagined a community should feel like, working together with a shared interest in making things better for everyone. It's nice.

Out of the corner of my eye I see Daniel smile and shake his head as Jack offers him a glug of the hip flask he's passing around. Margaret spots him too. 'Jack Germaine, will you stop that right now,' she hisses.

'What?' he asks innocently. 'I hope you're not trying to deprive me of a drink of water? I'm sure that's considered an essential human right.'

She fixes him with a glare and looks back at me. 'See what I have to deal with?' she says, a smile threatening to diminish her high levels of Jack-related irritation as she stabs the soil with a hand trowel. 'The slugs are the easy part.'

Daniel unwraps the tin foil slowly, as though he's waiting for a frog to jump out of the last layer.

'I hope you like chicken salad,' I say. 'I wasn't sure what we'd be doing for lunch so I thought it might be best to make us something.'

The Westholme Gardeners have stopped to refuel and Daniel and I are perched on one of the benches in the square where we're balancing the contents of our lunch bags on our knees.

Because I'm now following a budget, I knew I couldn't afford to find myself in a situation where I'd have to pay for lunch, so I made us both a packed one instead. I'd half-expected him to turn his nose up at it, but he seems grateful, touched almost, that I've bothered.

His eyebrows are raised as he continues examining the contents of the brown paper bag. Butties, a chocolate biscuit, packet of crisps, an apple … all standard fare, but he's picking up each one and studying them in turn.

'What's wrong?' I say, the frown puckering up my brow again. 'Don't you like it?'

'Oh no, it's not that,' he says, his voice unusually gentle. 'It's just that, well, it's been a long time since anyone made me a packed lunch, that's all.'

I tilt my head as I look at him. 'What *do* you eat then?'

He considers the question and shrugs. 'Whatever's on offer at the time. I'm usually out at lunch meetings, or if I'm stuck in the office my secretary, Candice, will run out and pick something up for me. There are plenty of good sandwich bars around Liverpool.'

I'm still looking at him, watching the way his Adam's apple bobs up and down as he chews and swallows the simple sandwich as though it's the best thing he's eaten that week. He must feel me watching then, because he looks back.

'What?' he says, brushing his fingers across the short black hairs on his chin, obviously expecting to find mayonnaise there.

I shake my head. 'Nothing,' I say. 'Just wishing I'd charged you for it now. At those Liverpool butty bar prices, I would have made a killing.'

I've always suspected that Margaret is an extremely smart cookie. So I'm not in the slightest bit surprised when, for our last task of the day, she asks Daniel and I to prune and water the magnolia tree.

'Young trees are like young people,' she explains as she hands me the pruning shears and Daniel the watering can. 'They need lots of love and care in order to grow into healthy adults. Without it, they might survive, but they'll never prosper. They'll never excel. They'll never bloom like they were truly meant to.'

The metaphor isn't lost on me. I'm just not sure which of us she's talking about.

Daniel does as he's told; pouring water around the base of the tree with such attention that you'd be forgiven for thinking he wasn't about to put its life in mortal peril by ripping it up and sticking it somewhere else.

I, aware of the significance of the task, handle its branches carefully as I follow Margaret's instructions on how to prune the redundant parts. 'When branches break, as this one has,' she points to a bough broken in two, the bottom part hanging by a smooth thread, 'through strong winds, or sometimes thanks to the kick of a ball, we have to prune them. Don't go mad,' she continues, as I position the pruning shears on the branch. 'Just prune it back to the main stem. The last thing you want to do is create wounds.' She looks at us both. 'They heal slowly, you know.'

And we finish off the day watering and pruning, putting our all into caring for a tree that each of us know is ultimately doomed.

———————

Westholme Community Facebook page:

Paul Gregory: Been looking at that new *Good News Gazette* online. It's nice to see something positive written about Westholme for a change. Some alright stuff on there.

Lisa Sheldon: Yeah, alright if you're interested in do-gooders running footie teams for toe-rags and auld women planting flowers.

Paul Gregory: Bit disrespectful that, isn't it?

Lisa Sheldon: It's fecking jobs we need, not flowers. Come back to me when there's some of those on offer.

Chapter Twenty-Seven

I t's hard to decipher who's more anxious as we drive in silence – if you ignore the noise of Tilly's exhaust – to our first ever football match. Charlie or me.

Not for the first time that morning, my heart melts as I look in the rear-view mirror and see my little boy sitting in the back in his red and white striped team football kit, seemingly in a world of his own as his eyes flicker at the houses flashing by in a blur.

'Hey, little man, you're not nervous, are you?' I'm aiming for a reassuring tone, but even *I* can hear the forced merriment in my voice.

He shakes his head, then says, 'Maybe just a little bit.'

'Don't be,' I say firmly. 'I'm sure your dad will turn up. Even if he gets held up and has to miss part of it, you're going to be great. And you know Sam wouldn't put you in the team if he didn't think you could cut it, would he?'

Charlie stays silent.

'Charlie?' I check the mirror again.

'Hmm?' he responds, still staring out of the window.

'Sam wouldn't put you in the team if he didn't think you were ready, would he?'

'I guess not.'

'Well then.' My voice is firm.

His gaze shifts from the window to the mirror where he finally meets my eyes.

'Unless it's because he likes you.'

I freeze. 'What do you mean?'

Charlie sighs. 'Likes you as in wants you to be his girlfriend.'

A hot flush rushes through my body, despite me being nowhere near the menopause.

'Oh, I don't think so, Charlie.' I laugh, my voice shooting up an octave.

'I do,' he says, his eyes back on the window now.

Taking a deep breath, I decide to test new ground.

'And how would you feel about that?'

'About what?'

'If Sam wanted me to be his girlfriend? Not that he does,' I add quickly.

'I dunno. We're here,' he announces, as I turn into the car park.

'Here he is, number eight,' says Sam, ruffling Charlie's hair as he joins the rest of the team for the warm-up exercises. I start to tell him that Charlie doesn't like having his hair ruffled, then realise, as he jerks his head away, that I'm too late.

Sam turns to me and issues a wink that awakens the butterflies in my tummy. 'Are you ready to see history in the making?'

I take up the thread. 'Absolutely,' I say, holding up my phone. 'And ready to record it for posterity. Good luck, Charlie!' I shout, and he waves me away while simultaneously looking for his dad.

Taking up my position at the edge of the pitch, I look too. I can see some mums, some dads and a mixture of both chatting to each other, all clearly stalwarts of the Saturday football league, but no Ryan.

Once again my stomach lurches and that feeling of anxiety kicks in. The feeling that, despite my efforts to be all things to my son, I've failed to give him a dad that will stand on the sidelines, cheering him on and laughing with the other parents.

But maybe today, I won't have failed at all. Maybe today will be the day that I don't have to meld myself into some sort of mum-and-dad hybrid, trying to be two people in one body and doing a convincing job of neither. Maybe today will be the day that Ryan finally pulls his finger out and at least pretends to be a dad for a few hours.

I crane my neck, searching the cars in the car park, my eyes seeking out the one that will make the difference between Charlie having a good day and a bad week. Even among the high-end lease cars on show, a Porsche would still stand out. But, to Charlie and I, it's the absence of one that's really making its mark.

I pull my phone out of my pocket and check it again. No text from Ryan. As Charlie moves into position on the pitch, I snap a photograph of him and text it to his dad. *Just getting ready*, I tap out. *He can't wait to see you. Hope you're very close.*

An ear-piercing whistle heralds the start of the game and it's then, at the very moment that the match kicks off, that Ryan texts to say he won't be coming after all.

———

I don't know whether I'm more upset or annoyed, but however you'd define the emotions swirling up inside me, you wouldn't call them good. I redial Ryan's number over and over again to demand an explanation, but he keeps dismissing the call just as easily as he dismisses Charlie and me. One tap, one press of a button, and puff, we're gone.

With his eyes mostly either on the sidelines looking out for his dad or throwing me many a questioning look that I have no idea how to answer, it's clear Charlie's head is not in the game. So it's little surprise that Sam waits no more than ten minutes before bringing him off the pitch.

Sam catches his arm as he marches towards us, but, with a quick flick of his shoulders, Charlie shrugs him off and, face like thunder, storms over to me.

'He's not coming, is he?' he says, his little nostrils flaring.

I crouch down and take his hands. The weight of what Ryan has done is almost too heavy for me to bear. 'I'm so sorry, Charlie. Dad texted me. His car broke down on the way so he couldn't get here, but he said to tell you how sorry he is and that he loves you so, so much.'

His chin trembles and his shoulders droop, arms hanging limply at the side of his mud-flecked white shorts. 'But he said he'd come,' he says, his wide, innocent eyes filling up now with tears that he attempts to brush away before his teammates spot them.

I try again. 'He really wanted to, it's just he's—'

In a sudden, violent gesture, Charlie shakes my hands away. 'No, he didn't,' he says, an edge to his voice I've never heard before. 'He didn't want to, he was probably never going to come, he, he…' His face is contorted as it dawns on him what he wants to say. 'He HATES me!'

I gasp as his words slice into me like knives being hurled in quick succession, the idea of anyone hating my son, let alone his dad, creating a rush of pain and anger that is almost too powerful to contain.

Charlie stares back at me defiantly, that same pain and anger reflected in his own eyes. There's surprise there too; surprise that he's finally managed to voice the emotions he's battled with for years, rage freeing him from the constraints of trying to protect my feelings.

Leading him away from the other parents who, probably assuming Charlie's substitution has caused his outburst, are whispering and nodding our way, I crouch down again so that I can look him in the eyes. 'Charlie, believe me, your dad *does not* hate you. He loves you more than life itself.' I suspect that last part might be a lie, but it's a completely necessary one.

'But he said he'd come, Mum,' Charlie wails, tears cutting like rivers through his red cheeks as they overpower his body, far too little, far too small to deal with such agony. He repeats himself then, flinging out one last anguished, '*He said he'd come,*' before his face crumples and his body heaves with howling, heartbreaking sobs.

I throw my arms around him, my body bent over his, tears streaming down my own cheeks now as I curse Ryan for being such a selfish and uncaring dad, myself for not protecting Charlie from the flakiness of his own father and the world for not ever giving either of us a break. We stand like that, huddled together, comforting each other over the failings of one man, until the whistle blows to mark half-time.

Mercifully, Sam brings Charlie back onto the pitch for the second half, which has the dual effect of keeping his mind occupied and turning me into the sort of football mum I always assumed I'd loathe.

Every time he gets within five feet of the ball, I shout with such gusto that I barely notice the sideways glances being issued by the other parents and when an opposing player fouls him, the only thing that stops me storming onto the pitch and taking him to task is a look, and an almost imperceptible shake of the head from Sam; a warning to leave it to the referee to sort out.

In the rare moment I'm not watching Charlie, I find myself sneaking a look or two at Sam. I'm used to his easy-going manner, so this unexpected show of command and passion as he shouts instructions to the boys and exchanges comments with some of the parents on the sideline is new to me. And not, I'll admit, unattractive. Then I remember that it's thoughts like that that put Charlie and I in the position we're in today and I shut down that part of my mind, determined it will never again see the light of day.

Confession time. Despite my loud cheers and groans at what appears to be the appropriate times, I have very little idea of what's actually going on throughout most of the match. The other side have the ball a lot. Then our side seem to get it back again. Charlie tackles some of the players a few times, his expression so fierce, so determined, that I almost don't recognise it.

There are a few mishaps, not least of all when one of the boys appears to forget the direction in which they're shooting and scores a blinder for the other side. But then finally, three minutes before the final whistle, something amazing happens.

If I were a football commentator, a player, or indeed any type of football fan, I'd be able to provide a detailed commentary on how Charlie tackles another player, dribbles the ball down the centre of the field and then shoots and scores a goal so mind-blowing that scouts descend from all corners of the field and start bidding to sign him up.

But I'm none of those and, anyway, that's not exactly what happens. It's more a case of Charlie turning around, seeing the ball next to him and giving it a wellie that by some fluke of nature ends up in the top corner of the net. And it is amazing.

All sense of decorum gone, I let my emotions take over, shouting and whooping for all I'm worth as those ever-present tears fall unashamedly down my face.

And when Charlie looks over at me after exercising his well-rehearsed and long-imagined victory dance, the look that passes between us reminds me that we don't need anyone else. Each other is enough. It's a moment that stays with me long after the final whistle is blown.

Once it becomes clear that the game has officially ended, I race over to where the boys are gathering for their team talk, only to realise, too late, that parents aren't invited to this particular gathering.

'Mum, stay over there,' Charlie hisses, mortified at my error and I skulk back to the sidelines, possibly the most humiliating walk of shame I've ever had to undertake.

A few minutes later he's at my side, his sweaty face a testament to his efforts.

'Did you see, Mum? Did you see my goal?'

Taking advantage of the fact that he's letting me hug him in public today, I squeeze him again, hastily sweeping my fingers under my eyes in an attempt to remove what's left of my eye make-up from my cheeks.

'You were amazing,' I say, 'Well done. I'm so proud of you.' And then, desperate to put a smile on his face and make him feel justifiably proud of his goal, I say, 'Why don't we go to Cath's? I'll treat you to anything you like.'

He considers his options. 'Can I have a blue slush?'

'Absolutely. I'll even get you a cake.' Despite my best

intentions, I'm not above drowning him in chemicals and refined sugar when the situation demands it.

'Okay then,' he says, his tone retaining just the right amount of an edge to let me know that he isn't entirely happy with the way today turned out, but his expression indicating that he'll let me indulge him anyway.

As parents and children say their goodbyes and wander off towards the car park, Sam strolls casually towards us. 'What do you think?' he says, smiling. 'He was great, wasn't he?'

I squeeze Charlie again as he tries to shrug me off. 'He was *so* good. I can't believe how far he's come in such a short space of time. You've worked wonders with him.'

Now it's Sam's turn to look embarrassed. 'Well, it's Charlie who's done all the hard work. I've just given him a few pointers.' He turns to Charlie. 'Did you enjoy that, mate?'

Clearly torn between emotions, Charlie simply nods, then, seeing a spare ball on the ground, starts doing kicky-ups with it.

Sam looks at me and frowns.

'Don't ask,' I mutter, rolling my eyes. 'Another no-show from his dad.'

I spot his jaw clench, and a flash of anger passes through his eyes. Then, as quickly as it appeared, it goes and he simply nods.

'So,' he says, 'what are you both up to this afternoon?'

'Oh, you know,' I reply, smiling. 'VIP tickets to a box at Anfield, all food and drink included, then a big night partying with the Liverpool players. What about you?'

Sam laughs. 'Same. I was thinking,' he continues, 'if your plans fall through, I'm having a little barbecue at mine later, just me and a few friends and their children. You're both welcome to join us if you'd like.'

Must say no, I remind myself. *Must say no.*

'I'd love to,' I respond, 'but I've actually promised to take Charlie to Cath's Caff for a post-match blue slush, which Charlie assures me is far more appetising than it sounds.' His face falls. Then, with the words hanging in the air I decide I might as well say them anyway, 'but you're more than welcome to join us if you'd like?'

Sam smiles. 'I'd love to, thanks.'

I dig my car keys out of my bag. 'Great. We'll see you there then.'

I really do have the breaking point of a Kit-Kat.

———

Within minutes of arriving at Cath's Caff, Charlie spots a friend from school and joins him and his family at their table, leaving Sam and I sitting alone.

'It's a good thing you came,' I say, 'or I'd be over there at the Chatter and Natter table hoping someone would join me.'

Sam laughs and glances at the group of strangers chatting as though they're old friends. 'I heard about this, but thought it must be a joke. I never had Cath down as the "chatter and natter" type.'

'It's incredible, isn't it? Adina's idea – apparently they did something similar in her old cafe in Bucharest.'

'And America.' Sam nods. 'I spent some time there doing soccer coaching after my footballing career came to an end and they had one in my local coffee shop.'

I feel my eyebrows shoot up, no doubt adding even more lines to my forehead. I concentrate on pulling them down again. 'Hang on, your footballing career? I didn't know you'd even had a footballing career.'

'Ah, yes,' he says. 'Slipped up there, didn't I?' His face relaxes into a grin and I wait, eager to know the next part of the story but pretty sure that heavy-duty questioning probably isn't the best way to do it.

'I was signed to one of the clubs here, so through various

contacts I was able to get into a club in Malaga. I did pretty well with them, but it's a ruthless business and they dropped me in the end. The offer to go to America and coach there saved me really and the rest, well, the rest is history.'

I take in this new piece of information. As if he hadn't already been the lead contender in Westholme's unofficial Bachelor of the Year contest, Sam has just wheeled out the big guns.

'Talk about a dark horse,' I say. 'Where in America did you coach?'

'San Francisco.' Sam smiles, but it seems like a sad smile loaded with nostalgia, rather than one that indicates it was a 'best summer ever when we partied 'til we couldn't stand up' type of trip.

I'm curious. 'Do you miss it?'

'Some elements,' he says and for the few seconds it takes for him to stir his Americano, it's as if he's miles away, taking an express return trip to another place and time.

'Was there a girl out there?' I say playfully.

There's a long pause as Sam considers how much to reveal.

Eventually he speaks. 'There was someone. But it was never going to go anywhere.'

'Why not?' I'm being so unusually direct that even *I'm* surprised.

Sam looks at the table. 'Let's just say a particular set of circumstances made it impossible for things to go any further. So, it's probably a good thing I ended up coming home. Otherwise we would both have been stuck in a catch-twenty-two situation for a long time.'

Again, I wait. He sighs. 'Okay, she was married.' He raises his eyes from the table to meet mine. 'Does that shock you?'

I shake my head. 'I'd love to say yes, but no, Sam, it really doesn't. Don't get me wrong,' I add quickly, noticing the shadow that crosses his face. 'That doesn't reflect badly on you. But if you're asking me if I'm surprised that someone's marriage didn't work out and that one of them strayed, then no, I'm not surprised at all. The more and more I learn about marriage, the more it seems that affairs are just part of the package.'

He frowns. 'I thought you'd never been married?'

'Oh no I haven't.' I bite my lip. 'I suppose what I'm trying to say is that these days everything's temporary, isn't it? Disposable. Whether that's takeaway coffee cups, clothes or marriage. Nothing's made to last anymore.'

'Hmmm, I'd have to disagree,' says Sam, cradling his mug with both hands. 'The situation in San Francisco? That wasn't a case of some bored housewife who fancied a bit on the side.' He stops himself and shrugs. 'It's life, isn't it? Like you say, it's not all a fairy-tale. But I do believe in happy endings, otherwise what's the point?'

I lean back into my chair and look over in Charlie's direction. 'And happy endings come in all shapes and sizes, don't they? There's mine, over there.'

Sam looks directly at me. 'Really?'

'Is Charlie my happy ending? Absolutely.'

'So, you don't think there's room for another person in that happy ending?' His eyes hold mine, a subtle plea for me to step up to the challenge, not to look away, not to fold.

I thread my fingers around the handle of the coffee cup and drop my eyes, concentrating with intense focus on the diminishing bubbles of the froth.

When it becomes clear an answer isn't immediately forthcoming, Sam tries again. 'And what comes after the end? Assuming that Charlie will leave one day, start a family of his own … what then?'

Still hanging onto my coffee like a life raft, I buy myself a few extra seconds by taking a sip of it. Then I put my mug down, smile and say, 'Then I'll just do what every other self-respecting spinster does. I'll get another cat.'

My joke forces the conversation onto lighter topics and I regale him with the antics of the salsa class in order to provide a few laughs, but for the rest of the day I can't get Sam's words out of my head. Am I destined to be alone for the rest of my life? Can I ever even think about inviting someone into mine and Charlie's lives?

As I curl up with the Love of My Life later on that evening, eating pizza and watching a movie, the answer comes easily. This is just how I like it, Charlie and me. He may not be here for ever, but he's here now. Everything else will just have to wait.

Westholme Community Facebook page:

Mike Oldhams: Some brilliant footie at the Westholme Football Academy v Presthill Under-Nine's match today, with a great goal from Number Eight. Carry on like that and they'll need their own cheerleading squad.

Leah Moreton: Hollie Cross is a brilliant cheerleader. You'll always find her in her cheerleading kit, waving her pompoms at Westholme's Walking Football Team matches, every Sunday at 11am.

Hollie Cross: Leah Moreton Will. You. Piss. Off.

Chapter Twenty-Eight

When I mentioned the salsa nights to Sam at Cath's the other day, he ended up asking if he could join me. And despite my determination that such an outing doesn't in any way constitute a date, even I can't help but admit that everything about my behaviour in the run-up to it points to the contrary.

My hair is freshly washed and curled, I've spent long enough on my make-up to feel confident that I look okay and even my jeans seem a little looser than usual. If this *had* been a date, the preparations couldn't be going more perfectly.

I hear a gasp and turn around to see Charlie, openly staring at this dolled-up woman who bears little resemblance to the old one.

'You look amazing, Mum,' he says, his eyes so wide that I feel bad for not making more of an effort on a regular basis.

I smile gracefully and bend down to kiss him. 'Thank you, Charlie,' I say, both surprised at and delighted by the unexpected compliment.

'Now all you need to do is get rid of that big wrinkle on your forehead, and you'll be perfect.'

Sam's there, waiting by the door, as I reach the parade. His long legs are clad in dark jeans, and he's wearing a pair of white trainers – a tell-tale sign that he's not yet experienced the joy of walking through rotting veg. He has his back to me and I notice again the strength in his shoulders, which are clad in a lightweight, navy blue jacket.

He looks up from his phone and something in his expression shifts as he sees me. 'Hey,' he clears his throat. 'You look … stunning.'

'Hi, Sam,' I smile, suddenly feeling uncharacteristically shy – and about thirteen years old yet again. 'You look good, too.'

We stand there for a second, like two awkward teenagers at a high school dance, when the door opens and Starr pops her head out.

'Are you coming in?' she says, an impatient note in her voice. 'Lawrence is waiting to start.'

'Absolutely.' Sam flashes her his most charming grin and winks at me. 'Lead the way.'

Sam has each and every member of the salsa group eating out of his hand.

We're only thirty minutes in and already he knows everyone's name, has promised Starr he'll pop round to hers to fix her leaking roof, and has practically made Paula melt with his compliments on her dancing skills.

He can literally charm the birds out of the trees when he wants to. And as if that wasn't enough, it turns out he can dance too.

'San Francisco,' he whispers by way of explanation. It turns out that one of his safe places with his ex over there was a salsa club where no-one they knew ever went. There, they could be the couple they always wanted to be, met only with joyful acceptance by their fellow unsuspecting dancers.

I'm sipping on a rum during breaktime, mulling over his words and wondering how I feel about his warm memories of the woman who was quite clearly The One, when he sits down beside me and squeezes my knee.

'This is fantastic,' he says enthusiastically, setting down another rum for me. 'I can't believe I didn't know all of this existed.'

'And I can't believe I didn't know you could dance,' I say, raising an eyebrow.

He turns to look me in the eye and his mouth forms a slow, sexy smile. 'You don't move so badly yourself.'

I giggle self-consciously, both aware of, and embarrassed by how much I'm behaving like a schoolgirl tonight.

'If I didn't know better, Sam Milner, I'd think you were flirting with me.'

He winks. 'If *I* didn't know better, I'd say you're right.'

My straw makes a gurgling noise to indicate that I'm literally sipping up the dregs of the rum now and I set it down. If I were more sober, I'd try and work out what that statement means, but I'm not, so I simply issue what I think is my most enigmatic smile and do a little wiggle of my shoulders that I immediately know I'll be horrified to remember tomorrow.

Satisfied that we've all had more than enough to drink, Lawrence cranks up the music and the Cuban beat that I've come to find so addictive pulses out of the speakers again.

I have to admit, in this dark and damp room, tainted by the smell of past-its-best veg and, quite possibly mould, I've found something of a haven, somewhere I can escape the never-decreasing mound of ironing, endless money worries and the loneliness that only those who parent alone can understand.

In a life that often feels a bit, well, grey, the salsa nights have brought colour, new friends, the unfamiliar sensation of adrenalin and, more often than not, intoxication. I love it.

I reach up to clasp Sam's hand, resting my other hand on his shoulder while Lawrence talks us through the next move of that night's dance and as Sam pulls me towards him, his arm around my waist and hand resting on the small of my back, I'm suddenly aware of the proximity of his hips to mine. Our moment in the office left a lot of unfinished business between us and his closeness is creating a heat in me that has nothing to do with the temperature in the room.

I'm pretty sure Sam can sense it too and we look deep into each other's eyes for a moment, oblivious to Lawrence's instructions until a light touch on our shoulders brings us back to our surroundings.

'Sorry, guys,' he says, looking at Sam and I with amusement. 'I hate to break up this little,' he waves his hand, 'whatever it is, but, Sam, we need you. Starr wants to put her own little spin on the move, and Dennis,' he gestures to a man at least half a foot smaller than Starr, 'can't quite support her through the hold. Would you be a love and swap partners for a moment?'

Our bodies snap apart and as we look across at each other, Sam's confused expression mirrors the bewildering mix of emotions he can no doubt see in my own.

Over the course of the next forty-five minutes, we're afforded the space we need to haul ourselves to our senses and by the time Lawrence calls the class to a close, our earlier intimacy has disappeared.

'Are you off home now?' Sam asks as we head out of the door.

'Yeah. Back to that mountain of ironing that keeps stalking me around the house.'

He laughs. 'If you need rescuing from it you could always come for a quick drink with me.'

I pause for a moment while my head and my heart battle it out.

'I'd better go,' I say, my thoughts far clearer now that the rum fog has cleared. 'Mum is babysitting Charlie and she'll be expecting me back.'

He looks at me thoughtfully, trying to read the situation. I look at the floor. 'Okay, then can I walk you home?'

'Sure,' I say, with more certainty than I feel.

Our slow meander through the mean streets of Westholme is filled with a mixture of words said and those left unsaid, meaningless chatter and meaningful pauses. The air is heavy with the questions he wants to ask and those I'm not ready to answer and I'm almost relieved when we reach my house.

He looks down at me, unsure of the best way to say goodnight.

'Well I think it's safe to say Starr is a fan,' I joke, referring to her reluctance to let him go at the end of the class.

'You think?' Just like that, his awkwardness has gone and the sexy smile is back. 'You think I might have a shot?'

'I do,' I say teasingly. 'You're definitely in there.'

He locks his gaze on mine, his smile fading. 'That's what I was hoping,' he murmurs.

I look into those green eyes and feel my insides stirring again. He's safe, dependable and absolutely gorgeous. And I'm so, so tired of being alone. Forgetting for a moment the many reasons why I shouldn't, I take a step forward, tilting my head up towards him, my eyes closing in anticipation of—

'Zoe,' my dad's voice interrupts the moment of near-bliss. 'Zoe!'

My head whips around in the direction of the front door.

'Dad? I thought you were at home.' The first stirring of panic whips around my chest. 'What's wrong?'

'Seriously, Zoe, what's the point in having a mobile if you never check it? We've got to get to the hospital. It's Charlie. He's been hurt.'

Westholme Community Facebook page:

Stephanie Porter: Anyone know what that ambulance siren was all about earlier?

Rob Horton: Maybe Cath's been having a go at paella again. Remember last year's attempt?

Billy Twistle: How could I forget? Didn't get off the toilet for three days afterwards!

Chapter Twenty-Nine

The amount of rum consumed tonight means that neither Sam or I are in any fit state to drive, so I jump into Dad's car, promising Sam I'll text him later and we head off in hot pursuit.

'So, tell me again what happened,' I demand, consumed with guilt at the thought of Charlie lying injured and me not there with him.

'I can only tell you what your mum told me,' Dad says, 'and you know what her mind's like at the best of times.' He taps the side of his head and rolls his eyes.

'She said she was watching TV when she heard a massive thud. She ran into the hall to find out what was going on, and there was our Charlie, flat out on the floor at the bottom of the stairs. She's got no idea how he got there like, and he was unconscious so she couldn't ask him.'

My heart lurches and I clutch at my chest. *Unconscious?* I think I'm going to be sick. Instead, I summon up enough strength to ask, 'What happened next?'

'Well, she called me, obviously and I told her to dial 999. You never know in cases like this, do you? One knock to the back of the head can leave you in a wheelchair for ever, if not worse.'

I swallow hard. 'Dad, just tell me what happened.'

'Oh yeah, sorry.' We join the motorway and he shifts the car into fifth gear.

'The ambulance came pretty quickly, apparently. Which is a miracle in itself. By the time the paramedics arrived, he'd come back around. I got there a few minutes later and the poor little fella was white as a sheet. Couldn't tell us what had happened and he had a little cry because his shoulder hurt, but he seemed okay overall. The paramedics just wanted to take him to hospital to double-check his head and make sure he hadn't broken anything.'

I remind myself to breathe. He must have been sleepwalking again. I can't believe I hadn't foreseen the possibility that he might hurt himself.

This is *exactly* why I can never take my eye off the ball when it comes to Charlie. It's too much of a risk. I think back to the near-kiss with Sam, which in reality only happened a few minutes earlier but already feels like a lifetime ago. I can't believe I lost focus. I let Charlie down. I wasn't there when he needed me. I'm a terrible, *terrible* mum.

We arrive at Alder Hey Children's Hospital and go through the usual administrative process before finding him looking every inch the wounded soldier on his way back from X-ray. As I catch a glimpse of his mop of dark hair and his weary expression, it strikes me that I have never been happier to see another human being in my life.

He's holding his arm close to him, but he's walking – which I take to be a good sign – and he even manages a sheepish grin as I approach.

I'm about to wrap him in a huge bear hug when I notice that his arm's in a sling. 'What happened?' I cry, managing instead to give him a half hug, concentrating on the half that isn't wrapped up.

'I don't know, Mum, honest. I woke up at the bottom of the stairs and Nana was there looking after me. But here,' he points at his collarbone, 'really hurts so they wanted to take a photograph of the bone to see if it was broken.'

He grins. 'I got to go in the ambulance and they even put the flashing blue lights on for me. And the nurse gave me a sticker for being so good when I had my X-ray taken.'

I hug him again, then look over the top of his head at my mum. 'I'm really sorry, Mum,' I mouth to her.

She shakes her head and frowns, knowing me as only a mum can know her daughter. 'You haven't got anything to be sorry for,' she whispers. Then she raises her voice to its normal level. 'Look at him, he's fine. Nothing a good night's sleep and a few days rest won't cure.'

Amidst the tears and the self-recriminations, we make our way back to the waiting area where Charlie has been invited to hang out until the doctors have had a chance to look at the images.

We've just settled into the chairs, prepared to settle in for the night, when Sam appears.

I can't explain the relief I feel at seeing him, his usual cheerful expression now twisted into one of concern, amongst the faces of strangers. As he walks in, it's as though someone has turned the lights on. And then I remember what we were about to do at the point that Charlie needed me, and I feel overwhelmed with shame.

'Sam. You didn't need to come...' I trail off. 'How did you get here?'

He flashes me that familiar smile and as I glance at the other waiting mums looking in his direction, I notice it's not only my head that's been turned. 'I called a cab. When I heard that my star player had been injured, I did what any good manager would do – I came to check on him.' He crouches down in front of him. 'How are you doing, Charlie?'

Charlie looks up from my phone, which I've given him free rein of in order to get him through the wait.

'I'm okay,' he says, issuing one of his trademark reassuring grins that I've recently realised he probably developed for my benefit, before resuming his game.

Mum shuffles along to make space for Sam next to me and he settles down between us, seemingly oblivious to the suspicious looks Dad's giving him three chairs along.

'How are you?' he says quietly. 'Not exactly the perfect end to the night, was it?'

I shake my head. 'Not exactly.'

He reaches for my hand and gives it a squeeze. I pull it away quickly. I already have the feeling that I'm going to be given the Spanish Inquisition by my parents tomorrow. I don't want to add any fuel to the fire.

I let my eyes meet his just long enough to see his forehead crease into a light frown, but then the doctor calls us back to give us the results of the X-ray and I forget all about it.

Mum, Charlie and I follow her through the double doors and into one of the treatment rooms, leaving my dad and Sam in the waiting area. I don't even want to think about the kind of things Dad might say in my absence, and I'm almost too tired to care.

'I've had a good look at the X-rays,' the doctor says, 'and it does appear that there's a little crack in the collar bone.' She looks at Charlie. 'So, I'm afraid we're going to have to strap you up for a few weeks in order to give it time to heal. Would that be alright with you?'

Charlie nods obediently and I marvel, not for the first time, at the secret powers that appear to be in the possession of these amazing NHS doctors and nurses, who manage to have kids eating out of their hands while simultaneously putting their broken limbs back together again. I want to kiss her, but realise that that might be somewhat inappropriate. I'm also being careful not to get too close, in case she can smell the alcohol on me and decides this might be a case for social services.

Once Charlie's been strapped up by a hilarious male nurse who appears to share his encyclopaedic knowledge of football, we trudge back to the waiting room, all more than ready to go home and sleep for a couple of hours.

All, it appears, except Sam and my dad, who look for all the world as if they're on a lads' night out. My dad is guffawing loudly over something Sam has said, and Sam's gesturing animatedly as he regales Dad with a story. All they're missing is a couple of beers and a football screen. My eyes flicker around the waiting room. Thank goodness there's hardly anyone left in here to witness this burgeoning bromance.

'Here he is,' Dad looks at Charlie. 'The walking wounded. Are you alright, Son?'

Charlie nods and yawns.

'Let's get home, Dad,' I say, my voice thick with both tiredness and the start of a hangover. 'Are you alright to give us a lift?'

'Of course, love. Sam's coming too – I've said I'll drop him off.'

I raise an eyebrow. My dad has *never* welcomed any of my previous boyfriends into the fold. Good grief, even he must now view my single status as something of an emergency.

We head to the ticket machine to pay the fee for the car park, and it's right then, as we're arguing over who's going to pay, that I see it.

Bundles of that day's edition of *The Northern News* are being wheeled past me towards the hospital's shop on a trolley.

And staring back at me from the front page is the very picture Westholme Council had promised was mine and mine alone. The picture that I was planning for the front page of *The Good News Gazette*.

The photograph of the town's brand-new wheelie bins.

Westholme Community Facebook page:

Pete Owen: Everyone seen *The Northern News*? Finally, Westholme's getting wheelie bins!

Jimmy Hunter: Just what you need when you've got a two-metre square back yard and your house front door is on the pavement. Cheers, all!

Chapter Thirty

As if it wasn't enough to be dealing with broken bones, the sniff of a romance I'm not sure I'm brave enough to embark on, and the town carnival which is meant to be the clincher in my campaign to convince Daniel to drop his plans; we're now less than twenty-four hours away from the printer deadline with absolutely no front-page story to file.

So, when I realise that sticking with my plan to take Daniel to Tarnhurst, which saw its fortunes transformed following the much-needed renovation of its shopping precinct, means I won't have a chance of finding a new story in time for our midnight deadline, I think I'm going to have to do the unthinkable – cancel our appointment.

Fortunately, one factor has been taken out of the mix; rather than wanting to stay at home and lick his wounds, Charlie wants to go into school and show them off, so at least I can spend the day in the office.

But I'm mortified to have to call Daniel and explain that delivering on one commitment means I might not be able to stick to the other. If he ever suspected that this single mum wouldn't be able to cut it in his world, I'm about to well and truly confirm that that is indeed the case.

Surprisingly, not only does he take it all in his stride, he also has a solution.

'You'd planned for us to spend most of the day together, hadn't you?'

'Yes,' I say miserably, mortified at having to cancel and worried about missing out on the opportunity to further convince him of the parade's worth.

'Well, why don't I come to your office this morning and observe what you do there? I've always been intrigued by the premise of *The Good News Gazette*. Then we can pop over to Tarnhurst for lunch and I'll drop you back at the office straight afterwards so you can carry on with your work.'

I hesitate. I can't say I relish the idea of working under pressure while Daniel watches me squirm, but I'm not sure how to get out of it and his idea does kill two birds with one stone, so, reluctantly, I agree.

I tex Ollie and impress upon him the importance of winning Daniel round with his charm, and by the time I arrive at the office after dropping Charlie off, they're both there. While I wouldn't exactly say they're chatting away like old friends, Ollie is at least taking the time to show Daniel how we're getting on with the first issue and Daniel is showing an interest.

We decided that in order to stick to our remit of publishing only good news, we couldn't lay it on too thick about the possible impending gloom and devastation that the demolition of the parade would bring. Instead, we've gone big on the sixtieth anniversary celebrations, devoting much of the issue to the people of the parade, past and present, and highlighting the many individuals who've benefited from its existence. A year on from now it'll either be a celebratory issue or a commemorative one. Right now, we're not sure which.

Ollie, mercifully, talks Daniel through the software he's using and other tech stuff that I don't yet fully understand, giving me time to phone around all my contacts for leads while simultaneously proofreading the last few pages.

After the tenth phone call, I'm starting to feel utterly beaten. It took long enough to find the first exclusive splash; there's little chance of landing upon a second in such a short space of time.

I look up to see Daniel studying me and quickly turn back to the proofs, assuming my 'busy and important' position. I might be going down in flames, but I'll be damned if he's going to watch it happen.

He clears his throat. 'Do you need a new front-page story?'

'No,' I say, keeping my eyes fixed on the proofs.

'Because I might be able to help you out with that.'

My eyes freeze on the page. Talk about being stuck between a rock and a hard place. But still, I'm not giving him the satisfaction of knowing I'm struggling. 'No thank you.'

'Yes please,' Ollie jumps in.

'Ollie!' I hiss.

'Well, we do,' he says, his voice rising as frustration threatens to get the better of him. 'We're – ooh, fourteen hours away from deadline and we haven't got a clue what's going on the front page. Zoe, don't be so stubborn. We need his help.'

Daniel leans back, a smug smile on his face. 'It's a good one.'

Ollie throws me one last, furious look.

'Okay.' I tut, throwing aside the proof. 'Tell me what you've got.'

'Oh, it's nothing really,' Daniel says, clearly revelling in the power he has to tease us with this carrot at the end of the stick. In fact, I've never seen him this playful. 'Just that, next year, a couple of A-list celebrities will set up camp in Westholme for a week or two to film scenes that are going to be part of a Hollywood movie.'

I stare at him open-mouthed as it dawns on me that he is an actual sadomasochist.

'That's not funny, Daniel,' I say, suddenly feeling as though I've completely lost my footing.

He stops smiling. 'It's true.'

'How would you know that?' says Ollie, clearly as unsure as I am.

'The director grew up here. I know him from school. He emailed me the other day to let me know he'd be back in town and to see if I wanted to meet up.' He scrolls through his phone and shows me the name of one of his contacts: Tony Hanlon. 'Google him if you don't believe me.'

I type his name into the search engine and skim the many entries on the first page. There he is. Tony Hanlon. Director. Location, Los Angeles. Wordlessly, I pull up the number for the local film office and ask to be put through to the press officer who, after some too-ing and fro-ing, confirms that there is more than an element of truth in the facts I've put to them.

Within two hours, the story has been researched and written, with quotes from each of the main parties.

'And that's how it's done,' I say, issuing Daniel with a wink as I close down the story and send it over to Ollie to place on the page.

'You won't give me an inch, will you?' Daniel smiles.

'Nope,' I say, picking up my bag. 'Come on, I'm hungry. Let's go for that lunch.'

Once again, I'm in the passenger seat of Daniel's BMW, and with the July sunshine out in full force today he's decided against switching on the heated seats, so there's no uncomfortable sensation down below either.

'How does it feel to be heading up your own publishing operation?' he asks.

'I wouldn't quite call it that,' I reply grudgingly. 'Not yet, anyway.'

He flicks his eyes from the road to me, then back again.

'Why do you do that?' he says.

'What?' I turn my head to look at his profile. He checks the rear-view mirror, careful not to meet my gaze.

'Put yourself down, sell yourself short.'

Goosebumps rise on my arms and the fingers of a strange chill unfurl along my back. I frown.

'No I don't.'

'You do. You do it a lot.'

I don't know how to answer, so instead I shake my head and we fall silent, each of us – or maybe just one of us – wondering if he's finally overstepped the mark.

After a couple of traffic hold-ups and a miscommunication with the sat nav, we eventually arrive at our destination.

Like Westholme, Tarnhurst was formerly a Sixties shopping precinct that, at best, could be described as jaded. But when a new forward-thinking owner bought the property a few years ago, they decided to invest rather than bulldoze. Now, it's a thriving, upmarket shopping centre where independent shops, bars and cafes sit alongside high street names. From its chic, white exterior to the quality of its retail tenants, Tarnhurst is a shining example of what can be achieved when you take something really ugly and throw a ton of money and ideas at it, all in one go.

Typically, Daniel doesn't say anything, but I can tell he's impressed. His eyes are everywhere, taking in the twenty-somethings enjoying lunch on the terraces of the trendy restaurants, the pretty gift shops with window dressings that could be art installations themselves and the bookshop-cum-coffee lounge where bohemian types digest both caffeine and culture from the comfort of its window seats.

I don't know what I'm expecting from him. Maybe I want him to take one look at the place and realise that this is exactly what he needs to do with the parade. To decide right here and now that he's no longer going to lease the land it to a supermarket – that instead, he's going to leave the parade intact and make it beautiful, just the way it should be, for the people of Westholme.

But even though we've now joined those people sitting in the pedestrianised area, surrounded by planters, the clinking of wine glasses and the delicious scent of garlic and herbs, he's saying very little. Even less than he usually does, in fact.

I don't want him to see how nervous I am about his opinion of this place, but after five minutes of failed small talk, I can't contain myself any longer.

'So … what do you think?'

He sips his coffee thoughtfully. He's not like me, Daniel. He doesn't appear to feel the need to fill every silence with words. Or, in fact, to even answer questions with them.

After an agonising wait, he speaks. 'I have a confession to make. I actually know the owner of this place. He approached me about investing in it when he was looking for funding for the regeneration project. I knew all about the plans, I saw all the figures, I appreciated him coming to me with the opportunity.'

I hold my breath. 'So why did you turn it down?'

He rubs his chin briefly and looks away. 'I didn't think it would work in the long term. Still don't, if I'm honest.'

I look around at the hustle and bustle and find it hard to believe what I'm hearing. It's thriving. Why on earth would he think it wouldn't work?

'There's a number of reasons,' he says, as if reading my mind.

'Obviously, online shopping is a big one. It's undermining investor confidence in bricks and mortar retail. Shopping parades like Westholme are becoming more and more difficult for commercial property owners to shift, which is where the supermarkets are coming in.

'Start-up retailers who want to operate from units like the women that Gloria's been working with? They don't stand a chance. I see it all the time – businesses coming to me with what, on the face of it, are great ideas, but if it's retail and it's based in a physical shop, I can tell them immediately that it's unlikely to work long term.'

I feel my nose scrunch up, like it always does when I'm confused. 'But you were so helpful to Gloria's women. You made them feel as though their ideas were viable.'

'I tried to be realistic. I pointed them towards the online opportunities as well as the physical ones they were talking about.' He sits back in his seat and looks directly at me. 'I might come across as an ogre, but I'm not about to trample on the dreams of enthusiastic would-be entrepreneurs.'

My cheeks colour at his accurate interpretation of my thoughts of him. But I've come too far to give up now.

'Yes, more people are shopping online,' I agree, 'but bricks and mortar is certainly not dead. The problem is that the old model of sticking the same old high street names in every shopping parade across the country just isn't working anymore. Tell me this, when was the last time you looked at the demographics of Westholme and checked to see whether the parade was actually an attractive proposition for the types of retailers that would do well here?'

He looks at me blankly. 'What do you mean?'

'Tell me about the people who live in Westholme,' I demand. 'Who are they? How old are they? What sort of jobs do they do? What do they do in their spare time?'

He shifts uncomfortably in his seat. 'Well, there are plenty of older people.'

'What about me?'

'And some families.'

'Lots of families,' I correct him. 'Carry on. What do they do for a living?'

He runs a hand through his cropped hair and squirms.

'I don't know, office workers, hairdressers, builders...'

'Journalists, senior marketers, financial advisers, entrepreneurs...' I add. 'And there's a reason why they're travelling to the likes of Presthill to shop. Presthill's high street is aspirational, pleasant to visit, with lots of independent offerings that take into account what will do well in the neighbourhood. Then the retail units are adapted to make them more attractive to those businesses. Where are Westholme's delis, wholefood stores, boutiques,' I gesture at our surroundings, 'nice restaurants?'

I wait for Daniel to interrupt, but instead he's looking at me, listening.

'The great news is,' I continue, 'that this can be fixed. All it needs is a few tweaks. Take Cath's Caff for example. Six weeks ago, it was just another old greasy spoon. Now look at it. All it takes is a bit of imagination. You just need to look at what people in the area need. What the *area* needs.'

He looks thoughtful for a minute then nods. 'Okay, I hear you and I'll think about what you're saying.'

I'm prevented from launching into another monologue by the arrival of the young, very glamorous waitress, who brings out mouth-watering dishes on contemporary white plates, looking at Daniel as if she'd like to offer herself up on one, before disappearing after promising to return with a range of condiments.

'Looks good,' he says approvingly. 'Now I don't know about you, but it's not often I get out of the office to enjoy a nice lunch with good company in the sunshine. Plus, this is my only brief respite in a long day that will end with a delightful conversation about rental rates with the Wilson's Butcher's boys. So, how about we park business talk for now and enjoy the fact that, for an hour at least, we're able to do so?'

My shoulders slouch at the missed opportunity to convince him to give the parade a chance, but there's very little I can do. Instead, I sit there eating my goats' cheese pasta, feeling the warmth of the sun on my back and pretend, for one moment, that people's very livelihoods don't depend on my ability to convince Daniel Lewis not to bulldoze the parade – or the very dreams it is built on.

It's not until a few hours later, when I'm in the car on the way to pick Charlie up from school, that I remember something I almost missed.

He said I was good company.

Westholme Community Facebook page:

Wilson's Butcher's: After twenty-three years at the parade, Wilson's Butcher's is relocating to 41 Westcote Road, opposite the new e-cigarette shop. We can confirm that we will still offer all of our usual produce from our new premises and we look forward to seeing you all there.

Pete Owen: Good luck in your new home, lads. Hope the landlord gets what's coming to him. Greedy bugger.

Chapter Thirty-One

'Ask me more football questions, Mum,' Charlie demands, despite the fact that we've already done two rounds of this game since I picked him up from school and neither was a success.

I try, honestly I do, to store up any little football facts I come across in my daily life, but there really aren't many and I've regurgitated the few I do have so many times that Charlie now hurls the answer at me before I've even finished the question.

'Okay.' I sigh. 'Which former Liverpool player is now a manager?'

'Mum, really? You've just asked me that one, and it's still Steven Gerrard.'

'Have I?' My eyes flicker towards the car park at the side of The parade as we drive past. There's no mistaking the black shiny BMW that's still there – or the guy crouched down on the floor next to it.

'Hold that thought,' I say, making an executive decision to stop off and check that Daniel's okay. I'm emboldened by the knowledge that Charlie and I spent ages yesterday cleaning the car after I spotted a mouldy sandwich hidden in one of the back seat doors, so as long as he doesn't spot the crumbs of Cadbury's Flake I dropped on my own seat earlier, I don't mind if he ends up seeing inside.

I pull up beside the BMW and, as I wind down the window, I hear Daniel swear under his breath as he peers at the extremely flat tyre, punctured in several places by shards of broken bottle. My heart sinks. He really doesn't need another reason to take against the parade.

'What's wrong?' I ask innocently.

He points at his tyre. 'I've got a flat. Broken glass bottle. Kids, probably.'

Leaving the engine running, I jump out of the car and hunker down next to him to look at it.

'Hmmm, would we really call that flat?' I say, hopefully. The wheel trim is sitting neatly on the ground. The tyre literally could not be any flatter.

He raises an eyebrow. 'Can you think of a more appropriate description for it?'

I look back at the tyre. 'Probably not, no.'

'Do you have a spare? There's often one in the underneath part of the boot.'

He coughs. 'Um, I'm not sure. Maybe.'

'I can change it for you if you like?'

He turns to me, eyebrows drawn together now. 'You can change tyres?'

'Of course,' I say indignantly. 'Can't everyone?' We're still crouched down in the shade that the narrow gap between my car and his provides, our faces much closer together than is normal, or natural. As my eyes meet his, it's as though a sudden burst of electricity passes between us, drawing us together while making it impossible to move away.

'No,' he says, his voice suddenly lower and huskier than usual. 'No, they can't.'

We stay like that for a few seconds, staring at each other, then he stands up abruptly. 'I called the rescue company a while ago. I'm waiting for them to arrive.'

I'm still crouched on the ground, aware of the rapid thumping of my heart and confused by the unexpected moment. Then, pulling myself together, I stand up and force myself to look at him as though it never happened.

'How long ago did you call them? I could always give you a lift home.'

He frowns and his voice has an edge to it. 'There's really no need. I don't need rescuing.'

I'm stung and surprised at his reaction. 'I don't for a moment think you do. I just know how long these rescue companies can take to actually, well, *not* rescue you … or your car,' I say pointedly.

'Well,' he says, and I see his expression soften as he looks up and down the road, 'they did say they might be some time.' Then he taps the bonnet of the car twice, as though he's just made a decision. 'Never mind, I'll call a taxi.'

'Don't call a taxi,' I say, ignoring the inner voice that's telling me to let him tough it out. 'It'll be at least a tenner to get to Presthill from here. Come on.' I climb into the driver's side and gesture to the empty passenger seat next to me. 'Jump in. I can give you a lift back here tomorrow to pick it up.' I look at the car. 'Then again…'

He knows what I'm about to say. 'No, I don't think it would be a good idea to leave it here overnight either.' He thinks out loud. 'I could always cycle down later after the rescue people have replaced the tyre. But what about your son?'

I twist around to face the back seat. 'Charlie's fine, aren't you, Charlie?'

He glares at me.

'Right, that's sorted then,' I say firmly. 'Let's go.'

The first few minutes are a little awkward. I keep trying to create conversations that involve Daniel and Charlie, both of whom seem more reticent than ever, but my attempts are falling flat.

Then Charlie unexpectedly comes to the rescue. 'Do you like football, Daniel?'

'I do,' he says, pulling down the passenger mirror so he can look at him as he answers. 'Do you?'

'I love it!' Charlie says emphatically. 'My favourite team's Liverpool. What's yours?'

Daniel's expression becomes very grave. 'If I tell you, do you promise not to tell anyone?'

'I promise,' Charlie says, putting a hand on his heart as if to solemnly swear that he would keep to his word.

'Morecambe FC.'

Charlie bursts into peals of laughter. Keeping my eyes firmly on the road, I raise my eyebrows and smile.

'It was my grandad's club,' he explains. 'My grandad was the only person who ever took me to watch football, so Morecambe became my club too. Even now, I still travel to every home game.'

'Wow, so you get to watch football all the time?' Charlie says, clearly in awe.

'I do,' says Daniel. 'Do you go and watch football too?'

'My grandad's going to take me when I'm nine,' he says. 'Mum says I can't go until then. She doesn't want me to hear the swearing.'

'Is that right?' Daniel asks me. I nod.

'Smart lady,' he says to Charlie and I hate myself for not being able to control the blush that follows.

'Do you know who the first ever player was to score an own goal in a World Cup final?' Charlie fires at him.

'Of course – it was Mario Mandzukic.'

And so begins a football quiz that bounces back and forth between the two of them all the way up to Presthill. I listen, a warm sensation creeping through my veins and hugging my heart. It's nice, this, listening to my son chatting to a male figure who's not his grandad and I wonder, not for the first time, if this is what it's like for children with dads who are actually around. Then I think of Emma and am reminded that the reality is not always what is seems. When I look again, the warm feeling has gone.

We drive through the pretty village of Presthill and I fight the urge to rubberneck at the people sitting outside the wine bars and coffee shops dotted along the high street.

Out of the corner of my eye I can see women in white jeans with glossy hair sipping drinks at bistro tables set out on the wide pavements while their mini dogs sit primly at their feet. Older couples are relaxing over a bottle of wine, enjoying the freedom that only retirement and a load of money in the bank can bring. Even the teenagers, stopping off for milkshakes on their idle walk home from school, look happy and relaxed. We're just twenty minutes' drive from Westholme, but a million miles away from our own reality.

It's not just me who's fascinated by the scene before us. Charlie seems transfixed by the place too and has paused his seemingly endless game of football trivia in order to peer out of the window and take in his leafy surroundings.

'It's fine, I like it,' Daniel had reassured me as I'd tried to call time on the game earlier, alarm bells going off in my head as my shy little boy chatted away to the very person who might be about to single-handedly destroy his home town.

A wave of nausea hits me as I'm reminded of the high stakes

challenge I'm knee-deep in. Daniel's not a family friend. He's our adversary. A fact that, at times, is becoming dangerously easy to forget.

———————

Eventually we turn off the main road onto a tree-lined avenue where varying styles of huge detached houses, each as jaw-dropping as the next, are framed by stone walls and stunning gardens.

'It's right here,' Daniel says, pointing, and I pull up in front of a pair of black wrought- iron gates, a small plaque on one of the gateposts indicating that we've arrived at Harper Lodge.

Out of the corner of my eye, I catch a glimpse of the house that lies at the end of the long driveway. It's rusty red brick, with rows of huge windows set symmetrically across two floors. Grey tiles cover the roof which slopes gently up on all four sides before falling into a flat line across the top, with two much smaller windows protruding from the front slope on what appears to be yet another floor. Wisteria falls over the grand entrance in a lilac haze as though nature itself is celebrating the very existence of the building. It's like something out of a fairy tale. I can't believe it's where Daniel calls home.

I'm momentarily lost in the beauty of the place when I'm suddenly hit with the words no parent wants to hear when they're outside the house of someone they barely know.

'I need the toilet.'

I turn around and glare at Charlie. 'No, you don't,' I hiss. His strategy to gain an invite into the house is so transparent it's painful.

'I do. I'm desperate, really desperate.' He screws up his face to demonstrate the intensity of his need.

'No you're not.' I say quickly. 'We'll be home in a minute. You can wait.'

'Not a problem, Charlie,' says Daniel, turning to face him. 'Just use mine.'

I feel the blood drain from my face. 'Honestly, Daniel, it's fine, he can hang on.'

But he's already pressed something on his key fob, and the electronic gates are slowly drawing back.

'Wow,' says Charlie, already transfixed.

'That's nothing,' Daniel smiles at him. 'Wait until you see the pool.'

I slump back into my seat, embarrassed and intrigued all in one go. Despite my best intentions, it looks as though we're going in.

———

'Would you like to look around?'

I feel Daniel watching me, looking for a reaction as Charlie and I hover by the front door, the very definition of grandeur with a triangular gable above it and Tuscan columns standing proud either side of the entrance.

His desperate need for the toilet seemingly forgotten, Charlie is running around the gravelled driveway, surrounded by grounds that run all the way around the house and far beyond, as though he's been fed glucose on a drip.

'No, thank you,' I say politely.

'Yes, yes, yes!' Charlie shouts.

'Charlie!' I gasp, horrified at this sudden change in his behaviour.

Daniel chuckles. 'Thought you might,' he says. With a jolt of his head, he beckons me inside. 'Come and see what I do when I'm not knocking down shopping centres.'

The place is unbelievable. I mean, truly unbelievable. A six-bedroom Queen Anne house with high ceilings, original cornicing and wood panels on the walls, it is the stuff that dreams are made of – and by far the biggest house I've ever been in that isn't owned by the National Trust.

A beautiful ornate ceiling is the crowning glory of the entrance hall and as I run my hand over the solid oak banister, it's impossible not to envisage just how beautiful the place could look at Christmas.

Huge windows flood the rooms with light, while ceiling roses and original wooden floors act as reminders of those who've lived here before, walked on these same floors before, sat in front of the stunning fireplaces before us.

I had assumed, on the odd occasion that I'd given Daniel's home a moment's thought, that it would be like him: aloof, cool, minimalistic, modern. But this isn't like that. This place is warm, welcoming and full of period feature charm.

'I bought it three years ago,' Daniel explains, 'when it was an absolute wreck. It used to be a country retreat for a wealthy family from Liverpool, but as it was handed down over the years it was used less and less. Then the remaining family members moved away and stopped visiting completely. It had been unoccupied for ten years when I took it on, an absolute shell of a place, but I knew the minute I stepped inside that it could be beautiful again.'

I'm staring at him, lost in his words, and realising my mouth is open slightly I shut it quickly. His eyes are shining and it's as though his mask has slipped for a second. It's the first time I've seen him look passionate about anything.

'There's still a lot to do,' he continues. 'And the fact that it's Grade II listed has made it a bit more of a challenge. But I'm getting there.'

I picture Daniel here in those battered jeans and that grey t-shirt, stripping old wallpaper, sanding down woodwork that needs attention, hammering nails into walls—

'Let me show you around,' he interrupts my thoughts and I follow him into the first of the rooms, our footsteps making a steady rhythm on the wood floors that's punctuated only by my whispered warnings to Charlie to stop wandering off and conducting his own tour.

Subtle sage greens and warm greys create a calming, neutral feel across the house that, despite its size, puts me instantly at ease. The decor is a combination of old and new, ancient chandeliers clashing beautifully with some seriously modern art and as Daniel leads us around the four floors (it turns out there's a basement too), laying a hand on a wall here, touching a curtain there, his pride at the place is clear to see.

There are areas that are unashamedly contemporary; the gym, with its complicated machines and massive blocks of iron is little short of an homage to masculinity and the pool and jacuzzi are just as impressive as you'd expect anything that has Daniel's stamp on it to be.

There are also numerous rooms he hasn't yet got round to furnishing and the vast but neglected garden with its stunning views across the valley would definitely benefit from Margaret's input.

But the whole house is filled with warmth and character and its restoration has quite clearly been a labour of love.

We reach the kitchen and he pauses at the island to take in my reaction.

'What do you think?' he asks. 'Have I done its former owners justice?'

'Of course,' I say. 'I'm just…' I hesitate.

'Surprised?' he cuts in. 'What were you expecting – an overpriced bachelor flat? All the mod cons but no charm?'

'Something like that,' I admit quietly. 'But this … it's beautiful, Daniel.'

'It will be,' he says, loosening his tie and undoing the top couple of buttons of his shirt. I find myself staring at the dark stubble covering his jaw and trailing towards the base of his neck, disappearing behind the grey fabric. 'There's a lot of late nights involved but,' he shrugs his shoulders, 'what else would I be doing?'

I drag my gaze back up to his face, where on closer inspection, I notice shadows under his eyes. He looks tired, vulnerable almost.

Somewhere in the background I can hear Charlie's delight at discovering even more rooms, but other than that it's completely silent. Daniel's eyes meet mine again and this time an electricity flows between us that's so powerful, so intimate that I am suddenly hit by the fear that he might actually be reading my mind. I feel an uncomfortable heat spread across my face and quickly look away.

He tilts his head to one side, observing me. 'You're blushing,' he says, quietly.

'What?' My hand flies to my face.

It's at that point that Charlie returns to the kitchen, and, noticing the change in atmosphere says, 'What's going on?'

Daniel shakes his head. 'Nothing.' He turns away and opens the door to a cupboard with several glasses set out neatly inside. 'Would you like a drink?'

'Yes please,' Charlie says politely, his manners having finally returned.

I smile, awkward, thankful for the disruption.

'We really don't want to keep you, Daniel, I'm sure you're very busy.'

'Never too busy for coffee,' he says abruptly, then delves into the fridge. 'Coconut milk and one sugar,' he says, holding up a carton of my favourite dairy alternative. 'That's how you like it, isn't it?'

Raising my eyebrows, I nod and for once, forget the fact that I don't drink coffee in the afternoon.

———

By the time we leave, we've seen every room in the house except his bedroom. He didn't offer and, mercifully, Charlie didn't ask. To see the place where he slept, dressed, had sex – probably lots of it – felt like a step too far.

'That was fun. Thanks, Daniel,' Charlie says, as we gather in the entrance hall. And then my son does something completely out of character. He hugs him.

Daniel looks momentarily startled. Then, without looking at me, he crouches down and hugs him back. I fight an overwhelming urge to cry.

'I had fun too, buddy, thank you. It's not often I have guests here.' He looks at me. 'It was nice.'

I smile. 'Come on, Charlie, let's go and get some tea.'

'Can Daniel come too?'

Not for the first time that day, I remind myself to have a chat with Charlie about boundaries.

'I'd love that, Charlie, but I still have a lot of work to do tonight,' he says. 'No time for tea, I'm afraid.'

I realise that Daniel may not eat at all this evening, and it's all I can do not to invite him to join us.

'Anyway, we'll be off,' I say, fumbling with the door. Then I feel him close in behind me, his arm reaching past me to pull it open with ease.

'Something else I haven't fixed yet,' he mutters, stepping quickly back.

We head out onto the drive and I turn to face him as we leave.

'So, I'll see you on Friday for our last parade venture?' he says.

'That's what we arranged,' I reply.

'I'll look forward to it.'

We say goodbye and I head towards the car, unable to resist adding a slight swagger to my hips as my heels sink slightly into the gravelled driveway.

It's only when I'm giving my appearance a quick once-over back at home that I realise one small but mortifying fact that Daniel will have seen in all its glory during my little sashay down the drive.

Those Flake crumbs I dropped on my seat earlier have left a pattern of very noticeable chocolate stains right across the bum of my trousers.

Westholme Community Facebook page:

Margaret Kemp: To the good people of Westholme, we're looking for raffle prizes for the carnival next week and I was wondering whether any local businesses might like to donate? All funds raised will go to local hospitals.

Beauty by Gemma: I'll throw in a voucher for a bikini wax.

Wilson's Butcher's: We can give a rump steak.

Westholme Wheels: Free MOT?

Claire Phillips: Who needs a lottery win with prizes like these on offer.

Chapter Thirty-Two

Three days after Ollie and I send the newspaper to the printers, our redundancy pay finally comes through.

I can't over-emphasise what this means for my stress levels. Not only will I now be able to pay the invoices I know will shortly arrive from both the printer and Ollie, it also means that Charlie, Lola and I will have a roof over our heads for a while longer yet.

But the best news is, it also marks the end of my employment by *The Northern News*, so I can register *The Good News Gazette* as a bona fide business and start invoicing the few businesses that have agreed to advertise too.

It's the one highlight in an otherwise bleak, yet typical, English summer's morning in which I feel mostly sick with nerves about what will happen once *The Good News Gazette* hits the streets in its newspaper form.

I proofread and re-read every page until my eyes glazed over before it went to print, but I'm still concerned that, once I have a hard copy in my hand, I'll suddenly see a glaring error that, despite my extensive edits, I had failed to spot.

Fortunately, I've arranged to meet Daniel today to talk him

through the plans I have for the parade – the conversation I'd wanted to have with him the other day before his eye contact with Sam killed the whole thing stone dead – so my mind will be mostly occupied with other things.

I still have no idea what happened that day. I *can't* ask Daniel again and I haven't seen Sam since the night of Charlie's accident when the question was pushed to the back of my mind by our near-kiss, so there's been no way of getting to the bottom of it. I make a mental reminder to mention it to Sam when I see him again, then realise there's probably a few other conversations he'll want to have first.

I arrive at Cath's at one minute past ten to find Daniel's already there, take-out drinks ready for us on the table. 'Good to see you've thought ahead,' I say, nodding at the coffee and smiling not only at him, but also at how much more relaxed I feel around him these days. 'You're learning.'

'We aim to please,' he replies, a smile playing on his lips. 'So where are we off to today?'

'We're staying right here at the parade,' I say. 'Leave your coat here and we'll head out into the square where it'll be easier for me to point out my plans.'

Daniel takes his wallet and keys out of his coat pocket and tentatively lays it over the back of a chair, looking around as if to try and suss out who might nick it.

I raise my eyebrows at him. 'Don't worry, it'll be quite safe. They only nick Armani round here.'

He looks uncharacteristically uncomfortable, then says quietly, 'It *is* Armani.'

'Tell you what,' I say, picking up the coat quickly and heading for the door, 'why don't we take it with us. Can't be too careful, can you?'

───────────

Once outside, I stand back from the parade's tired exterior and look at it in all its glory.

'So here it is, your empire,' I say to Daniel, smiling.

'Well, part of it,' he adds. I check his expression but he isn't gloating – simply stating facts.

'Anyway, as you may have guessed,' I continue, 'I have some ideas on how we could make it *so* much more workable.'

He raises an eyebrow.

'Right now, the very appearance of the parade is letting Westholme down. The grey concrete and grimy pillars are ugly, the boarded-up shops are hardly screaming "vibrant hub" and the overflowing bins are surely doing very little to attract retailers to the area.'

'It's up to shoppers to take home their rubbish if the bins are full,' Daniel says defensively. 'But they don't. They just dump it here, on top of the bin, then it gets blown away, then…' He shakes his head dismissively as if to castigate all those who've ever failed to take their litter home with them then turns to face me. 'We can only do so much. After that it's up to the residents to take a bit of pride in their local area.'

'But so many of them do,' I argue, feeling my blood pulsing quickly through my veins. 'Like Margaret and the Westholme Gardeners.'

'They're great,' he agrees, 'but they're in the minority. Most Westholme locals couldn't care less about how the parade looks. They just want to be able to buy their meat and two veg and be home in time for the afternoon TV shows.'

I shake my head and tut disapprovingly. 'You're wrong. They need something to feel proud about, that's all.' I inhale slowly, aware that I need to choose my words really carefully in order to make him listen to the next part. 'And actually, it wouldn't take much to do that.'

He waits for me to continue and I delve into my bag and fish out some A4 documents.

'What are these?' he asks, taking the computer-generated designs from my hand and looking through them.

'Images of how the parade *could* look. One of the cafe's hot-desk customers is a retail architect who often works from home. He's kindly mocked up images of how a relatively low-cost facelift could transform the place.'

Lines appear across Daniel's brow as he focuses on the pages, his eyes flitting across the many aspects of the design. It looks truly stunning, with the façade an off-white and new shop signage with black lettering setting out the names of each shop. Trailing ivy and jasmine tumbles over some of the shop fronts, while warm white fairy lights are strung across others. Black wrought-iron signs hang at a ninety-degree angle to each shop front, acting as signposts to shoppers walking along the parade. It really is pretty.

I start to speak, slowly and tentatively at first, fearful that my enthusiasm, if left unchecked, might scare him off.

'I've had a quote on this and, okay, it wouldn't be cheap, but the residents would be happy to crowdfund part of it if you would consider adding the rest.'

He says nothing, but continues to examine the design, then looks up at the parade, clearly trying to superimpose the facelift version onto the real-life one.

This is hopeful. So hopeful in fact, that I can barely contain myself. 'Look how beautiful it is. You can't tell me this wouldn't attract shoppers and businesses alike.'

Daniel goes to speak, but I cut in. 'Don't say anything yet. There's more I need to show you.'

One by one, I walk him past each of the shops, telling him about their history and the part each one has played in the community.

Where shop fronts are boarded up, I suggest unexplored possibilities, explaining how a sliding scale rental agreement for new businesses would be far more profitable than an empty shop, how a facelift would increase footfall and how tackling the issue of town centre regeneration would score massive corporate social responsibility points for Lewis & Co.

I've spent a lot of time working on my ideas for how the parade can generate more money and can reel the figures off the top of my head. Each suggestion is well thought out and feasible – something even Daniel can't deny.

By the time we agree to break for lunch, I'm convinced my enthusiasm alone must have beaten Daniel into submission. But it turns out I'm not quite there yet.

'You have some great ideas,' he says, 'but they all require significant investment, with questionable returns. I'm in the business of making a profit. When my assets aren't bringing in a return, I offload them. The parade is not making any money. Full stop.'

I bite my lip. I've used up all the arguments in my armour and I don't know what else to throw at him. So I hit him with this.

'How do you know Sam Milner?'

He jolts back, as if stung, and a cloud passes over his face.

'What makes you think I know him?' His expression has hardened and there's a coldness to his tone now that wasn't there before.

'The way you changed when you saw him the other day. It was as if you'd seen a ghost.'

He suddenly pulls the cuff of his white shirt up his wrist and checks his watch. 'I'm sorry, Zoe, I'm afraid I'll have to skip lunch today. I've just remembered there's somewhere else I need to be.'

I frown. Not again.

'Daniel, what is it? What's the big secret?'

He shakes his head. 'No secret, no problem,' he says, backing away as he speaks. 'But I really do have to go now.'

'Are you still coming the carnival tomorrow?' I say, raising my voice now so that it reaches him, adding forlornly and somewhat pathetically, 'You said you'd come.'

He pauses for a minute and looks away, his tall, suit-clad outline incongruous with his surroundings. Then his dark eyes find my face and he looks at me, *really* looks at me, for a beat too long, before nodding that yes, he'll come. And in that instant, something I can't put my finger on passes between us. A feeling. A missed heartbeat. A moment. And then it's gone.

Westholme Community Facebook page:

Paul Gregory: Anyone going to this carnival tomorrow then?

Heidi Ho: Yeah, all looking forward to it in our house actually. The two kids are on floats and all excited about dressing up.

Lisa Seddon: My son's quite excited about it too. Should be good.

Johnny H: Something'll go wrong. They always do at these things.

Chapter Thirty-Three

I'm awake from 4am in the morning of the carnival, partly with nerves but mostly with excitement. *The Good News Gazette's* print edition will finally be unveiled to its Westholme audience, the TV news team have confirmed that they'll be there to interview Starr and film her twerking in all her glory and if nothing else, it's going to be a great day for the community. All I need to do is not cock it up.

We've all worked so hard to get to this point and I'm hoping with every ounce of me that this will be the cherry on the cake that convinces Daniel once and for all that he needs to save the parade.

At 6am I hear Charlie stir and concede that the day has officially begun. I get up and take a shower, closing my eyes as the warm water trickles through my hair and praying that everything will turn out just as it's meant to. By which I mean perfectly, but I suspect it's best not to make it too specific and hope my prayer acts as a catch-all for the day's events to go my way.

Even Charlie, aware of what today means to me, is so agitated he declares he can't eat a thing, but still manages to stomach a bowl of Coco Pops and a pain au chocolat before we both head back upstairs to get dressed.

He's ready in minutes, having thrown on the tracksuit I laid out for him the night before. For me, it takes a bit longer, because as every woman knows, it's impossible to lay out a 'night before' outfit in the middle of a British summer when the demands of the following day could range from a sundress to a snowsuit, depending on what sort of mood Mother Nature's in when she wakes up.

If the weather forecast is anything to go by, and that in itself is debatable, jeans seem the most appropriate attire for the day. I add a completely impractical but flattering white t-shirt to show off the false tan I've applied especially for the occasion, while a pair of white trainers completes the look.

When I head downstairs even Charlie takes his eyes away from his Nintendo long enough to issue a quick 'You look nice' and, convinced enough by his faint praise that I must be doing something right, I treat myself to one last look in the mirror before I usher us both out of the house and into the car.

By the time we reach the parade, there's already a buzz of activity, with Adina serving tea and coffee at the outdoor tables while Antonio is setting up an outdoor bar.

'Courtesy of a temporary licence,' he says, winking at me and I wonder how early is too early to start on the wine.

Inside the cafe, I'm amazed to see Cath at the coffee machine, looking for all the world as if she knows what she's doing, and my jaw hits the floor when I see her serving a cappuccino with an imperfect latte art palm tree set out on the top.

'I teach her,' says Adina, squeezing Cath's shoulder as she

passes her behind the counter and Cath grants her a rare but warm smile in return.

Back outside, Charlie is kicking a ball around with Sean while Paula sets up the tombola prizes just feet away from where Margaret's doing something creative with the bunting. As I look around, I feel a lump form in my throat as it strikes me how far we, this little community, has come.

Across the square I spot Sam casually directing a couple of the football boys as they set up a goal for a shoot-out.

In tracksuit bottoms that skim his thighs and a blue t-shirt with sleeves that cling to his biceps, he looks good. The sun is picking up various strands in his golden-brown hair, creating a halo effect around his head and my heart gives a little lurch as I think about all he's done to help me in recent weeks. I don't know what I would have done without him.

I walk over to him. 'Hey, Sam,' I say casually.

He smiles broadly. 'Here she is, Westholme's very own Wonder Woman.'

'Hardly – the day's not even begun yet. Let's see how you feel in eight hours' time.'

Sam pauses to kick a wayward football back to the boys then looks back at me and winks.

'I'm pretty sure I'll feel exactly the same.'

By 10:30 the sun is beaming down on the parade and people of all ages in various forms of dress and fancy dress are starting to board the many floats lined up along the road next to the pedestrianised square.

Music is blaring from the outdoor speakers, a few kids have opted out of the procession in order to sneak onto the bouncy castle and a number of market stalls dotted around the square are selling everything from homemade candles to designer sunglasses. I'm convinced the sunglasses are knock-off but I've decided, in the interests of my already frayed nerves, to turn a blind eye to the questionable merchandise.

Despite having avoided all of the Friends of Westholme Parade meetings, even Beth and Emma have turned up bright and early and are in the process of being issued tasks.

There's no sign of Daniel yet, for which I'm hugely relieved. I want him to arrive when the event is in full swing: when the carnival parade is arriving back at the square, the dancers from the local dance school are in performance mode and at precisely the point that Starr is being interviewed by the TV reporter for a national news channel.

It turns out her video did indeed go viral. In fact, it ended up being shared more than 200,000 times, attracting media interest as far afield as America in the process. So, when a producer got in touch with me to ask whether I could arrange for Starr to speak to one of their reporters, I suggested that they come along to the carnival where Starr would be performing, hoping that they'd pick up on the story of the parade in the process.

The producer agreed and she's told me to expect someone here at around noon in order to capture the triumphant return of the floats and the general fun of the fair.

Or something like that.

At 11am, as planned, the procession sets off in a haze of music, laughter and multicoloured fancy dress. On every float, beaming faces smile down at the people who've turned out to see them and as I look down the road I'm surprised to see just how many residents are there, lining the streets and cheering.

Those left behind in the square heave a sigh of relief and

Antonio starts handing out hot drinks while I consult my schedule to check how long we have until the procession returns. Roughly an hour. Then a long line of local talent, starting with Starr, will make its way onto the temporary low-level structure that we're calling the stage to entertain the crowds. I take a deep breath. I can't believe this is happening. We've brought the Westholme Town Carnival back from the dead. And if the rest of the day runs as smoothly as this, there's a chance it might even be a success.

Daniel strolls casually into the square at the exact moment that the procession pulls in to the edge of the kerb, welcomed by a crowd of enthusiastic attendees. With the music playing, people queuing for the attractions and flags, bunting and other tat adding a festival of colour to the parade, it simply couldn't look more perfect.

He sees me immediately and makes his way over. Dressed in smart navy jeans, an off-white polo t-shirt that's cut just right around his broad shoulders and a pair of loafers, he draws at least a couple of glances as he strides towards me.

'Good afternoon, Zoe,' he says, smiling. He looks around at the festivities: at Antonio and Adina bringing out trays of food, at the group of small children screaming in glee as they fall like dominoes on the bouncy castle, at the stalls surrounded by customers.

'It looks as though you've pulled off quite an event,' he continues. 'Well done.'

I bite my lip, an attempt to hide the absolute delight I feel at having received a compliment from the hardest man in the world to impress.

'Oh, not really,' I say quickly. 'The Portaloos haven't turned up, the youth jazz orchestra have failed to return from their foreign

289

exchange trip after getting stopped at customs for hiding pot in the bongos and Margaret says the tombola prizes are disappearing but … all things considered, it's not going too badly.' I issue a little laugh to show him just how relaxed I am about it all, but when I glance at him, he's looking right at me, a slight frown replacing his earlier smile.

I would have thought that even *you* could see what a great job you've done here,' he says,'but apparently not.'

I'm trying to think of an answer when Mum and Dad turn up. 'Well will you look at this!' bellows Dad. 'Don't tell me this was all *your* doing. There's no way *you've* organised this.'

I shift from one foot to another, not sure what my response should be but fully aware that Daniel will be waiting to hear it.

'It looks good, doesn't it?' Dad continues, addressing Daniel as much as me. 'Would have been better with a few more stalls like. And I still think you should have done donkey rides. But you know our Zoe – likes things the way she likes them, doesn't she, Sue?' He turns to my mum.

'You've done a great job,' says Mum quickly. 'It all looks brilliant, Zoe.'

'Colin!' Dad suddenly yells down my ear. 'Oi, Colin, here a minute. I just wanted another quick word about those bats.'

'Dad!' I hiss, but he ignores me and heads off towards Colin.

'Bats?' Daniel asks, an eyebrow raised.

'Don't listen to him,' Mum says. 'He talks a load of rubbish.' She looks over at the cafe. 'Ooh, excuse me a minute. I need to ask Cath if she has any of that Victoria sponge in today.' She squeezes my arm and says, 'Well done, love, I knew you could do it,' before giving Daniel a polite smile and heading in the direction of the cafe.

I don't need to look at Daniel to know that he's still staring at me.

'What?' I ask again, this time a defensive tone creeping into my voice.

He doesn't answer, forcing me to look at him. 'What?' I say again, more quietly this time.

He shakes his head and fixes his eyes on mine. 'Nothing,' he says. Nothing at all.'

I stare at the floor, wishing it would open up and pull me – and my dad – under it.

Then Daniel does the strangest thing. He takes a step forward so that he's close, very close. Then he bends down and whispers in my ear, causing my heart to pound so aggressively I fear I might be about to have a heart attack.

'You've done a great thing today,' he says. 'No matter what happens next, never forget what you've achieved here. No matter *what* happens.' Then he turns and walks away.

Disaster strikes before the performances even begin. Starr's about to go on stage to execute her song and dance routine when she realises she's brought her cubic zirconia tiara instead of the emerald one.

I try very hard to reassure her that cubic zirconia will have an equally impressive effect on the crowd, but she's having none of it and sets off back home at a speedy pace with a promise that she'll be back in a jiffy.

I'm wondering how to fill her spot when a tall woman with long blonde hair turns up with a cameraman.

'Starr White,' she says loudly to no-one in particular. 'I'm looking for Starr White.'

I move quickly to speak to her. 'Hello, Zoe Taylor, event organiser, nice to meet you.'

The woman purses her ruby-red lips and looks me up and down.

'Hello,' she says, her voice a tone that even a glass-half-full kind of person would struggle to describe as anything more than cordial.

'Starr's just popped back home to pick up a different tiara,' I say, as though this is a completely normal occurrence. 'She'll be back in a few minutes.'

The tall woman rolls her eyes at the cameraman and then turns to me, a smile fixed on her lips.

'Okay, as long as we're not waiting too long. There's another job we've got to go to straight after this one.' She turns to the cameraman. 'The next one's a *good* one.'

Looking around impatiently, she spots Sam. I see her watching him for a minute, laughing with another one of the many boys he appears to be giving freebie turns to, then she licks her lips and turns to me. 'That man over there, he's another one of the organisers of the event, is he?'

I blink. 'Well, not exact—'

'Great,' she cuts in. 'I'll speak to him.'

Before I even have time to think of a response, she's off, her red kitten heels clattering across the square as she makes a beeline for Sam. I watch for a moment, waiting to see his response as she touches his arm and throws her head back in laughter. Then I remind myself that, as he's not my boyfriend, I really don't care what he does and turn back to my trusty clipboard.

―――――――――

Ollie is hanging around outside Cath's Caff, desperately trying to catch Adina's attention. I'm not sure if she's not aware or just not interested, but she still seems oblivious to the puppy dog eyes he's giving her.

I can see the look of frustration on his face. With his affable personality, good looks and questionable sense of style, it's very rare that Ollie fails to make his mark on a woman. But as I observe Adina serving the customers, her olive forehead wrinkled in concentration, I remember that this is no ordinary woman we're dealing with – and that it's going to take more than good looks and nice clothes for Ollie to convince her he's worth taking a chance on.

Margaret appears at my side then and follows my gaze. 'She's doing a great job, isn't she?' she says, nodding over at Adina.

'She really is,' I say. 'How's she settling in with you?'

Margaret smiles broadly. 'Honestly, she's brought the house to life again. She's forever cleaning and cooking and she's fantastic company too. It's fascinating hearing about her life in Romania. I know she was only supposed to be with me for a few days, but I'm so glad I convinced her to stay for longer. She's an absolute tonic.'

We watch her for a minute, admiring her easy charm with the customers, her ability to juggle numerous tasks in one go and her imperviousness to her own striking beauty. She couldn't be more different from the girl who cowered on the floor as the gang hurled bottles at her just weeks ago and it strikes me how ironic it is that the very person the cafe so desperately needed was standing just feet away from it all along.

At 13:30 prompt, having postponed the start of the performances due to Starr's absence, I pick up one of the copies of *The Good News Gazette* and step up onto the stage. My heart is still dancing with joy at the fact that, against all odds, we actually managed to meet the deadline and create our very own newspaper. Fresh from the printers, it still smells of the printing press and if you hold it in your hands for long enough, black ink leaves marks across your fingers. It looks great; it's jam-packed with good news and I couldn't be more proud of what Ollie and I have achieved.

I tap on the mic to make sure it's working, then tap a few times more. When a combination of taps and coughs has finally captured the crowd's attention, I start to speak.

'Hi, everyone.' Good grief, it's loud. I take a step back from the mic. 'I'd like to thank you all for coming today, to celebrate the sixtieth anniversary of the Westholme parade and to mark the launch of *The Good News Gazette*. As most of you know, the parade is currently under threat, so it's more important than ever that we're all here, demonstrating both our support to the shopkeepers and our desire, as a community, to keep our local high street alive and kicking.'

'I decided to start a newspaper that only focused on good newsas a result of being made redundant from my job. *The Good News Gazette* gave me something positive to focus on at a time when positivity was in short supply and I've loved hearing about your own good news stories along the way.

'There's been so much support for the website and now, finally, I am delighted to bring you the first issue of *The Good News Gazette* newspaper. You'll find copies at various points around the parade and in a number of other outlets across Westholme, so please feel free to take one and let me know if you like what's inside.'

I go on for a bit longer than planned, thank pretty much everyone I've ever met, then declare that the crowd should 'go forth and read' before stepping off the stage, adrenalin and embarrassment combining to make me feel exhilarated and mortified all in one go.

As I descend into a sea of congratulatory hugs and kisses, my eyes flit around the crowd, searching desperately for Charlie, seeking *his* approval above all others. Eventually I spot him with Mum and Dad, staring at me as though he's seeing me for the very first time. I head straight over to him, and while he isn't about to throw his arms around me in front of everyone in Westholme, when he squeezes my hand and says, 'Wow, Mum, you were amazing,' all the other faces fade into the background as the overwhelming power of love that connects a mother and her child gives me my own natural high.

For the first time in a long time, I feel so, so happy. Despite everything we've had thrown at us, Charlie and I are doing just fine. More than fine, in fact. And as I look around at the crowds of people enjoying the day with their families, I have never felt more like I am exactly where I am supposed to be.

Westholme Community Facebook page:

Elise Harvey: Lovin' this *Good News Gazette*!

Lisa Seddon: Yeah, I think it's Zoe Taylor from school that's behind it. Good, innit.

Paul Gregory: Brilliant.

Steve Crossley: Well done girl.

Eyelash Lucy: Love it!

Jimmy Hunter: Council propaganda crap.

Chapter Thirty-Four

T ypically, despite my mobile having been on charge all night, it promptly dies just before the performances are about to begin.

I've been trying to post regular updates on social media all morning and my phone clearly does not possess the constitution it needs to be able to withstand my demands, so I ask mum to keep an eye on Charlie and pop back to the office to plug it into the spare charger.

Glad of the chance to flop on the couch and re-charge my own batteries for five minutes – oh, and to take a quick swig of the emergency bottle of wine I keep in the fridge while I'm there – I head up the stairs and into my own little haven. Predictably, it's as I'm necking the vino, straight from the bottle, that Sam appears in the doorway. I cut my swig short, cursing inwardly as a couple of drips escape my mouth and dribble down my chin. Sam, for his part, doesn't flinch. He simply leans against the door frame, a lazy smile playing on his lips.

'What can I say?' I grin, raising my bottle in the air to hide the wave of horror washing over me. 'I'm a secret alcoholic.'

He walks slowly towards me. 'Or maybe an amazing but extremely harassed woman who needs a bit of Dutch courage to get through the rest of this particularly stressful day?' A high-pitched giggle that, even to me, sounds strange, escapes from my lips while my stomach flutters furiously and my mouth suddenly feels dry. My cheeks, naturally, are blazing.

Sam comes to a stop inches away from me and takes the bottle out of my hands, turning it over in his own.

'Pinot grigio,' he says, reading the label. 'I'll be sure to remember that.'

I look down at his hands, rough and tanned. Beneath them, I can see our feet, close together, toes almost touching. I smell his aftershave, feel the heat of his breath on the top of my head. I am suddenly nervous and scared to look up because I know when I do our lips will be close and will probably touch. And that won't end well for either of us.

'I like you, Zoe,' he says, his voice low and husky. He places the wine on the desk and gives his hands enough freedom to fall on my waist. Still, I dare not look up.

One hand moves up and around to my jaw. Firm fingers spread under my chin, pressing it gently upwards. It's only then, when there really is nowhere else to look, that I allow my eyes to rest on his face.

Slowly, tenderly, he dips his head and presses his lips to mine. I pull back, hesitating, then he does it again. This time I don't move. At first the kiss is gentle, slow, leisurely almost. But then, as his tongue parts my own lips and starts to explore my mouth, it becomes hungry, urgent, and the fluttering in my tummy turns into something much more primal.

I snake my arms up over his chest, my fingers squeezing into his shoulders, hips pressing forward to mould into his.

A loud bang from above cuts like a knife through our bodies, forcing us apart.

We stare at each other for a second, neither of us sure what will happen next, but certain that something will. And then it does.

'ZOE!!!' It's my mum, calling my name in a strangled voice that sounds so like her, yet at the same time so completely different .

Wordlessly, we move quickly towards the door.

I reach the bottom of the stairs first and head out into the square, glad of the cold chill of the fresh air on my flushed cheeks. Mum is there, in front of the office, her face drained of colour.

'Mum, what's wrong?' I'm breathless, and my hand involuntarily reaches for my heart to ease the palpatations.

'Oh, thank goodness you're here,' she says, pulling me a few steps further into the square and pointing upwards.

'It's your dad. Look!'

I follow the direction of her finger, and for a moment I think there's a very good chance I really might have a heart attack. Because there, balancing precariously on the roof of the parade and wearing a superhero outfit while holding a banner with the words 'SAVE OUR BATS' daubed onto it in black paint, is the only man in the world I can rely on to show me up at every available opportunity. My hero. My dad.

I freeze as my brain attempts to piece together what on earth is going on.

Around me, people are gasping and pointing. The blonde TV presenter has moved towards the scene, cameraman in tow, issuing directions to him as she pulls out her mobile phone, probably wondering whether to call her news desk or live stream the whole thing herself through social media.

'Dad!' I shout through gritted teeth. 'What are you doing?'

'I'm being Batman to raise awareness,' he shouts defiantly,

then gives me a pantomime wink. 'Of those bats that will be destroyed, DESTROYED, if Daniel Lewis goes ahead and knocks the parade down.'

He crouches down then and pulls something out of a plastic bag that's hanging off the chimney stack. Even the small act of him standing back up looks like a suicide mission. Then he starts to shout again. Only this time it's through a megaphone.

'Don't allow the murder of Westholme's bat population. Save our bats. SAVE OUR BATS.'

'I thought we'd agreed to forget the bat idea, dear?' Margaret whispers in my ear.

'We did,' I say, my head a crazy messed-up mixture of confusion and shame.

Then a man in the crowd that I vaguely recognise shouts to him.

'Terry, mate, what's going on?'

'I'm staging a sit-in – save our bats. I'm Batman.'

A wave of sniggers echo around the square.

'But Terry, that's an Iron Man costume.'

I look again at the mask over his face and the red skin-tight all-in-one that clings to his protruding belly. He looks like an adult in a Baby-gro. And he is, indeed, dressed as Iron Man.

Unperturbed, my dad battles on. 'No it's not, the fella said it was the new Batman one.'

The sniggers turn to undisguised laughter.

'Sorry, mate, but it's definitely Iron Man.'

Just as it dawns on me that not only is my dad single-handedly ruining the event, he's also doing it dressed as entirely the wrong superhero, I hear the first ear-piercing scream from the bouncy castle.

My head whips around in time to see a jumble of arms and legs as mums and dads drag their children quickly off the rapidly deflating contraption.

'There are kids stuck in there,' one mum screams. A flash of blue races past me. It's Sam, diving into the pile of flaccid rubber, emerging from the wreckage moments later with the two final toddlers, one perched on either hip.

I'm rooted to the spot. Not once in my search for a dummies' guide to staging a town carnival did I see any mention of how to deal with deflating bouncy castles – or furious attendees. I watch as all the parents involved examine their children for damage, claimable or otherwise. Once satisfied/dissatisfied that there are no immediately obvious grounds for a claim, they turn their rage in my direction.

'Hey, you, are you the organiser?' one of them shouts at me.

'Uhmmm, yes I am,' I reply in my most authoritative voice, which in all honesty is little more than a quivering whisper.

'What kind of set-up is this?' The dad's face is red with rage. 'My son could have been killed. Who provided this piece of crap? Get it on the cheap, did you? Absolute joke.'

'Sir, first of all, is your child alright?' I say, genuinely concerned.

'Well, he seems okay, FOR NOW! No thanks to you, mind. I knew this whole event would be a cock-up. From the minute I saw the advert, I said to Denise, "this won't work for a minute, this won't". And I was proved right, wasn't I?'

'Look, I can't apologise enough,' I say, trying to tune out the dulcet tones of my dad still chanting on the roof. 'I have no idea what's happened here but please, rest assured, I will find out. Now, can I get you and your son a drink and a cake by way of an apology?'

The man's upper lip curls. 'It's going to take more than a drink and a cake to make up for this,' he snarls. The crowd of disgruntled parents gathered behind him make noises of agreement as though they're about to lynch me on the spot.

'Alright, guys, that's enough.' Paula pushes her way to the front of the crowd, placating and soothing as she goes.

'Don't get involved, Paula. She nearly killed our Hayden,' a skin-headed short man shouts out.

'Come on, Rick, she's done her best to put on a nice day for us. Leave her alone.' Paula looks over at my dad, seemingly oblivious to the chaos going on below him and still shouting about saving the bats.

'Anyway,' she adds. 'I think she's got enough on her hands dealing with that crank, don't you?'

Paula then turns her attention to me. 'Let me take Charlie back to mine with Sean,' she says. 'You can pick him up when you're ready.'

I nod gratefully and watch as, one by one, the crowd start to disperse, still muttering threats of legal action.

Up on the roof, my dad continues to chant, albeit more quietly now, about saving the bats.

And me? Well, I'm left wondering what ever possessed me to think that staging the Westholme Sixtieth Anniversary Carnival was a good idea.

Eventually it's the fire brigade that help Dad down off the roof, right before they deliver him into the arms of the police.

By the time the arrest occurs, word has got round and most of Westholme appears to have congregated at the parade to witness the event. If the community day alone had generated this much interest I would have been over the moon. But knowing it was my dad dressed in a babygro – and not even, as it turns out, the *right* babygro – that has caused such a high turnout only serves to invalidate any success I might have otherwise claimed.

The performances have to be shelved. The stacks of

newspapers are left largely untouched. And telling Starr that her interview is no longer likely to happen when she finally returns with her emerald tiara has to go down as one of my all-time lows.

Daniel is there to witness it all, of course. As is Sam, the entire Save The Westholme parade group and, if the buzz on social media is anything to go by, every single follower of the Westholme Community Facebook page.

The market stalls start to pack away pretty soon after Dad's arrest, and when Beth comes over to tell me most of the raffle prizes have been stolen in the chaos, I'm ready to burst into tears on the spot.

Beth pulls me close to her and gives me the sort of massive hug that make best friends worth their weight in gold. 'Why don't I take your mum to the police station and we can wait there for your dad?' she says.

'Beth, would you mind? I don't think I can look at him right now, let alone rescue him from the hands of the law.'

She gives me another squeeze. 'It was all going so well,' she says, her voice filled with sympathy.

'It was a stupid idea,' I reply, extricating myself from her arms and unpinning some bunting from one of the shop walls. 'I don't know why I ever thought it would work.'

'Because it was a brilliant idea, and it *should* have worked,' she says.

Emma joins us. 'The best-laid plans and all that,' she says, the sides of her mouth pulled into a sympathetic smile. 'So, it didn't finish entirely as planned. Don't worry chick. It was still a great day and it did what you wanted it to – partly at least – by proving how great Westholme can be when everyone puts their mind to it.'

I sigh, unwilling to be placated just yet. 'But the idea was to impress Daniel and convince him not to knock the parade down. There's no way he's going to agree to it now.'

Emma looks over at one of the outdoor tables where Daniel

appears to be finishing a phone call. He puts his mobile in his back pocket, stands up and looks over in my direction.

'It seems as though you're about to find out,' Emma says. She signals to Beth. 'We'll leave you to it.'

I wave them off, then turn around to face Daniel. Step by step, he's walking towards me, ready to deliver his verdict on the fate of our town.

Westholme Community Facebook page:

Johnny H: Told yez something'd go wrong.

Chapter Thirty-Five

'Zoe. Can I have a word?'

My view of Daniel is blocked by Ollie. I peep round him to see Daniel coming to a halt just metres away.

'Ollie, can we speak in a minute?' My tone is despondent. 'I think Daniel wants a word.'

'Zoe, it's about that,' Ollie says in a commanding tone that I'm not used to hearing from him. 'And it's urgent.'

'Okay,' I say, steering him to the side of the square. 'What's wrong?'

'I've just got off the phone from a contact of mine, a contractor. Zoe, Daniel contacted him last week to ask him to work on flattening the parade, subject to planning approval being granted.

'There's something we missed. Daniel had a legal agreement in place with the supermarket operator before he even called the first public meeting. As long as the planning committee approved the plans, it was always going to go ahead. He has no intention of changing his mind. He *couldn't* change his mind even if he wanted to.'

I stare at him, my mind whirling.

'But why did he agree to let me try and convince him if I never had a chance?'

Ollie shrugs. 'I don't know. I have no idea what he's playing at. But one thing's for sure – as long as the council agree to it, this development is going to happen.'

The events of the past two weeks replay in my mind. The research I'd done, the places I'd taken him, the lengths I'd gone to, to convince him to drop the plans. All for nothing.

'There's something else, too,' Ollie says, lowering his voice even further. 'He's a known friend to the criminal fraternity and I believe his brother's in prison. I can't tell you any more at this stage, but it sounds to me as though he's some kind of gangster. You were right all along. He's definitely dodgy. Zoe, he's taken us all for fools.'

Out of the corner of my eye, I can see Daniel waiting, watching, taking in the expression on my face. I lock eyes with him and then look away, disgusted. I can't believe what I'm hearing. But then, I know the strength of Ollie's contacts. And I know he wouldn't pass on this news if he wasn't certain it was correct.

'Right, Ollie,' I say, 'thanks for telling me. I'll take it from here.'

'Alright, Zoe, but just…' He glares in Daniel's direction. 'Be careful, okay? We don't know what we're dealing with here.'

'I can handle it,' I say steadily. 'I'll talk to you later.'

Ollie heads back in the direction of the cafe and, satisfied that I'm finally alone, Daniel makes his way over, doing a double-take as he passes Ollie who has obviously given him one of his looks.

'So,' he says with a gentle smile. 'How are you doing?'

I glare at him. 'Why did you say you'd give me a chance if you had no intention of doing so?'

He freezes, all traces of the smile gone.

'What?'

'You heard me. Why did you pretend to be considering my

plans for the parade when you were actually lining up contractors to bulldoze it?'

He rubs his chin. 'Where did you hear that?'

'It doesn't matter where I heard it. Tell me why you did it.'

'Zoe, I—' He takes a step towards me. I move back.

'It's true, isn't it?'

'It's not as straightforward as—'

'I don't understand. Why would you make me think I had a might be able to do it? Why would you spend all that time with me if you had no intention of changing your plans? It doesn't make sense.'

His cheeks colour and he looks away, unable to meet my eyes, then his shoulders go back and he seems to grow a couple of inches as he regains his usual composure. 'I might have changed my mind. If I'd been convinced, maybe I would have found a way to get out of the agreement.'

I look at him steadily. 'But you weren't convinced, were you?'

'No,' he says, his voice quiet.

I narrow my eyes. 'I know all about you, Daniel Lewis. I know you associate with criminals, I know you employ criminals, and I know you're not as straight as you seem. You pretend to care about Westholme, about the community, but I know that, deep down, all you care about is lining your own pockets.'

He looks stunned. I've got him now.

'Oh yes, Daniel, I know about it all. And I'm going to make sure the whole of Westholme knows too.'

I shake my head at him, then start to walk away. As I do, he grabs my wrist. 'Look, Zoe, you're wrong about this,' he says. 'You have no idea how wrong you are. Let me explain. And as for the parade? It's not personal. It's just business.'

I wrench my arm away and fix him with my deadliest death stare.

'You don't know the meaning of personal. You and your

crooked mates may not be convinced by the downsides to bulldozing a community, but the council still hasn't delivered its verdict. Don't crack open the champagne just yet.'

As if I didn't have enough on my plate, I realise I need to pop home and feed Lola in order to stop her from nicking anyone else's steak before heading to the police station to find out what on earth's going on with my dad.

When I pull into the front path, Sam is there, leaning against the front wall like the world's best-looking and most-conspicuous burglar.

'Hey,' he says, an uncertain smile on his face. 'Things got a bit crazy at the parade and I thought … well … there are things that need to be said.'

I feel the last remaining ounce of energy drain out of me.

'You'd better come in,' I say wearily, gesturing for him to follow me into the house.

As I reach the kitchen, I turn to him.

'Would you like a drink? Coffee? Tea? Something stronger?'

'It's okay,' he says. 'I know you've had an afternoon of it, so I won't stay. I'll just say what I came here to say.'

I turn around and put my hand up to stop him.

'Sam, before you do, there's something I need to ask you.'

He looks at me expectantly.

'What *is* it between you and Daniel Lewis? Don't tell me it's nothing because I *know* it's something. I saw it that day at the cafe.'

I've clearly touched a nerve. Because right now, easy-going, cheery Sam is looking anything *but* that. Instead, he's shifting from one foot to another, hands stuffed in his pockets.

'You sure you want to know?' he asks, his eyes now not quite meeting mine.

I nod. 'I do.'

He takes a deep breath. 'Okay, Zoe, I'll tell you. But before I do, I want you to promise me one thing – that you'll judge me on the person I am now, the person you've got to know over the last few weeks, rather than the person I used to be.'

'Okay,' I say, my heart hammering. 'I promise.'

'I've told you I grew up in Westholme and I'm pretty sure you'll know by now that Daniel did too.' He looks at me, still seeking some sort of reassurance, but I can't give him any. Not until I know what his secret is.

'What I haven't told you is that we both lived on the Orchard Estate. And his name wasn't Daniel then, it was Jonno – Jonathan, I think. Our families didn't have anything back then. Obviously, my mum was single and Jonno – I mean Daniel's – family were pretty broke too. We're a similar age, we were in the same year at school… I suppose you could say we were pretty good mates.'

Prickles start to jab at the back of my neck, over my shoulders and down my arms. I don't like where this is going.

'Gangs on the estate are nothing new. There were gangs then, just as there are now. Daniel and I both belonged to the same one; we had each other's backs, engaged in a bit of petty crime, but nothing serious. His older brother was part of the scene too, but he was more into it than Daniel. He was a few years older and did drugs with some of the other lads.

'But then Daniel's dad's building business started taking off. He was getting bigger and bigger contracts and making more money. The older lads realised Daniel had a bit of money behind him and started demanding cash.'

I can't believe what I'm hearing. Posh, loaded Daniel growing up on the Orchard Estate and running around with the gangs? None of this makes sense.

'Obviously Daniel's dad realised he needed to get the boys away from the gangs and as the business was doing so well, he could afford to. Just before we went to secondary school, they all moved to Presthill. Daniel and I lost touch, but his brother had a regular supplier on the estate and kept coming back to get his fix.'

'I think Daniel realised as he got older that his brother was being used as a bit of a cash cow. He'd often get the bus down here to try and convince him to go home, but there was no point – he was always off his head anyway.'

'One night, when we were about seventeen, eighteen, I was hanging out with some of my mates at the parade and we saw Daniel walking back towards the bus stop.'

'I had a place at the football academy by then so I didn't do drugs, but that night the other lads were high and Daniel was on his own. He was overweight then – almost unrecognisable from how he is now. They started following him, taunting him, trying to get money out of him. He told them where to go, but they wouldn't leave him alone.'

He raises both hands to his face and starts pressing his temples. 'They hurt him, Zoe,' he says quietly. 'They left him for dead. I tried to get them to stop, but they were like animals.'

I feel sick. 'What happened?' I whisper.

'We ran, then as soon as I was away from the other lads I found a phone box, called an ambulance and went back to wait with him until it came. The minute I heard the sirens, I disappeared.'

'I knew Daniel was pretty badly injured, but I also heard on the grapevine that he'd recovered. It was his brother who never got better. He kept on doing drugs and one of the lads told me he ended up in jail a few years ago for armed robbery.'

'Daniel never pressed charges – I guess he knew better than to be a snitch – and I got out of the country pretty quickly after that. I didn't realise he'd changed his name so had no idea the Daniel

Lewis you were talking about was actually Jonno, until I saw him that day at the first planning committee meeting.'

I hang my head. Poor, poor Daniel. No wonder he wants to see the parade demolished. And Sam? What does that make him? A monster? A scared teenager? I have no idea which one is true.

'Look,' Sam's saying, 'I know this is a lot to take in – I get that. I'm also sorry that today worked out the way it did for you. I know how much you've put into this, and how much you were looking forward to finally giving *The Good News Gazette* the launch it deserves.'

He moves closer towards me, eyes fixed on mine.

'But I'm not sorry, I won't ever be sorry, that I kissed you, Zoe. I've wanted to do that since the day you came to interview me at the training session. And every time I've seen you since.'

'I think you're incredible. You're a fantastic mum to Charlie, you're so focused in the way you get things done, you're kind, caring and beautiful too. I know you're independent but, Zoe, I want to look after you. I want to make coffee for you in the morning, to be there for you at night when you've had a bad day, to help you out with Charlie. I don't want to be just friends.' He rests his hands either side of the worktop against which I'm leaning and bends downso that his face is level with mine. 'I want more. The question is, do you?'

I can't look at him. I'm picturing Daniel on the floor, left for dead. Sam, running away. Charlie and how I'd feel if anyone ever laid a finger on my son. And now this, this expectation that I might want a relationship with him. I finally lift my gaze to his and shake my head.

'No.'

He looks pained, as physically hurt as if I'd slapped him.

'This. You. It's just too much.'

He takes a step back. 'It's because of what I told you about Daniel, isn't it?'

'No.' I shake my head, then say, 'I don't know.'

He frowns. 'But I thought ... back at the parade...'

'I'm sorry about that. It was a mistake. I have a responsibility to Charlie. I can't go entering into relationships that will only end badly. And with the best will in the world, that's how it will end. I need to keep things on an even keel. I can't do that if I'm in a relationship.'

He hangs his head. 'I didn't realise you saw relationships that way.'

I nod slowly. 'I've learnt from experience.'

'But, Zoe, not all relationships end badly. Not all relationships end. You have to take a chance sometime.'

I try and ignore the dull ache settling in my chest. 'I'm sorry, Sam.'

He gives me one long, last miserable look. 'It's your call, Zoe,' he says, his voice steady. 'You know where I am if you change your mind.'

It's only after the front door slams shut that the knot in my chest finally unravels. Then, when I'm finally alone, the tears that have been forming for hours start to fall in big, fat lonely drops.

Westholme Community Facebook page:

Heidi Ho: Zoe Taylor your cat Lola's in ours again. Guessing you're probably a bit tied up right now so I'll feed her and keep her here 'til the morning.

Chris Scott: It's Zoe Taylor's dad who's tied up – in the cells at Westholme Police Station.

Chapter Thirty-Six

'Officer, he's a very confused old man. Let's just say the doctors haven't ruled out dementia at this stage.'

The policeman cocks his head as he tries to assess whether I'm pulling the wool.

'Wait here,' he barks, disappearing through the door behind the counter.

I hang around at the desk for a few minutes, then concede that the wait might be a long one and take a seat next to Mum in the waiting area instead.

Having reassured Beth that she could stand down from her duties, we're completely alone and Mum apologises for what feels like the hundredth time.

'Forget it, Mum,' I say, my tone more brusque than I intend. 'It's not your fault.'

We fall silent, me scrolling through my phone while Mum reads the crime prevention posters.

'What the hell was he thinking?' I blurt out, unable to contain my thoughts.

'I know, he's an idiot,' Mum says, her own eyes welling up. 'I promise I had no idea he had this up his sleeve.'

'But why would he do this, Mum? You both know how much this means to me. Why would he ruin it with one stupid act? If I wasn't already the laughing stock of Westholme before, I certainly am now.'

I go to stand up again, but Mum holds me down with a firm grasp of my arm.

'Wait a minute, what are you talking about? Why would you be the laughing stock of Westholme?' She looks genuinely confused, which in turn confuses me.

'Are you joking?'

Mum frowns. 'Zoe, I really don't know what you mean.'

'I know what people say about me. I know what *Dad* says about me. "Zoe, the one with the world at her feet until she got up the duff."'

'Your dad doesn't say that about—'

I fix her with a stare.

Mum leans back in her seat.

'I know,' she says. 'I know he does it. But he doesn't mean it. He's so proud of you and Charlie, so proud of how you've both turned out.'

'So why does he always joke about it? Why does he put me down?'

Mum moves her hand down to my wrist, then squeezes my fingers.

'Why do you let him?' she asks gently.

'Mum, it's not up to me to stop Dad from laughing at me. He's my dad. He's meant to support me, bolster me, not pick at my flaws and point them out to everyone else.'

'But, love, that's what *you* do.'

I pause for a moment. 'No I don't.'

'You do, love. I've wanted to speak to you about it for a while now. Your dad thinks it's all just a big joke when he does it. You seem to think it's real.'

'But that's my point, Mum,' I say, sniffing as the tears threaten to fall again. 'He's always laughing at me. Always has. The jibes about my weight, the comments about me getting up the duff when you and I both know the situation was far more complicated than that, the way he's always so ready to write off any plans I might have. Look at *The Good News Gazette*. He didn't think that would work, did he? And today. Making me feel as though I could have done better, while all along it was him sabotaging everything.'

Mum shifts her attention from my arm to the zip on her handbag, which she moves backwards and forwards repeatedly, the zip whirring as it flies from one end to the other.

Eventually she looks up. 'You're right, Zoe. You are right. Your dad shouldn't say these things. But, more importantly, you shouldn't believe them. You didn't make a hash of anything. You were let down by the man you loved. But look at what he left you with. Look at the life you've made for yourself and Charlie. Yet you still seem to think you've underachieved.

'You were made redundant, so what? You carry a bit more weight than you want to – although you seem to have lost some from what I can see – who doesn't? You wanted things to change and you've changed them. From where I'm standing, you're not a laughing stock, you're an inspiration.'

A kerfuffle behind the counter heralds the arrival of my dad, handcuffs off and looking somewhat sheepish. Still dressed in the Iron Man costume, now minus the mask, I have to smother a smile. He *does* look ridiculous.

'What's the verdict, officer?' I ask wearily.

'He'll have to appear before the court, but he's out on bail for now,' he says stiffly. 'Just try and stay off shop rooftops between now and then if you can manage it, sir.' His tone is formal, but he's smiling.

'Thanks, officer,' Dad mumbles. He trundles into the waiting room. 'I ruined it, didn't I?' he says, not quite catching my eye.

I nod. 'You did.'

'I'm sorry, love. I thought if we kept on about the bats then that Lewis bloke might give up and move on. I thought I was helping.'

A loud sigh escapes me. After the emotional highs and lows of the day I suddenly feel drained.

'Come on, let's go home,' I say, picking up my bag and making my way towards the station door.

'I don't suppose you're hungry by any chance, are you?' Dad says, following behind. 'I could just go for a chippy tea, and the *good news* is that if they've run out of paper to wrap the fish and chips in, we can just use the newspaper. There's enough copies of it left.' He chuckles to himself.

'Stop!' I turn around. 'Stop right there.'

Dad looks taken aback. Mum is holding her breath, wondering what's coming next.

'No more jibes, no more jokes at my expense. This ends *now.*'

'I'm only joking, love,' he says, looking surprisingly wounded. 'No need to be like that.'

'Well, I'm *not* joking, Dad. If you still want to be in my life after today, then you stop making jokes about it. Full stop. And to make it clear exactly how serious I am about this, you can walk home. In your Iron Man costume.'

He blinks in disbelief. 'You're not serious?'

I spin round and fix him with a stare. 'I've never been more serious about anything in my life. Come on, Mum, I'll drop you off.'

Without a word, Mum walks through the door and heads straight over to the car.

'Sue?' My dad can't believe she's leaving without him. 'Sue?'

'She's right, Terry,' Mum shouts over her shoulder. 'Anyway, you won't need a lift. With that get-up on, you'll be able to fly.'

Westholme Community Facebook page:

Harold Kiddle: The Iron Man jokes everyone's posting tonight are all very funny, but please can you remember to keep it clean. Vulgarities and swear words are not tolerated on this site and as an administrator, I do have the power to remove any comments that are not in keeping with the ethics of the Westholme Community Facebook page. Thank you kindly.

Chapter Thirty-Seven

The scent of body odour that hangs in the air of the planning committee's meeting room is testament to the number of people that have sweated their way through the life-changing decision-making processes over the years – and I am no exception.

All the gang are there – Ollie, Cath, Lawrence, Antonio, Adina, Mum and Dad, Emma and Beth, Margaret, Colin, Lynne and Starr. Even Neil's made an appearance. In fact, the only person who isn't there is Sam. He's kept his distance since the carnival and to save any uncomfortable situations, I've done the same, staying in the car to drop off and pick up Charlie every time I've had to take him to football.

I miss him more than I had anticipated. I miss asking him for advice, flirting with him, laughing with him. I miss his support, his sexy smile, just, well *him*. But it's for the best. Nothing good could have come of it.

On the other side of the room, Daniel and *his* gang sit on a row of seats.

As the planning committee file in, I glance at him and realise he's watching me. I try and shoot arrows at him through my eyes then, aware it may look as though I simply need glasses, I turn haughtily away.

There are a few points on the agenda to discuss before they get to ours, but after an interminable wait, we're there. The conversation that follows is long, drawn-out, peppered with clichés and uninteresting points of information that are so boring I almost switch off. And then finally, after a vote, a woman who seems to be in charge of everything delivers the committee's verdict.

'And so it is, that with respect to the proposed development, the application as set out by Lewis & Co. is granted.'

A gasp can be heard from our little group. Across the room, Daniel's team are congratulating each other and slapping him on the back. But he stays still, his eyes fixed on mine.

I feel winded, as though I've taken a sucker punch. I tell myself to breathe as I look around at the faces of those who've stood by me these past few months, supporting my crazy ideas, my unrealistic dream of transforming the parade. I'm not the only one to feel like that. As I look at the defeated expressions of our little group, I can see that every single one of us is truly gutted at the outcome. We put our heart and soul into saving the parade and we still lost. But I led everyone into this. It's up to me, in the face of a colossal failure, to lift their spirits and lead them out of it.

'We did everything we could,' I speak quietly as the committee members start to pack away, my voice calm and reassuring – adjectives that absolutely could not be used to describe how I feel inside.

'Zoe, I'm devastated,' says Margaret. 'I never really believed he'd actually win.'

Emma is muttering expletives under her breath.

Cath is trying to bring Antonio and Adina up to speed with the complicated workings of the English planning system by way of an explanation that is simply causing Antonio to shake his head.

Dad gets up out of his seat and squeezes my shoulder.

'Well done, love,' he says, in a voice that could almost be described as fatherly.

'Dad, we lost,' I reply.

'It doesn't matter. You tried. You put up a fight. That's why I'm proud. You saw an injustice and you tried to fix it. Good on you, girl.'

'Hear, hear,' says Colin, and the others join in, moving towards me one by one to pat me on the back and issue words of reassurance.

As we prepare to leave, I turn around and find myself face-to-face with Daniel, his eyes hollow, his expression unreadable.

'I'm sorry,' he says simply.

Slowly and deliberately, I pick up my handbag and fix it across my body.

'Don't be,' I say, arranging my own facial features to make them equally unreadable. 'It's just business after all.'

'Come on, Zoe,' says Cath, glaring at him. 'Let's go.'

And we file out of the meeting room, our motley crew, battered and bruised but in possession of one significant fact. Daniel Lewis might have stolen our town, but during his daylight robbery of our community, he's unearthed its most special feature – and it's the one thing he'll never have, despite his riches. A heart.

Westholme Community Facebook page:

Hair by Becki: Don't know if I'm allowed to post this on here so please take it down if not, but my little boy, George, is being bullied in school at the moment. He's crying every day and I don't know what to do. His birthday's coming up and I'd really appreciate it if people could send him messages to make him smile.

Westholme Castles: Really sorry to hear this, Becki. What's his favourite football team? We can provide a penalty shoot-out inflatable for the day if it would help?

Cakes by Paula: I'm the new caterer for Cath's Caff. I'd love to make him a cake if you want one.

Cath's Caff: Ciao, Cath's Caff can offer George a little party for a few friends.

Hair by Becki: Aw, guys… I can hardly type through the tears. What can I say? You're the best.

Irene Wilson: We look after our own here, love. Always have, always will ♥

Chapter Thirty-Eight

I t's Slim City day and despite having lost a few pounds in recent weeks, the number flashing up before me indicates that I've returned to form.

Granted, I've eaten three big bars of chocolate and sunk two bottles of wine since the council meeting last week but I had hoped that the scales would let me off due to mitigating circumstances.

Wendy finishes off writing up my weight gain into the little log book that acts as testament to my ongoing failure and casts her usual look of kindly sympathy on me.

'One and a half on. Don't worry, you'll have that off by next week.'

I swallow the urge to make a sarcastic retort and head off to join the girls.

'How'd you do? Emma whispers as Barbara starts her weekly roll call of shame.

'One and a half on,' I roll my eyes. 'You?'

'Six pounds off.'

I turn to face her. 'What?'

'Yeah, it's apparently the one plus point of being cheated on by your husband – you completely lose your appetite.'

Reaching out for her hand, I squeeze it tight. 'Have you spoken to him?'

Emma's eyes fills with tears. 'I speak to him regularly. He phones and texts every day, telling me how sorry he is, trying to work out what went wrong, then of course there's always kids' stuff to discuss. He's desperate to make it work again but … I don't know.'

'Do you miss him, Em?'

Emma nods. 'All the time.' Then she shakes down her hair and straightens her top. 'How did you do on the scales this week, Beth?'

Beth shifts uncomfortably in her seat. 'Three off.'

I groan. 'Not you too.'

She pulls an apologetic face. 'I'm trying to be good – you know – with the whole IVF thing. She hangs her head and looks at me apologetically. 'Sorry.'

'Don't be daft,' I say. 'Well done you. Where are you up to with it all?'

Barbara fixes us with a glare to let us know she can hear us talking and we turn our bodies towards her as though we've been listening all along.

After a minute or two, Beth whispers, 'It's all done.' Then, keeping her eyes firmly focused on Barbara, she murmurs, 'All we can do now is wait.'

'So, are you really going to do this then?' I ask.

'What, have a baby?'

'Actually do the diet. Treat it seriously rather than just coming here to buy the low-calorie chocolate bars and have a gab with us?'

'Well, yeah, I think I might,' she says.

'Right. Well, that's good, isn't it?'

As we settle into an uncomfortable silence, I can't help but feel a little betrayed. Beth, Emma and I eat too much rubbish, drink too much booze and then reaffirm our bond by talking about it. It's who we are. What does all this weight loss mean for me? Will I eventually be cast as the unattractive, slightly chubby friend that always acts as the sidekick to the leading lady in films? The single parent, struggling to get by, as her slim, gorgeous friends go on to live the life of their dreams? All too soon it's my turn on the roll call of shame.

'Zoe,' Barbara calls my name in the manner of a teacher checking students into detention. She checks her screen, tuts loudly, then looks over at me.

'You had a plan this week, didn't you, Zoe?'

'Yes, Barb.'

'You were going to eat less this week, weren't you?'

I sink further into my seat.

'Yes, Barb.'

Barbara pauses, clearly trying to keep her emotions in check.

'So how did that work out for you?' I silently curse her; she knows full well how it's worked out.

'Um, I had a pound-and-a-half gain, Barb.'

She puts her glasses on the table.

'Zoe, let's have a little chat after today's meeting.'

The whole class falls silent. It has been a long time since anyone has been summonsed for a chat. My stomach plummets, sparking a wave of nausea that continues throughout the rest of the session and only intensifies when Emma is awarded the City Slimmer certificate and handed a carrier bag of past-its-best fruit as a reward.

The girls flash me a sympathetic look and a promise they'll wait for me at Greggs as they leave and I make my way over to the table where Barbara usually welcomes new members.

'Ah great, you stayed.' Her features soften as she relaxes into a smile, gesturing for me to sit down.

Once seated, she puts her hands together as if saying a silent prayer. 'I just wondered if we might be able to have a little chat about what may and may not be working for you at Slim City and how we can help you to achieve your slimming goals?'

I laugh, a sound that convinces neither of us. 'Oh, I know, I've been terrible lately, haven't I?' I'm babbling. 'But don't worry, Barb, I'm onto it now, I know what I have to do and I promise I'm going to come in with a loss next week.'

Barbara pauses for a minute, the vertical lines between her eyebrows deepening as she chooses her words carefully. 'You know, losing weight isn't all about what we're eating.' She sees the look of confusion on my face and attempts to explain. 'What I'm trying to say is, unhealthy eating can be a symptom of lots of other types of issues. Stress, unhappiness, loneliness, depression. Not that I'm saying you're suffering from any of these things,' she adds hastily. 'But sometimes it's worth looking at what you're putting into your head rather than what you're putting into your mouth.'

A lump forms in my throat as, inexplicably, the urge to cry threatens to overwhelm me. 'Honestly, I'm—' I try to speak, but find myself choked.

Barbara reaches across the table to place her hand on my arm. 'Is there anything you'd like to talk about, Zoe?'

I supress a laugh. Where would I even begin? With the son who I love dearly but whom I've let down from the moment of his conception, with the life that had seemed so full of potential when I left from London but seems so limited now, with the massive cock-up I've just made with my sworn enemy, the confusing pull I'm feeling towards a man who seems determined to break down my barriers, or with the town that I just can't fix, no matter how hard I try?

Slowly at first and then gathering speed, the tears make their way down my cheeks, landing unedifying on the Slim City new member packs all ready for distribution to new hopefuls who could never predict that this might be the outcome of their own weight loss journey.

I shake my head, words seemingly pointless in this situation.

Barbara squeezes my arm. 'You're not alone, you know.' I raise my eyes to meet hers. 'I feel like this sometimes. I don't know if you're aware that my husband has motor neurone disease?' I gulp and shake my head.

'So, there are weeks when I struggle. Wondering what the point is, feeling like it's all just that bit too hard, getting through those days when you don't even want to get out of bed, let alone chop peppers and worrying that that one glass of wine will count against you on the scales when all you really want to do is neck the bottle.'

I look up at her, surprised, as the image of self-controlled, perfect Barbara lying in bed swigging bottles of wine and bingeing on chocolate pops into my head.

She looks at me. 'But you know what, Zoe, I just keep getting up. I keep chopping those peppers. And I keep counting the calories of the wine. Because do you know what? I know what the alternative looks like.'

She reaches behind her and pulls out her own before and after pictures. I supress a gasp. The large lady on the 'before' photographs is a world away from the woman who sits in front of me now. 'This was me before my husband got his diagnosis. We weren't able to have children. Never knew why. It devastated me. Still does, if I'm honest. As far as I was concerned, my body had let me down. It had failed in the most basic of tasks – to reproduce.'

'For a while, I hated it. I ate and ate and ate. In fact, for a couple of years I didn't stop. I think I was trying to punish it for not giving me the one thing I most desired. And then Frank became ill, and was eventually given his diagnosis. Overnight, I realised that the wallowing had to come to an end. I'd grieved for the life I would never have. Now I had to fight to keep the one I did have, to keep it going for as long as I possibly could.'

'I needed to be here for Frank. I needed to be around to chop the peppers. Because he didn't have anyone else who could. And over time, as I watched Frank's's body start to change, I became more and more thankful for my own. It seemed a crime to stuff myself with rubbish when my own husband would have cherished a fully functioning body like mine.'

She sighs, clearly exhausted at having revealed so much.

'So, when things seem that little bit too hard, as I suspect might be the case for you right now, don't punish yourself with food. Instead, nourish yourself with whatever you might need, be it time with your family, a walk in the hills, or a boxset binge, and think of all the blessings in your life, rather than the curses. I have my health, I still have my Frank with me, and I have this class. You are all my blessings. That's what keeps me going on those days when I don't want to get out of bed. So, think about those things and turn to them instead of food. You can do it, Zoe. And I'll be here to support you as you do.'

The door opens slightly and a head pops around it. 'Sorry, Barb,' a jolly man booms. 'Am I too early for the 11:30am class?'

Barbara smiles. 'Not at all, Bill, come in.'

Turning her attention back to me, she says, 'So, will we see you next week?'

I nod and smile. 'Definitely.'

'Good.' She shuffles her new member packs as I put my coat on and make my way towards the door.

'Oh and, Zoe,' she calls.

I turn around.

'Remember – you've got to fix what's going on here,' she

points at her head, 'before you can fix what's going on here…' She grabs her non-existent love handles.

I smile. 'Thanks, Barb.'

She winks. 'See you next week.'

———————

Westholme Community Facebook page:

Tori Hindle: I know everyone's feeling a bit low after hearing the news about the parade, so just putting some positive vibes out there today, guys, with this lovely saying that will hopefully make you feel a bit better: *Today is the tomorrow you were worrying about yesterday.*

Rita Hollingworth: Lovely Tori.

Stephanie Porter: Ah, that's nice hun.

Rob Brown: WTF????

Chapter Thirty-Nine

I t's surprising how quickly you learn to adapt to a new normal after everything falls apart. Following an overwhelmingly positive response to the first print issue, Ollie and I work flat-out to create the second while also uploading stories to the website and trying to bring more advertisers on board. Although, admittedly, finding good news at a time when all anyone is focused on is the imminent demolition of the parade is no easy task.

The situation has been made even more difficult by the death of Tilly. She stuck with me as long as she could, bless her, but when her exhaust pipe finally fell off on the drive back from Slim City, we both knew it was time for her to go to the scrapyard in the clouds.

Cath, Antonio and Adina are battling on against all odds, defiant in the face of adversity and seemingly determined to press ahead with their plans to give the cafe a new lease of life – even if that life might only last five minutes.

Poor Bob returned from his holidays yesterday. I watched him from the office window, standing in front of the shop that has been his life for so long looking utterly and completely beaten.

Ollie and I have decided that when the time comes, we'll move operations to my house and work on the kitchen table until we can afford to find a new space. It's not the perfect solution, but for now it's the only workable one.

Daniel appears to have disappeared off the face of the earth. Whenever I think of him, the jumbled thoughts make my head hurt, so I've decided not to bother right now.

Then there's Sam. We haven't had a proper conversation since the day of the carnival and I've done everything I can to avoid him since. More than once I've found myself questioning whether I made the wrong decision, whether there might be room in mine and Charlie's lives for a third person after all. And then something will happen to remind me that I'm only just keeping my head above water as it is.

I have Charlie. He has me. It's safer to keep it that way.

Ollie is pacing up and down the office as though he's trying to complete the ten-thousand-step challenge in just thirty minutes.

He's scratching his head to such an extent that I'm starting to wonder if he has a bad case of nits and he's so preoccupied with whatever's on his mind that he hasn't popped out to the cafe to fetch our morning coffees – an agreed part of the Adina Plan – once yet this morning.

Eventually, I can stand it no longer.

'Ollie, you're like an ant on speed,' I say. 'What's wrong with you today?'

He looks at me, eyes wide as though I've just caught him with his fingers in the till. Not that we have a till, or anything resembling a pot of money as of yet, of course.

'Nothing, absolutely nothing,' he says, issuing a forced laugh.

I narrow my eyes. 'Now tell me the truth.'

He makes a noise that sounds like he's been punctured and all the air is rushing out.

'I may have made a mistake.'

'What kind of a mistake?

'You know I told you about Daniel Lewis mixing with and employing convicted criminals?'

A sinking feeling starts in the pit of my stomach. 'Yes?'

'Well, I didn't get that wrong, that part is absolutely right.'

I stare at him. 'But?'

'There's the most fascinating interview with him in *The North West Business News* this month. I was reading it last night.'

I sit up straight. *The North West Business News* is the region's most prestigious glossy business magazine.

'Go on.'

'It turns out that Daniel makes a point of employing people who have served time. A bit of a second chance, if you like. He sets them up with work and accommodation so that they can get back on their feet straight out of prison.'

I compute what he's telling me.

'So, that's actually a good thing, isn't it?' I say.

Ollie tilts his head to one side and pulls a face.

'Many people might refer to it as that, I suppose.'

'I think it's fair to say that *most* people would refer to it as that, isn't it?'

He looks sheepish. 'I guess so.'

'So, when I basically told Daniel that I knew he was a crook, I was probably wrong, wasn't I?'

Ollie sits down and turns his attention to his computer screen, staring at it as if to indicate a high level of busyness.

'That may well be the case, yes.'

'And what he's doing is actually beneficial to the community, isn't it?'

Ollie scratches his head again. 'Ummm, yes, I think it might be. Hey, maybe we should do a piece on him for the next issue of *The Gazette.*

My head starts to throb. And as I think back to what Sam told me about Daniel's brother, the pieces of the jigsaw suddenly fit together.

I lay my head down on the desk as the horror of what I've done hits home in full force.

'Shit.'

I'm lying awake in the middle of the night thinking about what a mess I've made of everything when it dawns on me. I need to give it one last shot. I need to go and see Daniel.

The next morning, I walk Charlie to school then jump on the train and head straight to Liverpool's business and commercial district where the Lewis & Co. office is based.

I follow the directions on my phone's sat nav to find it's in a shiny glass building in St Paul's Square. It's trendy and modern and a world away from the renovation project he goes home to every night. But then probably not many people know that.

An achingly cool receptionist phones through to his office and then points me in the direction of the lift. I walk through the foyer over to the elevators and take a deep breath as I step inside the one that indicates it's going up. But once the doors close and I'm rising, floor by floor, through the glass construction, the knot in my stomach comes back and I start wondering whether this was such a good idea after all.

All too soon the doors ping open and I'm alone, standing in the foyer of the Lewis & Co. offices.

My armpits feel cold and clammy and I'm lifting my arm to check for sweat patches when I hear that familiar low voice.

'Zoe Taylor, what a surprise.'

I look up, arm mid-air.

'Hello, Daniel,' I say, lowering my arm slowly as though I'm actually engaged in some sort of one-armed yoga exercise.

He pretends he hasn't seen any of it.

'It's good to see you. Come in. Can I get you a drink?'

I'm tempted to say no on principle, but I can smell coffee somewhere in the distance and it smells really good.

'Coffee, please. No sugar.' I don't elaborate on the fact that I've finally dumped the sugar and he knows better than to ask.

He turns to a beautiful redhead as she walks past with a file in her hands. 'Candice, this is Zoe Taylor.'

Candice smiles and says hello.

'Please can you get her a coffee, no sugar?'

'No problem,' she says, her heels tapping on the floor as she starts to walk away.

'Oh and, Candice – can you see if we have any of that coconut milk left as well?' He turns to me. 'I take it *that* hasn't changed?'

I shake my head, watching Candice observe our exchange.

Then Daniel says, 'Candice?' and she grins.

'Coming right up.'

Daniel's office is neat, tidy and the size of the whole ground floor of my house. Everything seems glossy and streak-free, from the chrome chair frame to the floor-to-ceiling windows that offer an impressive view of St Paul's Square and the many office workers going about their business below. I stand in awe. It's been a long time since I've been in a room that's streak-free.

There are few personal touches though. No photos on the desk, no pot plants that he's barely keeping alive. Just files, laptops and phones.

Candice brings in the coffee and I sit down on one of the low red couches and sip it as he goes through the niceties, asking how I've been, how *The Good News Gazette* is doing, how Charlie is … everything, it seems, except the one thing I came here to talk about.

Eventually, I blurt it out.

'Look, Daniel, the reason I'm here is because, well, I've become aware that I've made something of a serious error of judgement.'

Daniel perches on the arm of the couch, his own coffee in hand. This must be how he does it, intimidating people into submission. It's all about the seating arrangements.

He nods gravely. 'You did.'

I squeeze my eyes shut for a second then start again. 'It has come to my attention that you are not, in fact, part of the criminal fraternity, but actually someone who is trying to help reform those who have found themselves in jail.' I'm thinking of his brother and trying so hard to use the correct terminology for people who have broken the law that I sound like the queen.

'That's true,' he says. 'But you're not the first person to misinterpret my intentions, and you won't be the last.'

I relax. 'I'm still annoyed with you and I still think you've made a huge mistake with the parade, but I do admit that I misjudged you slightly—'

He raises an eyebrow. 'Slightly?'

'Well, massively,' I continue. 'And I've come here today to apologise and to say that what you're doing – at least with the *people who have found themselves in jail* – well it's actually pretty impressive.'

Daniel's face relaxes to the point that he even allows himself a smile.

'Impressive enough to make it into the next edition of *The Good News Gazette*?'

I give him a look. 'Don't push it.'

Then I push my own luck.

'Also, I felt we never really had a final discussion about the parade.'

Daniel frowns. 'Ah yes. But the council has given its verdict on the parade. It's going to be demolished within weeks.'

My stomach lurches. 'I understand that. I understand that your plans have been given the go-ahead. And I now understand that you had a prior agreement with the supermarket. But I wanted to speak to you one last time to make sure you understand exactly what these plans will do to Westholme and to urge you to look for any hole in your contract, anything at all that would allow you to change your mind.'

He stands up and walks to the window, concentrating very, very hard on the square below.

'Zoe, the decision's been made. It's done.'

'I get that. What I'm not so sure about is whether you truly believe it to be for the best. You've got to know these people over the last few weeks. You've got to know *me*. Are you sure you're okay with destroying our livelihoods? Our town? Because – and I may be way off with this but – I got the feeling that you *liked* being part of Westholme again, even if it was only for a while.'

He stuffs his hands into his pockets. 'I'm not denying that there are some good people in Westholme and I'll admit, I enjoyed spending time with them.' *Now* he looks at me. 'But that's immaterial. The benefit to the community of the supermarket sale will far outweigh the losses. It will provide jobs and long-term prospects.'

'But what about the people that don't want a career in a supermarket, Daniel? What about the ones like Cath, who simply wants to growl at her customers? Or Bob, who provides fruit and veg to most of the town? Or Ollie and I, who don't particularly want to work from our kitchen tables? Don't we count?'

'Of course, you count. It's just…' His gaze returns to the scene outside the window, which is obviously much less threatening than the one inside.

'We have some spare desks here,' he says. 'You're more than welcome to move your operations into this office, if it would help?' I look around and for a moment I'm almost tempted by his offer. Then I remember that that wouldn't help anyone else.

'Thank you, but no,' I say, shaking my head. I take a deep breath. 'Daniel, there's something else.'

He looks up, completely unaware of what's to come.

'I know, Daniel.'

His blank expression indicates that he clearly has no idea what I'm talking about.

I shift in my seat as I gear myself up to deliver what I'm about to say. 'I know why you want to knock down the parade.'

Daniel frowns. 'Well yes, we've just discussed it. It's because—'

I lower my voice. '*Jonathan*,' I say. 'I know.'

He freezes. His pupils dilate and his skin suddenly loses its usual olive glow. I instantly regret bringing it up. But I *have* brought it up, and I have to go through with it now.

'I totally understand why you want to demolish the parade,' I continue, 'why you want to bulldoze it and never, ever have to walk through it again. But, Daniel, the shop owners, the residents at the parade … they weren't responsible for what happened. They'd never harm you. Not even Cath. They're good people, Daniel. Hurting them won't make you feel better – it'll make you feel worse.'

His body language is completely different now. His shoulders are slumped, arms folded across his chest, head dipped. It's as though I've just uncovered his darkest secret, which I guess I have, and for a moment I can see him as a young man. Overweight, scared and utterly, utterly vulnerable.

'How do you know?' he says quietly.

'Sam told me. He's sorry, Daniel, he's so, so sorry. He'd do anything to go back in time and change things.'

Daniel says nothing. Absolutely nothing. Then the telephone on his desk rings. He reaches down and picks up the handset.

'Right,' he says into the receiver. 'Okay, thanks. Show them up.'

As he replaces the receiver, his whole demeanour changes. Back go the shoulders, out puffs the chest and he finally looks at me. 'It's been really good to see you again, Zoe. But I think we're done here.'

'Wow. Okay,' I say, trying to get to my feet from the low-level couch without spilling the rest of my coffee.

He reaches out to take it from me and I pull myself up in an ungainly fashion, the wretched feeling of complete and utter failure wringing my organs inside out.

Unsure of how to close the meeting, I stick out my hand for him to shake.

'Thank you for your time,' I say, my voice stiff.

His hand closes around mine, like a big warm hug and I want to cry again.

'No, thank you for yours.'

I pause at the door.

'So, I guess I'll see you around?'

He nods. 'I'll see you around.'

And I leave, both of us knowing that our worlds are now so diametrically opposed that there's little chance we'll see each other around ever again.

———

The Good News Gazette

Westholme Community Facebook page:

Tori Hindle: Hi guys, I see the mood is still low so I want to bring you some more positive thoughts today. This one's by someone called Dodinsky: The key to being happy is knowing you have the power to choose what to accept and what to let go. Thanks, guys, now go and be the best you can be!

Paul Gregory: Tori, NOT TODAY.

Chapter Forty

It's a leisurely Sunday afternoon, the type that's tailor-made for picture-perfect families and their two point four children.

But Emma, Beth and I are in our own little way, a family of sorts. Emma's boys and Charlie are playing in the garden together and their laughter is filtering through to my kitchen where we're sitting around the table, post roast dinner, enjoying the final rays of the late summer sun streaming in through the windows.

With the boys unable to hear, we're finally able to ask Emma how she's doing, how she's *really* doing. She smiles but it's one of those 'I'm fine' smiles, rather than a real one. Then I see why; those same eyes are shiny with newly formed tears that she's trying so hard to blink away.

Eventually she can contain them no longer. 'I miss him,' she says simply, as the first tear of what looks set to be a torrent rolls down her face.

'I don't want to miss him. What he's done goes against everything I believe in, that I thought *we* believed in. But as much as I hate to say it, I also understand how it happened. I've been so busy trying to juggle work, kids, the house, so many nights away with Simon... He's been working long hours... I guess somewhere along the way we lost connection. We were operating like single parents in a two-parent household.'

I squeeze her arm. 'I can't relate to the two-parent household thing, but I can relate to feeling so busy that there's no space left in your head to accommodate the needs of another adult too. It must be incredibly difficult to squeeze romance in when there are so many other things going on.'

Emma's eyes narrow slightly and she focuses her attention on me. 'Tell me about Sam,' she says gently.

It's not a question I'm expecting and I pull my hand away from her arm and get up from the table to make a coffee, having finally given up on the afternoon caffeine rule.

I turn on the tap, deliberately keeping my back to them. 'What do you want to know?'

'What happened between you two?' Emma says. 'Before the carnival you mentioned him a lot. But since then, you've said nothing at all.'

The water container full, I move over to the coffee machine. Then I smile and turn back to her. 'No you don't, missy. We're talking about you and your situation here. Don't try and make it about me.'

'Zoe, my situation has done so many rounds in my head it's making me dizzy. Please do me the favour of letting me think about something else.'

I sit back down at the table and pick up one of the caramel slices Beth has laid out, ruining the carefully laid pattern on the plate. Then I have second thoughts and put it back.

'We were friends,' I say. 'He wanted more. I told him I didn't think it would work out. That's it, really.'

Emma and Beth exchange a look. 'What made you think it wouldn't work out?' Beth says.

I shrug. 'These things generally don't, do they? No offence, Em.'

Emma smiles. 'None taken. And I can't argue with you. Based on my experience, it seems that, no, these things don't tend to work out.'

'But sometimes they do,' says Beth. 'Okay, so not having a child when it's the thing you want most in the whole world is not exactly fun. But the good thing about this whole IVF journey is that it's brought Tony and I closer together. Regardless of whether we end up pregnant or not, the important thing is me and him. And I think now we realise that as long as we're okay, everything else will be okay too.'

Emma and I fall silent. 'That's beautiful, Beth,' I say, suddenly nostalgic for something I've never even had. 'Maybe one day I'll have my forever fling too.'

Beth's tender expression makes way for the giggles.

'Your forever fling?' she says laughing. 'What on earth is that?'

'You know,' I say with some indignance, because surely *everyone* knows what a forever fling is? 'Where you think it's just going to be a fling but it turns out to be forever.'

'That's how it happened with Dave and me,' Emma says, a tender look flitting across her face. 'We started off as friends with benefits. Just a fling. But after a while we realised we didn't think of each other that way anymore and it seemed more natural to be with each other than without.'

I nod, remembering all too well how Emma's tales of fantastic sex turned into stories of shared intimacies and thoughtful gestures. And then, eventually, a proposal.

'It doesn't have to be over you know, Em,' I say gently.

She looks straight at me. 'Zoe, you know I love you, but how can you tell me my relationship doesn't have to be over when you're not even giving yours a chance to get off the ground?'

I bite my lip as I scrabble around for an answer.

'Sorry, chick.' She squeezes my fingers. 'That was harsh.'

'Please, someone, eat these cakes before I do.' Beth pushes the plate forward, a small crease lining her forehead, unable, as always, to stand any kind of tension.

We all take one.

'I must admit, that kiss was incredible,' I say, lost for a moment in my own thoughts.

'There was a kiss?' Beth drops her cake. 'You never said anything about a kiss!'

'You dark horse.' Emma smiles. 'I didn't know it had got that far.'

'And he's so kind, so caring. Always trying to look after me.' I rest my chin on my hand, momentarily lost in thoughts of him.

'Maybe that's the problem,' says Emma, getting up to finish the coffee I'd started. 'You don't *need* looking after.'

Beth's eyes nearly shoot out of their sockets. 'What are you talking about? *Everyone* needs looking after!'

'Zoe's got us, she's got Charlie, her parents … she doesn't need anyone else to look after her. She can do that herself.' Emma hands me my mug. 'What she needs is to be challenged.'

'Challenged?' I repeat, a dull laugh escaping my lips. 'Do you really think I don't have enough challenges already?'

'I don't, actually,' says Emma. 'I think there's a whole load of potential in you that's currently being untapped. The right person would bring that out of you. Or maybe it's something you're more than capable of doing yourself.'

I let her words sink in and then dismiss them on the grounds that they're actually a little bit painful to think about.

'It doesn't matter now anyway,' I say. 'It's too late.'

'Not yet it isn't,' Emma says slowly. 'But if you *do* decide to go for Sam, it soon might be.'

I look at her with a start. 'What do you mean?'

'I overheard Sam at the football yesterday. That girl at the burger van with the massive lips was pretty much ordering him on a date. I think they were meeting for drinks last night. So if he *is* the one, you should think about telling him pretty quickly.'

Westholme Community Facebook page:

Irene Wilson: Pic here of my mum and dad, Burchell and Vera Alexander celebrating their Platinum Wedding Anniversary. Congratulations, Mum and Dad. Love you to bits.

Tori Hindle: I'd say something nice about how great it is that they've been married for seventy years, but don't wanna get my head bitten off. So will use an emoji instead ♥

Chapter Forty-One

B urchell and Vera Alexander are quite possibly the cutest couple I've ever met.

They're sitting on the couch of their sheltered accommodation together, surrounded by balloons and cards celebrating their landmark achievement and looking positively bemused by all the attention.

In the kitchen, their daughter, Irene, is bustling around making hot drinks and cutting cake, delighted that their anniversary is about to be captured for posterity in *The Good News Gazette*, while I'm in the armchair opposite them, notepad in hand, scribbling down the story of their life.

'So, I decided not to go back home and came back to Westholme to spend the rest of my days with Vera,' Burchell says, his eyes gleaming with pride as he peers through his glasses at his wife with her soft grey curls and bright blue eyes. 'Once I'd set eyes on her I knew I could never let her go.'

Vera, who after seventy years of washing, ironing, cooking and cleaning for Burchell and their three children clearly sees their coupling through far less rose-tinted glasses, folds her arms over her gently rounded tummy and says, 'He was kind and he had good teeth, so I thought it was worth giving him a chance.'

Irene steps out of the kitchen, drinks and cakes set out neatly on a tray, just in time to hear her mum add, 'And he was good in bed.'

'Mum!' Irene is clearly from a generation that doesn't talk about that kind of thing while it appears that Vera no longer gives a stuff.

'Please don't write that down,' Irene says, her eyes silently pleading me not to make her ninety-six-year-old mum out to be a woman of loose morals.

I shake my head, smiling. 'Of course not.'

In between sips of coffee and mouthfuls of cake, I piece together their life story; how they met at work, the different places within Liverpool they've lived together, how they still enjoy a spot of ballroom dancing now and again in the residents' lounge.

As with everyone's life, it's a patchwork quilt of good and bad times; moments they'd quite clearly like to forget and others that bring them so much happiness to remember.

They've had to endure three bouts of cancer, a heart attack and a lifetime of prejudice rallied against them. Because while Liverpool-born Vera is Scouse and white, her husband Burchell is Guyanese and Black.

'During World War Two, they didn't have enough engineers for all the war weapons they needed,' explains Vera, 'so men from the Caribbean volunteered to come over and help. Burchell was one of them.'

'They sent him to work at the factory where I was employed at the time and told me I had to help him.'

'You couldn't stand me when we first met!' Burchell laughs, his dark eyes twinkling with undisguised adoration for his wife.

'Who says I can now?' she shoots back, before flashing him a reassuring grin as he chuckles at her joke.

'I thought she was the most beautiful girl I'd ever seen,' Burchell continues, 'but she wouldn't even look at me at first.'

'I didn't know what to make of you,' she says. 'I'd never seen a Black man before. But then you started talking to me and eventually we became friends—'

'And then we fell in love,' Burchell finishes.

They touch, but don't dwell on the bad times; the fact that Vera's mum threw her out of the house, that her dad threatened to kill Burchell, that racist attitudes back then meant they had to move house several times before they found a community in which they were accepted.

Instead, they focus on their current health, their happiness and the family they clearly adore.

'So,' I ask them the question that is almost compulsory when it comes to interviewing couples celebrating landmark anniversaries. 'What *is* the secret to a long-lasting marriage?'

Vera looks at me then, her eyes still bright despite having been on the go for almost a century.

'Are you married?' she asks.

I shake my head and bury it in a notebook for a second. 'I have a son though.'

'Ah,' she says conspiratorially, and that one word indicates a shared understanding of how it feels when your set-up doesn't conform to others' expectations.

Burchell reaches over and squeezes her hand. 'She's my best friend. I can always rely on her. And she's the best partner a man could ever wish for. I am very, very lucky to have found her.'

Vera looks back at him and smiles then and the love that flows between them is so strong, so obvious, that it's almost tangible.

'That's it,' she says, nodding. 'He's always been there for me. He's never let me down. And he tells some really dirty jokes.'

'*Mother!*' Irene says again, and I smile so that she knows, once again, I won't write it down.

The couple shuffle along the couch so I can photograph them sitting together rather than with a half-metre gap between them and as they're manoeuvring into place, Sam's voice pops into my head, telling me that he wants to be there for me, to make coffee for me in the morning, to be there for me at night when I've had a bad day.

It's right then, as I'm staring true love in the face, that I realise what I've walked away from. A best friend, a partner, an alternative happy ending to the one that only involves Charlie and I. And my heart sinks as I realise that, out of everything I've got wrong over the past few days, saying no to Sam was the biggest mistake of them all.

It's been a long and depressing week and before I know it Slim City has come around again.

I queue up with Emma and Beth, the three of us devoid of the fun chatter we usually engage in while we're waiting for the scales of doom. We've all been through the wringer over the last fortnight and, as far as I'm concerned, I'm only there to avoid going into the office and packing up the last of my things.

'How did it go with Dave?' I hear Beth mutter to Emma. I whip my head around.

'You saw Dave?'

Emma nods. 'He came round yesterday. We talked all night,' she says. 'And I mean *all* night. I had to have three coffees before I felt awake enough to leave the house today, but it turns out there was a lot to discuss.'

'And…?' I search her face for clues as to the outcome.

'It's baby steps,' she says. 'But I believe there's something there to save. Call me an idiot – and I know many would – but I want to try again. I want to keep our family together.'

I give her a quick hug. 'You're not an idiot,' I say, dropping my voice to a whisper. 'And life's complicated. If there's one thing the past few years has taught us, then surely it's that.'

I slip off my shoes as Wendy beckons me forward. 'Hello, dear,' she says, then raises her eyebrows. 'Are you sure you want to keep your cardigan on?'

'Wendy, I've taken my cardigan, my belt, my shoes and my socks off for the past eight months,' I say. 'I think we're way past that point now.'

She considers this for a second, then agrees I'm probably right. 'Okay dear, step on.'

I shift my weight from the floor to the scales, keeping my eyes on the digital display screen on the table next to Wendy despite the fact that I'm already resigned to my fate.

When the numbers flash up, I do a double-take.

'Hmmm,' says Wendy thoughtfully. 'I thought the scales had been playing up today. Do you want to try again?'

I step off, wait a few seconds, and then step back on.

Wendy looks at the figures and shakes her head. 'Definitely playing up,' she says. 'I'll call Barbara.'

At Wendy's beckoning, Barbara makes her way over to the scales.

She greets me, then listens as Wendy explains the situation.

'Right, okay.' She nods, slipping her glasses down on to the bridge of her nose. 'Let's try again, shall we?'

I step back onto the scales, my face heating up nicely as I take in the number of women scowling at me in the queue.

Barbara's focused expression relaxes into a slow smile. 'No,' she says firmly to Wendy, 'that's definitely right.'

She addresses me. 'Half off this week. Well done.'

I blink. 'Half a pound?'

'No, Zoe. Seven pounds. Half a stone.'

I stare at her, trying to take in what exactly she's saying.

She speaks again, this time beaming from ear-to-ear.

'That's good by anyone's standards. But by *yours* – it's incredible!'

A wave of excitement ripples through me. Then another, then another. Then I'm actually buzzing with joy.

I watch with pride as Wendy jots down my weight loss in my little book and marvel at how the week I finally forgot about my weight was the one week that I actually managed to lose some.

Half an hour later, I'm called before the class – and my two best friends – to accept my City Slimmer award for having achieved the most weight loss that week. It's a small victory but a significant one and as all three of us boldly bypass Greggs on the way out, I'm reminded of one small but important fact.

I, Zoe Taylor, am nobody's joke.

Westholme Community Facebook page:

Barbara Forshaw: Well done to one of our long-standing members of the group who lost half a stone over the last week. And let me tell you that if *she* can do it, anyone can. Still spaces available for anyone trying to achieve a last-minute weight loss in order to fit into their bikini. Or mankini. Here at Slim City, everyone's welcome.

Chapter Forty-Two

Getting ready for the farewell party is like preparing for a wake. I'm looking forward to seeing everybody – and one person in particular – but am devastated at the reason it is happening in the first place.

One by one, we all file into the cafe, where, courtesy of Antonio, the cool jazz soundtrack has been exchanged for something a little more up-tempo. Coffee and tea are off the menu. Tonight, nothing less than a good dose of alcohol will do.

All of the members of the Save the Westholme Parade group are there along with the shopkeepers and we greet each other with the knowledge that we did all we possibly could to save such a crucial part of Westholme life.

It's good to see Neil, who appears to be very much in the company of the man I saw him talking to that day in the hot-desking space at the cafe. 'Zoe, this is John,' he says as he introduces me to a tall man in a flat cap and hipster jeans. 'It's John who's been running the Classics for Beginners sessions.'

'Lovely to meet you, John,' I say, winking at Neil who immediately turns crimson in response.

Cath, Antonio and Adina are at the counter, pouring wine, beer, gin and goodness knows what else for those who want to raise a glass to the concrete heap they've called home for so long.

Ollie is standing next to Adina helping her out with the drinks and I can tell by their body language that they're engaging in a spot of flirtatious behaviour. Ollie catches my eye and winks and I shake my head, laughing. I had a feeling he'd win her over in the end.

'Alright, love?' Cath greets me gruffly. 'What are you having?'

'White wine please, Cath.' I cast my eyes around the cafe, seeking out Sam and eventually spot him at the back of the room chatting to Margaret. Dressed in smart jeans and a light green polo top that accentuates his eyes, he looks so good it's all I can do not to grab him on the spot, but the space that's developed between us feels so tangible that it's hard to work up the courage.

Instead, I knock back my wine more quickly than I probably should and return to the counter for another, an act which in itself, takes quite some time due to the number of people who want to either thank me or commiserate with me over my abject failure to bring any type of positive change to the situation.

Despite my embarrassment, it's good to hear their kinds words of reassurance and we ponder on where we might meet up after the parade has been demolished and a supermarket erected in its place. The best we can hope for is that the supermarket will have a cafe, as there'll be precious little other eating establishments around. Cath seems to have lost the will to run a business anymore – I think knowing it could be ripped away from her so easily has made her wary of entering into an agreement on the new units and although there are a few pubs around the town, we've all agreed a pub just wouldn't be the same. Nowhere would, come to think of it.

Just when it seems we couldn't feel more low, the door opens and Starr walks in, accompanied by the awful TV reporter who covered the events on what I widely regard to be The Worst Day of My Life. And that's saying something.

'Hello, darlings,' Starr trills, effervescent as ever. 'I have some delightful news. After I lost out on my chance to recreate my famous twerk at the carnival, our lovely friend,' she turns to the reporter, 'what was your name again, dear?'

'Anna,' the woman says, a look of near-disdain on her face.

'Yes, Anna agreed to meet me here at the farewell party.'

I look behind her to where the cameraman is already filming.

'Hmmm, I don't suppose it had anything to do with wanting to film our final farewell to the parade, did it, Anna?' I say.

She issues an icy smile. 'Not at all. We definitely want to film Starr. We just thought that maybe we could get a few shots of the party while we're here.'

'Quite right too, dear,' says Starr, patting her hand. 'Now, let's have a little drink and then you can film me.'

Before Anna can object, a glass is shoved into her hand and she's left suspiciously eyeing up its contents as Starr gets stuck into some warm-up exercises, a precursor for the TV moment she always knew would one day come.

———

We're an hour or so into the evening when Cath climbs onto a chair in front of the counter and shouts for everyone to shut up for a minute so she can make a speech.

'I'd just like to thank you all for coming here tonight, to this fab party that most of us hoped would never happen,' she says.

'When I opened Cath's Caff thirty-two years ago, I thought all my dreams had come true. And in a way, they had.'

'There's been plenty of highs and lows over the years, but I've always thought of this place as my home and I know many of my loyal customers have too.'

'These last few months have been some of the best I've ever had here. I've been lucky enough to spend time with my lovely nephew, Antonio, and I've had the pleasure of welcoming Adina to our little family too. And, in turn, they've helped me turn the business into something exciting and new.'

She pauses, then when she speaks again her voice is cracking.

'We're all gutted to be saying goodbye to the parade, but we're not saying goodbye to each other now, are we? No matter what life throws at us, we'll still be here trying to put the world to rights.

'That's exactly what Zoe's been doing for us over the past few months and while that idiot may have won in the end, we couldn't have got this far without her.' She raises her glass. 'So, all that's left to say is Zoe, this one's for you.'

'For Zoe,' the crowd echo, and I feel my own eyes spilling with tears.

Suddenly, another voice cuts in.

'Excuse me, but that's not all there is to say.'

We all fall silent as we turn towards the source of the words.

There, standing by the door, looking as cool, calm and tall as ever, is Daniel Lewis.

Cath glares at him. 'Was there something you wanted? Because as you can see, we're currently in the middle of a *leaving* party. So, can I suggest that's what you do?'

Anna, who up to this point has been looking nothing but bored, is suddenly a hive of activity, gesturing animatedly to her cameraman to make sure he doesn't miss this.

'I will do exactly that in just a moment,' Daniel is saying. 'But there's been a change of plan and I thought you'd all want to be the first to know.' His eyes flit across the room, searching for something, then settle on mine.

'Over the past few weeks, your ambassador Zoe has highlighted to me just what an important part the parade plays in your everyday lives. She's also set out a number of proposals in order for it to prosper.

'In short, she convinced me that it would be far better for the community to keep the parade as it was. But due to pre-agreed contracts, I was unable to effect change.'

'However, I have had news today that a subsequent survey has revealed that the land is considered highly contaminated due to the presence of the nearby petrol station.' Spotting expressions of alarm, he says quickly, 'Please don't worry about this – it's not something that will ever harm you or even Westholme. It just puts restrictions on what can be built where.' He looks sheepish. 'This is something that should have been spotted by numerous people earlier on in the process, but for one reason or another, it slipped through the net. As a result, the supermarket has decided not to go ahead with the proposed development and after much deliberation, I've decided to change my own plans for the parade.'

At this, the room starts to echo with muttering and whispers. 'Get on with it,' someone yells, and I see Daniel's chest expand as he takes a deep breath.

'I will no longer be bringing in the bulldozers. Instead, my team will embark upon a programme of improvement with immediate effect, which will enhance our offering to retailers and will hopefully result in an increased footfall, an uptake in retail units and a much-improved public space.'

We all pause, working through his words and wondering if they really do mean what we think they mean.

'Er, sorry, lad, but I think you're going to have to translate that for us,' says Cath. 'Are you actually saying that you're not going to knock the parade down?'

'Yes.' He nods. 'I'm saying exactly that.'

'And our businesses are safe?' Bob pipes up.

'As long as you can pay the rent, there'll be no need to leave the premises.' Daniel nods again. 'Let me reiterate, the parade is not going to be knocked down.'

A rumble of excitement is felt before it's even heard. Slowly, the rumble turns into a wave of whispered chatter that spreads across the room as the information sinks in. Finally, the voices become louder, more confident, as it dawns on everyone what's just happened. We may have achieved it by default, but we've done it. We've saved the parade.

As we turn to each other to share our delight, I notice Daniel, satisfaction etched across his face as he watches the scene before him unfold. I excuse myself and catch him as he's turning towards the door.

'Daniel?' He turns around. 'What happened? Why the change of heart?'

He smiles. 'You may have struck a nerve with what you said the other day, but you had a point too. I'm not going to get into it now, but let's just say I was relieved when the supermarket pulled out. I'd realised by that point that I'd made a mistake. You made me see the parade – and Westholme – differently. I didn't want to knock it down anymore.'

'Wow, Daniel,' I say. 'I'm flattered.'

'I'm not a monster. I never wanted to make life worse for these people. Hopefully now we can make it better.'

I giggle and raise my glass to do a pretend 'cheers' to his shoulder, when really it's just an excuse to hide my shock in a gulp of wine.

'You showed me some interesting plans. Would you mind dropping by the office in the coming week and we can discuss the best ways to implement them?'

'Absolutely,' I say, aware that I'm now starting to slur just a teeny bit. 'I'll email you to arrange a meeting.'

He nods. 'Good. Well, it looks as though tonight's going to turn into a great party. I'll leave you to get back to your friends.'

Instinctively I place my hand on his arm. 'Will you not stay for one?'

He looks down at my hand and then at me. 'No thank you. I have work to do.'

'But it's Saturday night.'

'Business never sleeps.' He smiles.

I smile back.

'Okay well ... thank you, Daniel. I really mean it. Thank you.'

'You're welcome,' he says, looking slightly awkward. 'I'll see you next week.'

I nod. 'I'll drop you a line.'

And just like that, our final goodbye suddenly turned into a brand-new hello.

If I was looking to drink 'til I was merry before Daniel's announcement, then I'm ready to knock 'em back 'til I'm completely hammered afterwards. Within minutes I've become the hero of the hour, unable to walk two paces at a time without being slapped on the back, hugged, and generally made to feel as though I've saved the entire planet rather than the parade.

Eventually, as the crowd of well-wishers disperse, Gloria approaches me with tears in her eyes. 'My dear, you have no idea what this means to me,' she says.

'I do,' I reply, my own voice filled with emotion. 'I understand. The women that you've worked so hard with, the plans they had. Maybe now we'll be able to work with Daniel to help them access those boarded-up units.'

'That would be wonderful,' says Gloria, 'but my desperation to see the parade saved wasn't only about those fabulous women. It also came from a very personal place.' She reaches into her bag and pulls out an old black and white photograph of a man standing in front of the parade.

'My father,' she says, showing me the picture. 'The parade was his vision, his idea. He died years ago, but, for me, he's always lived on through it. To see it pulled down would be more than I could bear.'

'Oh, Gloria,' I say, hugging her. 'Why didn't you tell me this before now?'

'You already had so much pressure on your shoulders,' she says. 'The last thing I wanted to do was to burden you with any more. Thank you, my dear. You haven't just safeguarded this community's future, you've preserved its past too. And the preservation of memories, my dear, is something that money just can't buy.'

It's as I am making the endless journey back from the toilets that I come face-to-face with Sam. One minute I'm edging my way through the throng, wondering how I'll ever find him in the room full of people, the next thing he's there, right in front of me.

'Hi,' he says, guarded, cautious.

'Hi.'

There's been so many things I've wanted to say, wanted to tell him. And now, all of a sudden, I'm lost for words.

'So, you did it.' Dimples form in his cheeks as he relaxes into a smile. 'You saved the parade.'

'It appears that we did,' I admit, trying and failing not to beam.

'That's brilliant, Zoe. Well done you.' He gestures towards the counter. 'Can I get you a drink?'

'I've had a fair few already. But I won't say no.'

I follow him over to the counter where Antonio pours me another.

'For the most beautiful *donna* in the room tonight,' he adds, shouting over the cranked-up soundtrack to what is turning into a fully blown party.

Lawrence has pushed some chairs aside and is leading some of the die-hards in a salsa routine, while others are hanging around the edges, shuffling self-consciously to the music.

Drink in hand, I shout to Sam. 'I need to talk to you.'

'What?' he says, scrunching his face up to indicate that he can't hear me.

'I said, I need to—' Beaten by the volume, I grab his arm and pull him towards the door.

Once outside, he looks at me expectantly. The fresh air hits me and I'm reminded that I'm probably at my limit drinks-wise. But I haven't had enough alcohol to muddy what I want to say.

'I made a mistake, Sam, I don't want us to just be friends.'

He sighs and shakes his head and I realise he thinks I'm joking.

I step towards him and place my hand on his chest.

'Don't laugh. This is hard enough already without you laughing at me.'

Sam places his hand over mine. 'Zoe, I would never laugh at you.'

He looks down at me, green eyes sparkling as they catch the light from inside the cafe.

'I know I said that it wasn't what I wanted, but I was playing it safe. I lied. This – you – are exactly what I want. If you, well, if you feel the same?'

He purses his lips, pretending to consider what I've said yet never once taking his eyes away from mine. Then he takes my drink from me and puts it on the floor.

'Zoe,' his voice is filled with longing and he puts his hands on my hips and pulls me towards him. 'I understand exactly why you weren't ready, but I can promise you that I will never *ever* let you down. I—'

I reach up, cutting his words short as I pull his head down and resume the kiss that began the day of the carnival.

'Alright, you two, what's going on out here?'

As if destined never to happen, this time our kiss is cut short by the arrival of Emma and Dave, approaching the cafe hand-in-hand.

We pull apart, embarrassed. 'I was just, er...' I trail off and focus instead on straightening my dress.

'No need to explain,' Emma says with a wink. 'I heard what happened with Daniel Lewis – it's all over the Westholme Community Facebook page – so I think you're entitled to a little self-indulgence.'

I look over at Dave, who shifts awkwardly from one foot to another.

'Hello, Zoe,' he says quietly, his glance shifting to Emma for reassurance.

'Good to see you, Dave,' I say. If Emma's prepared to give him another chance then so am I.

I pick up my glass and wrap my arm around Sam's waist. 'Come on, let's go back in. I'm ready to dance like no-one's watching.'

And that's what we do, our little bunch of warriors, long into the night.

The Good News Gazette

Westholme Community Facebook page:

Lisa Seddon: To Zoe Taylor, the girl who started up *The Good News Gazette* and went on to save the parade. Can't thank you enough for everything you've done.

Rob Brown: We salute you!

Sam Milner: You're right – my girlfriend's amazing ♥

Epilogue

EIGHT MONTHS LATER

The spring sun is reflecting off the white walls of the Westholme Parade, creating a dazzling glare that threatens to blind anyone trying to look at the building straight on.

Charlie is revelling in his May Day leisure time, having fun in the small children's play area with some friends whose parents, like me, are enjoying the newly created pavement cafe culture that's being lapped up by locals and visitors to Westholme alike. I smile as I watch him, as carefree and happy as I always wanted him to be. Now and again the boys strip down to their shorts and run into the water fountain that springs up intermittently from the ground, their peals of laughter causing the onlookers to smile. Long gone is the bleak, soulless parade that formed the heart of Westholme a year ago. In its place is an area teeming with charm and character.

The shops that were once boarded up are now thriving independents, with a wine bar, Eva's vintage clothes boutique and, of course, Paula's bakehouse creating bread, pies and cakes so good that even the Presthill residents travel here to sample them.

Fairy lights have been strung around the various seating areas, making the square twinkle at night, while new shop frontage and signage in the monochrome shades that I'd suggested, give the entire parade an added classy edge.

Most touching of all is the memorial garden that's been created around the magnolia tree. Stan no longer has a lone tree to mark his existence. Instead, he has a whole garden area, filled with his favourite plants, flowers and, as promised, a bench where Margaret can sit and remember him.

Of course, it wouldn't have happened without Daniel. Once he'd made the decision to invest in the parade, that's just what he did; ploughing an insane amount of money into regenerating the shops and outdoor space to turn it into something beautiful. And *The Good News Gazette* covered it all.

He's just left here after a meeting with me to discuss the events he has planned for over the summer months, but I've stayed on, glass of wine in hand, enjoying the feeling of complete relaxation as I watch Charlie play with his friends.

A shadow moves over the sun and I look up to see Beth's large baby bump blocking the light.

'Hey you.' She beams, leaning over awkwardly to hug me.

'How are you doing?' I ask, jumping out of my chair and urging her to sit down. She shakes her head, indicating that she's in a rush and can't stop.

'Fantastic,' she says, cradling her tummy. 'Only a couple of weeks to go now. Can you believe how quickly it's flown by?'

'A lot has certainly changed in a short space of time,' I smile. 'Are you off home?'

'Yes, just needed to pick up some of these.' She pulls a pack of unflattering maternity knickers out of her bag and I wince at the memory.

'Oh yes, those,' I say, with no elaboration, determined to

preserve the secrets of the post-labour experience that mothers all the world over have guarded so fiercely for so long.

As I watch her waddle away, another figure comes into my line of vision. Sam and I have become close since that night at Cath's Caff and although Charlie and I still live very much alone, he has a regular presence at our dining table.

I return his smile as he approaches.

'Hey, beautiful,' he says, bending down to kiss me on the lips. 'How has your day been?'

'Good. I actually just finished a meeting with Daniel.'

I see Sam bristle as he pulls out a chair to sit down. While most of the original Friends of Westholme Parade have acknowledged a grudging respect for Daniel over the past few months, Sam still grits his teeth whenever his name is mentioned.

'He told me something interesting actually,' I continue, choosing to ignore Sam's reaction. 'You know the old cinema on the main road? An application for outline planning permission to turn it into apartments has been submitted to the council.'

Sam raises his eyebrows. 'Is that not listed or protected or something? It's a beautiful art deco building. I don't know if you remember inside, but it's absolutely stunning.'

I cast my memory back to my teenage years, the last time I remember going to the cinema before moving away and coming back to find it boarded up.

He watches me, his eyes narrowing. 'Oh no…' he says.

'What?' I say, lost in thought.

'Don't tell me you're thinking about making this your next project.'

I laugh. 'No way. I have more than enough on my hands right now.'

He tilts his head. 'Isn't that what you said about the parade?'

'I mean it this time,' I say defiantly. 'Anyway, you must be hungry. Have a look at the menu and see what you fancy for tea.'

He gives me a look. I wink. And as Charlie joins us, embarking on an in-depth discussion with Sam about the form of some footballer I've never even heard of before, I turn my face to the sun, cross my lean legs – courtesy of a continued programme of weight loss – and smile.

Far from being the girl who cocks it all up, it turns out I can make things happen for myself after all. It was believing it that was the hardest part.

And now I've conquered that? The world – or Westholme, at least – is my oyster.

Acknowledgments

The idea for *The Good News Gazette* came to me in late 2019, when the world seemed relatively normal and the power of positive news had at that time only been fully realised by pioneering editors such as Rebecca Keegan who had set up *Good News Liverpool* and others with similar visions.

Little did I know that within months everything would change, and that many people would start actively scouring the internet for good news that gave them hope at a time when there seemed to be very little in existence.

It was against this backdrop that I wrote *The Good News Gazette*, and while good news might have been in short supply during that particular time, it was not hard to find heartwarming acts of kindness that inspired many of the scenes. I, like so many others, will be forever grateful to those who found ways to make life easier, brighter, possible even, for others during those dark days, many of whom inadvertently drove this book.

Closer to home, my editor Charlotte Ledger became a real beacon of light at this time; knowing that she was patiently waiting for the story meant I had to keep writing it, even in those moments when it just felt too hard. I honestly don't think I would have finished it if it wasn't for her belief that it would one day come to fruition. Thanks so much to her, Bethan Morgan, Nicky Lovick, and the rest of the team at One More Chapter who helped to make the book better. I'm very grateful for all of your efforts.

The Romantic Novelists' Association played an important part in my journey too. I would recommend anyone interested in writing romantic fiction to join their New Writers' Scheme and thank them for their tireless efforts in supporting this special genre. Thanks too to Diana Beaumont, who was also incredibly generous with her advice when I was starting out.

There are a number of other people without whom this book probably would never have been completed, largely due to the help they gave me with my research. A massive thanks goes to Tony McDonough from Liverpool Business News for his initial feedback on whether the supermarket line was a plausible one, employment solicitor Lindsey Knowles for her expert guidance, the team at My Romania Community for ensuring Adina's voice was authentic and Francesco Zaralli and Lauren Gibson for providing the same support with Antonio. To the aforementioned Rebecca Keegan, thank you giving me such a fascinating insight into the inner workings of a good news newspaper.

Thanks also to Dr Jane Hamlin, President of Beaumont Society which carries out such important work on behalf of the transgender community, Kevin Gopal, Editor of Big Issue North, an amazing charity whose work is more important now than ever, and Dr Joe Nunez-Mino from The Bat Conservation Trust for fact-checking my character Colin's research on bats.

The Chatty Café Scheme was another welcome discovery during my research, and thanks must go to Jenny Bimpson who kindly supported my reference to such a brilliant initiative.

There were two other people who didn't want to be mentioned but helped me immensely in the research for this book. Thank you both – you know who you are.

To the magnificent Debbie Johnson who played such an important role in the creation of this book – including coming up with the title – thank you, thank you, thank you. You're an amazing friend. The same goes to Catherine Issac, whose advice and support, but most importantly her friendship, has been invaluable. You've both made it all seem possible at times when it has felt anything but. To Caroline Corcoran who has chewed the writing fat with me while digging in sandpits, crawling around in soft plays and, more recently, enjoying grown-up dinners, I'm so glad you moved back up North. Here's to many more conversations about books and babies.

To Kate Walker, who has spent the last twenty-odd years cheering me on, thank you. I love you to bits. To the Friday Playgroup girls; Laura Buoey, Jenny Maude, Sheila Matthews, Karen Day, Sandra Flynn, Sandra Browne, Zoe Kennedy and Gill Harris – you are the strongest, most incredible group of women I know. Laura, thank you so much for everything you've done for me in recent months and Sandra B, my first proper reader, thanks for the invaluable feedback!

Angela Anderson, my friend and mentor, I love putting the world to rights with you over our three-hour lunches. To Claire Grey, Sally Edgar, Rebecca Smullen and Laura Benjamin – thank you for the pep talks and listening ears.

To Paul, Hannah and Diane Hudson and Laura B; thank you for taking a chance on me and making me a part of your close-knit team. I look forward to many years of office banter with you all.

Thanks also must go to my mother-and-father-in-law, Glen and Viny Lynch, who welcomed me into their family a long time ago and have made me such a part of it, while also helping me to juggle work and family life. You are very special people.

To Jenny, my actual sister (and an integral part of the Friday Playgroup girls) and her family; I love and miss you all so much. I can't wait to see you again, and have in person the conversations we've only recently managed over the internet.

Mum and Dad… What can I say – except Dad, thank goodness you're absolutely nothing like Terry! You've both been there through the ups, the downs, the successes and the outright failures, but you've never doubted I'd get there someday. I owe you everything and love you more than I could ever express in words.

To the love of my life, Mike, who is the most amazing husband and dad anyone could ever ask for. Thank you for making me believe I could do this and helping to make sure I did. You are, indeed, my angel.

Finally, to Nathan and Natalie. I love you more than life itself. Thank you for making all my dreams come true. I promise I'll spend the rest of my life trying to do the same for you.

YOUR NUMBER ONE STOP

ONE MORE CHAPTER

FOR PAGETURNING BOOKS

One More Chapter is an
award-winning global
division of HarperCollins.

Subscribe to our newsletter to get our
latest eBook deals and stay up to date
with all our new releases!

signup.harpercollins.co.uk/
join/signup-omc

Meet the team at
www.onemorechapter.com

Follow us!
@OneMoreChapter_
@OneMoreChapter
@onemorechapterhc

Do you write unputdownable fiction?
We love to hear from new voices.
Find out how to submit your novel at
www.onemorechapter.com/submissions